D0604845

◆ The Lost Journals of Ven Polypheme ◆

# THE TREE OF WATER

FROM STARSCAPE BOOKS

The Lost Journals of Ven Polypheme
by Elizabeth Haydon

*The Floating Island*
*The Thief Queen's Daughter*
*The Dragon's Lair*
*The Tree of Water*

*The Lost Journals of Ven Polypheme*

# THE
# TREE of
# WATER

*Text compiled by*

ELIZABETH HAYDON

*Illustrations restored by*

BRANDON DORMAN

A TOM DOHERTY ASSOCIATES BOOK | NEW YORK

THE TREE OF WATER

Copyright © 2014 by Elizabeth Haydon

Illustrations copyright © 2014 by Brandon Dorman

*The Floating Island* excerpt copyright © 2006 by Elizabeth Haydon

Reader's Guide copyright © 2014 by Elizabeth Haydon

All rights reserved.

Endpaper map by Ed Gaszi

A Starscape Book
Published by Tom Doherty Associates, LLC
175 Fifth Avenue
New York, NY 10010

www.tor-forge.com

The Library of Congress Cataloging-in-Publication Data is available upon request.

ISBN 978-0-7653-2059-9 (hardcover)
ISBN 978-1-4668-6367-5 (e-book)

Starscape books may be purchased for educational, business, or promotional use.
For information on bulk purchases, please contact Macmillan Corporate
and Premium Sales Department at 1-800-221-7945, extension 5442,
or write specialmarkets@macmillan.com.

First Edition: October 2014

0  9  8  7  6  5  4  3  2  1

It is with the greatest of thanks and the most sincere admiration
that I dedicate the translation of this recently discovered volume
to
His Majesty, King Varoon de Muk Muk
of the sovereign island kingdom of Digitalis,
the only head of state willing to underwrite the expedition
to unearth the first of this newly found set of Ven's journals
and with equally sincere thanks
to
Roberto Eugeneve Hadoni
my rickshaw driver (and amateur rocket scientist)
who transported me from Mobile, Alabama to the streets of Rome
(as well as several extraterrestrial destinations)
without a whisper of complaint and who will always have
my enduring admiration and love.

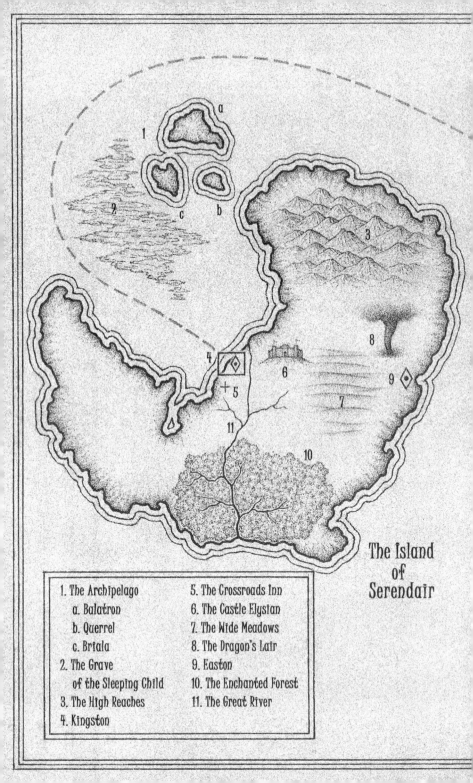

The Island
of
Serendair

1. The Archipelago
   a. Balatron
   b. Querrel
   c. Briala
2. The Grave
   of the Sleeping Child
3. The High Reaches
4. Kingston
5. The Crossroads Inn
6. The Castle Elysian
7. The Wide Meadows
8. The Dragon's Lair
9. Easton
10. The Enchanted Forest
11. The Great River

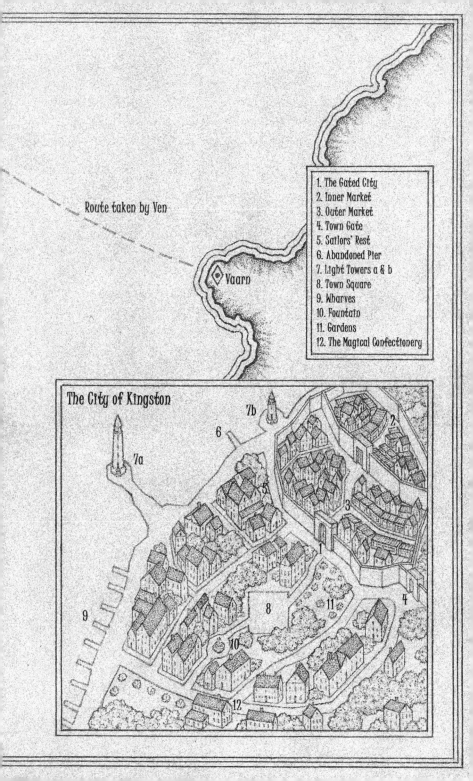

Route taken by Ven

Vaarn

1. The Gated City
2. Inner Market
3. Outer Market
4. Town Gate
5. Sailors' Rest
6. Abandoned Pier
7. Light Towers a & b
8. Town Square
9. Wharves
10. Fountain
11. Gardens
12. The Magical Confectionery

The City of Kingston

7b

6

7a

5

2

3

1

9

8

11

4

10

12

# PREFACE

Long ago, in the Second Age of history, a young Nain explorer by the name of Ven Polypheme traveled much of the known and unknown world, recording his adventures and the marvelous sights he witnessed. His writings eventually formed the basis for *The Book of All Human Knowledge* and *All the World's Magic.* These were two of the most important books of all time, because they captured the secrets of magic and the records of mythical beings and wondrous places that are now all but gone from the world.

The only copies of each of these books were lost at sea centuries ago, but a few fragments of Ven's original journals remain. Three of these journals were discovered a few years ago by archaeologists and were studied and tested at great length. Finally it was determined that they were, in fact, Ven's actual journals. Those three journals, *The Floating Island, The Thief Queen's Daughter,* and *The Dragon's Lair,* were then published. Included in them were the fragments of diary entries that had survived, reproduced in Ven's handwriting as they were originally written, along with the drawings that he had sketched and signed.

For some time it was believed that those three journals were the only surviving record of Ven Polypheme's research. But recently, a Mr. Dieter Bigglesworth of Ketchup-upon-Hamburg, South Germany, was on vacation with his wife, Euphemia, in the tropical paradise of Langerhan Island. Mr. Bigglesworth had buried Mrs. Bigglesworth (except for her head) in the sand of the pink beach of Langerhan, when suddenly her toes scraped against something rough and wooden. After receiving medical attention for splinter removal, the Bigglesworths returned to the pink beach and dug until they unearthed a small sea chest, bound in brass and very old.

The chest contained what appeared to be three more journals in the familiar handwriting of Ven Polypheme.

As before, the journals were given to internationally known archanologist Elizabeth Haydon, who was at the time attending a yak-milking seminar in the high peaks of Katmandont. After a very large coffee, she immediately began studying the newly found volumes and, at the end of a grueling authentication process, declared them to be genuine. This first of these journals, *The Tree of Water*, contains entries that are reproduced in Ven Polypheme's handwriting, as they were originally written. Some of them are little more than a few words, or a sentence or two. A number of sketches from his notebooks also survived and are reproduced here as well. Great care has been taken to reconstruct the parts of the journal that did not survive, so that a whole story can be told.

At the time of the original excavation of the first three journals, a separate notebook containing only sketches of dragons, plus drawings of what appear to be cards made out of dragon scales, is still being restored. It was found, buried with the journals, in a waterproof chest lined in gold.

It is perhaps the most deeply magical book of all Time.

The dragon scales appear to be cards in an ancient deck that allowed a special reader to see the Past, know the Present, and predict the Future. They apparently had older, deeper powers of magic, which we are just beginning to learn about. The archaeological dig is continuing in other places Ven was thought to have visited.

These few scraps of text and sketches provide a map back in Time to hidden places, where pockets of magic might still be found.

# Contents

~ The Lost Journals of Ven Polypheme ~

# THE TREE OF WATER

# – 1 –

# To Go, or Not to Go

The human boys had an expression back in the faraway city of Vaarn where I was born. It went like this:

> Curiosity killed the cat
> Satisfaction brought him back

I am a curious person. I was just as curious back in my early days in Vaarn as I am now, perhaps even more so, because my curiosity had not yet been given a chance to be satisfied.

The first time I heard this expression, I was very excited. I thought it meant that my curiosity could make me feel like I was dying, but it would let up if I discovered the answer to whatever was making me curious.

I told my mother about the rhyme. She was not impressed. In fact, she looked at me as if I had just set my own hair on fire on purpose. She patted my chin, which was woefully free of any sign of the beard that should have been growing there.

"That's very nice," she said, returning to her chores. "But just in case nobody told you, you are not a cat, Ven. Unlike you, cats have whiskers."

My pride stung for days afterward.

*But it didn't stop my curiosity from growing as fast as my beard should have been.*

*My name is Charles Magnus Ven Polypheme, Ven for short. Unlike the human boys in Vaarn, I am of the race of the Nain. Nain are somewhat shorter than humans, and grumpier. They live almost four times as long as humans, and tend to be much less curious, and much less adventurous. They hate to travel, don't swim, and generally do not like other people. Especially those who are not Nain.*

*I clearly am not a good example of my race.*

*First, I am very tall for a Nain, sixty-eight Knuckles high when I was last measured on the morning of my fiftieth birthday. I've already mentioned my uncontrollable curiosity, which brings along with it a desire for adventure. I have been blessed, or cursed, with quite a lot of that recently.*

*But as for the curiosity, while I've had a lot of satisfaction for the questions it has asked me, it doesn't seem to matter. As soon as one burning question is answered, another one springs to mind immediately. As a result, I am frequently in trouble.*

*So now I am about to lay my head on a chopping block, <u>on purpose</u>, and a man with a very sharp knife is standing over me, ready to make slashes in my neck.*

*I'm wondering if in fact instead of being a live Nain, I am about to end up as a dead, formerly curious cat.*

*Because now I have three whiskers of my own.*

V EN POLYPHEME HAD TWO SETS OF EYES STARING AT HIM. One set was black as coal. The other was green as the sea.

Neither of them looked happy.

The green eyes were floating, along with a nose, forehead, and hair on which a red cap embroidered with pearls sat, just above the surface of the water beneath the old abandoned dock. The brows above the eyes were drawn together. They looked annoyed.

The black ones were in the middle of the face of his best friend, Char, who stood beside him on the dock. They looked anxious.

In the distance a bell began to toll. Ven looked to his left at the docks of the fishing village to the south of them, where work had begun hours ago. Then he looked behind him. The sleepy town of Kingston in the distance was just beginning to wake up.

Ven looked back down into the water.

"Come on, Amariel," he said to the floating eyes. "I can't really go off into the sea without him."

A glorious tail of colorful scales emerged from below the surface, splashing both boys with cold salt water.

"Why not?" a girl's voice demanded from the waves. "He's a pest. And he isn't nice to me."

Char's black eyes widened.

"I—I'm sorry 'bout that," he stammered. "When I first met you, Ven didn't tell me you were a mermaid—" He shivered as another splash drenched him again. "Er, I mean *merrow*. I'm sorry if I made you mad."

"Hmmph."

"Please let him come," Ven said. "Captain Snodgrass gave him orders to keep an eye on me. So if I'm going to explore the sea with you, he kinda has to come along."

Char nodded. "Cap'n's orders."

"He's not *my* captain," said the merrow. "I don't take orders from humans. You know better, Ven. My mother will fillet me if she finds out I'm traveling with a human male. *Especially* if we are going to go exploring. There are very clear rules about not showing humans around the wonders of the Deep. And besides, it's dangerous. You have no idea how many sea creatures think humans are tasty. I don't want to get chomped on by mistake."

Out of the corner of his eye, Ven watched Char's face go white.

"We'll be careful," he promised. "Char will be on his best be-havior."

"I've seen his best behavior. I'm not impressed."

"Look," Char said. "If you get sick of me, you can always cover me with fish guts and toss me out as shark bait."

The merrow stared coldly at him.

"Oh, all *right*," she said finally. "But remember, there's a reason they call bait for sharks *chum*. 'Chum' is another word for 'friend.'" Her eyes stayed locked on Char. "And if you make a bunch of sharks angry, *Chum*—"

"I'll be chum," Char said. "Got it."

"So if you're coming, we have to find a fisherman named Asa with a red-bottomed boat." Amariel pointed south to one of the far docks. "He'll cut your gills, and we can get going."

Both boys grabbed their necks.

The merrow rolled her eyes. "Oh, come *on*. Do you want to be able to breathe underwater or not? Gills are the only way I know of to do that. I'm tired of waiting. Decide whether you're coming or whether I'm leaving."

"We're coming," Ven said as he let go of his neck. "Sorry—it's just instinct. Let's go."

Char nodded, but did not remove his hands.

The merrow disappeared below the surface of the water.

The two boys hurried south over the packed sand along the shore.

"Ya know, it's not too late to change your mind, Ven," Char muttered. "We could get a boat or somethin', and follow her out to sea, like we did when we were chasing the Floatin' Island, and then *dive* down to see whatever she wants to show us—"

"You can stay on shore if you want to, Char," Ven said, trying to see the merrow in between the waves. "But I promised her a long time ago that I would explore her world with her. It's now or never."

"Have it your way," Char said gloomily. "You always do anyway."

They followed the pebbly path in the sand south until the fishing village came into sight. Several long piers led out into the harbor, with docks along each of them. Small boats lined the docks. At each boat fishermen were hauling nets filled with flapping fish and cages with crabs and lobsters onto the piers. Seagulls flew in great wide circles above, screeching and crying, then diving for food.

"So how did she happen to find this Asa, and how does she know he won't just cut our throats?" Char asked as they picked their way among barrels and pieces of rope on the slats of the pier.

Ven shrugged. "No idea. But sailors and merrows have a pretty good connection." He pointed about halfway down the pier, where a small green fishing boat with a red bottom bobbed lazily in the morning tide. A wrinkled man in a wrinkled hat sat on a barrel at the edge of the dock, cleaning his morning catch of fish. "Could that be him?"

Char squinted. "I guess so."

"Come on. We may as well ask. If it's not Asa, he probably knows where to find him. Fishermen all know each other."

The two boys walked along the pier, stepping out of the way of men dragging lobster traps and heavy netting, until they got to the red-bottomed boat. They stopped behind the elderly fisherman, who did not seem to notice they were there.

Ven coughed politely.

"Excuse me, sir—are you Asa?"

The fisherman looked up from his work, his sky-blue eyes twinkling in the sun.

"Who's askin'?"

"Er, my name is Ven, sir. I was told I might find a fisherman at this dock who could, uh, cut gills."

The wrinkly man nodded. "Well, *Ven*, you've found 'im. But I can't say as I've heard of any recent wrecks."

Ven blinked. "Pardon?"

"Shipwrecks," said the fisherman. "That's the only reason I know of for a man to risk a slice in his neck—to salvage the treasure from the bones of a shipwreck."

"Oh." Ven and Char exchanged a glance, then looked off the edge of the dock.

In the water behind the boat, the beautiful tail of multicolored scales was waving at them from beneath the surface.

"Uh, we weren't really planning to dive for treasure," Ven continued, trying to block the sight of the merrow's tail. "We just want to do some exploring."

The fisherman's eyebrows arched.

"The sea's no place to explore without a good reason, lads," he said seriously. "Lots of bad stuff down there—believe you me. The only reason a man takes his life into his hands on a daily basis by going out there is to make a living for his family. Otherwise, we'd farm the land." The blue eyes twinkled. "If we knew how."

"Well, we'd really like to have gills, nonetheless," Ven said. "We've been told you know how to, er, cut them without too much pain—and safely. Is that true?"

Asa exhaled, then nodded.

"I suppose that depends on how much is too much where pain is concerned," he said. "That's really up to you. It's not my business what you're doing. We mind our own business on the sea. If you want gills, and you're willing to take the risk, I can cut 'em for you right quick." He held up a thin silver filleting knife. "Then I have to get back to cleaning my catch. So, what'll it be? Make haste, now."

Char and Ven looked at each other once more, then nodded at the same time.

"We're in," said Char.

"All right then," said Asa. He reached into the boat and took hold of the top of a small sea chest that held his tackle. He slammed it closed and put it on the dock in front of them. "Kneel down and put your heads on this chest, your left ears down."

The boys obeyed.

"Well, 's been good to know you," Char whispered as they positioned their heads on the chest.

"Shhh," Ven whispered back. "We're not being executed, for pity's sake."

"You hope we're not. You never know."

Asa wiped the filleting knife on his trousers, then came and stood over Ven.

"Hold very still, now."

Char winced and put his hand over his eyes.

Ven started to close his eyes as well.

Suddenly, from the end of the dock near town, a bright flash of rainbow-colored light blinded him.

And the world seemed to stop around him.

## - 2 -

# The Fortune Teller's Return

$V$EN LOOKED EAST INTO THE LIGHT OF THE CLIMBING SUN.

A tall, thin shadow was standing there where nothing had been a moment before. The rays of morning light made it look like the shadow was dancing in the air, which had suddenly become still and heavy.

Ven's eyes opened wide.

"Madame Sharra?" he whispered.

He blinked. The shadow came into focus.

Standing at the edge of the pier near town was a woman of great height, with golden skin and eyes. The eyes were watching him closely.

*This was only the third time I had ever seen her.*

*The first time was in a fortune teller's tent inside the Gated City, the magical, terrifying Market of Thieves behind high walls inside the city of Kingston. I paid a gold coin to draw from her deck of cards made from dragon scales, and in return she told me many things about my future that were both exciting and troubling.*

*The second time was at the abandoned pier in the north of*

*Kingston where Amariel and I meet. She had come out of the*
*Gated City, something I had not known was possible to do, with a*
*warning for me. She told me that the path of my footsteps into*
*the future was disappearing from her sight, a possible sign that*
*my life is drawing to its end.*

*And she gave me one of her dragon scales. It led to an exciting*
*adventure which almost made that prediction come to pass.*

*Now she is here again.*

*I guess I should stop being surprised by things like this.*

*Whenever she is near, Time seems to slow down around us. The*
*bells of the city stop ringing, the people freeze in place; even Char,*
*who is kneeling beside me, covering his eyes, does not seem to be*
*breathing.*

*But maybe that's because he was peeking through his fingers,*
*staring at the fisherman's knife.*

The golden eyes did not blink in return.

"Is this how you intend to bring my prophecy to its end, Ven
Polypheme?"

"Excuse me?" Ven stammered.

"You are allowing a man you just met to slash your throat? Why?"

Ven sat up, careful to avoid the knife in the fisherman's motionless hand above him, and began walking toward the golden woman.

"Er—well, I need to be able to breathe underwater." As soon as
the words came out of his mouth, Ven could almost feel them fall
foolishly to the ground in the heavy air around him. He swallowed
and tried again. "So I can go into the sea."

Madame Sharra's expression did not change.

"For what reason is a Nain, a son of the Earth, going into the
sea?"

Ven blinked again. His eyes felt as heavy as his tongue.

"Lots of reasons," he said slowly. "Amariel—the merrow over
there—she's my friend." He pointed to the motionless tail rising out

of the water, just the fluke fin visible. "I've been promising her for a long time I would come and explore the sea with her. It's her home. She came out of the sea to explore *my* world—she grew legs, in fact, and—"

"A good reason, perhaps, but good enough to risk death?" asked the golden woman. "Is there another reason?"

"Well, it's sort of my job." Even as he spoke the words, Ven thought they sounded silly. "King Vandemere—the ruler of this island—has asked me to make note of any magic hiding in plain sight in the course of my travels. He—he thinks I have the ability to see that magic, and he wants to protect it. He thinks there is a great magical puzzle, and when we have enough pieces, we can solve it, and know why the world was made and what we are supposed to do with it. I've been keeping notes in my journals—"

The golden eyes did not blink.

"There certainly is a great deal of magic to be found in the sea. A great deal of danger as well. You can find magic hiding almost anywhere you look. Why the sea?"

Ven's mind felt like it was slowing down along with the world around him. "Uh, well, you were the one who warned me that the Thief Queen in the Gated City was searching for me. It will be hard for her to find me in the sea, won't it?"

Madame Sharra let her breath out slowly. Ven thought he could see it sparkle in the air as she did. She glanced back over her shoulder to the north, where the Gated City stood within the walls of Kingston.

"If that is your reason, I suggest you leave as quickly as you can once I am gone."

Ven followed her glance.

The sky in the distance was darkening with what looked like thin black clouds. Ven stared harder.

Though they were barely moving, he could see that what he thought were clouds was actually a gathering flock of dark birds.

"Ravens," he whispered. "She knows I'm here. Felonia knows I'm here."

"Perhaps." Madame Sharra looked back at him, and her eyes narrowed. "Only one full turn of the moon has passed since last you and I met on the northern docks by the Gated City, Ven Polypheme. I warned you then that she and all her minions were seeking you. You left Westland to escape the Thief Queen's spies. For what reason did you return so soon?"

Ven coughed nervously. "I—had to get Amariel back to the sea," he said. "If I hadn't, she would have stopped being a merrow and been human forever."

"That seems folly. You don't appear to have spent too much thought on your reasons for making important decisions, Ven Polypheme." The golden woman looked down into her hands. "But then, one does not always know the reason at the beginning of a journey. Sometimes you find the reason in the course of it. What matters is that at the end, you know why you undertook the journey in the first place."

She extended her long, slender hand.

*In it were two clear stones that looked a little like the marbles I used to shoot with my brothers Leighton and Brendan back home in Vaarn. The marbles we had played with were made from bits of glass fired into balls when the glass was hot. There was something different about these two stones—they gleamed in the light so cleanly and brightly that my eyes stung. There was something so enchanting about them that it was all I could do to keep from snatching them out of her palm.*

"These will spare your throat, and that of your friend," Madame Sharra said. "Take them."

Ven obeyed. The stones were icy cold to the touch, and vibrated with what almost seemed like a hum.

"What are they?"

The golden woman smiled slightly.

"Hold your breath," she said.

Ven obeyed. He took air deep into his lungs and held it.

*Unlike most Nain, who fear the water, I can swim. In fact, I love to swim. Some of the happiest times of my life have been spent diving for pebbles and sea glass with Partch, a human school friend, in the shallow water off the docks in Vaarn, on the other side of the world where I was born. I can hold my breath for a pretty long time as a result of all that diving.*

*But as time went on I realized I had held it much longer than I ever had before.*

*And I didn't feel it was running out.*

*So I stood there, holding my breath, my chest loose and my heart steady.*

*For a very long time.*

After what seemed like five or more minutes, he held out his hands in question.

"Elemental wind," Madame Sharra said. "Living Air, left over from when the world was new. You don't need to breathe as long as it is on your person, so guard these carefully. They will breathe for you. If they are lost, however, the need to breathe returns immediately, no matter where you are, even fathoms deep in the sea. Should that happen, it is unlikely you will be able to return to the surface in time, and even if you do, coming up too quickly can be worse than drowning."

Ven let his breath out. "Thank you," he said. His voice was filled with awe. He put the stones in the buttoned pocket of his vest and rebuttoned it carefully.

"You still have one of the other gifts you have received from me," Madame Sharra went on. She pointed to his palm, where the image of an hourglass, thread, and scissors could still be seen. "You have chosen not to make use of the gift of the Time Scissors?"

*The image appeared in my palm when I chose a card from her deck during my reading in her tent. It came, she said, with the power to undo one thread of Time from my past, to change anything I had done. It's very odd to see a picture in my hand, a lot like the tattoos sailors sometimes get on their arms or chests. But for some reason, no one can see it but me. Well, I guess not no one—none of my friends have been able to see it except Amariel.*

*And she's a very unusual friend.*

"Not yet," Ven admitted. "I'm a little nervous about undoing something I've done in the Past. I want to make sure that there is no other choice when I resort to that."

"Wise of you. And the dragon-scale card? What have you done with that?"

Ven swallowed hard.

"I—uh—gave it to a dragon named Scarnag I met in the eastern lands past the Great River." When the golden woman remained silent, he pressed on. "It came from the, er, hide of his mother."

Madame Sharra was quiet for a moment. Then she reached into the folds of her robe and took out a thick oval stone casing, black as midnight, and handed it to Ven.

*My hands shook as I reached for it. I had seen a casing like that before. This was a sheath of Black Ivory, like the one that held the first dragon-scale card she gave me. A thin, sharp ridge stuck out of the top, just as it had before.*

*Black Ivory is a piece of stone so dead that every particle of magic has been stripped completely out of it. As a result, it can hide anything from any type of sight.*

*Which is good, because the only things I've ever seen in Black Ivory sleeves are very powerful and very dangerous. They seem to call out to the world in invisible waves of sound when they are not hidden away.*

*About the last thing I want to do with something in a Black Ivory sleeve is to pull it out.*

*But I can tell by the look on Madame Sharra's face that this is exactly what she expects me to do.*

He carefully ran his finger over the slit at the top.

The sharp ridge seemed to have vanished.

He tried again.

Nothing.

Ven looked at the top of the Black Ivory sleeve carefully. He could still see what looked like the ridge of a dragon scale, but when he tried to touch it, there was nothing there.

"Is it empty?"

"For the moment." Madame Sharra passed her right hand over her left. In the left hand a deck of dragon-scale cards appeared, spread out like a fan. Each was a dull gray, scored with scratches. The light of the morning sun, frozen in the sky, revealed all the colors in them, causing them to flash like the rainbow Ven always saw whenever Madame Sharra appeared.

*Ahh*, he thought. *It's not her—it's the scales that cause the flash. That makes sense.*

"Does one of these cards call to you?" Madame Sharra asked.

Ven stared at the deck.

At first he saw no difference between them. Then, after a closer look, one of the scales tucked within the fan began to glow and vibrate with a tinge of indigo blue. Deep in his ears, it felt as if a very large bell had rung and was vibrating still.

He pointed to the card.

"That one."

The golden woman nodded.

"Be certain of your choice, Ven Polypheme," she said. "Because if you choose incorrectly, you may never get the chance to make such a choice—or any choice—again."

# - 3 -

# Frothta

Ven's pointed finger shook a little, but did not move.

"That one," he repeated. "That's the only one whose tone I can hear."

The indigo glow disappeared.

"Take it out of the sleeve," she said.

Ven's brows drew together in confusion. Madame Sharra's gaze grew cold, so he quickly held up the Black Ivory sleeve and pinched the sharp edge sticking out from the within the black stone.

This time his fingers felt something solid.

He pulled gently.

At first what peeked out looked like a dull gray piece of wax with a finely etched surface and sharp, frayed edges.

"Is this the scale I chose? How did it get in here?"

Madame Sharra's gaze grew colder, but she said nothing.

Quickly, as carefully as he could, Ven took hold of the sharp edge and pulled it from the Black Ivory sleeve.

Another colored flash stung his eyes.

In his hand was a tattered, grayish scale similar to the one he had been given before, with fine lines and strange writing across its surface. It hummed with a music he could feel deep within his ears.

The scale was slightly curved, as the other ones had been. On the hollow side was a crude image of a tree etched into the surface, with what looked like waves above it. Beneath the image were symbols in a language Ven did not recognize. *What is this now?* he wondered.

"This scale is known as Frothta," Madame Sharra said. "The image is that of the tree of living, elemental water, old as the world is old. Legends say that once, long ago, in the Before-Time, it grew atop a tall mountain in the depths of the sea."

"And are those legends true?"

The golden woman shrugged slightly.

"My eyes have never beheld such a thing. My ears have never heard the words of anyone else who has seen it. It may have existed once, long ago. Many things born at the time that the world was new are gone now. Old magic has largely passed from the earth. I cannot say for certain that it no longer lives, but if it does, it has fallen away from the sight of the Deck." A smile flickered at the corners of her mouth. "Just as you are trying to hide from the eyes of the Thief Queen."

Ven's curiosity was burning so hot that his hair hurt.

"How would I find it? If it still exists, that is."

"If you are looking for lost magic that was born in the Before-Time, you will need to find a place that no one else could look for it. It might be in a place of extremes—the hottest and coldest part of the sea, the highest and lowest place in the world, the brightest and darkest realms, all at the same time." The Seer's smile faded. "Or you might have to accept that it no longer exists, as the rest of the world has. And that now Frothta is merely a symbol, just like all the rest of the runes and images on the scales of the Deck. A prediction of your future."

"What does it mean?"

The golden eyes grew brighter. "When this card is drawn in a reading it can have many meanings. Sometimes it warns of an impossible task. Perhaps it is a warning about the journey you are about to undertake." She smirked as Ven's eyes opened wide. "Or perhaps not. Sometimes it can mean bringing new power to an old or dead situation, the solving of what had been an unanswerable riddle or a lost cause."

"That would be better," said Ven.

"It can sometimes warn of something that is too good to be true," Madame Sharra went on. "Right side up, it can signify breathing underwater, while upside down it can warn of drowning. And sometimes, it just means 'the sea.'"

Ven stared at the image as long as he dared, then slid it quickly back into the sleeve. He held it out to Madame Sharra again. The golden woman shook her head.

"You are giving this to me?" Ven asked. "Why?"

"You seem to know what to do with it."

"No, really, I don't," Ven said quickly. "I have no idea what to do with this. Please take it back. I'm going into the sea, and as you have already pointed out, I really don't know what I am doing—"

"Be that as it may, the scale wishes to accompany you, at least for now." Madame Sharra glanced over her shoulder again in the direction of the Gated City. "Perhaps it will help you discover the reason for your journey into the sea, Son of Earth."

Ven looked down at the stone sleeve again. He ran his finger over the smooth surface. He imagined he could feel the vibration of the scale through the Black Ivory, even though he knew it was not possible.

"I'm afraid I will lose it in the sea," he said finally.

"It will not be the first time such a thing has happened to the Deck of Scales, nor will it be the last," Madame Sharra said. She looked more sharply at Ven.

"Do not be distressed, Ven Polypheme," she said. "You are confused, because you have not sorted out your reasons for doing what you do in life. I believe the scales are trying to tell you something."

"What? What are they trying to tell me?"

"I am not certain. But I can tell you this: in all the history of the Deck of Scales, from the Before-Time to now, they have never chosen someone to carry them as two of them have chosen you. The Deck has always been entrusted to a special tribe of Seren priestesses, Seers like myself, who read them as fortune-telling cards to anyone who can find us and pay us a gold coin. The mark in your hand that came from the Time Scissors scale has never been drawn by any of those people. There is something about you that is unique, totally unique in all the world. At least as far as the Deck is concerned."

Madame Sharra paused and drew breath again, as if it was becoming hard to do so in the heavy, still air.

"The fact that you returned the first scale to a dragon is *very* important. I have long believed, as did many of the Seers before me, that these scales should never have been marked with runes and pictures as they have been. They should never have been used to tell fortunes. They were sacred gifts, given for a sacred purpose, by creatures who were born at the beginning of Time. There are very few dragons left living in these days, Ven Polypheme—but you thought to return the scale you carried to one of them. And now another scale wants to travel with you."

Ven's curiosity was itching so fiercely that his head felt as if ants were crawling through his hair.

"Do—do you think this one wants me to find another dragon and return it as well?"

"I cannot say." The golden woman smiled. "That certainly seems an impossible task."

Ven was staring at the sandy ground, counting in his head.

"Impossible tasks, something too good to be true, bringing new power to an old or dead situation, breathing underwater, and the sea." When he looked up, his eyes were shining with excitement. "That sounds like a good forecast for our underwater adventure."

Madame Sharra's face lost its smile.

"Remember two things, Ven Polypheme: everything in the sea is food to something else. And the sea is always hungry."

Ven looked up in alarm. As he did, the rainbow light flashed again, searing his eyes and making him blink.

When he opened them again, Madame Sharra was gone.

Time was beginning to move once more.

And, in the distance, so was the storm cloud of ravens.

# - 4 -

# Eyes in the Sky

LIKE AN ARROW SHOT FROM A BOW, VEN DASHED BACK TO THE
end of the pier.

"Wait!" he shouted. "*Wait!*"

The fisherman's hand descended toward Char's neck.

With speed born of panic, Ven grabbed Asa's wrist in midslice.

And, in the process, accidentally booted Char off the dock and
into the shallow water beneath it.

The thin silver knife followed him off the edge. The loud *splash*
was followed by a tiny *plink*.

The old fisherman gasped, then grunted.

"Well, what—what—well—"

"I'm sorry," Ven stammered. He looked off the end of the pier,
where the water was bubbling, but saw no sign of Char.

"By the Great Blowhole, what was *that*?" Asa demanded. "You could
have cut my bloody *hand* off! Not to mention your friend's throat.
And how did you—weren't you—"

"I'm sorry," Ven said again as Char's head broke the surface,
shaking like a dog's.

He looked north toward the Gated City. The black mass in the
sky was quickly spreading south like oozing tar. Then he looked
back at the furious expression on the fisherman's face.

"We—we have to hide from them," he said, pointing at the approaching ravens. "I apologize. I hope your hand's all right."

"Ven—what the *heck*?" Char's voice was full of salt water.

The fisherman followed Ven's finger. "No need to worry about them, lad. They fly this beach every morning, then fan out to the rest of the island. They're messy and loud, but they won't bother you." He turned back and stared at Ven. His pale blue eyes narrowed. "Unless they're looking for you."

Ven said nothing.

Asa let out a low whistle. "Man alive—they're—they are! They're looking for *you*?"

Ven nodded. His words had dried up.

The fisherman took in a deep breath. "You've angered the Thief Queen? Well, then, you'd best get off my dock."

"Yes sir." Ven started back toward the sand.

"Not that way." Asa's arm shot out, and before he knew it, Ven was falling backward, joining Char in the shallow waves.

He came up coughing.

Asa's face appeared above them over the edge of the wooden planks.

"Get under the dock, lads. Hurry."

Ven took hold of Char's arm and pushed him into the striped shadows under the dock, ignoring his sputtering.

The black cloud of ravens had reached the northern edge of the fishing village. Their harsh screams filled Ven's ears, freezing his muscles. He tried to move his feet, but they slipped on the seaweed-covered rocks and shells in the sand below them. The retreating waves tugged him back deeper into the harbor.

"Out of sight, boys," said Asa. "Their eyes are sharp—if they look your way, they can see you from where they are."

At his words, the stripes of sunlight on Char's wet face and shoulders disappeared.

The sky turned dark above them. The harsh cawing of the birds grew louder as they came closer.

"Come on!" Char yelled. He grabbed for Ven's hand, but slid in the seaweed below the dock himself and missed.

"Too late," the fisherman shouted. "Better to stand still—if you move, they'll surely see you now."

*I did as he said, but not because he said it.*

*I didn't really have any other choice.*

*No matter how hard I tried, I couldn't move.*

*Almost from the time I have been on the Island of Serendair, those birds have been chasing me.*

*Felonia, the Queen of Thieves, is the mistress of the Raven's Guild in the Gated City. She has thousands of ravens in her command, acting as her spies.*

*If they see us, Felonia will have found us.*

*That possibility is the worst thing I can imagine at the moment.*

*And I have a pretty good imagination.*

The fisherman sighed. He picked up the bucket of fish guts and tossed the contents onto the planks of the dock. Then he grabbed a tarp and ducked beneath it.

Suddenly, a tornado of gray and white feathers swirled above Ven's head. The cawing of the ravens was drowned in a much louder, much higher-pitched screeching.

From everywhere along the water, over the wharf and all along the beach, seagulls appeared. There were thousands of them, diving and swooping at the dock. Fighting for every scrap of fish skin and bone, they engulfed the old dock and the air above it, flapping and fluttering, then returning to the skies for another dive.

The dark cloud of approaching ravens veered away from the gray and white tornado of hungry gulls and headed east, out of the bird storm.

"Get under the dock!" the fisherman shouted from beneath his tarp.

Char grabbed Ven's arm and yanked him beneath the planks.

The two boys clung to the wooden support beams, trembling from cold and fear. The shallow waves sloshed over them, pulling at their feet.

Almost as quickly as it had begun, the storm of gulls was over. As soon as the contents of the fisherman's bucket had been devoured, the birds took off, scattering into the skies, looking for more food.

Ven waited until he could no longer hear their shrill cries. Then he poked his head cautiously out from under the dock.

"Are you all right, Asa?"

"Eh-yup. They're gone—the ravens, that is."

Ven and Char pulled themselves out from under the dock, making their way around the small dinghy, and waded to shore. Their clothes, soaked with seawater, weighed them down as they climbed back onto the dock and walked down to the end.

All along the decking were gray and white stripes and blots that matched the ones on Asa's tarp. The fisherman was gingerly removing it from his head, a look of disgust on his face.

"Oh, man," Char whispered. "Have you ever seen so much seagull poop?"

Ven shook his head.

"We are so sorry," he said to Asa as the old man tossed the tarp into the dinghy. "We owe you our lives."

The fisherman turned back to them, his hand shading his blue eyes from the sun.

"You also owe me most of a day's catch and a filleting knife."

From the water below the dock, a girl's arm emerged. There was a slight webbing between the fingers of the hand, which was gripping a small silver knife.

Ven bent down over the edge and took it, then gave it to Asa. The merrow's hand disappeared into the waves.

The fisherman stared at the knife in amazement.

"How'd you do that?"

Ven shrugged.

"I always try to pay my debts," he said. "I will come back and work for you, if you'll have me, so that I can replace the day's catch as well."

"Me too," added Char.

Asa wiped the knife on his trousers, glanced over the side of the dock, then turned back to Ven.

"Never mind the catch. I suppose in place of the lives you owe me, I would take a story," he said. "I don't know what you boys are up to, but anyone who's angered the Queen of Thieves that much must have a whale of a tale to tell."

"It's getting to be pretty interesting," Ven admitted. "But I'm not sure it's going to turn out very well."

"I'd like to hear it nonetheless," said the fisherman. "But not today. I'm way behind in my work now, and you are going to miss the outgoing tide if you wait much longer. If you want to get to a wreck, or wherever else you're off to in the sea, you'd best be on your way. The ocean is dark and frightening enough in daylight. You don't want to be caught out there after the sun goes down—it will make every nightmare you ever had seem like the pleasantest of dreams, believe me."

"When we return I will come and tell you the tale," Ven promised.

Asa laughed.

"A man of adventure should learn the difference between *when* and *if*, lad," he said merrily. "But I do admire your spunk. Do you still want those gills?"

"No, thanks all the same," Ven said hurriedly. "I think we can make do without them today."

Asa laughed again.

"A wise choice. Well, come and tell me your tale sometime, Ven. But make sure you come early—a fisherman does a whole day's work before the sun even comes up. Morning's my busy time—I can't afford to be buried in seagull filth every day."

"Sorry about that."

"And stay clear of Felonia—I'm looking forward to hearing what you did to gain her anger, and whether you survive it or not."

"So am I," said Ven. "Thank you again, and sorry for the mess."

The fisherman waved a dismissive hand at him and went back to trimming what was left of his catch.

"Good luck, boys," he said. "May the waves be kind to you."

"And you as well," Ven said. It had been a long time since he had heard the expression, but it was one that had been said to him many times before, by the sailors on the *Serelinda*, and back in the harbor town of Vaarn, where he was born. It made him feel homesick. "Goodbye."

They hurried down the dock and back onto the beach, scanning the shallow water for a sign of the merrow.

They could not have felt the gaze of the spyglass that was watching them now from atop the wall of the Gated City far to the north of the dock.

# - 5 -

# Thrum, Drift, and Sunshadow

*By the time we made it back to the abandoned dock at the northern edge of town, our clothes had stopped dripping, though it would have been wrong to say they were dry.*

*The look in the green eyes that were floating above the surface of the water off the end of the dock, however, was hot enough to make it seem as if all the water had been blasted out of them.*

"Now, Amariel, don't be angry," Ven began. The words dried up immediately in his mouth. He could see he was too late to prevent that. He swallowed and tried again. "I—"

"Why didn't you let Asa cut your gills?" the merrow demanded.

"Well, because I have these—this—"

"Does it have something to do with that golden woman?"

Ven's mouth fell open.

"You could see her?"

"Who?" Char asked, confused.

"Of course I could see her," Amariel said. "Do you think I'm *blind?*"

"What are you *talking* about?" Char asked again.

Ven held up his hand, and Char fell silent.

*I'm not sure why Amariel can see things that none of my other friends or the people I know on the Island of Serendair can see. First it was the image of the Time Scissors in my palm, and now she has seen Madame Sharra, around whom Time seems to stop. Amariel is able to see magic things.*

*Maybe it's because she's magical herself.*

"Just what did you see, Amariel?"

The merrow shrugged, her long hair falling over the colorful scales that came up to her armpits.

"At Asa's pier, there was a sunshadow of a tall, golden woman swimming in a pool of sparkly air."

"Sunshadow?"

Amariel spat out a stream of water in annoyance.

"Don't pretend to be stupid, Ven. You talked to her. You took something from her!"

Char threw his hands up in confusion.

"All right, everybody calm down," Ven said. He cast a glance over his shoulder, scanning the skies for dark birds. "Let's meet under the pier—we'll be out of sight there."

The merrow gave him a grudging look, then dived.

"Come on," Ven said to Char. He sat down on the rotten planks of the pier and pushed himself off into the shallow waves.

"We just got dry," Char grumbled, following him.

A moment later they were up to their waists in seawater, their toes gripping the slippery stones under the dock.

The merrow's head broke the surface of the water in front of them. She still looked angry.

Ven waded over and grabbed on to one of the salt-encrusted posts holding up the dock. He reached into the buttoned pocket of his vest and carefully took out the stones of elemental air.

"I saw Madame Sharra again," he said. "You've not met her, Amariel, but Char has."

Char spat out the seawater from the wave that had filled his open mouth.

"Madame Sharra? *Where?*"

"As Amariel said, at the end of Asa's pier. Just as he was about to cut our gills, I saw that rainbow flash, and Time seemed to stop. She gave me another dragon scale—and these." He held his fist up out of the waves and opened his fingers slightly.

The stones that had glowed in the heavy air of stopped Time now looked like little more than shiny soap bubbles.

Amariel and Char looked down at them. The merrow shrugged, and Char shook his head.

"These are bits of elemental air," Ven explained. "If Char and I carry them, and don't lose them, we will be able to breathe underwater without gills."

"What's wrong with gills?" Amariel demanded.

"For you, nothing—you were born with them. But sooner or later the kind that Asa can cut seal shut on a human or a Nain, and if that happens deep underwater—well, we're unlikely to make it back to the surface safely. So if we carry these, we should be able to follow you wherever you want to go."

The merrow exhaled. "Well, all right then. There won't be any blood in the water, either, which is always a bad thing. Sharks can smell even the smallest amount of blood in the water."

Char grabbed his neck again.

"Put this in your pocket," Ven said as he handed Char one of the air stones.

"I don't have a vest," Char protested. "And my trousers' pocket doesn't have a button like yours."

"Fill your pocket with stones on top of it," Amariel suggested. "The extra weight should hold it down, and help you keep underwater."

"Good idea," Ven said. He bent down and began gathering pebbles from beneath the dock. "You said you saw a sunshadow, Amariel—what is a sunshadow?"

Amariel stared at him for a moment, then sighed. The fury went out of her green eyes.

"I had forgotten that you really don't know anything about the sea," she said. "All right. Let's have a quick lesson, and then we should go if we want to catch the outgoing tide."

Char finished filling his pocket with pebbles, then grabbed hold of a post as well, shivering.

"Under the sea," Amariel began, "the sunlight breaks the surface now and then, and goes down very far, leaving a bright, fuzzy beam. If there is any thrum in the way, it causes a sunshadow."

"Thrum?" Ven interrupted.

"Thrum is the special vibration that comes from each creature, each thing on earth. Land-livers don't know about thrum, because the vibrations are caught by the air and the wind of the upworld, and so you can't usually feel or hear thrum there. But in the sea, beneath the waves, you can feel thrum all around you. When a school of whales goes through, you can hear the thrum for miles. Volcanoes, giant sharks, sinking ships—all of them give off thrum. That's how I met you, Ven—my school could hear the explosion of your ship, and we came, looking for a party in the wreckage."

"I remember," said Ven.

*It seemed a million miles away and many years ago, even though only a few months have passed since then. I blew up a ship my father had sent me to inspect, the Angelia. Amariel rescued me from drowning, and Captain Snodgrass, along with the sailors of the Serelinda, had rescued me from the sea. That's how I met Char, and came to live on the Island of Serendair.*

*And now my two best friends and I are off to explore the wonders of Amariel's world.*

*My curiosity is on fire.*

*Even the water all around me can't put it out.*

"Do you hear thrum?" Char asked. "Or do you feel it?"

"It's hard to say whether you feel it or you hear it," Amariel said. "But it's the way the entire ocean makes noise. You don't need to talk with your mouth underwater—your thrum does it for you. And your thoughts are a large part of thrum. If you happen to be in a shaft of sunshadow when you are thinking strongly about something, your thoughts sometimes appear as pictures in the hazy water. It can be very embarrassing."

"I'll bet," Char muttered.

"So unless you want everyone and everything around you to know what you are thinking, try not to get too excited or think too hard about something near a sunshadow. You wait until you're in regular drift before doing that."

"Drift?"

"Drift is just the normal current of the sea, the movement of the water. When there's no storm, drift is just like being in the air of the upworld. You feel tugged by it when you are close to shore because of the tides, but once you are out in the Deep, you are barely aware of the drift around you unless it changes suddenly. And that usually means trouble is coming."

"Why did you think Madame Sharra was a sunshadow, then?" Ven asked.

Amariel shrugged. "She looked like she wasn't real, exactly. She seemed to be in a shaft of light that came from behind the walls of the Gated City. And while that beam started out in the Gated City, it ended in your head. Which was, I might add, lying at the moment on a box waiting to have gills cut in the neck below it."

"Really?" Ven exclaimed.

"Yes. Very powerful people—like the Sea King—can use sunshadow to send messages or even objects across wide expanses of ocean, just by the strength of their thoughts. So it seems to me that this golden woman who you saw in your head is really in the Gated City, but she was sending you a message, and perhaps your bubble and shell, using a land sunshadow."

She took a deep breath.

"All right. Enough mouth talking. It's making me tired. The tide's going out—are we leaving with it?"

"Absolutely," said Ven. "Let's go."

"Hold up a minute," Char said quickly. "Can we at least try out these bubble-stone things before we get in over our heads?"

"Sure," said Ven. "Hold your breath, and we will just walk out behind Amariel into the harbor. If it works the way it should, the stone should breathe for you. You'll know whether or not that's happening pretty quick."

Char sighed. "That's really not what I meant."

"Follow me," said the merrow. "And, for goodness' sake, if we come upon a shark, hold still and don't make any noise or movement until I discover if it's one of my friends or not. They can tell where you are by your movements. And your smell, of course, especially if you're bleeding. If you're bleeding, my friends might eat you by mistake—or even me. Blood in the water kind of cancels out any notion of politeness or friendship."

Ven thought back to a sight he had witnessed aboard the *Serelinda*, the ship that had rescued him from drowning, on which Char had served as a cook's mate. A giant fin, tall as the mainmast, had surfaced from the Deep, belonging to a prehistoric creature that had caused the hardened sailors of the *Serelinda* to freeze in terror.

"What about a shark like Megalodon?" he asked. "Isn't he so big that our blood would be of no notice to him? He's longer than the biggest ship I've ever seen moored at my father's factory."

Amariel shook her head.

"His pilot fish would notice even the smallest amount of blood," she said. "Megalodon is frightening, but the pilot fish is said to be utterly evil. He clings to Megalodon, helping guide him through the sea, and feeds off the scraps left behind from whatever Megalodon devours. And there always are some. You better hope we only meet sharks that are friends of mine."

Char swallowed nervously.

"I don't suppose Megalodon is a friend of yours," he said, half joking, half hopeful.

Amariel's voice was cold as frost on winter ground, clear in the air of the upworld.

"Megalodon has no friends," she said. "Even the pilot fish isn't his friend. The whole ocean fears him. Fortunately, it's a big ocean, and he lives fairly deep in it, down in the Twilight Realm. He only comes up every now and then to hunt. You have both seen Megalodon once already in your lives. It's pretty unlikely, unless you are *very* unlucky, that you will ever see him again. Especially if you don't call his name once you're underwater. Now, come on. The tide won't wait."

*At first I was very afraid.*

*I have been swimming most of my life, something about me that my family finds very upsetting, because Nain aren't supposed to be able to swim. I learned to swim in salt water, because my family's home and factory were in the seaside city of Vaarn, down on the harbor.*

*So I am used to my eyes stinging from salt.*

*It was hard to get out from under the dock. The small waves were more powerful than they seemed. They pushed us back toward shore even as they dragged at our feet. It took a few minutes to get out to where the water was over our heads.*

*Because Char is a little taller than me, it happened to me first.*

*The water closed over my nose and mouth. I tried not to panic and kept my mouth closed, but my breathing did not change. A moment later it was up over my eyes and ears, and that's when I felt a big difference.*

*Once my ears were under the water, all the sound of the upworld was gone. There was nothing but a pounding, like a heartbeat, in my head.*

*I looked above me, and was surprised to see that the sky was still visible beneath the water's surface. It moved and danced above the waves, which made me feel a little dizzy.*

*Suddenly, something slithered across my hand and my attention was drawn away from the sky. I was surrounded by schools of small fish, darting in between Char, Amariel, and me, zipping back and forth with perfect speed. Amariel waved them away like a swarm of flies in the upworld.*

*Char and I were so busy watching the fish that it took us several moments to notice that we were breathing underwater without any problem.*

"Let's keep going."

Ven could hear Amariel's voice in his head. She was smiling, and her lips had not moved, but he had heard her as clearly as if she had been standing right beside him.

"Lead on, Amariel," he thought to himself.

The merrow smiled more broadly, then nodded that she had heard him as well. She turned and headed out into the depths of the harbor, into the blue-green darkness streaked with dusty shafts of light.

Char looked at him. Ven could feel his best friend's sigh of despair in his skin. Then the two of them began swimming, as if walking in the air of the upworld, after her.

The thrum of the ocean was so slight, so distant, that they did not notice the schools of fish suddenly stop, then scatter quickly into the deeper shoals.

As if in fear for their lives.

# ~ 6 ~

# Kingston Harbor

I have always liked words.

It would not be honest to say that I was a great student back in Vaarn. Whenever the teacher was telling tales of history or geography, of places far beyond the small city in which I lived, he always had my complete attention. There was nothing more exciting to me than the prospect of exploring the world, or fighting in great battles, or solving riddles and puzzles. But when the lessons turned to mathematics, or spelling, or something else that failed to fire my imagination, I often found myself watching out the window of the schoolhouse, searching for pictures in the clouds.

My mind wanders easily.

My body wanders too, though much less easily, especially these days.

But I have always had a fondness for words. When I was at school I spent many nights writing down each new word I learned that day by candlelight. This made my brothers, Leighton and Brendan, who shared a room with me, hurl shoes at my head. By the time I turned fifty on my last birthday, making me about twelve in human years, I had a very thick journal of nothing but words that had tickled my fancy. I have been told I have a good vocabulary for a lad my age.

*But nowhere in that thick volume would I have been able to find words that could describe what I saw all around me in the world beneath the waves.*

*Because there are none.*

THE FARTHER THEY GOT OUT INTO THE HARBOR, THE LESS THE sand on the bottom shifted. The water around them became clearer, and bluer. Seaweed floated everywhere, and the boys watched how Amariel flipped her tail and waved her arms to get it to move out of her way as she swam.

"Not sure how we're supposed to do that," Char grumbled, slapping a patch of slippery weeds away. "I've only been in the sea a few minutes, an' already I can see you sorta have to have a tail to survive here."

"Not everything in the sea has a tail, Chum," said Amariel. The anger was gone from her voice now, replaced by excitement. "Only the lucky ones. If the crabs can survive without one, so can you."

Ven was not paying attention. He was watching a huge school of bright blue-and-yellow fish swim in and out of clumps of seaweed, above skittering shells that drifted toward the shore with each big wave.

"The colors in the sea are so much different than they are in the upworld," he said, marveling at a large, flat, many-legged creature, orange and flower-shaped, moving quickly along the bottom.

"Careful of that," Amariel warned. "That's a sunflower starfish. It may look pretty, but it's one of the hungriest creatures in the sea. I don't know if you can hear the thrum, but there's a whole colony of sea urchins screaming in fear up ahead. They can feel it coming, and they know that very few of them will escape being its lunch. They just can't move fast enough."

Ven shuddered. "Madame Sharra said that everything in the sea is food to something else, and that the sea is always hungry. It was the last thing she said to me."

"That's good advice," said the merrow. "If you don't pay attention, it *will* be the last thing she said to you."

As the thrum of her words died away, a long pointed shadow appeared on the surface above her head.

It was moving toward them, gliding in from deeper in the harbor, blocking the light as it passed. It dwarfed the school of fish swimming beneath it.

Ven felt his heart pound hard against his rib cage.

*Shark*, he thought. *Shark.*

Instantly, the blue-and-yellow fish vanished.

The sunflower starfish, now almost out of sight, froze. It buried the tips of its many legs into the sand and lay flat, all but disappearing into the bottom of the harbor.

Char's head whipped around, catching a clump of seaweed in his hair.

"*Shark?* Where, Ven? *Where?*"

Amariel spun around as well.

"What? Where's the shark? Hold still, for goodness' sake, Chum."

Ven stopped moving as well.

*Above you*, he thought, trying to think quietly.

Amariel's head did not move, but her eyes looked up. Then they returned to Ven. The thrum of her voice echoed in his ears, the tone sarcastic.

"Sharks don't have rudders, Ven," she said. "That's a fishing boat."

Ven looked up as well. Just as the merrow had said, what had looked like a tail on the shadow was just a piece of wood, like the hundreds he had seen manufactured in his family's factory.

Even in the cool seawater, he could feel his face turn hot.

"How embarrassing," he said. "I'm very sorry."

The merrow shrugged. "Don't tell me—tell *them*." She pointed at the hundreds of fish, now staring at him from within the seaweed. The sands at the bottom shifted as the sunflower starfish angrily pulled out its tentacles and shook them.

"Sorry, everyone," Ven repeated.

The school of fish regrouped and swam off in a huff. Ven could feel their annoyance in their thrum. The starfish crawled away, its fury clear. In the distance Ven thought the sea urchins had made use of his mistake to gain some time and escape. Their thrum was farther away, and less frightened.

"Well, at least the urchins made out well," he said to Amariel and Char, who were floating next to him.

"That's not funny, Ven," said the merrow sternly. "A shark warning is taken seriously by everyone in the sea. A false alarm doesn't make you any friends, trust me."

"I'll try to be more careful," Ven promised.

"You had better be. Come along, now."

The two boys followed the merrow as she swam farther out into the depths. The deeper they went, fewer shells dotted the sandy ocean floor. The sky, while still visible through the watery ceiling, was growing hazier. Only the sun was still clear, its rays spreading out in the green water, making shafts of light and shadow.

"Where are we goin', Amariel?" Char asked. "I've lost all bearings. Can you tell directions in the sea?"

"Of course." The merrow's voice was disdainful. "Seafolk have a lot better sense of direction than land-livers do."

"I think what Char meant to ask was what are you taking us to see," Ven said. "I'd like to know that as well. The harbor looks very different from underneath." He looked up at the surface of the water and marveled at the number of ships and small boats sailing by above them, unaware of everything that lay beneath the waves.

Just as he had been when they were on the decks of the *Serelinda*.

"Well, besides showing you the harbor of your own land, I thought we might go outside it and explore the coral reef," the merrow said. "This island is surrounded on almost every side by a huge wall of living creatures that protect it from storms and high seas. It might be nice for you to get to see them—and maybe say thank you."

"Good idea," Ven said.

"It will take a while to get to the reef—especially with you two slowpokes. We'll be lucky if we get out of the harbor by nightfall. We're heading north, so I guess we can make for the skelligs and sleep there tonight, then head west to the reef in the morning, when you can see all the colors and the creatures that live there."

"Skelligs?"

The merrow sighed. "Black pointy hills in the sea off the coast. You sailed right past them on the way here."

"Oh, yes," Ven said. "They look like dark teeth sticking out of the water not too far from shore." *Covered in mist*, he thought.

"A lot of merfolk and sea creatures like to hang out on the skelligs. Sea lions especially—merrows have to be careful of them, because the males are stupid and often mistake us for giant fish. It's the last part of the upworld you will see for a while once we get there. After that we head out to the coral reef. The water there is still pretty shallow. The reef is very large, so it will take a while to get to the edge of it and out to the True Deep."

"What does that mean, True Deep?" Char asked nervously. "You mean the bottom of the sea?"

"Don't worry—we will never leave the Sunlit Realm, the shallowest part of the ocean," Amariel said. "That's where all the normal creatures and plants live, because the sunlight shines through the water there. Most of the ocean is far too dark and cold for anything but monsters to live there. No self-respecting sea creature goes below a hundred fathoms."

"Do merfolk use the same measure of a fathom that sailors do?" Ven asked.

The merrow scowled. "I don't know what sailors use. They're *humans*, remember?"

"Right, sorry. A fathom's about six feet by human measure, about the size of a human man."

"That sounds about right. So the reef is very shallow, just a little bit over your head, for the most part. Once we're past it, we will be in the True Deep, anywhere from five to one hundred fathoms to the bottom. That's where the Sunlit Realm ends, and the Twilight Realm begins. We don't want to go there—it's a frightening place with very little light. Some really strange creatures live there that we would never want to meet up with. Twilight goes about five hundred fathoms deep, and then you're at the place where all light dies, the Midnight Realm. But that's very far away from here. *Way* too far for us to go, not that we would want to."

"I think exploring the Sunlit Realm sounds perfect," said Ven. "The skelligs and the reef sound like great fun."

"Then, maybe, if you're very good and things go well, we can travel past the reef and into the Sea Desert. That's a challenge, because the desert is a pretty scary place. A lot of the big predators, the sharks and giant octopi, live there—and most of them are *not* my friends. But if we want to go to the Summer Festival—which we *do*—we'll have to cross the desert. Believe me, it's worth it."

"The Summer Festival? Isn't that where you said you wanted to be a hippocampus rider in the great races there when you get older?" Ven asked.

Amariel smiled. "You *were* listening, then," she said. "I told you those stories when you were lying on that piece of driftwood after the explosion that blew up your ship. I wasn't sure you were awake."

"I was somewhere between awake and asleep. But I remember those stories very well. I've never seen a sea horse—er, hippocampus—especially not a giant one big enough to be ridden. I think that would be a very exciting thing to see."

"Me too," Char said.

A thought suddenly occurred to Ven.

"Do you know where there are any sea dragons, Amariel?" he asked.

"No," said the merrow. "Why?"

"Because I think I am supposed to return the scale Madame Sharra gave me to a sea dragon," Ven said. "She said it was important to discover the reason I am making this journey before it's over.

I think that may be part of the reason—to return this scale to the dragon who owns it, just like we did with Scarnag."

The merrow stared at him.

"I thought the reason was to explore the Deep with me, as you've been promising to do since we met," she said huffily. "I didn't realize you needed another reason."

"I don't," Ven said quickly. "But I think perhaps Madame Sharra does. Or at least she expects me to do something for her while I'm here."

"Well, there's no point in annoying anyone who is powerful enough to send things through a sunshadow," said Amariel. "We can always ask around about the dragon. But I warn you, if you're intentionally approaching a sea dragon's reef, I'm not going with you. Sea dragons breathe the same sort of fire that Fire Pirates use—it is not put out by water, and it burns like a thousand of the fires you have on land. Sea dragons, like any other dragon, are very protective of their reef lairs, and everyone stays clear of them. So if we learn of where one is, you can go visit it—as long as you do it by yourself."

"Fair enough," said Ven.

"What's goin' on over there?" Char's thrum sounded even more nervous than it had before.

Ven and Amariel turned in the direction he was pointing.

In the distance to what Ven guessed was the north, a great disturbance of sand and weed was churning.

Amariel's face lost its smile.

"That's the place outside the Gated City," she said. "It's a sort of undersea tunnel. When I first followed you to Serendair, I used to see people going in and out of there all the time, sometimes with barrels and crates, sometimes alone. It was closed for a while. It looks like they have it open again."

"Those are Felonia's people, I'd guess," Ven said. "It's one of the leaks in the Gated City—like a hole in the wall. That place was built to be a prison a long time ago, but it's clear that she has contact with the outside world. In fact, it seems like everyone in both the Inner and Outer markets has some way to get past the gates."

"My, you have a lot of interesting enemies," the merrow said. "I say we stay as far away from that as we can."

"Good idea," said Ven. "It's a shame. There are a lot of nice people trapped behind those walls that can't seem to get out, and yet the most evil of them, like the thieves and assassins in the Raven's Guild, don't have any trouble at all. It's disgusting."

"I guess everything in the upworld is food to something else, too," said Amariel. "Let's be on our way—the merfolk all know to stay well clear of that place."

"Amen," said Char.

Amariel turned and gave a strong sweep of her tail, heading back out toward the depths of the harbor. Char followed quickly behind, but Ven lingered for a moment, staring at the place where the underwater tunnel entered the market.

*The excitement I felt at finally getting to explore the Deep had dimmed a little.*

*When Char and I, along with our other friends, first went into the Gated City, we were dazzled by all the magic and the beautiful sights we found inside the walls of the Outer Market, where the townspeople of Kingston go to shop on Market Day. Everywhere we turned we saw bright colors, golden spangles, and odd animals that we never knew existed. We smelled rich meats roasting, spicy perfumes, and baked goods that made our mouths water from several streets away. And we heard sweet, entrancing music everywhere we went. It was such an interesting, exotic place that it was easy to forget that it wasn't a safe place. It was not until we were beyond the keyhole-shaped gate that led into the dark, misty streets of the Inner Market that we understood how the bright magic could mask deadly danger.*

*For just a moment, I felt a flash of that feeling again.*

*Then it was gone.*

*I wondered if seeing the tunnel into the Gated City was bringing back old, scary memories.*

*Or if the exotic call of the sea was masking a deeper danger.*

*But either way, it was too late to do anything about it.*

"Are you coming?" Amariel demanded.

Ven shook off his thoughts.

"Yes, sorry," he thought quickly in reply. "Lead away, Amariel. Show us the coral reef."

Amariel nodded, then turned and swam off into the sunshadows of Kingston Harbor.

Ven followed as fast as he could.

In the distance, he heard the familiar thrum once again echo against his ears, far away.

And then it was gone.

# - 7 -

# On the Skelligs

I T TOOK FAR LONGER TO REACH THE OPEN SEA THAN VEN COULD have imagined.

The drift was stronger the deeper out they went. Both he and Char could swim, but neither of them had ever had to do so for long. They found themselves getting tired easily.

"Weaklings," Amariel muttered as they took a break near some broken lobster traps at the bottom of the harbor. "Sheesh. How do you walk around in the air of the upworld when you are having so much trouble in the sea? The sea carries you. This shouldn't be so hard, Ven."

"We'll get used to it," Ven promised.

"Or die trying," Char added.

"Careful what you say," the merrow cautioned. "The sea is full of wishes. Yours might be granted by accident."

"What do you mean?" Ven asked.

"A lot of humans wish on the sea for luck," said the merrow. "They send messages in bottles or toss coins over the sides of ships. They even swear oaths by the sea, which is the truth in its purest form, a very powerful thing. Sometimes those wishes and oaths get caught in the waves and float around, trapped in the sea. If you happen to swim through one when you are wishing for something yourself, well, you may just get your wish. I don't think you want that one to come true, Chum."

"No, indeed," Char agreed. "Thanks. I'll be more careful."

"I had no idea Kingston Harbor was so busy," Ven said, looking overhead at the surface. Boats and ships of every shape and size passed over frequently now, darkening the surface with their shadows. The seaweed was thicker farther out from shore. Fish swam by in schools, pausing long enough to stare at them, then swam on.

They stopped frequently to rest. Finally Amariel turned to both boys.

"You're working far too hard," she said. "You're fighting the sea. Don't be surprised when the sea wins. If you want to survive down here, you need to learn to trust the drift. You weigh so much less here in the Deep than you do in the upworld. The tide is going out, which means the drift is pulling you naturally out to sea. Hold still a moment. Let it pull you with it. Take a look around you, then close your eyes."

Ven exhaled, then looked to Char, who nodded.


*When I relaxed my muscles, I could see what she meant.*

*Now that we were away from the shoreline, the tug of the sea was more gentle, less frightening than in the breaking waves. The air stone was filling my lungs without effort, which still felt unnatural in the water. I closed my eyes and let the drift carry me forward for a few seconds.*

*Amariel is right.*

*Trusting the drift, allowing it to carry you, makes traveling beneath the waves so much easier than trying to swim against the current.*

*But I can't help it.*

*I'm Nain, a Son of Earth. I have a very hard time putting my trust in the sea.*

*Especially after hearing that wish thing.*

"Now open your eyes."

The boys did as they were told.

Ven looked around. The seaweed that had been beneath their feet a few moments before was gone. They were hovering over some broken barrels and a long piece of slime-covered rope in the sand.

"Crikey," Char's thrum whispered.

"See?" said the merrow. "You've been making everything far harder than it needs to be, as always. Relax. We have a very long way to go, especially if you want to sleep on a skellig tonight. Now, let the drift carry you and come on."

Ven and Char followed her.

Even with the discovery of riding the drift, it still took a very long time to get out of the harbor. The shafts of sunshadow were growing shallower and fewer, by the time Amariel waved them to the surface.

"Let's go up to the air," she said.

The boys followed her. As they got closer to the surface, they could see the sky above had turned to colors of the sunset. Streams of red, orange, pink, and yellow light made the foamy top of the ocean look like clouds bursting with rainbows.

*Have I ever seen anything so beautiful?* Ven thought as he swam through the colorful water.

He could feel Amariel chuckle. "Keep your eyes open," she said. "I told you the sea has wonders that you could never imagine. Before you're on land again, you'll see glorious sights."

"Yeah, a lot of green water, gray fish, and slimy seaweed," Char said.

"You had best learn to keep your thoughts to yourself, Char," Ven said. He could feel how angry his friend's comments had made Amariel. "Thrum keeps no secrets, it seems."

"Sorry," Char mumbled. "It really is pretty here, Amariel."

"Hmmph."

They broke through the surface of the water, and Ven found himself gasping. The air of the upworld was thinner than he remembered, unlike the rich, sweet air the elemental stone had been providing. It took them a moment to adjust. Then the merrow pointed back toward where the shore had once been.

"I thought you might like to see the lighthouse," she said.

Ven looked off into the distance. Kingston's three great light towers were marvels of the Known World, Captain Snodgrass had told him. The tallest of the three stood at the opening of Kingston Harbor. The beams it threw guided ships into the safety of port from many miles away, often in some of the most terrible storms. He remembered the day they first sailed into Serendair's capital, how overwhelmed and excited he had been.

Now that giant tower was little more than a twig in the distance, far to the south. The bright flags that snapped merrily at the end of each pier in the harbor were nowhere to be seen.

Ven swallowed hard. He remembered how grand the harbor had seemed the first time he had seen it, sailing on the *Serelinda* with Char and Captain Snodgrass and the crew that had rescued him from the sea. There were so many people scrambling over the wharf, unloading cargo from hundreds of ships, just like the ones he had seen passing overhead, that the harbor looked like a giant ant-hill.

Now, as he floated in the sea beyond it, the harbor seemed like little more than a memory.

All around him was nothing but water for as far as he could see.

"Looks like the evening will be nice tonight," Amariel said. Ven looked up into the sky, where the colors of the sunset were fading to a beautiful green-blue at the horizon. Stars were winking in the dark blue beyond. A burning ball of orange hung over the western horizon, looking ready to drop into the waves. "The sea lions will be moonbathing on the skelligs. We should hurry if we want to make it there before Total Dark."

"Total Dark?"

"That's what merfolk call nightfall after sunset and before moon-rise. On nights when the moon is visible before the sun goes down, it's called a Brazen Moon.'"

My mother had used that word a good deal when I was back in Vaarn, and never in a good way. "Brazen" in her mouth meant cheeky or rude, something or someone that did not know its place, or that spoke out of turn.

But I could tell by the sparkle in Amariel's eyes that "brazen" was a good thing.

A brave thing.

A thing that's not afraid to be wherever it wants to, whether it is supposed to or not.

A lot like Amariel herself.

It's strange how so many words have different meanings on the land and in the sea.

"How far to the skelligs?" Char asked.

The merrow pointed north along the coast.

"If you squint you might be able to see them in the distance," she said. "Of course, I keep forgetting that humans—*and* Nain—seem almost blind when compared to the sharpness of merfolk sight. Follow the coastline to the horizon. Eventually you will be able to see them."

"It's getting dark," Char said, nervously looking into the sky.

"Come on," Amariel said. "We'll travel much faster under the water." She dove into the waves.

"Got your air stone?" Ven asked Char as he patted his vest.

Char felt around in his pocket.

"I think so. The pebbles are still there. It should be wedged at the bottom of 'em."

"Let's go, then. If you have a problem breathing, just head back to the surface and I'll catch up with you."

"Right," said Char.

The two boys followed the merrow into the depths.

The gloriously colored shadows of the sunset were all but gone from the green water of the sea now. Ven fixed his eyes on Amariel's multicolored tail as it swept through the waves, struggling to see in the darkening water. He tried to keep his mind clear of thrum, but he could not drive the words of the fisherman from his thoughts.

*The ocean is dark and frightening enough in daylight. You don't want to be caught out there after the sun goes down—it will make every nightmare you ever had seem like the pleasantest of dreams, believe me.*

Even without being able to see him, he could feel Char's nervousness beside him as he swam.

"Try to stay calm," he thought to his best friend. "Let the drift carry you if you can."

There were no words in the thrum of Char's answer, but Ven caught the meaning all the same.

After what seemed like forever, the merrow stopped in the drift, turned and hovered there.

"Now to the air," she said.

The boys followed her up.

They broke the surface together, gasping in the thin air of the upworld. Then they gasped again.

Rising out of the darkness just beyond them was a small mountain of black stone wrapped in thin white fog. The sun had left the sky, leaving only the faintest blue at the horizon. The last lingering light caught the gleaming slopes of the skellig, making them shine eerily in the darkness.

A terrifying howl was echoing off the caves and canyons of the tooth-like rock. It sent shivers through Ven, who was already trembling from the cold of the sea.

The merrow didn't seem to notice.

"This one is Skellig Elarose," she said matter-of-factly. "It's named for a type of undersea flower that grows on its rock roots below the surface. You'll see a lot of elaroses on the coral reef. The smaller one farther out near the reef is Skellig Lilyana. It was named for a merrow who was crowned Sea Queen once. She was from my school. We were all very proud."

"Once?" Char asked. "How often does a Sea Queen get crowned?"

"A new one gets crowned at the beginning of each Summer

Festival," Amariel said. "The Sea King and Queen only reign during the Festival. The ocean is far too big to have one king and queen all the time."

"Amariel, what is that horrible wailing?" Ven tried to see through the mist that was wrapping the skellig in a foggy veil, but the waves kept whacking him in the face, blurring his vision.

The merrow spat out a thin stream of seawater.

"Sea lions," she said. "They're pushing each other around, trying to get the best sleeping and moonbathing positions. They're in a *swell* mood tonight. We may have to slap a few around. Great. See, this is what happens when you come late. Oh well, let's get onto the beach."

"Slap around?" Char whispered to Ven. Ven shrugged. He swam hurriedly after the merrow, who was disappearing into the mist around the base of the skellig, Char close behind.

The mist thickened the closer they came to the rocky roots of the skellig. Ven peered through the haze as they approached the sea mountain's shore and saw a wriggling mass of black, slick bodies writhing on the slanted ground. The horrible noise bounced off the mountain's upper faces, scratching against the inside of his water-swollen ears.

The merrow had already reached the skellig, and was dragging herself onto the shore.

"Come on!" she called. "It's pretty flat here—you should be able to hold on once you've beached yourselves."

"*Beached* ourselves?" said Char aloud to Ven. "What are we now, whales?"

Ven was climbing ashore, following Amariel.

"No, I don't think whales can breathe underwater like we can," he said, pulling himself onto the slippery black rock face. The slap of the waves all around him threatened to pull him back into the sea. He made a grab for a rocky outcropping, but it slid through his hands and he fell, dangerously close to the water's edge.

Only to find himself face-to-face with a pair of beady eyes and a set of whiskers.

A deep howling bark almost shattered his eardrums as the putrid smell of fish blasted up his nose.

"Get away, you blighter," he heard Char shout from behind him.

"Careful," the merrow cautioned as she crawled closer. "He can bite your nose off."

"Easy," Ven said to the shiny animal as it waddled closer. "Down, boy."

"Yeah, that'll work," the merrow said sarcastically. "Hold still." She rolled onto her side. Then, with lightning speed, she wrenched her lower body around and slapped the sea lion directly across the face with her tail.

The beast wiggled backward, barking and whining in pain.

"Shove off," the merrow ordered. To add emphasis, she let out an earsplitting sound, part bark, part howl, that rattled off the peaks of Skellig Elarose. The sea lion froze in shock.

The merrow spat in its eye.

The sea lion's aggressive bark withered into a whimper. It turned and ran awkwardly away, its flippers slapping against the rocky shore as it retreated.

Amariel stretched out on the beachfront.

"Warn your friends," she called after the sea lion. She yawned and stretched, then put her webbed hands behind her head and grinned at the boys, her porpoise-like teeth gleaming in the night. "I'm guessing they won't bother us again, but sea lions, as I already noted, are stupid. You might want to get to sleep as quickly as you can. The moon will rise soon, and once it does, they become calm and happy. Sea lions are in love with the moon."

"Good idea," Ven said. "Thanks for the rescue, Amariel. Good night."

"Don't mention it. Good night, Chum."

Char, who was wet and shivering with cold, only nodded.

By the time the moon rose over the wave-swept island, the only sound howling around the skellig's peaks was the whine of the wind.

And the crash of dark waves.

## – 8 –

# Firstlight

W HEN VEN AWOKE THE SKY WAS GRAY. THE SUN HAD NOT YET come up, but night was waning. The moon was gone, and the eastern horizon was brightening slowly. The men he had sailed with called this time of the day Foredawn. When the first ray of the sun finally did crest the horizon, it was known as Firstlight.

In his sleepy haze, Ven felt certain that Firstlight was still a good way off.

*I had been dreaming of home.*

*Not the home in Vaarn where I was born and raised and lived with my Nain family, but my home at the Crossroads Inn on the Island of Serendair.*

*My second home, and the place I consider my home now.*

*In my dream I was standing in the center of the inn, in front of the roaring fire on the enormous hearth. That's where McLean, the blind Lirin Singer, can almost always be found, playing music on his strange stringed instrument for the Spice Folk, invisible fairies who live in the inn as well.*

*Only in my dream, there was no one to be seen in the inn.*

*I could hear banging in the kitchen, where Char works when we are home. I went to the kitchen, but when I opened the door there was no one there, either.*

*But I could smell the most delicious food cooking in the kitchen.*

*I shouted for Char, and then Felitza, the girl Char has a crush on who does most of the kitchen work.*

*No one answered.*

*Finally I called out the name of the innkeeper, the lady who has been most like a mother to me since I left home.*

*"Mrs. Snodgrass?"*

*In reply, I could hear her voice, though I still could not see her.*

*"Kitchen's closed, Ven."*

Ven's stomach was gnawing at him by the time Foredawn came.

The heavy mist of Skellig Elarose was cool against his eyelids, which stung from the salt of the seawater. He still had not opened his eyes, but he could feel Char stir beside him. He reached over and poked his best friend, who groaned and rolled over.

"You awake?" Ven asked sleepily.

In response, Char stuck his cold, wet nose into Ven's face and belched loudly.

The odor of fish and unbrushed teeth filled his nostrils.

Ven's eyes popped open wide in shock.

All around him was a sea of shiny dark fur and brown whiskers.

Ven sat up.

The entire slanted side of the skellig was covered in sea lions, hundreds of them, some stretching and groaning, some lying still. There were so many that the black rock of the tooth-like mountain had turned glossy brown and looked as if it had been covered completely in fur.

He glanced around to find his friends. He saw Amariel a stone's throw away, her arm tucked around the middle of an enormous sea lion sleeping on its back. Char had taken shelter nearby beneath a rocky outcropping on which four more sea lions were stretched out, still sound asleep.

And beside him, an enormous female was snuggling against him, burping every now and then.

"Er, Amariel?" Ven whispered.

The merrow sighed but did not respond.

He looked back at Char, but he was even farther out of earshot. He tried sending thoughts to him, the way thrum worked under the sea, but then remembered what Amariel had said.

*Land-livers don't know about thrum, because the vibrations are caught by the air and the wind of the upworld, and so you can't usually feel or hear thrum there.*

*I had absolutely no idea what to do.*

*Amariel had said that the sea lion I came face-to-face with last night could have bitten my nose off. From the size of the teeth on the female sleeping next to me, I could see that she was not joking.*

*And we were surrounded by hundreds, if not thousands of them.*

*Sea lions for the most part seem to be fairly harmless, playful creatures. But one thing I have learned from our journey in the sea so far is that most of the animals that live in the drift are much stronger than we land-livers, because the water is so much harder to just <u>exist</u> in.*

*The slap of Amariel's tail in the sea lion's face last night was eye-opening. I had always known she was strong. I had forgotten this when she chose to grow human legs and walk on land, as merrows can, because being in the upworld made her fragile and nervous. But in the water, she is powerful, like the other creatures of the sea we had come upon.*

*So while the sea lions may appear silly and awkward on land, in fact they weigh more than we do, and most of that weight is muscle.*

*I had no idea how to warn my friends of the danger we were in without bringing that danger down upon us.*

*Then, before I could come up with an answer, it was too late anyway.*

A tiny ray of sun appeared at the edge of the eastern horizon. Firstlight.

The sky near that sunbeam lightened to a pale blue, while the rest of the world remained gray.

A bellowing bark sounded from the top of the skellig.

A moment later, hundreds of harsh voices took up the reply, echoing off the rocky island and making the ground shake. The noise battered Ven's eardrums, then was swallowed by the heavy mist of the sea.

Like an avalanche, the slippery brown beasts began sliding down the sharp hillside, rolling into the water, howling and barking with glee. They dove into the waves, chasing their breakfast, taking rocks, pebbles, plants, and everything else in their path with them into the sea.

Including, Ven noted with horror, the merrow.

"Amariel!" Ven screamed as her beautiful tail tumbled past him. The multicolored scales caught the light as the merrow rolled toward the water beneath a landslide of excited sea lions. "Amariel!"

"Ven!" Char's voice rang out over the clamor. "Get out o' the way! Hurry! Get over here!"

Ven pushed himself away from the giant female, who was flapping her flippers, preparing to slide. He stumbled to his feet just in time to see Amariel's tail disappear into the crashing waves at the base of the skellig.

"Amariel!" he shouted again.

"She can swim, ya idiot!" Char called from beneath the rocky outcropping that had served as his shelter through the night. "You're about to get *crushed!* Get over here!"

Ven dodged a trio of slithering sea lions as they slid past him, then ran as fast as he could toward the rocky shelter. The sun was beginning to crest the horizon now, and as the sky grew lighter, more and more sea lions took up the barking shout, hurrying down the pointy hillside. He dove for cover just in time to avoid a wall of slick brown fur and whiskers as more than a dozen of the hungry animals hurried past him into the rolling white foam of morning.

"I barely remember crawling over here in the dark last night," Char said. He grabbed Ven by the shoulder and hauled him further back in the small cave of stone as sea lions rained down from the top of the skellig on either side of them. "I don' think I've ever been so cold."

"I didn't notice," Ven said as he scanned the waves, looking for a sign of the merrow. "But of course I was being a sea lion's pillow, so I guess all that thick fur and blubber kept me from feeling the chill." He looked past the rolling tide of sea lions into the misty distance. "There's land! We must be off the northern coast, up past the Gated City. I thought we were farther out to sea than this. Amariel brought us back pretty close to shore."

Char had spotted the merrow and was pointing past the waves.

"There she is!"

Ven followed his finger, and a moment later could see her waving from beyond where the colony of sea lions were fishing. She was signaling for them to go around to the other side of the skellig toward the open sea. He crawled out of the rock cave and stood up.

"Let's go," he said, shaking the sand and pebbles from his clothes. "The sea lions will be back soon, and will probably want to nap in the sun. I think we should be out of here before that happens."

Char stopped him.

"Ven, haven't we seen enough? We're miles from home as it is, and I don't know about you, but I think I've had enough explorin' of the depths for one lifetime. We're lucky we didn't run into a shark or somethin' equally nasty down below the surface. You're one of the few men—er, Nain—that went into the Deep at night and lived to tell about it. How's about we head back now? Besides, I'm starvin'."

"Me too," Ven admitted. "But I think we've barely seen the edge of the sea, Char. From all the tales Amariel as told me, we've barely seen anything. I know she wants to go to the Summer Festival, which sounds like a lot of fun, and I have to discover what I'm supposed to do with the dragon scale, as well as why I undertook the journey in the first place. That journey may involve returning this scale to a sea dragon, the way we took the first one back to Scarnag. If you want to go home, I understand completely. But I'm not ready to go back yet."

Char sighed. "I knew you would say that. All right, let's get 'round to the other side."

The boys made their way to the beach, which, while slanted like the rest of the rocky island, was a little flatter. The waves crashed in, rolling up the jagged sides of the skellig, then slipped quickly back into the churning ocean.

"What's that?" Char asked as they crawled away from the land side of the skellig and over to the side that looked out onto the open sea. He was pointing to a rocky shoal at the edge of the beach which was being battered by surf. A shiny object was bobbing around in the waves as if it were dancing, leaping up against the rocks and then being pushed back again.

"I don't know," Ven said. "Let's have a look."

Carefully they climbed onto the black rocks at the water's edge. Ven waited for the waves to roll out, and in the moment before the next breaker crashed in, he made a grab for the object. His fingers wrapped around something smooth and cold. He had just enough time to seize it and step back onto the beach before he was drenched in surf to his knees. He closed his eyes, but the salt spray caught him in the face anyway, and he had to wait a moment until the stinging stopped.

He opened them again and looked down in his hand.

He was holding a small green glass bottle, its cork sealed with wax. Inside it a slip of parchment was rolled around something that rattled and clinked when he shook the bottle.

"Well, I'll be tied to the keel and fed to sharks," Char murmured. "What do ya suppose is inside there? Most people only put messages in bottles if they're gonna toss 'em into the sea."

Ven shrugged. "We can always find out. I'll need to pry the cork out with one of the tools in the jack-rule, but I can't risk taking it out now, especially since Amariel is waiting for us. We'll open it after we catch up with her."

The hairs on the back of his neck bristled for a moment, as if a cold wind had caught them.

Ven looked behind him.

All he could see was the waves crashing on all sides of Skellig Lilyana, foaming and whispering over the rocky black sand. In the distance the land was swallowed in morning fog, too far to see anyway.

He ran a hand over his neck.

The feeling was gone.

Ven exhaled. He tucked the small green bottle into his pocket and made his way over the rocky shoreline to where Amariel was waiting. Char followed glumly.


FAR TO THE SOUTH, ATOP A WALL THAT SURROUNDED THE Gated City, a man in a hooded cloak exhaled at the same time.

He collapsed the spyglass through which he had been watching the sea to the north, tucked it back inside his garment.

And smiled for a fleeting moment.

As the smile faded he wiped the spray of the sea off his bushy eyebrows and hooked nose, drew his cloak closer around him, and disappeared into the shadows that always lingered inside the walls of the Gated City.

Even in morning's light.

# ⚜ 9 ⚜

# The Herring Ball

By the time they reached the seaward side of the tooth-like rock, the merrow was looking impatient.

"Come on!" she called as the rolling breakers splashed over her. "We're late for school!"

"School?"

"Of course! Every morning you can find a school lesson in the sea. There's so much to learn each day that you can never get bored. Are you hungry?"

"Starving!" both boys called back in answer at the same time.

"Well, there's a lot of herring past the waves, or if you're not in the mood to eat it raw, there is some lovely spiny seaweed and a big patch of kelp out here as well."

"Yum," said Char sarcastically as Ven's face fell. "I had forgotten in all the excitement that we would need to eat. I was dreamin' of Felitza's cornbread. I imagine the taste of seaweed might be a little less appealin' for sure. "

"It can't be that bad if the whole ocean survives on it," Ven said. "Come on, Char, cheer up. We're going to have an amazing adventure together, as we always do. And you will have tales to tell the crew of the next ship we sail on that will keep them entranced through even the roughest of storms or the longest days without wind. You might even get out of swabbing the decks when you tell them. Make sure your air stone is still in your pocket, and let's go."

"Aye, aye," Char muttered as he followed Ven into the waves. He patted his trousers and sighed. "Yep. Still there. That's a good thing, at least."

"You're in luck," said the merrow when they finally made it past the surf to where she was waiting in the drift. "The lesson in school this morning is Herring Ball. That's always a sight to see."

"What does that mean?" Ven asked. He was glad to be able to communicate with thrum once again.

"It's a defensive lesson for fish, but it can be useful to anyone who travels in a group. I think you, Chum, and I can learn a lot from the lesson, even though the predators that would threaten us are not the same as the ones the herring are trying to avoid."

"Who's teachin' this lesson?" Char asked.

"Well, this morning it's a four-year-old herring schoolmaster. As herring go, that's very old. I was chatting with him a few moments ago during breakfast, and he told me about the lesson."

"What did you have for breakfast?" Ven asked.

"Herring, of course."

"You were, er, eating his fellow herring?"

"Yes." The merrow looked surprised. "Why?"

"Didn't that upset him?" asked Char.

"Goodness, no. In the sea you eat whatever you can to survive. No one takes it personally."

"Oh," said Ven. He thought back to Madame Sharra's warning.

*Everything in the sea is food to something else. And the sea is always hungry.*

"Well, I suppose if I get eaten, I won't take it personally either." He watched as all the color drained from Char's face. "Just kidding. Where's the school, Amariel?"

The merrow pointed out to sea in the direction of the other skellig, this one smaller and darker than Skellig Elarose, its peak blanketed in soft mist.

"Just past Skellig Lilyana is the beginning of the coral reef, that wall of living creatures I told you about. Between here and the reef the water is deep enough for the herring to practice forming their Ball. The reef near the skelligs is thinner than it is around the rest of the Island of Serendair. Once you get past the reef the ocean floor drops off sharply, and that's where the krill are."

"Krill?"

"Tiny shellfish that everyone in the ocean feeds on. They hatch in swarms, bazillions at a time, and when they do it's a huge feast. The herring like the krill because they are about the only food in the sea smaller than herring. But since whales, sea lions, dolphins, salmon, and all kinds of other creatures feed on the krill, too, it's important for the herring to stick together. When predators show up, the herring form a gigantic ball to protect themselves—although depending on the kind and number of predators, it sometimes doesn't help much. But it makes them feel less defenseless, and it's fun to see. Sometimes a Herring Ball can be a mile wide."

Char whistled. "That's a *lot* of herring."

Amariel nodded. "Millions. There will be fewer this morning. The herring are eager to get out to the krill beyond the reef. So if you want to catch the lesson, we have to go now. The schoolmaster will be looking for sunwater to demonstrate the technique—you've seen sunwater, it's that fuzzy light beneath the surface. Thrum, in combination with sunwater, causes a sunshadow."

"Is that where your thoughts look like pictures in the water?" asked Ven.

"Yes, so be careful what you are thinking if you are swimming through it." The merrow pointed to a spot where the early-morning rays of the sun were reflecting on the surface of the sea. "That seems to be a likely place—and, as you can see, the birds are gathering, so I assume the Herring Ball practice will be there. Come on."

She dove beneath the surface.

"Got your stone?" Ven asked. Char nodded.

"All right—then let's go."

They followed the merrow through the swirling water. The waves around the skelligs were violent, crashing in many different directions, so the boys sank as deep as they could, away from the surface, to the skittering sand of the ocean floor where the drift was not so strong.

All around them, denser curtains of small, thin fish were swimming, mostly in the same direction, making the green water flash with the reflection of sunlight on their silver scales.

Ven peered into the hazy light where the sun had broken below the water's surface. A long, thin fish, more gray than silver, was hovering at the light's edge.

"That's the schoolmaster," Amariel's thrum whispered.

"Oh," Ven thought back. He watched as the hazy water turned clearer.

Suddenly the drift was filled with a moving picture. In the image were millions of small silver fish like the ones watching the lesson. They hovered in the water for a moment, then went from the flat formations in which they normally swam into a series of circles that eventually formed a giant ball in the sea, spinning like a globe. It revolved in the water, the different sections rotating inside the ball, taking turns at being away from the vulnerable outside.

*I can't really explain how I knew that I was watching a lesson, but it was unmistakable.*

*With each new movement, each new strategy, there was a thrum that instructed the movement. From the vibration that returned from the immense curtain of fish, it was obvious that the herring were understanding the instruction. The directions were clear and simple. It made me wish my teachers back home had been able to communicate our lessons in thrum.*

*A few moments later, when the sunlight above the surface shifted, the image in the sunshadow faded.*

*The huge wall of fish that had been hovering in the water,*

*watching the lesson, began to move into the patterns that the schoolmaster had directed.*

*All around me, the wall of silver scales shimmered, then formed a sphere that spun in the water just as the lesson had shown.*

*I could feel the approval of the fish teacher vibrate in my head.*

*Very good, it seemed to say. Tighten up those corners, now. The top is a little sloppy.*

Amariel was smiling broadly.

"See?" she said as the gigantic ball of herring rolled past. "You'll never see anything on land do that."

"No," Char admitted. "But there are some pretty amazin' things done by land animals. Have you ever seen a bunch of ants build a hill?"

"I've seen a family of crabs make a tower almost a hundred fathoms tall. Don't try to top the merfolk, Chum, you land-liver. Our animals are bigger and smarter, our mountains are taller, our trenches deeper—you can't begin to match what's in the sea."

"So what happens now?" Ven asked hurriedly, swimming quickly to get between them. Char had started to open his mouth, then choked, forgetting to use thrum in the heat of the argument.

"Well, now that the herring know how to make the Ball, they will head for the coral reef, then out past it, where a storm of plankton is blooming. We can go watch and see if they make it."

Ven and Char looked at each other blankly.

The merrow sighed.

"All right, let me see if I can put it in land-liver words you can understand. Imagine that the harbor was the city of Kingston, and that here, around the skelligs and the coral reef, is like the inn where you live. Out there, past the reef, is like the Wide Meadows beyond the inn. Does that make sense so far?"

The boys nodded.

"Good. Now imagine that on one day, every flower, vegetable, and seed that acts as food in the Wide Meadows ripened all at the same time. That's what a plankton storm is like—a giant banquet of food in the sea."

"Got it," Ven said. Char looked doubtful but his thrum was silent.

"So, on land, if every bit of food was suddenly available in one place, all the animals that need that food would appear, wouldn't they? Mice, rabbits, rats. squirrels, bugs, all those nasty little creatures I saw when I was on land with you, would show up in droves, looking to gobble the food up. Right?"

"Yes."

"Well, those vile little animals are like krill. And everything that eats those creatures, from cats to coyotes and wolves, would come to the feast. It would be one big disgusting picnic. And, of course, wherever there is food, there are birds. Whether it's seagulls or ravens, there always seem to be birds."

Amariel pointed up to the surface. Ven looked up. The flocks of seagulls he had seen before entering the sea that morning had grown until they covered the blue of the sky. He thought he could hear their harsh cawing even below the waves as they circled above, diving occasionally for herring that had ventured too close to the surface.

"Sky rats," Char murmured.

"So if you were a mouse that needed to cross the Wide Meadows in the middle of a feeding frenzy like that, the only way to do it would be to join forces with a lot of your friends and try to make it through all the predators," the merrow continued. "That's what the herring do. Obviously a lot of them are not going to make it, and that's as it should be—I mean, the bigger fish need to eat, too. But many of them do, because there's safety in numbers."

"I kinda wish we had brought along the rest of our friends from the inn," Char said. "Nick and Saeli and Clem and Ida—well, maybe not Ida—"

"They would have had no way to breathe," Ven interrupted. "I think it's best that we just tell them the story when we get back."

"*If* we get back," said Char gloomily.

"That's the spirit," said the merrow. "Let's get going—the herring are starting to head for the reef. They must feel that there aren't many predators, because they're swimming in sheets. That's a sign that they have clear seas—so we had better take advantage of that while we can. And if they make it, the herring will throw a party, and we'll be invited, of course. It will be a huge celebration."

"Let me guess." Char's thrum sounded sour. "A herring ball?"

The merrow blinked. "Well, yes. Herring are great singers, and they dance pretty well, too."

"Of course they do." Char looked at Ven, who was scowling at him. "All right, let's go."

"If you listen, you can hear the herring singing," Amariel said as they followed the great silver cloud of fish through the drift and out to sea. "Their thrum is pretty."

Ven listened. At first he didn't hear anything, but after a moment he could feel in his skin a pleasant tingling, as if he were being brushed by a feather. Then he realized the thrum was all around him, echoing through the sea.

"That *is* pretty," he said.

"It can confuse predators, if there are any nearby," Amariel said. "Soothing sounds and smooth gestures go unnoticed. A whole school of fish can swim right past a shark if they are singing nicely. It's jerking movements and thrashing around that comes when a creature panics that will catch its attention." She gave a thrust of her powerful tail to catch up with the herring.

"We'll keep that in mind," Ven thought out loud. He let the drift carry him as Amariel had showed him, and found that he was able to follow the fish fairly easily.

He was paying such close attention to keeping up with the curtain of herring that he didn't notice the change in the seafloor.

Until something large and dark as night with wings like a giant bat passed directly beneath him.

Waving a sharp weapon that gleamed menacingly in the light of the sun.

# ~ 10 ~

# The Coral Reef

U H, VEN," THE MERROW SAID. "DON'T MOVE."

*She didn't have to tell me twice.*
*In fact, I'm not sure she had to do so even once.*

The immense creature glided along the ocean floor, which Ven could see now was alive with strange formations in many shapes, sizes, and colors. Some looked like plants, others like stone, but Amariel had told him enough stories that he was fairly certain he was now hovering above the coral reef the merrow had told him about.

Coral formations made up of billions of tiny animals.

The bat-like beast came to a halt just above the coral bed. It turned to face them, then puffed its back like an angry cat. Its dark hide was mottled with flecks of gray and white, and it looked hollow as it watched them, its gills opening and closing quickly. Ven guessed it was bigger than the bed he slept in back home in the Crossroads Inn.

*It's a marble ray.* Amariel's thrum echoed in his head. *A stinger. You've startled him. He doesn't want to hurt you, but he's frightened, and he will if you make him feel threatened. And he can kill you very easily. He*

{ 86 }

*can break your leg with a swipe of his tail, and that barb is like a land sword—it can run you through.*

Ven held still. He hovered next to Char in the drift, who was frozen beside him.

"Sorry to have bothered you," Amariel said to the ray. "All a mistake. No problem here."

The enormous fluid creature stared at them, but didn't move.

*Sorry.* Ven thought as he hung motionless in the drift. *Very sorry.*

The ray stared at them a moment longer, then turned and floated away, its rubbery body and whiplike tail with its shiny barb skittering over the glorious colors of the reef below them. Ven heard its thrum in his head, two separate thoughts, as it left. One he could understand easily.

*Idiot.*

The other was harder to pin down, but as best he could tell it was an observation that each of the sea creatures they had met had made.

*Out of place.*

I couldn't argue with that. We certainly were outsiders in this vast, foreign world. It was clear that the inhabitants of the ocean found us even more odd than we found them.

Even though the ray was gone, I still was unable to move.

But now it was not fear that froze me, but amazement.

Below me the ocean bottom had changed from the sand-strewn floor with patches of seaweed and the broken trash of humans to what looked like a living painting. Here in the depths, away from the beating of the surf, a magnificent wall of color and life was spread out as far as I could see. Coral of all sizes and forms danced in the drift, some shaped like the horns of reindeer, some like great tubes, and others like the wispy fronds of ferns in a watery forest.

And within the plant-like arms of the coral, brightly colored fish darted. A school of beautiful orange and white ones with ruffled fins swarmed below my feet. Their thrum was curious.

"Those are clown fish," Amariel whispered in his head. "They're very friendly."

Ven smiled. "You have clowns under the sea as well?"

"Well, of course."

"I'm afraid of clowns," Char said. He had wrapped his arms around himself and was hovering in the water, trembling slightly.

"You would be," said the merrow disdainfully. "You have no common sense, Chum. Clown fish are some of the only things in the sea you don't have to fear."

"I don't mean the fish," Char continued awkwardly. "I mean the ones in the upworld that put on creepy face paint and weird clothes with ruffles and bells and pom-poms. They had a lot of them in the Gated City, in the Outer Market. I don't like *nothin'* with a permanent smile. You can't tell what it's really thinkin'. "

"I bet land-liver clowns got the idea for their ruffled clothes from clown fish," said Amariel. She waved her web-fingered hand, and the clown fish scattered back to the arms of some purple coral that looked like cabbage leaves.

"I guess we are going to have to swim until we get past the reef," said Ven. "I imagine we shouldn't walk on the coral."

"Of course not. Would you want some human walking on *your* family?"

Ven thought back to his sister, Matilde, and his eleven brothers, his business-like father and his stern mother. Even though Nain were shorter than humans, they were stockier, and generally sturdier. They were also a good deal grumpier, with thorny personalities, and tended to bounce their bellies off anyone who got in their way. *Definitely not*, he thought to himself. *I wouldn't want to see humans' feet get bitten off.*

Char chuckled, and Ven remembered that his thoughts were no longer his own in the sea.

"Come along," said Amariel. "Let's explore the reef."

The water above them was clearer and bluer than Ven had seen since coming into the sea. The sun shone down steadily through the surface, brightening the colors of the coral and the creatures that lived within it. The sight reminded Ven of the lair of the dragon Scarnag, the beast he had met in a great serpent-shaped cave in the Wide Meadows of Serendair. Scarnag had hoarded books, globes, and maps as well as gems and coins in sparkling towers. Ven wondered if the beautiful reef and its creatures could be the hoard of another dragon, one whose scale he might be carrying at that moment in the buttoned pocket of his vest.

As he was thinking about it, they swam through a patch of bright, hazy light caused by the sun beating down from the sky above. Before he could stop his thoughts, an immense sunshadow image of a dragon appeared.

The beast's mud-colored hide was striped in colors of green and red, purple and blue and seemed to have been formed from Living Earth itself. His head was roughly shaped, with cruel spines all the way down his back to a tail that had softly rounded spikes on it. His stone-like claws were jagged, and gray smoke curled from his nostrils, almost covering the tiny pair of glasses that were perched on the end of his nose.

Scarnag, whose name meant *scourge*, was in truth really a fairly pleasant dragon librarian when he wasn't torching the countryside.

Ven's head almost exploded as the thrum of every living creature around them gasped and screamed at the same time.

Including all the tiny creatures forming the massive coral reef.

The sheets of herring swarmed around them, then sped off the reef toward deeper water.

Char's body snapped in shock, then curled up into a ball in pain.

"Gee ma-nee, Ven!" he moaned. "What the *heck*?"

The merrow spun in a similar fashion. She clutched her head and let out a sound that was half screech, half gurgle.

"By the Blowhole!" she shrieked. "Get out of the sunwater, and think of something *else!*" She let go of her head long enough to give Ven a violent push with her tail.

Furiously Ven paddled, flailing his arms and kicking his legs hard. He swam as fast as he could into bluer parts of the water until the thrum from the reef subsided. He looked back over his shoulder.

The image of Scarnag had vanished.

The merrow was glaring daggers at him.

The reef was bare of fish.

And Char was still curled up in a ball, sinking slowly toward the bottom of the sea.

"You know, I can't take you *anywhere*." The merrow's thrum vibrated against his eardrums. "You are *so* embarrassing. Don't even say it," she added as Ven started to apologize. "Get your thoughts under control, Ven, or I'm going to abandon you here in the middle of the coral reef. You are getting to be a danger to associate with."

Ven swam quickly down to where Char was floating helplessly, and grabbed his arm.

"I'm so sorry," he thought, trying to keep his brain from conjuring up any more ferocious images. "Are you all right?"

"Awwwggh" was the answer from Char's thrum.

"I don't know what to say," Ven thought to Amariel. "I didn't mean to think of Scarnag—I don't know what to do, how to apologize to an entire coral reef—"

"Stop." The merrow's thrum sounded a little less annoyed. "Just keep a quiet mind for a moment."

Ven's face was red and hot, and it was all he could do to keep from throwing up. *I should never have come*, he thought, trying to keep his mind from wandering. *We're very far from land, and one more false move might doom us out here.* He looked down into the palm of his hand at the magical image of the Time Scissors, the sign of his ability to redo one moment of his Past. *Maybe I should undo this whole journey, and take my chances with the Thief Queen on land.*

The thought of Felonia made him shiver. He looked around quickly to make sure he wasn't floating in a patch of sunwater, then tried to make his mind go blank. But his curiosity was burning so intensely that he could not stop the images that were flooding his brain.

Then, his head suddenly cleared.

Around him was a thrum that was both magically distant and familiar, a haunting song of a sort that wrapped him in a gentle vibration. He knew he had heard it before, but he could not place it.

He turned to Char, who obviously could feel it as well. His best friend was staring ahead of him.

He pointed. Ven followed his finger.

He was pointing to the merrow.


Amariel was singing.

Instantly I knew why the thrum was so familiar. Her voice was different underwater than it had been in the air of the upworld, when she sang me songs and told me stories to keep me awake so that I would not slip off the broken piece of driftwood on which she had tossed me to save me when the Angelia blew up. But it had the same tone, sweet and enchanting and calming.

As she sang, the fish and other creatures of the reef that I had frightened away began to emerge from holes in the coral and return. They were gathering around, listening to her, too.

The song did not sound like anything I had ever heard. It had no words or choruses, just a sweet, pleasant melody that made the air from the breathing stone feel cleaner. My head felt light and woozy, and at that moment I would have done anything she asked of me.

I remembered the stories human sailors tell on dark nights about merrows, or mermaids, as they call them, and their songs. They say that they are so magical, so enchanting, that many men who sail the sea meet their doom following those haunting songs to rocks and reefs where their ships are lost, run aground. Hearing her call the frightened fish back to the reef, I could believe it. Then I realized what she was doing with her song.

She was apologizing for me, trying to keep the creatures of the reef from attacking me, or seeing me as an enemy.

I've never been so embarrassed in my life.

In a section of the coral of reef below him, many tiny plants suddenly swelled and bloomed between the rocky structures. They opened like flowers blossoming in the sunshine, splashing the coral with their colors of soft orange and vibrant pink and a purple so intense that Ven could actually hear it as it grew. They moved in time to the merrow's song, almost as if she were calling them with her melody, and they were answering her.

He could hear the plants sing, each in its own colors.

When Amariel had finished her song she turned back to them in the drift. She smiled when she saw Ven and Char watching the new colorful garden exploding in the coral at their feet.

"Elaroses," she said.

"They're beautiful." Ven pumped his arms to raise himself higher as the plants shot up even taller. "Thank you for singing to them—and to everyone else." He watch as more fish, bright blue and yellow with noses that looked like the beaks of birds, and a small herd of pink-and-white-striped shrimp emerged from the coral bed. "You have saved me from myself once again, Amariel."

The merrow's face lost its smile.

"I know," she said. "And I hope you understand what a dangerous thing it was to do. Because someone is going to pay for it now, probably with their lives."

# ~ 11 ~

# A Deadly Song

**W**HAT—WHAT DO YOU MEAN?" VEN STAMMERED.

The merrow shrugged. "I've told you that merrows—well, female merrows, anyway—are some of the most beautiful and wonderful creatures in the sea. Everyone knows that. And, as you have seen several times, merrow songs are very powerful. Goodness knows they've saved your backside more than once. We aren't supposed to sing unless it's an emergency, because so many creatures, including human males, get silly and lose control of themselves when we sing. That's the reason we are allowed to save human men if they're drowning, as I told you the night I saved you. We're not supposed to have contact with humans at all, but if a merrow has been singing, it's possible that the human jumped into the sea or sailed into rocks to follow the merrow's song. So if they do something foolish, we're allowed to save them, but we're not supposed to talk to them."

Ven looked up at the surface, where the sun was turning the water a spectacular shade of aquamarine. The drift was clear of any sign of a vessel passing overhead. "Do you think a passing sailor or ship might have heard you?"

"Maybe. I have no idea. But sailors are not the only thing—or even the most important thing—that is attracted by the song of a merrow." She pointed at the blooming elaroses below them. "As you can see, everyone and everything that hears it wants more of it. The elaroses don't hear well down in the coral bed, so they grow just be to close enough. The fish, who ran from your sunwater mess-up a moment ago, braved what they thought was a sea dragon, one of the scariest creatures in the sea, to hear it. A merrow's song makes most creatures forget their common sense completely, because they are entranced. All they want to do is follow the song—and that can mean terrible trouble."

"So somethin' else is going to show up?" Char asked nervously. "Something dangerous?"

"Quite possibly. There are all sorts of deadly creatures on a reef that listen to the music of the sea—and not all of them are predators. We had best move along. The plankton are storming nearby, and there are a lot of krill not far from here. That means just about anybody could be around. That's why merrows are supposed to be very careful about singing, especially under the water. We only do it if it's an emergency. You seem to be good at making emergencies, Ven. Now everyone has forgotten the dragon in the sunwater—but we've just potentially made our journey to the Summer Festival a whole lot more dangerous."

Ven sighed. "Sorry."

The merrow shrugged again. "Can't be helped. That's what happens when you go to a place you're not really supposed to be in. You land-livers call someone who is out of place a 'fish out of water.' We have an expression for the same thing—'a man in the sea.' Either way, it's not the best situation to be in. I guess that's the risk you take when you explore each other's worlds."

Ven thought back to the words of Asa the fisherman.

*The sea's no place to explore without a good reason, lads. Lots of bad stuff down there—believe you me.*

Madame Sharra had questioned him as well.

*For what reason is a Nain, a son of the Earth, going into the sea?*

His answer sounded even more weak in his memory than it had in his ears at the time.

*Lots of reasons. Amariel—the merrow over there—she's my friend. I've been promising her for a long time I would come and explore the sea with her. It's her home. She came out of the sea to explore my world—she grew legs, in fact, and—*

*A good reason, perhaps, but good enough to risk death?*

"Watch your foot by that hole, Chum." Amariel's thrum had a tone of urgency.

Char jerked his legs quickly up.

A split second later, a triangular head with rows of pointed teeth attached to a snake-like body shot out of the small cave in the coral, its mouth snapping fiercely. It missed Char's foot by a hair.

"Swim a little faster," the merrow cautioned. "That's a moray eel. Its bite can make you very sick—he only missed you because he's still woozy from the song."

Char tucked his legs up as high as he could and doubled his arm movements.

Ven's curiosity burned hot in his skin as they traveled the reef, seeing new and marvelous sights with each glance. Amariel's thrum whispered in their ears, telling them the names of and interesting facts about each of the creatures or plants that they passed.

The fish with the beaks they had seen were known as blue parrots according to the merrow, and were sand makers, grinding coral and rocks down to white sand with their powerful jaws. The large pale yellow mass of jelly that looked like a soft snail was a hooded sea slug, very proud of its strong. sweet odor that the merrow assured them made the rest of the creatures on the reef gag, but everyone was too polite to thrum about it for fear of hurting the sea slug's feelings. "Just because we occasionally eat each other doesn't mean we want to be unpleasant to one another," she told Char, who looked at her doubtfully.

Ven listened as the merrow named each animal and plant along the beautiful reef, from the giant pink, white, and orange sponges shaped like a human hand to the wispy purple corals that looked like tube-shaped trees. And everywhere was coral—coral shaped like the horns of stags, mushrooms, ferns, bubbles, cabbages, honeycombs, brains, plates, spiders, anything and everything Ven could imagine. One word kept forming in his mind, over and over again.

*Magic.*

The merrow heard his thrum and smiled.

Char rose up in the water as a small, ugly fish with spotted skin and yellow fins below him began to suddenly inflate, forming itself into a round ball.

"Whoa, careful of him," Amariel cautioned. "He's a puffer—and he's poisonous."

Char kept his knees drawn up and paddled gingerly away from the fish. "Yikes," his thrum whispered. "How did he do that?"

"His stomach is very stretchy, and he can fill it with water or air to make himself look bigger," the merrow said as they passed beyond the puffer. "It helps keep him swimming upright as well." Her thrum lowered to what seemed like an embarrassed whisper. "He's a little slow and awkward. Try not to think badly of him."

"Sure," said Char. "No problem."

Above them, the surface was surprisingly close, Ven noted. He judged the water to be only a few dozen feet deep. At each turn, the reef grew more colorful, with tiny lemon-colored fish darting in and around red anemones that looked for all the world like the daisies in his mother's garden, even though their thrum assured him they were animals.

While they were admiring the beauty of the coral forest, in the distance, explosions of light and color appeared in the drift ahead of them. They twinkled and glowed in the darkness beyond the edge of the reef ahead.

"Fireworks!" Char exclaimed.

"Fireworks under the sea?" said Ven.

The merrow shook her head. "That's the plankton. Sometimes it gives off blue and red sparks to attract some of the bigger predators. We must be getting near the edge of the reef. Be careful, because the bottom will drop off and the water will get much deeper fast once the reef ends."

"Wait—the plankton *wants* to attract the bigger predators?" Ven asked. "Why?"

"Because right now it's being chewed on by bazillions of tiny krill. The krill are being chewed on by millions of herring. If the plankton can attract some bigger predators, like yellowfin tuna or salmon, to the storm, those predators will pick off some of the things that are eating the plankton."

"Ah," said Ven. "That's very clever."

"Well, of *course*," said the merrow. She looked below them as the main body of the reef bed thinned and came to an end above a more sandy bottom dotted with fewer coral formations. The ocean floor, as she had predicted, dropped off sharply, with deeper, greener, cloudier water beyond the reef.

"You can see a lot from here," Amariel said, hovering over the edge. "Sometimes it's nice to look under the reef and see how cleverly it's made."

The boys floated over the edge beside her, then turned to look back at the underpinnings of the coral barricade.

The merrow continued her tour. She pointed out a number of striped fish, known as reef sharks, swimming smoothly through the blossoms of a patch of coral that looked like bright pink broccoli.

"There," she said to Char. "You've seen your first sharks—reef sharks. Are you afraid?" She didn't give him a chance to answer before launching into a long story about how the color of coral came from tiny plants living inside each coral polyp. Ven listened, fascinated, as she explained that hard coral were friendly builders forming communities together that eventually turned into reefs, she said, "sort of like the Gated City or the farmers who live in the Wide Meadows of Serendair." And the soft coral, which looked like friendly, innocent plants in an immense, colorful garden, actually had tiny barbed tentacles coated with venom that they occasionally put out to spear krill or even small fish like the ones Ven could see taking shelter in their supple arms right now.

"But only when they're really hungry," Amariel noted as Char pulled his feet up even higher. "Or really bored. And mostly at night. The big corals will usually eat the little ones before they turn to eating fish. "

"Ugh," said Char.

"What?" Amariel demanded. "What's 'ugh' about that? Everybody's got to eat."

"Speaking of eating," said Ven, "we forgot to take care of that on the skelligs. I'm starting to get pretty hungry."

"Yeah. I'm starvin'."

Just as he heard Char's thrum in his mind, the same words came crashing all around Ven, echoing in his ears and skin. The joy and excitement was unmistakable.

*Starving! Starving! Starving!*

Amariel looked around quickly.

"Oh no," she whispered.

"What is it?" Ven looked around as well, but couldn't see anything coming. "What's starving? What's happening, Amariel?"

Suddenly, ahead of them in the green water beyond the reef, the sheets of herring let loose a high, frightened scream, their thousands of tiny silent voices making the drift shudder around them. Then the voices began chanting a single word.

*Ball! Ball! Ball! Ball!*

The clear blue water above the reef buzzed and swirled.

Char squinted through the sunwater.

"Something big is coming," he said. "A whole *bunch* of big somethings. And *fast*."

"Quick—take cover in the coral!" the merrow urged. "Careful not to cut yourself. If you do, and you don't clean the wound properly, coral can grow *inside your body*."

Ven dove for a patch of long-armed plants the color of dry wood, trying to block the sound of Char's horrified thrum from his mind.

He dragged his friend into a space within the branches. The merrow followed them.

Just as she was pulling her tail inside the shelter, a streak of blue and silver gray shot past them.

Then another.

And another.

Then a dozen more.

"Dolphins!" Char exclaimed, trying to avoid the waving arms of the corals as a whole school streaked by. Their thrum was full of joy and excitement, as if they were laughing and hunting at the same time, filling the water around them with a squeaking, whistling music of their own. "Oh, Ven, look! Remember how they used to chase the *Serelinda* and play games in the water around the ship?"

Ven laughed in relief.

"Yes!" he said happily. "Thank goodness it was something friendly and harmless that heard Amariel's song, instead of a shark or a big predator or something."

The merrow looked at him sourly.

"Friendly and harmless? I guess that depends on your point of view. Look."

She pointed into the deep, green water past the reef.

The thousands of herring they had followed since school that morning had formed themselves into an enormous Ball. They were swimming frantically, trying to keep moving, as the dolphins swept by, snapping at the outsiders. The schoolmaster's thrum could be heard above it all, calmly but nervously.

*Tighten up those corners, now. The top is a little sloppy.*

"Oh no," Ven whispered. "No."

"I imagine the herring would disagree with your definition of 'big predator,' mate," said Char.

"This is gonna get ugly real fast," said the merrow. "Cover your ears and heads."

Ven watched, part in amazement, part in horror, as the school of dolphins swept in from every side, taking out whole quadrants of the Ball. The thrum from the green water beyond the reef was at the same time thrilling and terrifying, amid sparks of blue and red flashes set off all around by the plankton. *It looks like a great celebration*, he thought sadly as silver scales began appearing in places where a few moments before herring had been. *And I guess to the dolphins it is.*

He couldn't help but feel sorry for the herring.

The feast seemed to go on for hours, but in reality it was over in a matter of minutes. A few surviving herring hurried out to sea. Ven thought he saw the schoolmaster among them, but he couldn't be certain in the cloudy water. The dolphins sped off, singing in their whistling voices, cackling happily.

Ven rose from within their coral hiding place and floated back to the edge of the reef and to the green water just beyond it.

The plankton had ceased setting off their sparks, and now the afternoon sun glittered hazily on an empty sea.

The screeching thrum was gone, replaced with the blurry silence of the drift and the quiet music of lapping waves.

Silver scales floated slowly down around him to the ocean floor below like snowflakes.

And nothing more.

His friends followed him to the reef's edge. Amariel's thrum echoed in their heads. "I told you someone was going to pay for my song with their lives. At least it wasn't us. I'm glad."

"Well, I guess we're not gonna be dancin' at the herring ball," Char said.

Ven sighed. "That was terrible."

The merrow rolled her eyes.

"What you call 'terrible,' most people would call 'lunch.' Snap out of it, Ven. You knew the rules when you came in—'everything in the sea is food to something else, and the sea is always hungry.'"

Char nodded.

Ven looked down to the ocean floor. The silver scales were skittering on the sand, almost as if they were dancing. He watched as the drift picked them up and carried them slowly away in all different directions.

He sighed again.

"So where to now, Amari—"

His words were cut short by the sight of what looked like human eyes staring at him from within the coral bed.

Above the shiny metal point of a weapon.

# – 12 –

# Coreon

*My mother always told me I should learn to think before I speak.
After many years of embarrassing examples of why I needed to
learn to do this, I finally started counting to three before I said
anything, at least when I remembered to.*

*But here in the sea, with thrum taking away the ability to
think something that you don't want to say, I have no idea
whatsoever how to contain my thoughts.*

*I don't know how to think before I think.*

*My curiosity has long gotten me into trouble. I have a hard
enough time controlling it in the upworld.*

*In the sea, I have no chance at all.*

W HO ARE YOU?"

Ven's surprise was so great that his thrum came out like a
shout. It vibrated through the water, causing the soft arms of the
coral and anemones to rustle, and his friends to stare at him in
shock.

A head emerged from behind the coral bed.

*It belonged to what appeared to be a young boy about my age, perhaps twelve or so in human years. He was hidden by the shadows, but through the sunwater he seemed to have skin the color of tea with a lot of milk in it. His eyes were the shape of almonds and dark as well, though I could not tell what color they were. His brownish hair floated about his head like seaweed, and his ears appeared to be slightly pointed, like those of the Lirin on land. He stood up, and I could see he was carrying a weapon. It was shaped like a land crossbow, flat, with a barbed point in front that looked a little like the harpoons sailors use on ships.*

"That's pretty nervy," he said. The thrum of his voice varied as if it had not decided how high it wanted to be. "You come into *our* realm and then demand to know who *we* are? Who the heck are *you*?" He pointed his weapon at Ven.

"My name is Ven. My friends and I mean you no harm—really."

The almond eyes narrowed even more.

"I can't say the same. What are you doing here?"

Ven blinked. His eyes were still becoming used to the salt.

*What reason should I give?* he wondered. *Hiding from the Thief Queen? Probably not a good idea. Exploring the depths? If they mean us harm, that makes us sound like we are out of place. They may use that against us, There are so many answers, and Madame Sharra was right— none of them sound very good.*

"Coreon!"

The thrum was similar to the voice of the boy, but older and deeper.

"Coreon! Where are you?"

The dark-eyed boy did not move his lips, but words came out of him and hung in the water.

"Here. I've found some land-livers."

Thousands of tiny colorful tentacles in the coral bed waved, and a man's head came into view, atop broad shoulders and a bare chest that seemed to have seaweed instead of hair. He, too, was armed, but with a long spear with a cruel-looking barb that curled like a sharp seashell.

"What are you doing here?" The thrum sounded threatening. "You do not belong here."

*Out of place*, *again*, Ven thought.

"They're my friends." Amariel's underwater voice washed over Ven as she rose up from their side of the reef. "Please excuse their staring. You are the first Lirin-mer that they have ever seen."

Ven's eyes opened wide, the edges stinging from the salt.

*Lirin-mer*, he thought. *Sea Lirin.* He tried to keep his body steady in the drift, trying not to seem threatening. On land, Lirin and Nain were often mortal enemies. He hoped that was not the case in the sea.

The man stared at Amariel.

"You're far from your school," he said. "What is a merrow doing keeping company with land-livers?"

"We're going to the Summer Festival." Ven could tell by her thrum that she was nervous. Amariel had told him many times that merfolk were not supposed to show land-livers the wonders of the Deep.

"Why are you traveling with land-livers and not your school?"

"I—I needed their help to get past the Gated City." Amariel glanced at Ven and Char. "I didn't want to try to get around the disturbance in the north of the harbor alone."

The man shook his head, his hair floating like sea kelp.

"The land-livers in the Gated City have tunneled out into the harbor again," he said. "For a short time their route into the sea was blocked, but now they are back to their old evil ways. There is great danger near the shore. You would be well advised to stay as far away from there as you can." The sea-Lirin man looked over at the boys. "All of you."

"Believe me, we try," Ven said.

Behind him, Char said nothing, but Ven could feel the temperature of the water around him grow warmer as the sun shifted above, causing a patch of sunwater to shine down on them.

"Oh boy," Amariel muttered.

Ven turned to see Char clutching his head, trying to block his thoughts, but it was too late.

The sunwater cleared. Within it Ven could see an image of the inside of the Gated City and the tunnels beneath it that led to the dark realm of the Downworlders, human rat-like people who lived there. He saw Char's memories of the Outer Market, where bright colors, sweet music, and the rich scent of food abounded, where magical goods from the world over were sold to people who came through the gates on Market Day. And he saw the water tremble with the thrum of Char's thoughts about the Inner Market, the deadly part of the city past the enormous keyhole gate.

The water around them swirled. The sea-Lirin man was beside them in a moment. He seized Char by the arm and swept the spear through the water, where it came to rest at Ven's throat.

"You must be *from* the Gated City," he said, dragging Char across the sandy bottom closer to him.

"No, no!" Ven said hurriedly. "We've only been there once."

"Please don't hurt them," Amariel pleaded. "They're good people, and they don't mean any harm."

"We'll leave that for the Cormorant to decide," the sea-Lirin man said. He gestured at Coreon to set his sights on Ven. Coreon lifted his strange crossbow and pointed it at Ven's heart.

"Come, merrow," the man said to Amariel. "You will soon see why you and your like are warned to stay away from humans." He turned and started away, deeper out to sea.

"Ven's not human," Amariel protested as she swam behind them. "He's Nain. I would never consort with humans—my mother would have my fluke."

"What do you call *that*?" Coreon asked, pointing at Char.

"I call it *Chum*," Amariel said gloomily. "He's like a barnacle on the Nain's backside."

"Cease thrum," the man said. Ven could tell by his tone that he was demanding silence.

The two sea Lirin led the two boys northward along the edge of the reef. The merrow followed sullenly behind. Ven could tell she was angry more than frightened. Char, on the other hand, had the man's shell-tipped spear in between his shoulder blades, so his thrum was a lot more nervous, to the point of almost panicking.

Now that they were traveling along its north-south edge, rather than crossing it east to west, the coral reef seemed almost endless. It stretched to their right, beyond them and behind them, as far as he could see. When they were crossing it, the reef had looked like a garden full of magical plants, or a jewel box full of brightly colored gems.

Now that they were being led along its edge, with a sharp drop off to a deeper seafloor to their left, it looked like a wall, a barricade between the shore and the Deep.

Ven wasn't sure which side it was trying to protect.

They traveled in silence for what seemed like hours. By the time the sea-Lirin man came to a halt, the sun had passed from directly overhead to deep into the western sky, and the shadows of the depths had darkened to a deep green. The sunshadow had begun to pick up sunset colors, breaking the surface with pink and orange haze.

The man held up his hand for the boys and Amariel to stop. Then he nodded to Coreon, who swam ahead into a darker part of the reef. He returned after a few moments.

Behind him was a line of sea-Lirin men, all armed with the same kind of cruel spears and crossbows.

At the front of the line was an enormously tall sea-Lirin man with dark kelp-like hair. His shoulders were wide, and he wore a shield-like chest plate made from what looked like black rock carved like wings, the tips of which rose above his shoulders. It was clear to Ven immediately that he was the leader of the men who were following Coreon.

Thrum pounded against their ears, as if his voice was harsh and deep.

"I am the Cormorant," the man said. "The leader of this outpost. What are you doing in the sea, humans?"

"They are with me—" Amariel began.

"I *did not ask you*, merrow." The Cormorant's thrum darkened, and Amariel's undersea voice choked off immediately. He turned to Ven. "I will ask you again—*why are you here?*"

"We are going to the Summer Festival," said Ven. It seemed the best of his many bad reasons.

"Coreon says you have knowledge of the inside of the Gated City," said the Cormorant. "Is this true?"

"We've been there once," Ven admitted. "Char and me, that is— not her." He pointed at Amariel.

"You will tell us everything you know," the Cormorant said. "Which is the one who caused the sunshadow?"

The sea-Lirin man gestured at Char.

"That one."

The Cormorant floated over. Ven could see that, like the merrow, the Lirin-mer had webbed fingers, but instead of a tail they had legs clothed in trousers that looked as if they had been made from sheets of kelp, and webbed feet. What would have been the whites of his eyes on a human were tinged in green. The Cormorant stared down at Char as if waiting for another sunshadow.

"Well?"

"Urk," said Char. It was the only sound he was able to make.

"Tell me of the Gated City," the Cormorant demanded.

Char opened his mouth. Nothing came out, but seawater rushed in, and he began to choke.

Ven tried to get to his friend's side, but the first Lirin man swept him back with his shell-tipped spear.

The Cormorant's nostrils flared in anger.

"Enough of this," he said. "Take them to the Drowning Cave."

## ~ 13 ~

# The Drowning Cave

STAY CALM, CHAR," VEN THOUGHT AS TWO OF THE SEA LIRIN
seized his friend. Two more grabbed him a moment later. "We
haven't done anything wrong."

"Yeah, that seems to matter a lot," Char replied. "Sorry, mate. My
mind went totally blank."

The Cormorant turned in disgust and swam off to the north. In
the blink of an eye he was gone.

The sea-Lirin soldiers pressed their legs together, then gave a
powerful kick that looked like the tail of a dolphin as it swims. Suddenly Ven was being dragged through the drift faster than he had
ever swum. He swallowed hard, hoping that his vest pocket would
stay closed and its contents remain safe.

The soldiers swam faster and faster until after a while the only
thing Ven could do was to try to keep from being sick. The sweet air
from the stone in his pocket kept bouncing hard against his nose
as he was dragged along, making his stomach turn. And behind him,
the merrow was following as quickly as she could.

Ven closed his eyes to keep from seeing the look on her face.

Then all at once the sea Lirin stopped.

At the reef's edge was a dark hole, hard to see amid the coral. It
was barely large enough for a human man to crawl into.

The soldiers pointed at the hole.

"In there."

"I—I'm not sure I'll fit," Ven stammered.

The soldiers dragging Char pushed him forward.

"Let him go first," said the bigger of the two.

"Swell," Char muttered. He got down on his belly gingerly, with care to avoid cutting himself on the coral around the hole. "Well, Ven, I have to say it's been good to know you. I have to say that because you're my best friend, and I'd rather say *I told you so*, but I don't want that to be the last thing you hear from me before we drown."

"Many thanks," Ven replied. He smiled at the merrow, who was hovering in the drift, fighting back tears. "Don't worry, Amariel."

"Of course not," said the merrow sourly. "I think I'll polish my scales and braid my hair instead."

One of the soldiers guarding Ven turned him loose and tapped him with his spear.

"You're next," he said. "Get moving."

Ven exhaled, then got down on his hands and knees. The coral beneath his fingers darted out of the way, and he recoiled as he touched it. Then he put his hands down again on the rocky spine of the reef and crawled into the darkness of the hole.

And, to his shock, tumbled out of the drift and rolled down what felt like a long rocky hillside.

Surrounded by air.

Ven sat up.

Char was beside him on his hands and knees, fumbling around. It took Ven a moment to remember that Char was human, and blind in the dark. He touched his friend on the shoulder. Char gasped and moved away.

"It's all right," Ven said aloud for the first time since they left the skelligs that morning. "We can breathe. I don't know why, but we can breathe."

A spark flared as a flame was lit.

The Cormorant was standing in front of him, a lantern in his hand. The gills on his neck were flapping slightly, a little like a fish out of water. In the shadows cast by the lantern, Ven could see that more sea-Lirin soldiers stood nearby, each armed with a spear. Coreon and his father were among them, watching silently.

They were in a cave of some sort, with a high ceiling where something was moving in the dark above them. The cave seemed to be filled with splashing noises and what looked like casks of rum and water in barrels all around its edges, as well as sea chests and other goods that once rested in the holds of sailing ships.

"Welcome to the Drowning Cave, human filth," the Cormorant said. In the air, his voice was very different than his thrum, and harder to understand. "This is the place we bring sailors and others of your kind who have run afoul of the sea. It is a place where many lives have been saved—and just as many lost. What will happen with yours remains to be seen."

"Are—are we really breathing air?" Ven asked.

"You are." The Cormorant held up his lantern.

Above them they saw an enormous wheel like the waterwheel in the Great River that turned a grindstone in a mill. Along its circular edge, however, where a waterwheel would have buckets, were many clamshells of great size. As the wheel descended, the shells swung down with it, then swung flat again as they made their way back up. The pink and white interior of the shells gleamed in the dim light as they passed by.

"The airwheel," the Cormorant said, guessing their question. "It scoops air from the surface and deposits it in here as it comes down, then pushes water out as it goes back up. Now, my patience has come to its end. Arrogantly you humans ply the sea in your ships, and we allow that without disturbance. But all that is beneath the surface is our realm, and you are trespassing within it. You appear to be younglings, but looks are deceiving. It is clear that you know what lies within the Gated City. This can only mean that you are inhabitants of that place, criminals of the worst sort, and most likely spies. Before we put you to death, you will show me everything you

know about that city—it streets, its walls, its weapons. If you coop-
erate, we will see to it that your ends are quick and painless. If you
refuse, you will see another reason why this is called the Drowning
Cave."

A loud *ooof!* followed by the sound of a body falling heavily rattled the ceiling of the cave.

Ven, Char, and the sea Lirin looked up.

Amariel was rolling down the cave wall, her tail spinning end
over end as she fell, until she came to a bumpy stop in front of the
Cormorant.

The sea-Lirin commander glared at her and gave her a poke with
his spear.

"Did I not tell you to remain on the reef?" he demanded.

"You did," said the merrow huffily. "But if you're going to drown
my friends, you may as well drown me too."

"That would be a first," said Coreon. His speaking voice cracked
a little in the air.

"No, it wouldn't," said the Cormorant. "A merrow can be drowned
fairly easily."

"I will tell you what you want to know," said Ven quickly. "But
first, will you please tell me why you want to know about the Gated
City?"

The green-tinged eyes of the Cormorant narrowed.

"Your people in that city—"

"Wait, please," Ven interrupted. "With respect. I swear to you,
though we have been inside the Gated City, I *swear to you* we are not
its citizens. My name is a Ven, and this is my friend Char. We live at
the Crossroads Inn outside the city of Kingston, and I work for the
human king, Vandemere. In the course of my travels for the king
I have been many places, and one of them is the Gated City. That's
why I know what's inside it. But, as you can see, I was able to leave.
If I was a resident of that city, that would have been impossible."

"You are a fool, *Ven*," the Cormorant said. "Humans who dwell
within those walls make their way out of that city *all the time*. As you

undoubtedly know, they have built a long tunnel outside the harbor in the King's town, a tunnel that has destroyed a good part of the reef. They crawl like sea slugs beneath the sand, ripping up the reef, killing millions of coral and creatures of the sea. But that is about to end."

"You are going to seal the tunnel?"

"Yes—after our army has used it to enter the city and destroy every human that lives there."

## - 14 -

# The Airwheel

Y OU CAN'T MEAN THAT," VEN SAID. HIS VOICE SHOOK.

The Cormorant's kelp-like eyebrows lifted in surprise.

"I do," he said. "Merfolk are a peaceful people, but we are also a strong one, and we do not tolerate the destruction of our realm, the murder of our people and fellow creatures, and, most important, the devastation of the sea. Every land-liver within the walls of that city is a criminal—*every single one*—so there is no need for mercy. And there will be none."

"It's not true that everyone within the Gated City is a criminal," Ven said. "There are good people there as well, and—"

"Lies." The Cormorant's voice was as harsh as a slap across the face. "The Gated City is a prison colony. Those living behind its walls were sent from other places because they were the *worst of the worst*, so dangerous that the humans in the lands where they came from did not even want them in their realms. They came in a prison ship, the *Athenry*, specially made to hold them securely, locked away behind bars so that they could not escape into the sea. They were offloaded into the city in chains, by armed soldiers. Each time the *Athenry* approached our reef we saw them, linked together with iron loops. Then, finally, the last load of criminal slime was delivered.

The gates were sealed, and the ship sailed away, never to return. Do you deny this?"

"No, I don't deny it." Ven's heart was beating so fast that his words came out sounding like he had the hiccups. "But that was hundreds, maybe even thousands of years ago."

The Cormorant blinked. Then he looked at the other Lirin-mer, who looked at each other and shook their heads.

"Years?"

The merrow cleared her throat.

"Er—storm seasons. There are four storm in a year." She looked at Ven. "Those that live beneath the sea don't count time in human years, Ven. I only know what you are talking about because merrows can breathe both on land and under water, and we spend time sunning ourselves on rocks in the air. We see more of the human world, so I know what you mean, but they don't."

"Four storm or four million, it doesn't matter," said the Cormorant. He signaled to two soldiers whose gills were flapping heavily. The men made their way over to the airwheel. The first one caught hold of a giant shell as it passed by and pulled himself into it. The other soldier waited until a few shells had passed, then caught one and rode it to the surface as the other man had.

*They must only be able to stay out of the water and in the air for a short period of time*, Ven thought as he watched them leave the cave.

"With respect, it *does* matter," he said when the Cormorant was looking at him again. "After hundreds of years, every criminal who came on that ship is long dead."

His words echoed in the Drowning Cave. Then the only sound was the noise of the airwheel and the thrum of the drift outside the cave entrance. The sea Lirin stared at him.

The Cormorant finally spoke.

"Why? What makes you think that?"

"They, er, well," Ven stammered, "they, just *are*. It's been hundreds of years."

The merrow cleared her throat again and addressed the Cormorant.

"Even though they look like Lirin-mer, land-livers are more like, er, herring," she said. "A few hundred storm, and they, well, wear out. They die of old age."

"Old age? After a few hundred storm?"

The merrow shrugged. "They're weak and without much value, I guess."

"Thanks," Char muttered.

The Cormorant looked as if he did not believe her. "How can a human—or any land-liver with a soul—only last a few hundred storm? Coreon—how many storm have you seen?"

The Lirin-mer boy thought. "Twenty-four hundred and seven."

The Cormorant nodded. "As I thought. A man would not have even lost his air-voice after a few hundred storm."

"When Lirin-mer are young, they can still speak and breathe easily in the air," Amariel explained to Ven and Char, who were looking baffled. "As they age, it becomes harder for them to do either one, unless they are Lirin-mer of great power, like the Cormorant. Lirin-mer almost never go up to the surface."

"Ah," said Ven. He watched as several more soldiers caught rides to the surface on the airwheel. *No wonder none of them speak,* he thought. *A little like kittens, who are born blind, or frogs that start life as tadpoles, with a tail and no legs, losing the one and gaining the others.*

*I don't know why any of this surprised me.*

*Since Nain live about four times longer than humans, we tend to think of them as weak and fragile, too. A Nain boy usually starts growing his beard, his most prized feature, when he is about thirty in human years. By the time he is forty-five, his entire Bramble, the short growth that covers his entire chin, is almost always fully grown in. Only the very slow-to-grow, like me, are past fifty when their whiskers start appearing, and that is* very embarrassing. And I still only have three of them, one for each adventure I've undertaken since my fiftieth birthday.

Now I understood why the Lirin-mer hated the occupants of the Gated City so much.

But they were hating people who had been dead for centuries.

"The original prisoners from that prison ship have been dead a very long time in human years," he said again. "The people who live there now are their descendants, their great-great-great-great-grandchildren. Many of them are just as evil as the ones that came before them, but a lot of them aren't. Many of them are just prisoners of circumstance, with the bad luck to have been born in the wrong place. There are quite a few children inside those walls. It's not their fault they were born there. And while you probably see all land-livers as humans, not everyone in the Gated City is human, just as I am not human. There are many races in the Gated City—including Lirin. If you kill everyone, while you will be getting rid of some very bad people, it's true, you will also be taking a lot of innocent lives. Isn't that the same as what the humans in the Gated City are doing to the coral reef?"

The Cormorant stared at Ven in silence. His gills were flapping more quickly now. Finally he signaled to the Lirin-mer soldiers.

"All but Coreon, depart," he said. The soldiers obeyed. He turned to the sea-Lirin boy. "You will stay and guard them. I will return shortly. If they give you any trouble, stop the airwheel and flood the Drowning Cave."

Coreon nodded. He walked over to the airwheel and took up a guard position beside it. Then he raised his weapon and pointed it at Ven.

The Cormorant started for the airwheel. As he passed Amariel he paused and looked down at her on the coral cave floor.

"You may find, merrow, that when you try to live in two worlds you are at home in neither of them," he said curtly. Then he strode to the airwheel and caught hold of a giant shell. He hung from it by one arm as it lifted him to the surface, then disappeared from sight.

"Well, this undersea adventure just keeps gettin' better and better," said Char, stretching out his arms.

Coreon sighted his crossbow. "Silence," he ordered. His voice squeaked as he spoke.

"Oh, shut up," said Amariel.

The sea-Lirin boy's eyes opened wide in surprise.

"You're not exactly in a position to disobey," he said when he could speak again. "You're out of the sea, merrow, in case you hadn't noticed. I bet your tail is drying out about now."

"Why don't ya come over here and tell her that again, up close this time?" Char said. "There's a sea lion with a broken nose on a skellig who thought the same way you do yesterday. He's changed his mind."

Amariel glared at Coreon. "Don't you dare try to bully me," she said. "You think you're important because you have a barb, but your voice is changing. Pretty soon you'll be just like the rest of them, and the Cormorant won't have any use for you. Leave us alone."

Ven sat down on the hard coral floor between his friends and the sea-Lirin boy. As he did, something in his pocket pressed up against his leg. He reached into the pocket of his trousers and pulled out the small green glass bottle. The cork was still in the opening, the wax seal unbroken. He held the bottle where Amariel could see it.

"Look what I found this morning in the surf on Skellig Elarose," he said quietly.

Char's expression brightened. "Oh, yeah! I'd forgotten about that," he said. "I guess you can open it now, since we're out of the sea for a moment."

The merrow's brows drew together as Ven pulled his jack-rule from his vest pocket.

"What are you doing?"

"The cork is sealed with wax," Ven explained as he extended the knife from the odd folding tool. "It looks like it has a message written on paper inside it, wrapped around something hard that clinks." He shook the bottle gently to demonstrate.

"What are you doing over there?" Coreon asked suspiciously.

"In case you're interested, you are about to hear the sound of a human, a Nain, and a merrow ignoring you," said Amariel. "Be careful with that knife, Ven."

"I will," Ven said. He slid the knife carefully around the cork seal. The wax seemed old, or at least hardened by the sea, so it took a good deal of prying before he could reach the cork. The wooden plug cracked and dissolved into pieces as he tried to pry it loose, so he shook it out onto the floor of the Drowning Cave, then gently pulled the little scroll of paper out of the bottle.

Before he could unroll it, something dropped into his lap from inside it.

Ven held it up in the shadowy light of the lantern.

It was a thin piece of metal, straight like a sewing needle but with a curve near the end with what looked like a tiny tooth at the very bottom.

At the top of it was a small carved metal skull, its hollow eyes blank and its toothless mouth grinning blackly.

"By the Blowhole," Amariel whispered.

"What the heck is that?" Char asked.

"I don't know," said Ven. "It looks a little bit like the lock picks in the weapons store in the Gated City, the Arms of Coates, remember, Char?"

"You mean those tools that thieves use to open locks without keys?"

"Yes. Or maybe it's a key itself." Ven held the tiny tool up closer to get a better look.

"A skeleton key?" Char shrank away.

"What's a skeleton key?" Amariel asked.

Char wrapped his arms tighter around his knees.

"I've never seen one, but the sailors tell stories about them sometimes. Pirates are said to have 'em. I think it's supposed to be able to open *any* lock, even a really complicated one."

"Hmm," said Ven. He handed the key to Amariel, who took it gingerly, then carefully unrolled the small scroll of paper.

It was an old piece of oilcloth, scratched and dulled with time, that smelled of salt and leather. On it one word was printed in ink that had smeared slightly.

*Athenry*, it said.

## - 15 -

# An Uneasy Truce

WHILE THE BOYS WERE EXAMINING THE SCRAP OF OILCLOTH, the merrow was examining the key.

"There's some writing on this, too," she said. "Very small."

"What does it say?" Char asked.

The merrow glared at him.

"Let me have a quick look," Ven said. He knew that Amariel could not read human script.

The merrow passed him the key. He held it up in the lantern-light. The letters were tiny, but he could read most of them if he turned it slowly.

"*'Free the only innocent prisoners she ever held,'*" he read.

"It says all *that*?" The merrow let out a low whistle.

"Criminey, whatdaya s'pose *that* means?" Char wondered aloud.

Suddenly, a loud *thud* echoed through the Drowning Cave.

Something large and heavy had fallen from the same hole in the coral ceiling through which they had entered. A few seconds later, the Cormorant entered as well, followed by sea-Lirin soldiers, their gills flapping more shallowly now.

Ven and Char scrambled to their feet. Ven tucked the key and the tiny oilcloth scrap back into the bottle, and the bottle back into his pocket. Char stepped forward and stood in front of Amariel, trying to keep her hidden from the entering Lirin-mer, but the merrow gave him a shove.

"Get out of the way, Chum," she said impatiently. "I want to see."

"I was trying to protect you," Char protested, but the Cormorant was now standing in front of him.

The Cormorant stared at each of them for a moment, the greens of his eyes glistening in the fading light of the lantern. Finally he took in a breath, then exhaled through his gills.

"You wish to go to the Summer Festival?"

The children looked at each other.

"Yes, sir," Ven said.

"Then you will tell me, as you agreed to, everything that I need to know about the Gated City. It will be easiest if we return to the drift to do this, so that you can picture the streets in a sunshadow so that we may all have an accurate view of the inner workings of the city."

Ven's stomach turned over. His head felt numb, but he managed to nod.

The Cormorant looked at him sharply.

"But before we return to the drift, I want you to tell me the names of all the good people in the Gated City," he said. "I need to know where they live, so that we can spare them if possible when the battle begins."

Ven swallowed hard.

"I—I don't know how to do that," he said. "I know the names of a few of them, but there are so many—"

"Tell your tale, Ven," the Cormorant said darkly. "My patience is thin and wanes with the sun—which is beginning to set, in case you are interested."

*So I started talking. I told the Cormorant all the things I could remember about the Gated City.*

*First I told him about the Outer Market, about the street vendors who roasted meat over open fires and cooked squash soup* inside a pumpkin shell the size of a wagon. I told them about the clowns, and the storytellers and jugglers, and all the people selling magical and wondrous wares. I told him about the puppet shows in the streets and the people who had been kind to me there when our friend Saeli was missing.

Next, I told him of the Inner Market, a darker, more evil place, where Felonia, the Queen of Thieves, had held us captive in the labyrinth of the Raven's Guild hall. While I imagine the people of the Outer Market are the descendants of the cutpurses and con artists who first came on the <u>Athenry</u>, I suspect the members of the Raven's Guild are probably the great-great-grandchildren of a worse sort of criminal.

But I don't know that for sure.

Finally, I told him about the Downworlders, a ragtag group of outcasts who lived in a vast maze of tunnels beneath the streets of the Gated City, hidden away from the sight of the world. I told them of Macedon, the Rat King, who was their ruler, and how they had helped us when we were lost in the Inner Market, running for our lives from Felonia's goons.

"So you see," he finished, "there are so many people who are good, or *could* be good, in the Gated City that it would be impossible to name them all."

The Cormorant watched him a moment longer, then turned and started for the airwheel.

"That's a pity," he said. "Oh well. I'm sure you tried your best."

"Wait!" shouted Char. His voice came out louder than he expected, and it echoed through the Drowning Cave. The gills of the merfolk fluttered at the sound. "Madame Sharra—there's a fortune teller, tall and thin and she has golden skin and eyes. She's a good person. She should be saved."

"And Mr. Coates," Ven added. "Mynah Coates, I think was his full name. He's a weapons maker, and he has two dogs, Finlay and

Munx. He was very kind to us as well." His voice got quieter as he thought about the last time he had seen the Arms of Coates, the weapons shop, empty, its door ajar, all of the security traps sprung, thin streaks of blood everywhere. "Actually, I'm not sure he's even still alive. He may have paid for helping us with his life."

In the back of his mind, something Mr. Coates had said to him early in his visit to the Gated City came back to him.

*There are many layers within any prison; remember that. It all depends on who's guarding what. Not just anyone can go at will out of the harbor tunnels, believe me. If they could, I—*

The weapons maker had never finished his thought.

"Mr. Coates told me that even though everyone in the Gated City knows about the harbor tunnels, not everyone can use them. So some of the people who live there are also prisoners of their fellow prisoners."

The Cormorant stopped. The children watched as he stood in thought for a long time. Then he returned to where Ven was standing.

"I have never seen a Nain," he said. "But if you are, in fact, Nain, then you are a son of the Earth. You are out of place in the sea, *Ven*."

Ven sighed. "So I have been told."

"Perhaps your connection to the land will help us make sense of the problem with the Gated City," the Cormorant continued. "I have no desire to slaughter the innocent. But it is my responsibility—my *first* responsibility—to prevent the destruction of the reef and its inhabitants. This riddle is beyond my ability to solve."

He signaled to the sea-Lirin soldiers. They picked up the heavy object that had fallen before they entered and carried it over to him, depositing it at his feet.

It was what looked like a canvas bag like sailors used to carry their gear in, clearly made at one time by humans, with a series of cords tying it closed.

The Cormorant opened the bag and pulled out three knapsacks, which he placed on the coral cave floor in front of them. Then he drew forth two barbed weapons like the one Coreon was holding, and two short spears.

"I suggest if you meet the Sea King at the Festival, you stay out of any sunshadows near him, especially on Threshold, the last day of summer," he said. "His power is at its highest on that day, the last day of his reign, and he makes great use of sunshadow then. You would be well advised to stay clear, or you might find yourself transported to another part of the sea on the other side of the world."

"I don't understand," Char said.

"I need to send a message to the Sea King," said the Cormorant. "I need his guidance about who to kill and who to let live within the Gated City. I do not have the ability to send such messages through sunshadow, but he will be able to send one in return to me that way."

"And you want us to deliver your message to the Sea King?" Ven asked excitedly.

An expression of disbelief crossed the Cormorant's face.

"Hardly," he said. "I want you to accompany Coreon while *he* does it."

## ~ 16 ~

# Back to the Drift

Coreon's green-tinged eyes opened in surprise. "Me, sir?"

"You may as well go with them," said the Cormorant. "They already have your name." He sounded annoyed. "You will take them past the kelp beds to the Underwater Forest, then through the Sea Desert and beyond to the Festival. Deliver this message to whoever has been crowned king of the sea this storm." He put his webbed-fingered hand on Coreon's forehead. The sea-Lirin boy closed his eyes, as if listening, then nodded. The Cormorant picked up one of the knapsacks and handed it to him, then tossed the other two at Char and Ven.

"You will find dried kelp and the un-salt water humans drink in there," he said. "There should be enough to get you safely to the Festival. After that, you will have to provide for yourselves."

"What about Amariel?" Char asked.

"A merrow is more than able to find food and drink in the sea. To laden her with provisions would make her clumsy, endanger her. You may take the weapons—she does not need one of those, either. Her weapons are part of her."

"Yep—ask any sea lion ya happen to come across," Char murmured.

The merrow smiled smugly.

The Cormorant signaled to the soldiers again. Different ones stepped forward this time and handed Ven and Char what looked like a piece of cloth from an old sail wrapped around something soft. Ven opened it to find a piece of cooked fish.

"Thank you," he said.

The Cormorant nodded. "We remember the stories from the Before-Time, when Lirin-mer still lived on the land, about drying fish in fire before eating them," he said. "It has never made any sense to me, but if it is your tradition, well, then, it is."

"Thank you," Ven repeated. "But, er, fish? Isn't this one of your, well, your—"

The Cormorant shrugged.

"Everyone has to eat," he said. "It's nothing personal."

"See?" Amariel said. There was a hint of triumph in her voice. "I told you so."

"Finish it quickly," said the Cormorant. "The sun is diving, and soon it will be night. You'll want to find shelter in the Deep while you still have a bit of light, and we still need to see your thrum about the inner workings of the Gated City."

Char was licking his fingers already. He cleared his throat uncomfortably.

As soon as Ven had eaten, the Cormorant signaled to one of the soldiers, who hoisted Amariel off the floor, ignoring her protests and squirming. The Cormorant led them to the airwheel, seized one of the giant shells, and held it still, temporarily stopping the wheel while the soldier deposited the merrow into the shell bucket. Streams of seawater immediately began to rain into the cave when the wheel came to a stop.

"It took many storm for the wheel to drain the Drowning Cave and fill it with air," the Cormorant said as he released the wheel. Amariel's shell began rising toward the ceiling of the cave. "If the airwheel were to stop for more than a few moments, the cave would be completely submerged."

Ven could hear Char gulp behind him.

"You still have your stone?" he whispered to his best friend. Char nodded.

"You're next, human," the Cormorant ordered. "Take your time going up from the cave—you should always go slowly toward the surface." He waited until the merrow had disappeared over the wheel's top, then stopped another shell. Char scrambled inside, and the Cormorant released the wheel again.

"Hold your breath," Ven advised as the shell headed for the ceiling.

"Believe me, I am," Char retorted. "I have been all along." Then the shell disappeared over the top of the airwheel.

Ven watched anxiously as his friends faded into the darkness. Then he grabbed his pack and weapon and hurried to the wheel, knowing the drill.

"When you leave the air, find the nearest patch of sunshadow as soon as you get into the drift," the Cormorant instructed. "Night is falling, and it may be hard to find one, but the light that breaks the surface at the end of the day is often the most powerful. A storm is coming; it will rain soon, and the morning will be gray. Clear your head and get your thoughts straight." He turned to the sea-Lirin boy. "Coreon, bid your father goodbye."

*As soon as I got into the shell I could feel the salt in my nose and eyes again. It still stung, harder now, because I had been away from it for a short time. I could feel the weight of the sea above me, and it made my stomach turn flips.*

*And the curiosity run wild in my veins.*

*Because we were going to the Summer Festival.*

*Amariel had told me stories of it, as I lay cold and shivering on the broken piece of driftwood that had once been part of the* Angelia, *a ship that never got a chance to be christened because I blew it up to keep it from the Fire Pirates. Before the driftwood sank I carved what would have been the name into it with the knife in my jack-rule.*

*It seemed like the story of my life then—too little, too late.*

*But perhaps now things were changing.*

*We were about to set forth on an important mission, even if it was Coreon's. Our efforts might lead to the saving of the innocent people of the Gated City, the people Mr. Coates had described as being trapped by the many layers of their prison home.*

*I hope he's still alive.*

*I hope the Tree of Water is still alive.*

*Most of all, when all this is over, I hope Amariel, Char, and I will still be alive.*

The shell, which had been tilted at an angle and sealed upright against the inside of the airwheel, rolled up so that it was lying flat. With a sickening rush, the sea grabbed Ven from within the smooth inside and dragged him into the drift again.

Fighting panic, he took a breath.

Instead of choking, as he had prepared for, the sweet elemental air filled his lungs once more.

In the patchy light to the west he saw the merrow and Char waving to him, surrounded by the sea-Lirin soldiers. They looked much more comfortable now that they were away from the air and back in their watery home.

*I wonder how they came to be here, away from the Lirin of the upworld,* Ven thought as he watched their gills open and close smoothly in the drift. *Maybe Coreon knows the story. We will certainly have time to trade tales on the way to the Summer Festival.*

The Cormorant was beside him a moment later. His kelp-like hair and brows floated in the drift, making him look even more terrifying. He signaled to the last sunny place where hazy light broke the surface, and Ven swam over as quickly as he could before the light shifted.

"Tell me," the Cormorant commanded. His thrum was even more powerful than his voice.

So Ven recounted what he knew about the structure of the Gated City. He had never seen the northernmost wall, nor the one that surrounded the far eastern section, but he was able to call to mind a fairly good picture of the rest of the place. He thought about the Outer Market's streets, laid out neatly in a circle around a center area, and the Skywalk, an elevated pathway in the air above the streets built of wooden planks and ladders that stretched from the Outer Market inward. Finally he pictured the Keyhole Gate, the frightening doorway through which they had passed into the Inner Market. He showed them a sunshadow of the Raven's Guild hall, where Felonia ruled, and the well in the center of the dark streets where they had met the Downworlders.

"I have no idea what their tunnels look like from above," he said as the sunshadow faded. "It was a giant maze. Only the Downworlders themselves can travel those underground routes and not be lost forever."

"Understood." The Cormorant waved to Coreon to join them as he emerged from the underwater cave. "Follow the sun as it travels across the sky—the Festival grounds are due west, beyond the great Sea Desert. Cross the desert carefully—there are fewer creatures living there, but those that do are often large and hungry. Be respectful and pass quietly."

"We will."

"Good. Remember to give the Sea King my message—it is the only thing that will save any good people who might live within the city's walls, if any such people really do exist. I will wait to attack until the last day of summer. If I have heard nothing by then, I will assume you have failed in your mission and have become part of the sea. Then I will do what I have to do. Are we clear?"

"We are," Ven replied. "Thank you for your help."

"Shoulder your packs and keep your weapons out," the Cormorant advised. "Clear drift and low waves to you."

"Thank you," all four of the children's thrum answered.

As Ven pulled the pack onto his back, it brushed against his pocket. The green glass bottle inside bumped against his leg. He called quickly after the Cormorant, who had already formed his legs into the dolphin-like position.

"Sir?"

The Cormorant turned around.

"The *Athenry*—the prison ship you mentioned? Whatever became of it?"

"I do not know the answer to that question," the sea-Lirin commander said. "Once its last load of prisoners was delivered, it departed, never to be seen again. I've heard tales that it sank, but I have never seen its bones on the reef or beyond it in the Deep. Perhaps a sea dragon has them in its lair. Other than that, I cannot say."

Thoughts were beginning to race in Ven's head.

"Do you know where a sea dragon lives?"

The Cormorant shook his head.

"Even if I did, I wouldn't suggest you visit one," he said. "They are among the most vicious creatures in the sea, and do not take well to strangers approaching their lairs. I'm told each dragon in the world collects something different in its lair. I've heard tales of one who lives near the great Icefields to the south that collects casks of rum, but that is a visit from which you would not return, for many reasons. I suggest you learn to rein in your curiosity, *Ven*. I know it plagues you—I could feel the thrum of your head when we first met. Curiosity can be a valuable tool, but it can also make you vulnerable. And in the sea, vulnerability means death. Remember that. I am not the least bit sorry that I do not know the whereabouts of any sea dragons."

With a strong kick, he was gone.

When the vibrations of his leaving had settled into the drift, and his thrum could no longer be felt, Coreon turned to the others.

"I know where one lives."

# ~ 17 ~

# Into the Deep

H<small>OLD ON,</small>" <small>SAID THE MERROW.</small> "<small>VEN, FORGET YOU HEARD</small> that."

"What she said," Char agreed. "Which way to the Summer Festival?"

Ven didn't hear them. His ears were filled with the words that hung in the water from Coreon's thrum. His curiosity blocked out the sound of anything else.

*I know where one lives.*

"Where?"

"It doesn't matter," Amariel interrupted before the sea-Lirin boy could answer. "We're not going there. We're heading for the Underwater Forest, then out to the Sea Desert. You'll love the kelp beds there, Ven. The forest is a magical place. I told you a little about it when you were half dead on that piece of broken ship."

Coreon shrugged. "Have it your way. I can visit him anytime. And we may see him anyway, since he lives *in* the kelp forest."

"How ferocious is he?" Ven asked.

Coreon thought for a moment. "He's pretty peaceful, though he can be cranky if you surprise him."

"A little like Scarnag," Char said. "An' I'm not sure we're up to takin' on a dragon at this point in time, Ven, even a peaceful one.

We have a set time to get this mission done, and to get an answer back to the Cormorant. I'd hate to see all the innocent folks in the Gated City pay with their lives because we took a detour to see a dragon. I still feel guilty enough about the herring. The second lesson they teach you in Don't Be an Idiot School is 'Keep away from dragons that ain't botherin' you.'"

"What's the first lesson?" Coreon asked.

"Lesson Number One: 'You can't trust *anybody* in a thieves' market,'" Char said. "We learned that one up close." He shuddered at the memory.

"But what about the scale?" Ven asked. He looked around to be certain nothing nearby was listening, but the drift was empty except for some floating kelp and a few minnows that were not paying attention. "Madame Sharra said that she had never seen one want to accompany anyone before. It wants me to do something important with it, I'm sure. The last time we returned a scale to a dragon we stopped at least three different wars. If we can do that under the sea—"

"What are you talking about?" Coreon demanded.

"Ven has this thing about dragons, having met *one*," Amariel said. Her thrum felt furious against Ven's skin, like a stinging slap. "That particular one was in the upworld. As you know, everything in the upworld is much weaker and far less powerful than what lives in the sea. So he thinks it would be interesting to meet a sea dragon. He doesn't have the first clue about the dragons of the Deep. My mother said she would rather see me marry a human than talk to a sea dragon."

"Whoa," Char whispered. "That *is* bad."

"Yes it is," said the merrow. "I told you at the beginning of this journey, Ven, that if you were seeking out a sea dragon, you were on your own. At least sharks eat you raw. I have no desire to be roasted alive before I get swallowed."

Coreon's kelp-like eyebrows drew together.

"I really doubt he would swallow you," he said.

"Well, pardon me if I don't want to take your word for it," Amariel said huffily.

Coreon shrugged again. "Suit yourself. Why don't we just head over the kelp beds to the forest and if we happen to see him, we can say hello, but we won't seek him out."

"That seems reasonable," said Ven.

"You really aren't listening to me, are you?" Amariel asked.

"Not really," Coreon admitted. "But that's mostly because Lirin-mer fathers tell their sons to never pay attention to merrows, because they're selfish and thoughtless and will lead you into trouble."

The merrow's mouth dropped open, and her thrum went flat in shock.

"Let's head for the forest," Ven said quickly. "The Cormorant said we would want to find cover for the night before dark. Do you think the Underwater Forest would be a good place for that?"

"Probably," said Coreon. He swam ahead of the merrow, who was still staring, aghast, at him. "This way."

Char looked doubtfully from Amariel to Ven. The merrow had recovered from her shock and was looking as if she were preparing to spit.

"Whaddaya think?" he asked.

"I think Coreon should decide where we go," Ven said. "This is his mission. And he's the one who knows the way to the Summer Festival."

The Lirin-mer stopped in the drift, then turned around and coughed awkwardly. "Well, sort of. I've been *told* the way. I've never actually been myself."

"Oh, swell," Char muttered.

"Well, at least we should find shelter," said Ven. "Let's go."

"If this mission is so important, why did the Cormorant send someone who had never been to the Festival before?" Char asked as they left the reef.

The Lirin-mer boy stopped swimming and hovered in the drift.

"You *really* don't get it, do you?" he said harshly. "This mission isn't important to anyone but *you*. The Cormorant doesn't care about the people in the Gated City. He doesn't believe *any* of them are worth saving. He has no reason to believe that we are even going to reach the Summer Festival. He probably assumes we will get eaten by predators in the Sea Desert. Didn't you hear what he said to me?"

Char and Ven were silent, but the merrow nodded.

"That's what he meant when he said that Coreon may as well go with us, because we already had his name," she explained to the boys. "I keep trying to tell you two how important it is to guard your name in the Deep, to not throw names around lightly. When someone has your name, it's like they have power over you. That makes you vulnerable."

Coreon added. "You wouldn't know my name if I hadn't messed up and followed you on the reef. My father called out to me because he didn't know where I was. I'm a vulnerability now, useless. To my people, I'm part burden, part danger. So the Cormorant decided to send me away with you. If we get through to the Festival, and we successfully deliver his message, he will have the Sea King's guidance and blessing about the Gated City. And if we don't, well, he can do whatever he already has planned. The Sea King is only king until Threshold, the last day of summer, so the Cormorant can also ignore what he says and nobody will be the wiser. You've given him all the information he needs to invade the city. So he wins either way."

"Oh man." Char's thrum came out like a whisper.

Ven fought down his anger.

"Well, then, I guess we'll just have to make certain we get to the Summer Festival, won't we," he said. "Hopefully the Sea King will be a wiser leader than the Cormorant."

"That all depends on your point of view," said Coreon. "The Cormorant is not a bad leader. He has a job to do, a reef and a people to protect. From his perspective, you asking to save a few good people in the Gated City would be like someone asking dolphins to spare certain fish in a Herring Ball."

"I hope the schoolmaster made it out," Char said. The Lirin-mer looked at him strangely.

"Let's be on our way," said the merrow. She started off into the darker green water, where only the smallest amount of light was breaking the surface now.

Ven and the others followed her into the deeper part of the sea, leaving the reef and its colorful wonders behind them.

Beyond the shallows, larger schools of fish moved about in between patches of kelp, spotty at first, but growing thicker as the water deepened and grew colder. A squadron of large, bat-like rays like the one Ven had startled on the reef swept past. They streaked toward the surface, leaping out of the water, then splashed back down, filling the drift with bubbles and stunning the fish.

As they watched the rays suck the dazed fish up into the mouths on the flat undersides of their bodies, a strange creature skittled along the ocean floor below them. Its head was shaped like that of a land snail, but its ray-like body had formless sides covered in green bristly growth.

"Oh!" exclaimed Amariel. "Hello, Elysia!"

The strange creature flapped its soft sides and scurried on.

"That's Elysia," the merrow informed them. "She's a green sea slug, part animal, part plant. But don't ever mention that fact around her, because she's a little sensitive about it."

"Part animal, part *plant*?" Char demanded. "How's that possible?"

"I dunno," said the merrow. "But she only needs to eat algae once in her lifetime, and then she never has to eat again. All she has to do is sunbathe, and she can make her own food, like a green plant. She must have been up at the surface soaking up the sun's rays."

"The sea sure is a strange place," Char muttered.

The merrow said something in return, but Ven was not listening. In the distance, the familiar thrum had brushed against his skin again. He tried to remember where he had heard it before, but the answer eluded him.

There was another thrum masking it, a buzzing on the surface above them, lighter and wider spread.

"It's raining," Amariel said, reading his thoughts. "A storm is coming. The drift is starting to churn. The winds must be picking up."

"We had best find shelter," Coreon said. "Come on. It's not too much farther to the doorway of the Underwater Forest."

They swam over kelp beds that grew thicker the deeper in they went, with large clusters of seaweed floating in the drift. Ven could see crabs hurrying along the ocean floor among the kelp, burrowing into the sand ahead of the storm. The light had left the sky, and the sea was now dark except for a little remaining surface blue.

The way ahead of them was even darker.

*I could see a little bit, but only a little bit. The sandy ocean floor was no longer bare. It appeared to be strewn with what looked like algae-covered rocks. And farther ahead there seemed to be something hovering in the drift, but I could not make out what it was.*

"Ven, we should prolly stop." Char's thrum sounded nervous. "I'm all but blind now. I can't see a bloody thing."

"That's a good idea," Coreon said. "We might want to settle at the bottom and ride out the storm, and get some sleep. Especially considering we're now in the area where the sea dragon lives. He could be anywhere around here."

"And you would never see him until it's too late."

# – 18 –

# The Underwater Forest

A storm at sea is a frightening thing when you are on a ship. The waves can rise higher than the decks, spilling slippery salty green foam over the sides while the ship pitches up and down. The winds howl madly and the cloth of the sails sometimes tears. The ripping sound when that happens makes you feel as if your skin has been torn from your body. It's all you can do sometimes to hang on and not be swept into the sea, let alone remain standing.

Under the sea, a storm is a different kind of frightening.

Unless it is a very violent storm, sometimes the only part of the sea that is affected is near the surface. The closer to the bottom you are, the less the drift moves. The winds may be screaming in the upworld, and the waves crashing, but a few fathoms deeper it's almost like nothing is happening.

Except for the pressure.

The storm on that first night was little more than rain and wind, Amariel said. We did not go up to the surface to see if she was right, but I trust that she knows what she's talking about. We took shelter in the first few rocks we found at the forest's edge, and tried to sleep.

*That was almost impossible.*

*The thrum of the storm echoed through the Deep. The sea pressed against our heads, making them ache, weighing us down in the drift and the dark.*

<u>*Storm. Storm. Storm,*</u> *it seemed to say.* <u>*Storm. Storm.*</u>

*Every now and then, a flash of lightning brightened the surface of the sea above us, casting ghostly shadows all around. The Underwater Forest looked haunted in the drift beyond the rocks where we were hiding. Coreon and Amariel did not notice. They were sleeping peacefully.*

*Char and I, on the other hand, lay awake, our eyes wide open, feeling the rumble of the thunder burbling through the water.*

*It was a little like old times on the* <u>*Serelinda*</u>.

*Only we were under the waves the* <u>*Serelinda*</u> *had sailed over.*

*Finally, when the winds let up, the thrum of the storm changed. The lightning stopped flashing, leaving behind nothing but the patter of rain on the ocean's surface. It sounded like raindrops dancing off the world's biggest roof.*

*It sort of reminded me of home.*

*Vaarn is a rainy city, so the patter of raindrops is nothing new to me. In fact, it's a comforting feeling. I closed my eyes and thought back to my bedroom at home, a tiny attic room I share with two of my brothers, Leighton and Brendan, both of whom work in smelly parts of the family factory. In the summer when the window is open the rain washes the air of our bedroom.*

*It's a great improvement over the regular smell of Leighton and Brendan.*

*So now, at the bottom of the sea, once the winds had gone, the thunder and lightning had ceased, leaving nothing but rain, I finally found it possible to sleep.*

*When I woke up, I was in a completely different world.*

VEN COULD FEEL THE SUNWATER EVEN BEFORE HE OPENED HIS eyes. His eyelids had almost become accustomed to the salt, so the warmth felt good on his skin.

He opened them carefully.

Then he blinked.

The dark and frightening place they had taken shelter at the edge of had transformed into a realm of immense, unearthly beauty. He and his friends were stretched out on what seemed like endless rocky ground covered in emerald algae swirled with soft colors of purple, yellow, and red.

Towering above them were what looked like trees, with thick broomstick-like trunks the width of his arm and others wider than his waist, around which large, lush green leaves stretched up to the surface above. The rising sun made the drift around those trees look misty and eerie, like an enchanted forest at dawn in the up-world, but alien and watery.

A pathway of sorts stretched out before them, lit by dusty sunlight.

Amariel yawned and stretched beside him.

"Morning," she murmured.

"Good morning," Ven said, looking around in wonder. "So this is a kelp forest?"

The merrow rubbed some sand out of her eyes and nodded. Then she reached out and tore a leaf off of a tall kelp tree and crammed it into her mouth.

"What are you *doin'*?" Char's thrum sounded sleepy.

"What does it look like I'm doing? I'm having breakfast." Amariel's brows drew together at the expression on the boys' faces. "For goodness' sake, it's *kelp*. It grows more than two wrist-to-fingertips a day. Calm down. Your thrum is so negative. You'll scare the nymphs and bother the water sprites."

"Not to mention the sea dragon." The feel of Coreon's thrum

was annoyed. "Please try not to embarrass me. I've had enough hu-miliation for one storm season, thank you."

"Ven," Char whispered. "Look." He pointed into the Underwater Forest.

Ven peered into the deep velvet green of floating leaves and branches glistening in the sunwater. At first he saw nothing.

Then, just as his eye was moving to another area, he saw a flash of movement.

But no color.

"What was—" Char began.

"Shhhhhh," cautioned Amariel. "It's only the Vila."

Ven watched, still as he could. The thick green leaves of the kelp danced in the drift. The sun's rays broke the surface, filling the for-est glen with moving patches of hazy light.

Then, slowly, a woman's face peeked out from behind the trunks of the kelp.

Then another.

And another.

But while they resembled human women, the creatures had no color, no solid form. Instead they looked almost clear, like the jel-lyfish that floated on the surface of the sea.

Amariel rose up into the drift. She smacked her tail on the rocks they had slept on. The sharp impact sent ripples through the water, causing the wide green leaves to flutter.

And the clear beings to disappear into the kelp.

"What did ya do *that* for?" Char demanded.

"To make them leave." The merrow brushed algae off her tail fluke. "Are you in the mood to dance?"

"Dance?" Ven edged a little farther into the kelp forest, but saw no sign of what Amariel had called the Vila.

"Never," said Char. "Why?"

"Well, that's often what Vila want land-liver males to do." Ama-riel ran her fingers through her hair and brushed her hands over the scales that came up to her armpits. Then she put her finger in her mouth and swished it around. She pulled it out, making a popping sound. "Are we ready to go?"

"What exactly are Vila?" Ven asked as he picked up his knapsack and weapon. He ran his hand through his own floating hair to clear it of sand and algae.

"Fairylike spirits, a little like the Spice Folk in your inn, but bigger and more obnoxious," said the merrow.

"There's somethin' in this world more obnoxious than Spice Folk?" Char said. "I don' believe it."

"I told you, Chum, *everything* is more extreme in the sea."

"The Vila don't belong here," said Coreon. "They're out of place. I hear they live in the clouds and somewhere on land in the up-world."

"The summer must be dry in their homes in the land wilderness," said Amariel. "They only come to the sea to gather rain for their clouds."

"Or to cause mischief," added Coreon. "It's said they can summon storms. They may have even called the one last night. They are nothing to toy with. My father has warned me about them many times. They're strong, and they can take many shapes, mostly of animals. It's not a good thing that we have already caught their interest."

The merrow snorted. "I'm not afraid of Vila. Let's be on our way."

She swam ahead into the frizzy shafts of sunlight that filled the forest pathway in front of them to the west. The boys looked at each other, then shouldered their weapons and knapsacks and followed her.

As they journeyed through the kelp forest, Ven kept his eyes open as wide as he could in the salty drift. The coral reef had been magical, and once they had left it he could not have imagined another sight as beautiful. But the forest of kelp had a different thrum, a sleepy, gentle call, almost like a merrow's song. It was even more hauntingly beautiful.

"Be careful," Amariel warned as that thought crossed his mind. "Vila have voices that can be enchanting to land-livers, and the kelp itself sings. This is a drowsy place. The injured and the sick are often brought to kelp forests to heal or recover, because the water is so rich here. Sometimes it's hard to get out once you go in. So stay sharp and pay attention."

"Right," said Coreon.

"Will do," said Ven.

There was no response from Char.

"Chum? Are you awake?"

"Hmmm?" Char's response was dreamy.

The merrow stopped suddenly in the drift. She swam swiftly to Char, grabbed him by the shoulder, and spat in his eye.

A howl of pain, followed by coughing, rocketed off towering kelp plants, disturbing the quiet of the forest and making all the fronds and leaves shake.

"Wake up!" Amariel commanded. "I'm not kidding. Next time, it'll be the tail."

"She's right," Coreon said hurriedly as Char glared at the merrow. "You land-livers have to be especially careful. If the Vila get hold of you they may drown you, just for fun."

"You spat at me," Char said. "You *spat* at me." His thrum shook with rage.

"Sorry. Next time I'll just break your nose."

"That's it, Ven, I'm done." Char dropped his barb and his pack. They floated down in the drift to the forest floor. "I'm goin' home."

"Yeah. Good luck with that," said Amariel.

"Excuse us a moment," Ven said to the Lirin-mer and the merrow. He took hold of Char's arm and pulled him away from the path to a patch of what looked like giant kelp ferns. He leaned close to his best friend. "Look, I'm sorry she did that, but she was trying to keep you safe."

"You don' have to thrum-whisper. Both of them can still hear you, ya know," Char said. "I don't care if she hears me. Coreon too.

I've had enough, Ven. We've only been at this a couple o' days, and I'm already tired of seaweed and talkin' in my head. I'm sick of the sting of salt and my underwear always being wet. And I'm beyond being sick of being treated like fish guts by a merrow who, as far as I'm concerned, *totally* lives up to the warning sea-Lirin fathers give their sons. Coreon says the Cormorant is going to do what he wants to, no matter what the Sea King advises. So why don't we just go back an' tell King Vandemere about what's goin' on in the harbor? Maybe *he* can do somethin' to help the good people in the Gated City. This isn't our problem, Ven. You did what you promised Amariel—you've explored the bloody Deep. Let's go home. I'm gonna, whether you go with me or not."

Ven took a deep breath. There was something in Char's dark brown eyes he had never seen, a glint of anger that had not been there before.

"You're not thinking clearly," he said slowly, trying to have his thrum sound patient and reasonable. "First, you and I cannot get home alone. We don't know where we are, but wherever that may be, it's miles away from any place we would recognize. Second, even if we did know how to get home, there's the little matter of actually *surviving* in the sea while we're getting there. We're in a place where plants sing and fish carry weapons. There are teeth and tentacles and poison everywhere you turn. We don't have a chance. Third, assuming we can drag ourselves safely out of the sea in Kingston Harbor, the moment we return, Felonia's spies will be all over us. We can't go back now, Char. We have things we have to do, like it or not. I'm sorry she spat at you. But we don't have a choice. We have to go on."

"*You* may hafta go on," said Char. "I can do what I want. I may be your best friend, but you're not my master, Ven. Good luck. I hope you find whatever you're lookin' for out here." He turned and started eastward back along the path out of the kelp forest.

Ven's whole body flushed hot with panic.

"So that's it? So you're going against the captain's orders, then?"

Char stopped. He hung in the drift, his back to the others.

Ven waited. A wave of hostile thrum from his friend washed over him, wordless.

Finally Char turned around.

"That's low," he said. His thrum felt steely against Ven's skin. "That's pretty low, Ven."

"Captain Snodgrass ordered you to keep an eye on me at all times," Ven said. He tried to keep his desperation out of his thrum, but it crept in anyway. "If you want to go, I can't stop you. But I never thought you would be one to disobey an order from the captain."

"I've followed your sorry hindquarters over most o' the Island o' Serendair," Char said. "I've put my neck on the line for you just about every bloody day."

"I know. And I owe you my life. So when we get back to the upworld, if there's any place *you* want to go, I'll be by your side, all the way. But, like I said, you're not thinking clearly. The pressure of the sea is probably getting to you. You have to come with me. We have to stick together and see this through."

The angry light in Char's eyes burned brighter.

"There ya go, tellin' me what I hafta do again," he said. "You say you don't have a choice, but you've already made one. I guess you're choosin' Amariel and her world over me—your best friend—and *our* world. You can't live in two worlds at the same time, Ven, no matter how much you may want to. Go ahead, then—go farther into the Deep, go look for your sea dragons an' your Summer Festivals an' your long-dead legends about watery trees. Just remember what they keep tellin' you here—you're *out of place*. If that's what you want, so be it. I'm *done*."

He turned away and began swimming back out of the kelp forest.

Ven started after him "Char—"

"Kiss the keel, Ven."

Ven stopped in the drift. The expression was one sailors used. It was the suggestion to throw oneself into the sea under the bottom of the ship.

And was only said to someone considered an enemy.

"At least take your knapsack and your barb," Coreon called. "You don't stand a chance without them."

"He doesn't stand a chance with them, either," Amariel muttered. "He's *chum*. Shark bait."

Ven felt the corners of his eyes sting in the salt, and his throat tightened.

"Char—" he called as his friend swam away into a sunshadow that crossed the pathway.

His thoughts were choked off by the strikes of movement in the water where he was watching.

Three streaks of light shot out of the floating kelp thickets on each side of the pathway, clear and formless. They were accompanied by the thrum of high-pitched, tittering laughter.

The vibration scratched the inside of his brain, terrifying him.

As the sun shifted he saw three filmy figures, female and colorless, circle in the drift around his best friend.

He felt the thrum behind him from Coreon and Amariel almost as if they had spoken the word at the same time out loud.

*Vila!*

In a hideous swirl of motion, the fairy spirits seized Char and dragged him off toward the surface, spinning and dancing frightfully. They flipped him upside down and righted him again, laughing as he struggled helplessly in their grasp. As they did, Ven saw a tiny glowing ball of intense blue light fall from Char's pocket and slowly float down toward the bright algae on the ocean floor below.

"Oh no," he whispered, his lips moving silently. "Oh *no*."

It was Char's breathing stone of elemental air.

# ~ 19 ~

# Spicegar

THEY'RE GOING TO DROWN HIM!" VEN SHOUTED.

"Not necessarily," Coreon said uneasily. "They could be taking him back to the clouds."

"Doubtful," said the merrow. "The Vila are pretty strong, and Chum's pretty skinny, but he'd be too much of a load to haul all the way up to the sky."

"He can't breathe." Ven swam over to the stone of air and picked it up from the patch of algae where it had dropped. It seemed fragile, little more than a bubble in the sea. He looked up to see the swirling creatures passing Char from one to another, spinning him in a freakish dance. His friend's face was turning purple, and his eyes were open wide in fear. "Amariel, what do we do?"

"If we can get them to turn him loose, I can take the stone to him faster than you can," the merrow replied. "But my tail would go right through them. I can't slap him free from their grasp."

Ven looked about desperately.

*There have been many moments since my birthday, when I first left on the Inspection of the Angelia and never returned, that I have been really scared.*

*But I have never been as scared as this.*

*If you put all those other moments together, they still did not scare me as much as this.*

*When Char swam away from us, heading east, I was just beginning to wrap my head around the possibility that he might die if he didn't change his mind and come back.*

*But I didn't really believe it.*

*Then, without warning, he was fighting for air in the grip of the Vila.*

*Dying before my eyes.*

*And I could do nothing about it.*

Coreon swung his barbed crossbow from over his back to his hands. "Spicegar?" he said. "Are you anywhere around here?"

For a moment there was silence. Then Ven felt a thrum against his temples that was like the rustling of leaves.

A soft, low voice answered. As it spoke, it was as if its vibration did not disturb the drift around it at all.

*Yes. Nearby.*

"Who is Spicegar?" Ven asked.

"The sea dragon," Coreon replied. His thrum sounded as if he thought the answer was obvious. He redirected his thrum to the kelp forest. "Can you do something to distract the Vila?"

Ven thought he felt the forest sigh.

*Oh, I suppose so. You know how much I detest doing that.*

Ven's head all but exploded with excitement at the sea-dragon's thrum.

"I know, but we would appreciate it." Coreon gestured with his head to Amariel. "Come on—bring the stone."

The merrow reached out her webbed hand, and Ven put the air stone into it, not understanding what they were doing. She followed Coreon up to where the swirling dance of the Vila was spinning closer and closer to the surface of the sea.

Suddenly, the drift was alive with a loud hum, a clicking sound that instantly reminded Ven of something familiar he couldn't quite place. It was a thrum so deep and widespread that it made his breathing slow down.

Then he recognized it.

It was like the purring of a giant cat.

The sound filled the forest so completely that the kelp leaves moved in time with it. The gentle, drowsy thrum became almost hypnotic.

Above his head, the swirling circle of Vila must have felt it, too. The dance slowed, and then stopped. The filmy women hovered in the drift, Char hanging between them, struggling for breath.

"Awwwwww," the first one said. "Listen."

"Awwwwwwwwww!" the other two echoed.

"For goodness' sake," Ven murmured.

With a powerful kick, Coreon was beside them a moment later. He pointed his barbed crossbow at Char's heart.

"Let him go or I'll shoot him," he said to the Vila.

Ven inhaled sharply. "Er, Coreon—I'm not sure that's such a good idea—"

The sea-Lirin boy held the crossbow up to his eye and sighted it.

"You're right," he said to Ven, loudly enough for the Vila to hear him. "The blood will ruin the rainwater. And it will bring the great whites. I hear their bite is so ferocious they can even tear through spirit folk like nymphs, and water sprites—and even Vila."

The three fairy spirits looked at one another. Then, dreamily, they dropped Char's arms and flitted smoothly away, leaving him hanging, like wilted kelp, in the drift.

"Quick!" Ven urged Amariel. "Get him the air stone!"

The merrow gave two quick sweeps of her tail. She was at Char's side in an instant. She pressed her hand with the air stone against his chest.

"He's not breathing, Ven."

Coreon slid his barbed crossbow over his back again. He took hold of Char's limp arm and pulled it around his shoulder.

"You take the other side," he said to Amariel, "but don't drop the stone. I've never seen one like it. I was wondering how humans were breathing underwater."

"They could have had *gills*," Amariel said pointedly, "but you can't tell them *anything*." She and Coreon descended to the floor of the Underwater Forest, where Ven was waiting anxiously.

"C'mon, Char, *breathe*," he said, pressing his hand against Amariel's. "You've got the air back. Let it into your lungs."

Char did not respond.

"No," Ven whispered, pushing harder. "C'mon, Char, don't give up. Breathe. *Breathe.* Please."

Coreon watched thoughtfully for a moment, then looked around at the glowing forest.

"Spicegar?"

The purring stopped.

The forest seemed to sigh again.

Suddenly, a harsh barking sound filled the sleepy kelp bed, sharp and quick and so loud that Ven's ears popped.

Amariel and Coreon looked stunned.

A school of yellow and white fish that had been passing through, taking their time, leapt and scattered, leaving the drift empty where they had been a moment before.

And Char gasped.

Then coughed.

Then choked.

Then took a few ragged breaths.

Ven patted his friend's back in relief.

"You're back! Welcome back."

Woozily Char put his palm to his eye.

"What—how—"

"Don't try to talk," Ven said. "Just rest and take some easy breaths."

He looked above at the waving fronds of kelp, which seemed to have grown a few Knuckles taller in the short time they had been in the forest. The gentle music had returned, and the kelp trees were swaying peacefully in the drift once more. "Er, Coreon—where's your, er, friend?"

The Lirin-mer boy looked around. He shrugged.

"Spicegar?" he called again. "Would it be acceptable for these landlivers and this merrow to meet you?" His thrum sounded a little bored, but perhaps it was just the cracking of his voice.

"Uh—just the land-livers," said Amariel quickly. "No offense—I'm supposed to steer clear of sea dragons. My mother said so."

*No offense taken. I understand completely. My mother told me to steer clear of merrows.*

"Where are you?" Ven asked.

*A little deeper in, past the stump, then to the north beyond the purple ferns.*

"Follow me," Coreon said. "I know just where he means."

Amariel clutched at Ven's sleeve.

"Don't go," she whispered. "Please. It's been a rough morning. I don't want it to get worse by having one or more of you get eaten."

"Yeah, I hate it when that happens," mumbled Char.

Coreon smiled for the first time since they had met him. It made his face look totally different.

"Are you coming?" he asked. "Not a good idea to keep a sea dragon waiting."

"Right. Let's go," said Ven. He glanced at Amariel. "Please come with us," he urged. "If we learned anything from all this it's that we should stay together and help each other."

The merrow shook her head violently.

"I don't want to leave you here," Ven continued. "How can we get to the Summer Festival if you won't pass through the forest with us? We still have to cross the Sea Desert after this. Please come along."

The merrow crossed her arms and turned away.

Coreon rolled his eyes.

"Oh, come *on*, Amariel. Spicegar, can you promise not to eat the merrow? Just this once?"

Silence filled the peaceful glen. Then the thrum voice spoke, and it sounded confused.

*I don't understand.*

"She's afraid you're going to eat her."

*Ah. Well, tell her I'm a vegetarian.*

The sea-Lirin boy turned to the merrow, who was glowering stubbornly. "Hear that?"

"Yeah, I heard it," she said. "If you believe that, you go on ahead. Maybe he thinks a sea cucumber is a vegetable."

"Isn't it?" Ven asked. Coreon shook his head.

Another deep sigh rumbled through the beautiful forest.

*Madam, you are trying my patience. You're also disturbing my nap. Now, I give you my word that I shall not harm you. Either come visit, or pass on your way. But get on with it.*

"Yeah, as I said before, it's not a good idea to keep a sea dragon waiting," said Coreon. "Let's go."

Ven took hold of Char's arm. "Can you help me carry him for a while, Amariel? I think his little Vila dance took a lot out of him."

"Hmmph," said the merrow. She glanced around, then took hold of the other side grudgingly. "All right, Ven, you win. But if I get roasted and eaten I am *never* going to forgive you, remember that."

"I will," Ven promised with a grin. He hoisted Char's arm around his shoulder and the merrow did so with the other. Then they followed Coreon down the forest pathway to the west, where the rising sun was casting dusty streams of light through the surface where it pooled on the top leaves of the kelp forest canopy.

They traveled in silence for a while. The deeper in they swam, the quieter the forest became. Occasionally a small school of colorful fish, larger than those they had seen on the reef, glided by, or a starfish crawled past, and once an enormous sunfish larger than the four of them put together sailed above, nibbling at the kelp. Otherwise the forest seemed almost empty.

And all around them, they could hear its song, low, easy, slow.

Char's color was starting to improve, and while he looked very tired, the unhealthy black circles under his eyes were beginning to fade.

"You all right?" Ven asked after a while.

Char nodded. "What's that up ahead?" he whispered.

Ven tried to see farther down the pathway. On the ground, a large, low object seemed to be taking up the entire floor of the path.

"Can't tell yet," he replied, "but we'll be there soon enough. It doesn't seem alive, at any rate."

When they finally got close enough, Ven could see that it was what appeared to be an old, overgrown stump, the trunk torn from it long ago. But unlike the trees of the kelp forest, the largest of which had trunks as round as he was, this had been a tree of immense size, bigger around than three oxcarts side by side. It was covered with colonies of rainbow algae and lichen. Its dead roots stretched out in all directions over the forest path and into the glades of kelp and algae to the north and south.

But, strangest of all, it did not appear to be the stump of a giant kelp plant.

Instead, it looked like it had once been the base of an enormous tree of the variety that grew in the upworld, but seventy or so feet below the surface of the sea.

Unquestionably dead for a very long time.

Ven's stomach clenched, though his curiosity was roaring inside him. He floated up high enough to pass over the massive stump and kept swimming, supporting Char until Coreon stopped next to a large bed of floating kelp past a clump of purple ferns.

Within the forest drift over the bed of kelp, small white puffballs that looked like milkweed seeds were floating. When Ven looked closer, he could see that they were actually tiny fairylike creatures, clear like the Vila, but much smaller and delicate.

"Water sprites," Amariel said quietly. "They usually can be found near where magic is strong. They're harmless. Thank goodness. But they're a sign that the dragon is around here somewhere."

Coreon pointed toward the bed of floating kelp.

"Here," he said simply. "Spicegar, these are my companions, the merrow, the human, and the Nain."

*Pleased to meet you.* The familiar soft voice seemed to come from all around them. *What is a Nain?*

Ven blinked to clear his eyes, but he saw nothing but the bower of kelp.

"Er, me, sir," he said as politely as he could. "A son of the Earth." *Perhaps Spicegar is invisible, and this seaweed is a pillow for his, er, claw?* he wondered.

"Where's the dragon?" the merrow whispered.

Coreon's kelp-like eyebrows drew together.

"Right in front of you," he said. "Can't you see him?"

*I looked as hard as I could, but all I saw was a leafy mass of floating weeds.*

*Then a few of the tiny leaves rustled.*

*I stared at them.*

*And then, above what looked like a twig the size of my thumb, was a tiny eye.*

*Smaller than the smallest button on my shirt.*

"Can you come out a little?" Coreon asked. "I think they're having trouble seeing you."

Another sigh filled the drift.

*Oh, all* right. *I suppose so.*

The seaweed rustled again.

A tiny creature no longer than Ven's two hands side by side floated up out of the weeds. It was shaped a little like a sea horse, but bony. Hanging from it were appendages that looked almost exactly like leaves of seaweed, so much so that had the creature not come out of hiding, Ven knew he never would have seen it there. It had a few small spines that resembled stripes and a long, thin snout, but otherwise it looked more like a loose piece of floating seaweed than an animal.

"What the heck is *that*?" The merrow's thrum exploded, disturbing the peace of the forest glen and scattering the water sprites.

Coreon pulled himself up straighter, his kelp-hair bristling in anger.

"This is Spicegar," he said. "A little respect, if you please."

"I thought you said he was a sea dragon."

"I did," Coreon insisted. "And he is."

An ugly sound, half laugh, half choke, came out of Amariel's throat.

"That's no dragon," she said. "That's—that's a *fish*!"

The low, soft thrum voice cleared what sounded like a throat. The small creature ruffled its foliage.

*I am no fish, madam. If anything, I am related to the hippocampus. But I assure you, I am indeed a sea dragon.*

"That's impossible," the merrow said. "Sea dragons are enormous creatures of immense power. They're the size of sailing ships, giant serpents that collect hoards of treasure and defend those hoards with fiery breath that burns like acid. At least that's what I've been told."

*And I've been told that merrows are lovely creatures with sweet voices and nice manners. So I guess we have both been somewhat misled.*

"Amariel," Ven said quietly, "stop it."

"What kind of a dragon *purrs and barks*, Ven? This is ridiculous."

"You are embarrassing yourself, and us. And especially Coreon. Now stop, please."

"Fine," said the merrow. "Fine. At least I'm glad to know that Coreon thinks a floating *salad* is a dragon, and I was frightened out of my mind for nothing."

"Well, at least you didn't have to go too far to be that frightened," said Coreon angrily. "Your mind is obviously pretty small."

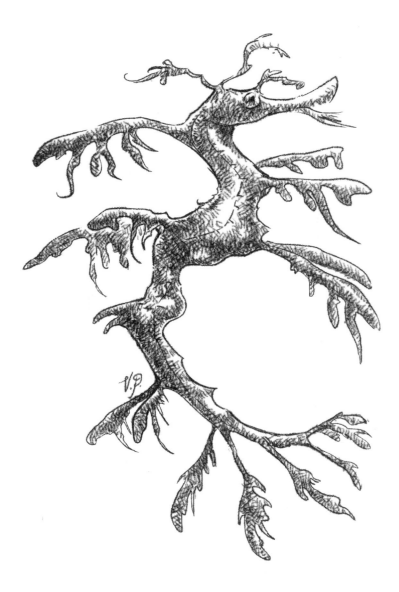

The merrow dropped Char's arm, gave a sweep of her beautiful tail, and swam off deeper into the forest. Ven watched as the small, leafy creature sank back into its seaweed bed again.

"I am terribly sorry," he said. "I apologize on behalf of myself and my friends. The situation with the Vila scared everyone and has left us all out of sorts. Thank you for what you did to save Char."

*Don't mention it.* The thrum of the sea dragon's voice was courtly, almost as if he was amused.

"We really do appreciate—"

*No, really, don't mention it.* The thrum had become slightly more annoyed, and the kelp around the fern bed shook with the vibrations of Spicegar's undersea voice. *I'd like you to move along now, if you please. You are drawing attention to my hiding place.*

"Of course. Sorry. Thanks again." Ven nodded to Coreon, who grabbed Char's other arm, and the two of them swam off, helping him along. "Thank you."

"That was embarrassing," said Coreon as they continued on the path. "If that's the way she's going to be, I'm not introducing her to any more of my friends."

"I'm sure she didn't mean what she said." Ven peered into the lush green of the forest ahead of them where the movement of the merrow's tail was making a wake in the water. He looked over his shoulder one last time at the giant stump.

"Coreon, by any chance have you heard of a tree named Frothta?"

The sea-Lirin boy nodded. "Just the old legends."

"Do you think it still exists?"

Coreon thought for a moment, then shook his head.

"Don't think so. I'm not sure it ever did. I haven't been too far off the reef, but I know lots of Lirin-mer who have crossed the desert and even have been down into the Twilight Realm. They tell great stories of the amazing things they've seen, but no one has ever mentioned seeing Frothta, or even any sign of it. Lirin-mer have been around a *very* long time. Most think that it may have always been a myth."

Ven sighed.

"I wish I knew what happened to it," he said.

They were too far away, too deep into the sleepy forest of waving towers of kelp, to hear the thrum of Spicegar's reply.

*Well, if you had asked, I could have told you.*

# - 20 -

# The Desert Beneath
# the Sea

After that it was just day after day of swimming through kelp.

The days blended into each other. Amariel and Char apologized, in their own ways, to one another, and went back to the
same uneasy companionship they had always shared. They both
apologized, sort of, to Coreon, who continued to be silent and
helpful, guiding us past places he thought were dangerous or
through others he thought were especially interesting. We showed
him the key that we had found in the bottle, and the paper with
the word <u>Athenry,</u> but it didn't mean any more to him than it
did to us.

It was sort of sad that he had so little of the Cormorant's
respect, I decided after a while. I knew how that felt. Each of my
siblings has a job in my father's factory, a specialty all his or her
own. My father had made me train in all of those specialties, and
just when I was getting competent in one, he would appear one
morning at the door, signaling for me to get my tools and follow
him. He was actually training me in each different department to
be his Inspector all the while, but I didn't know that.

I only know it made me feel useless.

Until the albatross who has been watching over me since the

morning of my birthday brought me a letter from my father, explaining his plan for me, that is.

The Inspector is one of the most important jobs in the family business. That's the one I may have someday, when I finally return to Vaarn.

Because to the Nain, there is nothing more important than being good at your job, and doing it well.

Maybe this mission will redeem Coreon in the eyes of the Lirin-mer. Maybe he will be seen as a great leader. Maybe he will be the Cormorant someday, who knows.

He certainly would make a better one than the current fellow.

Finally, after more days than we could count, we came to the end of the forest. The lush growth of kelp began to thin, then grow sparser, until it was just occasional clumps of seaweed and schools of fish passing through.

And a lot of sand and empty water once again.

It's hard to put in words how we knew that we had reached the desert's edge.

In spite of that, each of us did know it.

The drift changed first. We had been swimming so long that it took a while to notice. Tired as we were, we missed the early signs, like the seaweed growing paler, the schools of fish fewer. The sun beat down on the water's surface, creating great patches of moving sunshadow, which made it hard to see into the distance.

And yet, when we were at the desert's edge, we all knew we were there.

All four of us came to a halt at the same time on a sandy ridge as smooth and clean as a beach in the upworld, without a shell in sight.

The bottom of the ocean before us was almost completely free of plant life. There were no wrecks visible, no coral reefs like the one where we met Coreon, just silence and empty blue water as far as we could see.

And, for some reason, that water felt <u>heavier</u>.

*L*OOK AT ALL THE NOTHING."

Amariel's thrum echoed in Ven's ears. He took a deeper breath of the elemental air from the bubble around his head. He remembered the last time he had heard her use those words.

She was describing a place her father had taken her, a sea beneath the sea.

And she had described it as the most frightening place she had ever been in her life.

"What do you know about this place?" Ven asked Amariel and Coreon.

"Just what the Cormorant told you." Coreon's thrum was steady, but high. Ven wasn't sure if that was a sign of nerves, or if his undersea voice was just unsure what its pitch wanted to be. "If you want to find out if the Tree of Water still exists or is just a legend, the only one who may know is the Sea King. You have to cross the desert if you want to get to the Summer Festival."

"It's so quiet here," Char said. "I don't feel any thrum at all, just the drift. Maybe it's completely empty, like the vast deserts of the upworld."

"They say no desert is completely empty," Ven said. "They just look that way. I once heard tales of a great desert from a storyteller who came to the town square outside my father's factory in Vaarn. I was working in the front office that day, so I got to hear some of his tales through the window. He said that there are as many creatures living in that wasteland as there are stars in the desert sky. By day the desert animals hide in caves from the sun, but at night they come out looking for food."

"Well, it's the same in the sea," said Amariel. "Only it doesn't have to be night here. The Sea Desert is so vast that you never know when you might come upon one of the great predators—the big sharks, octopi of enormous size, even—"

"Megalodon?" Char offered helpfully.

The merrow's eyes widened. She balled up her webbed fingers into a fist and punched Char in the forehead.

"Don't even *think* his name, especially this far out in the Deep." Her green eyes glittered as she glanced all around the emptiness. "You *still* don't get it, do you, Chum? The sunshadows shift very easily here. Thoughts can carry a long distance."

"Yeah, but there's nothing around here," Coreon said. "While it's true you can run into one of the big predators, you can also go for days without seeing anything. My dad says that as long as you stay quiet and low and don't flap around a lot, they don't even see you. Merfolk and sea Lirin cross the Sea Desert all the time without a problem. Members of my clan have gone to the Summer Festival every year, and we haven't lost anybody in a really long time."

Char swallowed, rubbing his forehead.

"That's encouraging," Ven said. His thrum didn't sound much like he meant it.

"Well, most of the time a big predator is like a storm at sea," Amariel said. "You can usually hear and feel it coming. The bigger something is, the louder the thrum it makes. Does anybody feel something like that?"

Ven closed his eyes, trying to concentrate. The constant drift had become part of his brain, or so it seemed. The invisible bubble of air around him hissed or whistled from time to time when something swam too close to his ears, but most of the time the ocean had a background of low, musical swishing and very little sound, except for the slight thrum he had heard as they submerged, and that had been in the back of his mind ever since.

Here, at the vast edge of nothing, all of that background noise was gone.

"Not me," he said after a few moments. He looked at Char and Coreon. Both of them shook their heads as well.

"Well, then let's go," Amariel said. "I want to get to the Festival as soon as we can—I know the games have already begun, and I would hate to miss the hippocampus races. If I go all the way across the desert and they've already awarded the Grand Trophy, I'm going to spit." She eyed Char darkly.

"Well, we certainly wouldn' want *that*," Char muttered.

"No, indeed," Ven agreed, smiling. Heavy as the water felt, his mood seemed to be lifting. The sun in the upworld was high and bright, and the desert was empty and quiet. True, the white sand and absence of sea life meant no cover, no place to hide, but it seemed that nothing was around to hide from anyway. "Let's be on our way."

"Remember that most sharks and other big predators only eat when they're hungry," Coreon said as they started out over the sandy ridge above the clean ocean floor. "Even if one comes into view, it doesn't mean it's hunting. The best thing to do is not to panic. Panic makes your heart beat louder, and creatures tend to jerk in fear. Those sort of vibrations can catch the interest of a perfectly harmless predator that was otherwise minding his own business."

"Easy to say," Char said. "It's kinda hard to control your heartbeat."

"Maybe it's best if we stop talking and just think positive thoughts," Ven suggested.

"I'm all for stopping talking," said the merrow. "Especially Chum. I'm *always* for him being quiet."

"You know, you're not the only one that can spit," said Char.

"I'd like to see you try it underwater."

"Knock it off, you two," Ven thought, trying to keep the annoyance out of his thrum. "You're putting us in unnecessary danger. Think about the Summer Festival, and we'll be there before you know it."

Amariel nodded curtly, and, with a great sweep of her multicolored tail, she started off into the patchy light of the Sea Desert.

They swam in the nearly silent sea all afternoon, only seeing signs of life every now and then. The sun beat down on the watery surface above, casting loose beams of light into the depths that they tried to avoid whenever they could.

From time to time a large fish would appear like a shadow against the sun overhead, only to swim off into the murky dark, uninterested in them. Coreon pointed soundlessly as a large one with a long, saw-like nose glided by.

Char's thrum appeared in Ven's head.

"Reminds me—do you still have your jack-rule?"

Ven patted his vest pocket and nodded.

Char nodded in return, and the question in Ven's head disappeared.

"We're getting better at speaking in thrum," he thought. His legs were growing tired, and his throat was dry in spite of all the water around him. "When we finally stop for the night, Char and I need to go up to the surface and eat some of our provisions, and have a bit to drink."

"Amen," Char echoed.

"You both certainly are a lot of work," said Amariel. Coreon snickered but said nothing.

As the day wore on, the patches of sunshadow grew fainter and fewer. The heavy water grew even more quiet and green as the sun began to set over the rim of the world.

"We should find a place to sleep." Amariel's thoughts rattled the silence in their heads. "Night will fall soon, and the predators can smell a lot better in the dark than we can see. Keep your eyes out for a shipwreck or some rocks at the bottom. We are too deep now, too far from shore, to find the kinds of skelligs we rested on before. Who knows—we might even find a piece of the *Athenry*. It would be funny to find the broken bones of a ship we have a *key* for."

The three boys nodded in wordless agreement.

On they swam. The hazy shafts of light disappeared when the sun turned orange at the horizon, causing the water to go gray as the dusk deepened. Ven could tell that both Amariel and Coreon were growing nervous by the quickening of their heartbeats, but neither said anything until Amariel's thoughts burst into their brains.

"We need to swim faster. If the sun sets before we find shelter, we'll have to take our chances out in the middle of the desert floor."

All of their tiredness was suddenly gone.

"Set the pace," Ven thought back at her. "We'll keep up as best as we can, but do what you have to do. Don't wait for us."

The boys doubled their strokes, dragging their arms and legs through the drift as fast as they could.

Finally, when the light was all but gone from the sky, Amariel stopped for a moment, hovering in the water.

"Wait here."

She sped away into the gray sea before them, returning a few moments later.

"Shelter up ahead." Her thrum seemed a little nervous. "It's not pleasant, but it will do. Follow me to the surface so you can eat and drink, and then we'll settle in. I can feel some big things in the distance, and I want to get out of their way as quickly as we can. Follow me."

The merrow spun away toward the air of the upworld.

Char and Ven exchanged a glance, then obeyed. Coreon followed close behind.

*We took our time going up to the surface, as Madame Sharra, the Cormorant, and even Amariel had cautioned us. It took everything we had to keep from swimming up too fast, because as frightening as it is to have a predator above you, it is vastly more scary to not know whether you have one under you or not.*

*When we finally broke the surface, the air of the upworld stung our lungs. It felt thin after the richness of the air we had been breathing from the elemental stones, and both Char and I began to cough. As a result we swallowed a good deal of bitter water before our lungs adjusted and we could begin to breathe normally again.*

Four heads bobbed above the water's surface.

Ven looked around. There was nothing but ocean waves for as far as he could see. The sun was little more than a toenail of light at the edge of the horizon. Stars hung in the colorful clouds, rose-pink and aquamarine in the evening sky.

Amariel held out a packet of kelp and Coreon handed over a flask of fresh water.

"Land-livers. Sheesh. Hurry up and eat." The merrow's voice was cross. "See, if you had let Asa cut your gills, we could have done all this below in shelter."

"Yeah, but at least this way we don't have any scabs, any last drops o' blood," Char muttered between bites of seaweed. "Therefore, no blood to attract any passing sharks." He chewed, made a hideous face, then swallowed as if he were choking.

"No, you're right," the merrow agreed. "No scabs. Just four rather obvious floating objects at the surface. *Hurry up.*"

Ven was gulping water from the flask as quickly as he could. He passed it to Char, who took it and drank greedily. Then he gave the flask back to Coreon.

"Come *on*," the merrow urged. "The longer we're up here, the farther we'll drift away from the bones."

"Bones? You found a shipwreck?"

Amariel shook her head. "Not exactly. Ven, take my hand— Chum, grab hold of Coreon. You won't be able to see well enough to swim on your own now." She seized Ven by the shoulder and dove, dragging him with her.

The water closed over his head before he could catch his breath.

*Deep in my memory I recalled something like this that had happened not all that long ago. On my fiftieth birthday when the ship I had been inspecting, the <u>Angelia</u>, blew up, I was thrown into the sea without warning. I must have hit my head—I remember almost nothing.*

*Except sinking into green waves, down, deeper into the depths. Then the grasp of a webbed hand under my shoulder.*

*And being dragged through the water, though I couldn't see anything.*

*The coolness of the air as I broke the surface.*

*Being thrown on a piece of drifting wreckage. Shivering in the cold night wind.*

*The cry of an albatross, the giant white bird that had circled above me as the ship went down.*

*And, before I passed out, green eyes staring at me from the water's edge.*

*The same green eyes that were now scanning the bottom of the ocean desert in the last rays of light, looking for the shelter they had found a few moments before.*

Ven could feel Amariel's thrum being directed at Coreon.

"There. At the bottom, right ahead of you."

In response, the sea-Lirin boy stopped and hovered in the water, holding Char's foot. Ven could feel the dismay in his response.

"Oh. When you said *bones*, I thought you meant a shipwreck. You—you actually meant, er—*bones*."

# ~ 21 ~

# A Cage of Bones

Sometimes I forget that humans can't see in the dark.

I forget this because normally I can.

Nain have the ability, like foxes and owls and other animals of the night, to see heat in darkness. When that heat is within a living thing, what Nain are seeing is the energy caused by a beating heart, by the blood spinning through a warm body.

We can also see another kind of heat in the darkness, however.

Because Nain are children of the Earth, we can see parts of the world that are alive. Aboveground in the dark, this can be the sap flowing in trees or the sparks left behind in the ashes of a campfire. It's like we carry our own daylight with us. I can't imagine what it would be like to be human, and to be all but blind at night.

Within the Earth itself, deep in the mountains or tunneled below the ground, the world is even more visible to Nain. We can see the life within pieces of stone and rock, objects humans view as lifeless. Some stone is cold, almost dead, like basalt or marble. Some is warmer, like coal, with more energy still inside it. I've even seen rivers of boiling metal, liquid gold that flows with life. Like all Nain, inside the Earth I can see almost as well as I can in broad daylight. The Earth sings to me, the way the coral sings to Amariel.

*But here, in the watery world, I can only see when the sun is in the sky above the water. Even when the day is bright in the upworld, with clouds reflecting the light back at the sea, my vision below the waves isn't very good. I imagine it's a little like being a bat, or a human in the dark. When the light is gone, I am almost blind.*

*Especially in this place, this desert, where even those who were born to live here can't see very well.*

*So in the sea I have almost no chance of seeing something that is actually <u>dead</u>, like Black Ivory.*

*Or lifeless bones.*

*Even when they are giant bones.*

$V$EN, TAKE OUT YOUR AIR STONE. I NEED SOME LIGHT."

Amariel's thrum was quiet, as if she was trying to whisper. She stopped in the drift and hovered there, still clinging to Ven's shoulder.

Beside her, Coreon and Char came to a halt as well.

Carefully Ven reached into the pocket of his vest. His fingers trembled as he touched his great-grandfather's jack-rule. It was his greatest treasure, the last gift his father had given him on his fiftieth birthday not so very long ago. He dug around the measuring tool until he touched what felt like a smooth, round stone. It hummed in the skin of his fingers.

*Please, please don't lose it*, he thought to himself. *We're fathoms deep now, and I'll never be able to find it in the dark before my air runs out.*

He gripped the smooth object and brought it forth from his pocket.

Then almost dropped it as a burning blue light stung his eyes.

He could feel the startled thrum of his friends as they winced in pain as well.

"Geez, cover it," Amariel commanded. She pinched his shoulder sharply.

Ven cupped his other hand over the stone.

The blinding light dimmed to a blue glow. It hovered hauntingly in the water around them, casting ghostly shadows at the edge of their vision.

Amariel's strong hands seized Ven's waist. She swam around behind him and pushed him forward, like a giant Nain-shaped lantern, scanning the ocean floor.

A few moments later, she stopped.

"Here," she said.

Ven held the air stone in his clutched fist up a little higher.

Then he gasped.

At first it appeared as if they were in a giant broken cage the size of an immense building. Large curved bars in lines on both sides of them reached up toward the surface, black and pointed like enormous fence posts. It looked as if they had been neatly planted in the sandy white floor of the sea.

Except they were attached to a long knobby road that Ven could tell almost immediately was a spine.

A spine they were almost standing on.

A spine that was longer than the widest wing of the Crossroads Inn.

He could feel Char trembling beside him, and turned to see his best friend staring at an upside-down skull, bigger than a wagon, partly buried in the quietly shifting sands.

"What—what is this?" he asked Amariel.

The merrow was scanning the water above them.

"Whale skeleton," she said. "Probably a blue whale—I've never seen a humpback this big. Put the light away—*now*."

Ven obeyed quickly.

Once the stone was buttoned safely back in his pocket, the ocean turned a murky black. Ven felt Amariel's hand leave his shoulder and grip his own once again. She led him down to the ocean floor, where the knobby spine looked like a great line of barrels set up top to bottom on their sides, buried in the sand.

"Settle in," her thoughts murmured in his ears. "I feel serious thrum around here now. We need to take cover quickly and smoothly so as to not attract attention." Ven could tell that Coreon and Char had heard her as well, because as soon as she had spoken they began digging into the curves of the whale bones, trying to find shelter.

*It's just like a big shipwreck*, he thought as he blindly patted the sand near the spine. *Whatever living creature it belonged to is long gone. Try not to panic.*

"Stop thinking, Ven," Coreon whispered. "Sleep if you can—your thrum is way too loud."

"And stop being such a baby." Amariel's undersea voice sounded annoyed. "I always thought you were pretty brave. If I had known you got afraid so easily, I would never have taken you into the Deep. There's nothing scary about old bones, Ven. What you need to fear is swimming nearer to us now. You really have your priorities mixed up. Calm down. You too, Chum. You're making my scales itch."

"Try breathing slowly and quietly," Coreon advised. "Works for me."

Ven shifted his shoulders, trying to settle into the bony hollow. The sand on the bottom of the ocean floor skittered around him, but he had almost gotten used to that.

The heavy drift settled on him, almost like a blanket falling upon his head and shoulders. The air from the elemental stone filled his nose and lungs, still absent of smell.

Ven looked to his right. The merrow had found a comfortable spot and was gently covering herself with sand, using her tail as a whisk broom. To his left, Coreon and Char had dug in and were lying still. The whites of Char's eyes, and the greens of Coreon's, were the only parts of his friends he could see in the dark.

*Morning can't come soon enough*, he thought.

In his head, he could hear the others agree.

Now that he was still and quiet, the swishing sound of the open sea returned. The music was still there, but it was no longer far off and merry. The strange thrum he had been hearing in the distance since entering the water was very much louder now, but other sounds seemed closer. In addition to the buzzing vibrations, he felt a sort of pressure, almost as if he could sense the weight of the creatures in the water as well as their thrum.

By the intensity of the pressure, the creatures seemed large.

*Like a coming storm, Amariel said*, he thought. *This must be what she meant.*

"Shhhh," the merrow whispered. "Stop thinking so much."

Ven lay back and opened his eyes as wide as he could. The surface was much too far away to be seen, but a vague, hazy light hung in the water in one place. He guessed that the moon had risen since they had been to the top of the waves to eat and drink.

A long shadow swam across that hazy light, blotting it out for a moment, then swam on. Ven could feel its thrum pass with it, like the ticking of a clock.

He let his breath out slowly.

*Shark. Big shark.*

*Maybe one of Amariel's friends*, he thought. He could hear Coreon's words in his memory.

*Even if one comes into view, it doesn't mean it's hunting. The best thing to do is not to panic. Panic makes your heart beat louder, and creatures tend to jerk in fear. Those sort of vibrations can catch the interest of a perfectly harmless predator that was otherwise minding his own business.*

A second shadow, then another, crossed into and out of the hazy light.

*Like kites*, Ven thought.

*When I was little, really little, one spring my father took me on my first and pretty much only trip outside the seaside city of Vaarn where I was born. Strange as it is for Nain to live in the* upworld in cities, the place my father brought me was even stranger. We rode in a giant wagon drawn by eight horses, out into the forest lands, to buy timber to build our ships.

The countryside was alien to me, almost as if my father had taken me to the moon. There were more trees in a quarter-mile's travel than in all of Vaarn, and my eyes stung from looking at all the fresh greenery. In addition, my nose was on fire with the fresh scents of pine and hickory, and sweet air that was not clogged with factory smoke or the salty smell of the sea.

I was being trained on that trip to work in the factory, even though I was too young to know it then. My father wanted me to watch his meetings with the lumberjacks and foresters, to see how a good businessman conducted himself, to even learn a few tricks of the trade.

But my curiosity was drawn instead to the kites.

At the forest's edge, where the children of the lumberjacks lived, was a meadow. It was a little muddy, because the snow had just melted. The grass was pale green, and the wind was high and strong.

So the children of the foresters were flying kites.

I had never seen a kite before. In Vaarn the buildings are very close together, the streets are cobbled, and there isn't much room to play with something like that. So I peeked out of the wagon and watched, fascinated, as the forest children worked in pairs to put these toys made of wooden frames and colorful paper, tied with string, into the air. After a few tries, the entire sky was filled with dancing kites, spinning in different directions at the whim of the wind.

It was the first time I remember seeing magic hiding in plain sight.

One of the forest children saw me watching, and invited me to come and play. When my father nodded, I climbed out of the wagon and went over to the middle of the field. The children were all human, and I could tell, even as young as I was, that they *found me interesting, but there was none of the threat that someone who is different can sometimes feel. One tall red-haired boy let me hold his kite string, but he had to keep a hand on it, because even with his strength, the wind pulled me off the ground a little bit. I decided then it was a better idea to follow the example of some of the other kids, and lie down on my back to watch the kite dance.*

*I don't know how long I lay there, but too soon my father came to collect me, dragging me off of the green spring grass by my collar.*

*"Your coat and the back of your trousers are filthy, Ven," he said. "What do you think your mother will say?"*

*I knew the answer, and began to tremble.*

*Then I looked in his eyes, and noted that he was as scared as I was.*

*Then we both laughed.*

*Everyone I know is afraid of my mother.*

*So now I am lying on the sandy floor of the Sea Desert, on the spine of a long-dead blue whale, in the middle of a broken cage of bones, staring up at large shadows swimming above me. I am aware of the danger each of them poses.*

*But for some reason, all I can think of when I see them is kites.*

His cheek buzzed.

Ven held his head still, but looked to his left side.

A shark was swimming past within the cage of bones a few feet away. Its thrum was steady, but the pressure from its wake made Ven instantly aware of its strength and power. He tried not to tremble.

*Kites*, he thought. *Kites.*

The beast was beside him now. He could feel the menace in the dark, the slap of its tail through the drift, the long muscle of its body.

*Kites. Kites. Kites.*

He lay there, still as he could, until the shark swam past and out of the cage of bones.

He let out the breath he did not even realize he had been holding. A webbed hand reached into his.

"Sleep, Ven," Amariel whispered. "Please—for all our sakes. It's all your thinking that made him come down here to see what was going on."

Ven swallowed, then closed his eyes. Thrum was spinning all around him, but it was high above, and slow. He thought about home, about his family, and how they could never imagine what he was doing at this very moment. *I shall have to tell you all the tale one day*, he thought.

With that promise came sleep.

Dreams came quickly. In them he was back in beautiful forests of kelp, staring at the giant stump that had filled the pathway near Spicegar's lair.

*You want to know where Frothta lived?* The tiny sea dragon's thrum echoed in his head. *Here is the spot. This is all that's left of her.*

It seemed like only a few seconds later that the water turned gray-green again.

Ven opened his eyes.

He could see the bones of the whale skeleton quite plainly now, reaching hopelessly up toward the distant surface above them like curved, branchless trees. Within the broken cage of bones, small schools of fish passed by as close as the shark had been the night before.

No predators swam above them.

*It's morning*, he thought. *We've made it through the night.*

Beside him, the merrow stirred. Her webbed hand was still in his. He could hear Char's thoughts as he wakened as well.

"Mornin', Ven."

Ven smiled as a school of fish swam past his face. "Good morning, everyone. It seems we've made it."

Char yawned broadly, stretching his arms up into the drift. "Yep. Seems so."

Coreon sat up quickly.

Between him and Char, the sand shot up in a storm, blasting them away from the spine.

As the floor of the sea began splitting open.

# ~ 22 ~

# The Octopus's Garden

BEFORE ANY OF THEM COULD MOVE, A SWIRL OF EIGHT SAND-colored tentacles, each the length of a human man's leg, spun up from the ocean floor between the bones of the spine.

One reached out and seized a fish from the school going by.

Then the rest of the creature blasted up from the sand between Char and Coreon. Its bag-like head sucked in and out as the two boys clambered away. The fish in its grasp wriggled, then went limp with a soft *pop* as the octopus swam off into the murky green outside the cage of whale bones, leaving a thin trail of black ink.

"That's odd," Amariel noted as the three boys hovered above her in the drift, trembling. "Usually they prefer crabs."

"Maybe there aren't too many crabs out this far," said Coreon as he settled back down on the ocean floor. "This desert is pretty empty."

Char up looked at the surface above, then gestured to Ven, who was treading water, trying to return to calm.

"You all right?"

Ven nodded.

"Well, don't look now, but there's something big coming." Char pointed to the surface above Ven's head.

"Oh, crab," Coreon said. "I hope that's not a another shark."

Ven sank back down to the spine and looked where Char was pointing.

A vast shadow, longer than the blue whale's skeleton, was approaching. It slashed through the surface, splitting the waves into a great white swirl.

Ven broke into a wide smile.

"It's a ship!" he thought to the others. "Look—you can see the bowsprit, and the keel!"

Char swam down beside the others onto the sandy floor.

"Maybe we should try to catch a ride," he suggested. "They could prolly take us quickly 'cross the desert to where the Summer Festival is so we can skip the whale bones tonight."

Amariel looked at him disdainfully. "I sincerely hope you are joking," she said.

"No, I'm not," Char insisted. "C'mon, Ven, don't you think it's a good idea? We can swim up quickly, shout and wave. If there's a lookout in the crow's nest they may see us, pull us aboard, and—"

"You think that ship's crew is going to drop you off somewhere in the middle of the sea?" Amariel demanded. "First, for all you know, it's a pirate ship. They'd sell you into slavery or worse. Second, you can't get to the surface quickly enough for them to see you. Third, even if you could, and they're not pirates, if they pulled you aboard and you told them what you've been doing, they'd think you a loon and toss you in a nuthouse once you got back to land. Ships are full of *humans.* Don't you know by now that you can't trust them?"

"*I'm* a human," Char retorted. "And I'm rather tired of you talkin' us down."

"For goodness' sake, both of you, settle," Ven said. "We're here to explore the Deep—good and bad. We don't need a ride, Char. Just be quiet while the ship passes."

Char crossed his arms over his chest and leaned up against the spine. Coreon sighed and did the same. Amariel glared at Char, then settled back next to Ven. The green-gold sea turned dark again as the moving ship blotted out the sun.

"I remember being on the deck of the *Serelinda* and wondering what was below the waves," Ven said as he watched the barnacled hull go by above him, towing a large, crusty anchor. "In fact, I wondered the same thing back in Vaarn, standing on the dock. I even wondered about it when I was doing the Inspection of the ship that I, er, sank, the *Angelia*. I've had dreams all my life of what lay below the surface of the sea. But I could never have imagined how grand it really is."

"Grand. Yes, that's the word I would use," said Char, wiping fish guts from the octopus's meal off his shoulder. "Grand. That's it. Yes."

As the ship passed over the far side of the cage of whale bones, the light returned from above.

Near the skeleton's enormous head, something glittered brightly on the ocean floor.

The four children blinked.

As the ship sailed away, and sunshadow filled the cage, many more sparks twinkled around the skull.

"Did ya see that?" Char whispered.

"Yes," said Amariel. "Let's go see what it is."

They rose from the sandy bones and swam over to the upsidedown skull. As they approached, a trail of shiny objects sparkled beneath them.

"Look at this," Coreon marveled, running his hand along the glistening path. "A sea chest, gems, polished pebbles, a comb, abalone shells, pieces of mother-of-pearl—what is all this stuff?"

"That's a pretty big sea chest," Char said, pointing at a brassbound box near the skull. "I bet it weighs a ton."

Amariel stopped above a circle of gleaming coins, buckets and chamber pots, polished to a shine.

"I know what this place is!" she exclaimed. "This is an octopus's garden!"

"An octopus's garden?" Ven glanced into the murk where the sea creature had sped off.

"Yes. Octopi love shiny things. They spend most of their lives sweeping the ocean floor for objects that strike their fancy. Then they bring those objects back to their lairs and tend to them, like fussy little old human ladies."

Char was staring at the sea chest.

"I don't think that octopus could have carried this chest in from anywhere," he said doubtfully. "It's twice the creature's size."

"Of course it could," Amariel continued. "Octopi are very strong, you know, and very smart."

"You're right about that," Ven agreed. "I used to hear fishermen talking about them in Vaarn, and the sailors of the *Serelinda* as well. It's very hard to bring home an octopus from the sea. They can open locks on their cages and squeeze through the tiniest of holes much smaller than would seem possible. The mariners have an expression for it—'harder to pin down than an octopus' means someone is slippery or great at escape or avoiding things."

Char was shaking his head. "I still can't imagine that small guy gathering all this stuff."

"Shhh," said Coreon, looking toward where the tail of the whale would have been. "Listen—I think we have another visitor."

Ven closed his eyes and concentrated. From where Coreon was pointing he could feel the thrum of something approaching.

This time, however, the regular ticking he had heard the night before was gone. The thrum was higher, harsher, scratching against his eardrums. It sounded young and impatient. There were no words, but he could hear the intent nonetheless.

*Hungry. Hungry. Hunting, hunting. Hungry.*

Nervously the four children slid back against the spine, trying to blend in.

Ven's eyes went to Amariel. The merrow had dug her tail into the top layer of sand. He thought a single word in her direction.

"Friend?"

The merrow shook her head.

Ven exhaled.

A moment later, a shadow emerged from the darkness beyond the cage of bones. It was thin and agile, about five feet in length.

"Oh boy," came the thought from Coreon. "It's a great white— a small one, but bigger than any of us."

Unlike most of the sharks the night before, this new predator was swimming deep. It glided into the cage of bones at the tail end. As soon as it did, the thrum became louder, faster.

Excited.

*Hunt. Hunt! Hungry. Hungry.*

Ven swallowed hard. The high-pitched thrum was jumbling his thoughts. After a few seconds, it changed.

*Prey!*

He knew each of the others had heard it as well. All four of their bodies stiffened in their hiding places. They lay as still as they could. The blue-white beast swam past, the hollow eye on the side of its head twitching as it did.

Then it circled around the skeleton head.

And came back for another pass.

This time closer.

Amariel, who was on the end closest to the shark, began to shake. The sand covering her tail swirled in the water in little clouds. Ven reached out, shaking too, and took her hand.

With a powerful thrust of its tail, the shark lunged forward.

Ven heard the merrow gasp. Unable to hold still, he turned toward her and found himself staring into the black eyes and slightly open mouth, teeth gleaming in the sunshadow that was raining into the cage of bones.

Speeding toward them both.

Amariel's hand ripped out of his.

Before he could stop her, the merrow bolted from his side and swam past the startled boys, away from the beast.

"This way," her thrum called out in terror. "Follow me."

The shark obeyed.

"Amariel, no!" Ven screamed. His mouth opened, and the sea

rushed in, choking him. The great white's tail grazed him as it bore down on the merrow, its sandpaper skin slapping him across the face, leaving it raw and bleeding.

The three boys could only watch, helpless, as the merrow tried to outswim the shark.

It was clear to each of them that she would not be able to for long.

Coreon raised his crossbow and took aim at the great white. His hands were shaking violently. Char grabbed his elbow, trying to steady him.

"Don't hit her, whatever you do."

Coreon lowered his weapon.

"I can't see her," he said sadly.

Just as the chase reached the center point of the spine, the ocean floor began to rumble again.

Only much more violently this time.

Before their eyes, what had looked a moment before like the middle of the spine rose up out of the sand and untwisted itself. As it did, its color changed from the bone white of the whale's skeleton to a more orange hue. Great tentacles flexed and snapped out into the water, longer than two boys together.

A giant bulbous head rose from the ocean floor, opening to show a huge, parrot-like beak.

The arms of the enormous octopus lashed out like whips as the merrow swam past. It seized the great white and wrapped around it quickly, stopping it in its path, spinning it upside down.

"Blimey!" Char's thrum shouted. "I *knew* that little one couldn'a carried all that stuff!"

"Amariel!" Ven screamed again.

"Move! Move!" Coreon shouted, pushing them both out of the way of the lashing tentacles.

The boys swam as fast as they could away from the battle that was now raging on the ocean floor. The shark, caught unaware, was rolling and pitching in the grip of the giant octopus, which had wrapped at least four of its arms around the great fish's body.

The remainder of its tentacles were slashing through the water inside the cage of bones, long enough to reach any of them.

"We've got to get out of the cage," Coreon said. "Come on—swim for it."

"I'm not leaving her," Ven said, his eyes scanning the green water for any sign of the merrow. "You go."

A moment later, two screams ripped through their brains.

The first was low and raw, the sound of a sea creature battling for its life.

The second was high and piercing.

They knew the thrum instantly.

"It's got me!" Amariel's thoughts pierced the water, which was now cloudy with storms of sand from the ocean floor. "Ven, *it's got me!*"

Ven's hand went to his pocket. He patted the front of his shirt, fumbling for the button, then realized that the jack-rule's small knife would do nothing against either of the creatures of the Deep.

"Hang on!" he thought back. "We're coming."

He tried not to look as the octopus pulled the blue-gray body into its gaping maw, then swallowed it whole.

The parrot-like beak snapped shut.

"It's been here all along." Char's thoughts were so terrified that feeling them made Ven's head and skin hurt. "We were *leaning up against it*, for cripe's sake!"

Its breakfast consumed, the immense beast spread its arms through the water of the cage. The muscles of its tentacles rippled as it leisurely waved them around in the drift.

There was no sign of the merrow.

"Where is she?" Ven thought desperately.

"I don't see her." Char shielded his eyes from the sand that now floated in the drift.

Coreon was counting the arms.

"Six—I think I see seven."

"Come on," Ven said, swimming at the edge of the cage. "We've got to find her."

"Hold still a minute." Amariel's thrum washed over their ears. It felt edgy, but not as terrified as it had been a few moments before.

"*Where are you?*" Ven demanded.

The gigantic orange octopus raised its eighth arm slowly over its head.

The merrow was wrapped it its coils. The fluke of her beautiful tail stuck out beneath the suckers.

"Don't panic," she said as the boys stared at her. "She likes me."

"She?"

"Yes, she. Octopi are very intelligent—obviously. And they apparently like merrows. She saved me from the shark—she clearly wasn't all that hungry, or none of you would be here."

"Did—you know she was here all along?" Ven asked. He watched as the octopus turned Amariel upside down and swirled her back and forth in the drift.

"Of course not. Octopi are masters of disguise. Their camouflage is some of the best in the ocean. Do you think I would be *leaning on her* if I knew she was here?"

"Is she going to turn you loose, do you suppose?" Coreon's undersea voice sounded both relieved and cross. "I'd like to get out of this place and on toward the Festival."

The merrow shrugged, then looked questioningly at the giant octopus. The creature seemed to sigh, its massive tentacles drooping slightly. Then, amid a great swirl of sand, it dragged the rest of its enormous body out of the whale spine and scuttled across the ocean floor toward the skull.

"Where is it taking her now?" Char whispered to Ven.

"It looks like the octopus wants to show her its garden," Ven said.

"You obviously—*oof!*—do not realize—*oof!*—what an—honor that is—*oof!*" the merrow puffed from within the beast's coiled arm as it bounced her along. "Human treasure is very valuable under the—*oof!*—sea. Why do you think my whole school turned out when we heard your ship was sinking, Ven?"

"I thought it was for the rum," Ven admitted. "And the apples and parsnips floating in the wreckage."

"See? Human—*oof!*—things. If I hadn't seen the albatross circling over you, that's what I would have been—*oof!*—going after, too."

The octopus reached over with a tentacle and brushed the sand from the shiny objects on the ocean floor. It slid the end of its arm through something and dragged it up out of the sand, then placed it in the merrow's hands.

Amariel held the gift aloft in the drift. It was a ring, with a silver band and set with a stone that looked like an enormous diamond. It seemed clear as it passed through the drift, but when the light from the surface above hit it, the stone appeared white and solid.

"A human ring—how pretty!" the merrow said to the beast. "For me? Really?"

The enormous eyes blinked. Ven could feel its thrum answer.

"Well, thank you," said Amariel.

"Why is she givin' you that?" Char demanded. "She doesn't want to marry you or somethin' creepy like that, does she? That's what humans use rings like that for."

"Of course not. I told you, Chum, she just likes me."

"Why?"

"She has good taste," said Amariel. She patted the enormous tentacle on the side without the suckers.

"Maybe she just thinks you taste good," suggested Coreon.

Char was adjusting his pack. He squinted. "Ven—are you bleeding?"

Ven reached up to his stinging forehead. The skin was sore to the touch, raw.

"The shark grazed me—it's nothing." He looked up at the watery ceiling above the Sea Desert. "The day is moving on, and so should we if we're to get to the Summer Festival." He turned to the merrow, who had tied the human ring into the locks of her hair and was showing it to the admiring octopus. "Are you ready, Amariel?"

"Yes."

"Is she going to let you go?" Char asked nervously.

Amariel nodded.

"Then let's be on our way," said Coreon.

"Thank you for the ring," said the merrow as the great orange creature slowly turned her loose and patted her head with an enormous tentacle. The suckers made a whispering sound as they passed through her hair.

The boys thought their goodbyes, then followed Amariel out of the cage of bones and into the shadowy light of the seemingly endless desert beyond.

The wound on Ven's forehead had all but stopped hurting. It felt so much better, in fact, that he didn't notice the three small drops of blood that he left hanging in the drift behind him.

But not long afterward, something else did.

## ~ 23 ~

# In Coral Cathedrals

For a long time after we left the octopus's garden, our thrum was silent. It's not that I had stopped thinking. Actually, my thoughts were racing faster than ever. But the heaviness of the water, the emptiness of the desert, and the endless blue-green of the deepening ocean seemed to swallow all the sound in the world.

Finally, as noon passed, and the sea was growing deeper, we saw something up ahead in the distance. At first I thought it was seaweed.

But then I realized it wasn't moving in the drift.

**W**HOA."

Char's thrum broke through the heavy silence. The three other children flinched.

"What?" Coreon demanded

Ven squinted. Ahead he could see thin, dark lines in the water, reaching from the seabed toward the light above, but little more.

"What you suppose that is?" he asked Amariel.

The merrow smiled. "I don't have to suppose," she said briskly. "I know what it is. It's nothing dangerous. In fact, it's very beautiful. Come. I'll show you." She swam away with a great sweep of her tail.

"Hope she's right about the 'not dangerous' part," Char murmured as they struggled to keep up with her. "It'll be nice to meet *something* in the Sea Desert that isn't."

It took longer than Ven expected to get to a place where they could make out the lines more clearly. Everything in the sea was farther away than it looked, he realized.

And bigger.

Eventually the lines began to take form. As they approached, Ven could see that they were wispy rocks, or what looked like rocks, in soft, glowing colors of white and blue, pink and purple. They stretched from the seafloor up toward the surface, forming beautiful arched patterns that were dotted with nooks and holes. At the edge of his vision he could see them all around, so many that they turned this part of the ocean rosy in the afternoon sunshadow.

*What is this?* he wondered

"Cathedral coral," Amariel's thrum replied. "A cousin of the reef coral you met before, where Coreon lives. Even though it seems fragile, it's actually much stronger because it lives where the water is so heavy. It's also very old—the pillars near the bottom have been dead for a long time. It's alive closer to the top, and sharper."

"It's a lot like some of the great buildings in the upworld," said Ven as they passed under an intricate archway. "The spires of the castle Elysian aren't as tall and beautiful as this!"

The merrow rolled her eyes. "Of course not. They're on *land*. How many times do I have to tell you? Everything is better and more beautiful under the sea."

Char coughed but said nothing.

"Is it singing?" Ven asked. Once they were inside the field of cathedral-coral spires, he could feel a vibration in his skin that was musical and pleasant, much like the song of the Underwater Forest.

"Yes," said Amariel. "Don't get too enchanted, though. The music masks other thrum around it. Its sound is very soothing to fish and krill. They love to hang around cathedral coral. And you know what that means."

"Predators," Coreon said.

"I don't see many fish," said Char.

The merrow looked behind her. "You're right. That's not a good sign."

Ven closed his eyes and concentrated.

Past the pleasant tickle of the coral's vibration on his skin he could feel something sharper, something higher. The shark in the cage of bones had the same kind of thrum, a clean, harsh sound that made his blood run cold.

The sound of hunting.

He could feel the thrum coming from different places.

All following them.

And, atop it all, there was another sound he recognized.

That ancient, familiar thrum he had been hearing since entering the sea.

Only much, much louder.

And this time, it was coming closer.

Quickly.

"We're in trouble," he said to the others. He could see in their eyes that it was not necessary to tell them.

Out of the green darkness behind them three shadows appeared, swimming rapidly. They had the unmistakable movement of sharks, with the same thrum as the great white in the cage of bones.

But they were much bigger.

"*Slowly.*" Amariel's thrum was urgent. "Careful, Chum. Your heart's pounding like a drum. If I can feel it, you can bet they can."

"Take cover," Coreon advised. "There are some ship bones ahead. Beyond the cathedrals, but I don't think we'd make it in time. Press up against the coral, but not too hard. It can cut you, and the last thing we need is blood in the water. It'll lead them right to us."

Ven touched his forehead. *Oh, man,* he thought. *It's me. I brought them here, like a beacon on a lighthouse.*

Amariel grabbed his hand. With two strong, smooth sweeps of her tail they were up against a trio of tooth-like stalagmites. Char and Coreon took cover in another clump nearby.

The wispy coral arms reached above them, looking helpless, as if pleading to the sky for help.

The afternoon sun cast shadows from above as the sharks swam overhead. Ven closed his eyes, trying to blot out their hunting thrum as they circled above the tips of the cathedral coral.

But he couldn't.

Louder and louder above the high, harsh thrum of the circling sharks, the older drumbeat was drawing closer as well.

Suddenly, the three great whites split and swam off into the darkness.

*Where are they going?* he thought.

"Shhhh," Amariel whispered. Ven could tell by the size of her eyes that she was terrified.

He pressed himself up against the ghostly coral structure, its glowing formations hard as rock, though Ven knew it was actually a mass of the shells of sea creatures, some of them still living. He tried not to shudder as something wiggled against his back.

Above them, the stalagmites tapered up toward the surface, growing lacey and fragile as they reached above into the patchy darkness toward the hazy green light. The higher up they grew, the thinner and wispier their purple and white arms became. They reminded Ven of the frail threads of spun sugar that he saw from time to time in the Magical Confectionery in town, where the most delicious and beautiful candies and baked goods were made.

Just then, the light disappeared as an enormous black shadow passed overhead, blotting it out.

The thrum he had been hearing from the moment they came into the sea echoed in his ears, chilling his heart. He finally recognized the vibration.

*Megalodon.*

He had seen the giant shark once before, while aboard Oliver

Snodgrass's ship, the *Serelinda*. The lookout in the crow's nest had shouted the beast's name, and suddenly every sailor fell silent and stood utterly still.

Their eyes looked exactly as Amariel's did now.

The last time he had seen the beast, it was nothing more than a giant fin the size of the mainsail of the *Serelinda* and a shadow that passed beneath the hull. Now that he was in the water, feeling the pressure of its wake as it swam above him, it felt as is the moon itself had fallen out of the sky and was going to crush them into the sandy ocean floor.

He could feel Amariel's hand slip into his own, the webbed fingers trembling. He remembered her voice, clear from being in the air, just before they had submerged.

*And, for goodness' sake, if we come upon a shark, hold still and don't make any noise or movement until I discover if it's one of my friends or not. They can tell where you are by your movements. And your smell, of course, especially if you're bleeding. My friends might eat you by mistake if you're bleeding—or even me. Blood in the water kind of cancels out any notion of politeness or friendship.*

*I don't suppose Megalodon is a friend of yours,* Char had joked.

Amariel's voice in reply was as cold as Ven had ever heard it.

*Megalodon has no friends. Even the pilot fish isn't his friend.*

And now it was tracking his blood.

Ven took slower breaths, trying to keep his heart from beating too loudly. He looked as far to the right as he could by just moving his eyes, but he couldn't see Char. He could feel him, however, because the spidery fronds of the cathedral coral were shaking violently just like Char did whenever he was really frightened. *He must be leaning against it,* Ven thought. *Good, then at least he's still behind me.*

He could not see or feel Coreon at all.

*Keep going, please keep going,* he thought. *We're so small—a shark that eats ships has no interest in us. If we just stay still, like the sailors did on the* Serelinda, *it should pass us right by, looking for bigger prey.*

After what seemed like forever, the hazy light appeared above them again. Ven looked up and could see the very end of the enormous tail fin, waving back and forth as the beast moved beyond the dead reef, heading out into the darkness of the depths once more.

He squeezed Amariel's hand in relief.

"Thank goo'ness he's gone," he heard Char mutter behind him.

"No joke," Ven agreed. He smiled at the merrow, only to lose that smile an instant later when he caught the look on her face.

She was staring behind him, her eyes even wider.

He glanced over his shoulder.

At the edge of the light, he could see the giant shadow turning.

"The pilot fish," Amariel whispered. "It's seen us."

# ⁓ 24 ⁓

# Feeding Frenzy

W**HILE THE OTHERS WERE STARING OFF INTO THE DARKNESS,** watching the giant shark turn, Coreon was looking overhead.

"Holy crab," he said. "Ven?"

"What?"

"Not to make an already bad day worse, but our friends are back."

Ven glanced above.

The three great whites that had fled when Megalodon appeared had returned. This time they were swimming deeper, ten fathoms or so below the surface, less than two fathoms above Ven's head. Their thrum was sharp and loud, the hunting rhythm Ven had heard in the cage of whale bones. It was scattered, as if each shark was hunting alone, rather than in a pack, so it was even more frenzied.

*Prey! Prey! Prey! Prey! Prey!*
   *Prey! Prey! Prey! Prey!*

"Man, there's not even going to be enough of us left to look like snowflakes, the way the herring did," Char muttered. "Well, at least Megalodon won't be getting us—we'll be being digested before he gets back here."

The mention of herring gave Ven an idea.

"Herring Ball, you guys," he said as he pulled Amariel back-to-back with him. "Get into a circle, so someone's watching forward at all times."

"Because that worked *so* well for the herring," said Char.

"No, it's a good idea," said Coreon. "Sort of like having eyes in the back of your head." He swam over to Ven's side and turned his back, so that now they were facing three different directions. He pulled his barbed crossbow over his shoulder in front of him.

Reluctantly Char took the last position. "You know you can't kill a great white of that size with a barb, right? You'll be lucky if you scratch 'em."

Coreon smiled. "Don't need to kill them," he said. "*He'll* take care of that." He gestured with his head toward the massive shape approaching from the darkness.

"Why would Megalodon eat another shark when I'm the one that's been bleeding?" Ven asked. "It's my blood he's been tracking." He pointed to the wound on his forehead.

"Because they'll be bleeding more than you." Coreon sighted his weapon and fired as one of the large great whites swept past, missing it by a hair.

Understanding awoke in Ven's mind like a candle being lighted.

"A feeding frenzy!" he exclaimed. Char must have come to the same conclusion as well, because both boys pulled their crossbows over their shoulders at the same time.

"A feeding frenzy is not a good thing, Ven," Amariel whispered as the second and third sharks circled closer. "Sharks go crazy—they eat anything in sight." She ducked out of the way of a tail fin as it swept past her, narrowly missing her head.

"We're on the menu at the moment anyway," Coreon said. He reloaded his crossbow as the first shark came around for another pass, closer this time. "But a couple of tons of shark will make a much better meal for Megalodon than we will."

"Sometimes it probably doesn't hurt to be the smallest things in the water," Ven agreed. He was keeping his eye on the approaching monster in the shadows.

Hovering above its gigantic dorsal fin was a fish of enormous size, though it was tiny by comparison to the shark. It had scales that were blue with thick dark stripes, an angry-looking jaw, and eyes that gleamed in the dim light. Ven remembered Amariel's words when they first were entering the sea.

*Megalodon is frightening, but the pilot fish is said to be utterly evil. He clings to Megalodon, helping guide him through the sea, and feeds off the scraps left behind from whatever Megalodon devours. And there always are some.*

He was not certain, but it felt as if the pilot fish was watching them closely. As its excitement grew, the blue of its scales was turning white. Its thrum, unlike that of the sharks, was careful and intelligent, and the feeling in Ven's body when that thrum connected with him made his blood run cold.

As if it could read his thoughts.

Coreon took aim as the first shark suddenly swung wide, lining up for a direct run.

"Crab," he whispered. "It's coming at us head-on."

"Ven," Amariel said. It was the only thought that she could form.

Megalodon appeared at the edge of the sunshadow, streaking toward them in the sunlight. It was moving faster than anything he had ever seen before, sweeping great currents of drift ahead of it.

Char turned as the other two sharks passed again and fired his barb.

The bolt sped through the water, a direct hit against the great white's vertical gills.

And bounced off, useless.

"I have no shot." Coreon's thrum filled their heads. "It's coming straight at me!"

"Get ready," Amariel said. "Hold just where you are."

Before Ven could stop her, she shot out of the Herring Ball

formation and swam straight across the field of vision of all three sharks.

The first two immediately stopped their slow circling and gave chase.

"Amariel! No!"

"Aim for the eyes!" Her thrum echoed through the water. "And don't shoot me."

She streaked past Coreon, her tail beating the water as fast as Ven had ever seen it. The shark that had been heading for him veered to the side and followed her, with the other two right behind it.

Coreon fired.

Ven spun, taking his eyes off the pilot fish, and sighted his weapon on the last of the three sharks. Its hollow eye was twitching as it passed, close enough, it seemed, that he could reach out and touch it.

He tried to keep the crossbow from shaking as he aimed for that eye.

And fired.

Beside him, he could feel the vibration as Char's crossbow let loose as well.

Suddenly the water was filled with commotion.

One of the three great whites reared up like a bucking horse, thrashing around wildly. The other two stopped following Amariel and veered back, their tails twitching in excitement.

A streak of black blood hung in the drift outside the cathedral coral.

The merrow was by his side an instant later. She grabbed him by the elbow and pulled hard.

"C'mon! We have to get out of here *now!*"

The water around them was suddenly almost too heavy to swim in. A terrible pressure filled the drift as the enormous beast roared toward them like a sailing ship being pushed through the sea by a hurricane.

Ven looked down at the ocean floor as Megalodon's approaching shadow darkened it. He saw the pieces of the small shipwreck that Coreon had pointed out earlier get swallowed up in the dark.

"Quick," he said. "Take cover in the bones of those ships."

Coreon lifted his crossbow again. "I'll cover you—go!"

"Grab hold and don't move," Amariel ordered, holding out her arms. "Don't breathe, either—no thrum, or we may get caught up in the frenzy."

Char and Ven each seized one of her arms. The merrow straightened herself, moving only her powerful tail, and glided down to the sandy ocean floor, followed within a moment by Coreon.

Above them, the water began to swirl, thrumming violently.

It seemed to take forever to reach the shipwreck. Difficult as it was, the merrow took her time, moving as little as possible in the whipping drift that was turning darker and bloodier by the second.

The broken pieces of what had once been a fishing trawler were small, just two barrel-sized parts of the hull. As they approached a crusty porthole, Amariel pushed Char loose and in through what had once been a window in the ship's side. One smooth flap of her tail, and she and Ven slid under the other pile of broken boards. Coreon followed Char into the porthole.

"Shhhh," Amariel whispered as she and Ven sat down on the ocean floor. "It's about to get *really* ugly."

"You know, you say that an awful lot." Ven peered out from under the broken boards into the porthole of the ship bones where the others had taken shelter. He could see both Coreon's and Char's eyes glittering in the darkness below their piece of the dead ship.

*No noise, no movement*, he thought as loosely as he could, trying to keep from making any disturbance in the drift. He was aiming his thrum at the other boys, but it might as well have been a reminder to himself.

The pressure around us was even worse than when Megalodon had first passed overhead. Pieces of shark were beginning to rain down from above like the silver scales of the herring had, making the water around us cloudy.

It occurred to me as we crouched there, waiting for some sign the frenzy had ended, that we would never know which of us had hit the shark that had started it all.

I knew in my heart that was a very good thing not to know.

While the three great whites were distracted by the blood in the water, they did not have the ability to flee Megalodon.

Once he got there, it must have all been over pretty quickly.

Because that hideous pressure only lasted a few moments.

And then the thrum I had been hearing since we entered the sea began to move away.

We waited until it was so far gone that we could no longer feel it in our skin. But I could still hear it, way in the back reaches of my mind, just as I could from the beginning when I did not know what it was.

I'm not sure if I will ever be able to clear it from my mind completely.

What really scares me is that I'm not sure if the thrum I am hearing is that of Megalodon alone—or of the pilot fish, the only sea creature that has ever looked at me and smiled as if he knew my fear.

When the pressure of the drift had returned to normal, and none of them felt any predator thrum nearby, they slowly began to emerge from the shipwreck pieces, first Ven, then Char, then Coreon, and finally the merrow, who needed to be assured that there was nothing hovering above them.

"Well, that was disgusting," she said, swimming over a chunk of shark meat on the ocean floor amid scattered shark teeth, including one as large as her hand. "What a messy eater."

"When you're the size of the Crossroads Inn, I s'pose it's easy to miss a piece of your lunch now and then," Char said. "Yuck."

"I meant the pilot fish." The merrow brushed her scales with her hands, as if trying to erase the memory. "It's his job to clean up the scraps."

"Let's be glad he missed a few," said Ven. "If he had come down to pick them up, he might have seen us. He gives me the creeps."

"Hey, Ven, do ya think this might have been part of the *Athenry*?" Char asked, looking back in the window of the shipwreck from the outside.

Ven shook his head. "Too small, probably a fishing vessel."

"What do ya think that message about freeing 'the only innocent prisoners' meant?"

"I've no idea. Maybe someone was falsely accused of a crime, and came with all the other criminals. But that was so long ago that it hardly matters. All those people are dead by now."

"Maybe the key is really old, too. Maybe none of it matters anymore." Coreon looked around, his crossbow ready. "I think we better get out of here. A feeding frenzy causes as much thrum as a thunderstorm, and soon there will be a million scavengers here looking to feast on shark remains."

"Good point," said Ven. "Do you know the way to the desert's end, toward the Summer Festival?" He bent down and picked up the giant tooth.

"We just have to keep heading due west, following the sun, like the Cormorant said."

Amariel looked into the shadows where Megalodon had turned around to come back at them. "I wish I knew which way he went for certain."

"Speaking of following the sun, it's beginning to dive," Coreon said.

Ven looked up to the surface and saw that he was right. They had remained in the shipwreck for a much longer time than he had realized, and now the light above was beginning to fade. The water of the Sea Desert had turned from a clear blue to a cloudier green as the sunlight dimmed, and now the ocean was full of shadow.

What was more, he was beginning to feel the thrum of many things approaching from the east.

The direction in which Megalodon had been traveling.

"You're right. Let's get out of here." He stuck the giant tooth in his pack.

Without another word, they shouldered their knapsacks and weapons and began to swim, heading due west.

As quickly as they traveled, the sun was winning the race across the sky, and the sea grew darker with almost every breath. Every now and then, as Ven and Char began to slow down, the two ocean dwellers would grab them by the arm and pull them along in the drift, keeping them moving quickly.

Finally, at the edge of the last light of day that was shining on the surface above, just before the sunset, Amariel stopped and squinted.

"What is that?"

Ven squinted too. He saw what looked like a vast curtain of seaweed in the drift ahead, blocking their path.

"Another kelp forest, perhaps?"

"Maybe," said Coreon. "Thank goodness the moon is already high in the sky. In a moment it will be Total Dark, but we may have a little moonlight to see by until we find shelter."

"Shelter would be good," Char said. "Anybody else feel that?"

Ven listened. The thrum he had heard from the east was getting closer. It did not sound like the ancient music he now knew as Megalodon's thrum, but it seemed to be coming from a great number of creatures.

Large, strong creatures.

"Keep going!" he urged.

They were swimming as fast as they could toward the upcoming forest of what looked like kelp when the light of day gave out completely, plunging the ocean into darkness.

As Coreon had noted, the moon was hanging in the sky, almost full. The surface of the sea took on a silver glow, casting a tiny bit of light below to the drift. They swam more carefully now, even though whatever was following them did not slow at all.

Suddenly, just as they were within reach of the forest, Amariel stopped sharply.

"Oh no," she whispered. "No. Look."

Ven stared into the murky green darkness. At first he couldn't see anything except the occasional strand of light glistening down like colorful strings of pearls in what looked like moonshadows, even though night was just beginning to take hold. He thought he could even see the clouds hovering above the crest of the waves. *Strange*, he thought. *The clouds are hanging low tonight; it must be getting ready to rain in the upworld.*

Then he looked closer.

The strands of light were not from the sky above the water's surface.

They were tentacles.

Long, stringy curtains hanging in the drift.

Bazillions of them.

And the clouds at the top of the water's surface were not clouds but great colorless creatures, loose and puffy, like giant mushrooms. There were so many gathered there in the drift that they looked like a forest of shiny thread.

"Jellyfish," Ven murmured. It was the only word his thoughts could form.

"Men-of-war," the merrow corrected tersely. "Giants. One sting of those tentacles will kill any of us."

"Guess we're not going through *there*, then." Char's thrum shook as it vibrated against Ven's ears.

"We can't," Coreon agreed. "Our chances are better against the sharks that are chasing us."

Ven glanced behind them.

In the moonlit waters of the Sea Desert he could see great dark shapes speeding toward them now, faster than before.

Many, many more of them.

A terrifying thrum rose from the forest of men-of-war. It pounded against his skull and skin, making him shake uncontrollably. He understood its meaning perfectly.

*Death is coming. Death is coming. Flee—flee. Death. Death. Death.*

# ~ 25 ~

# The Summer Festival

Char whipped around and looked behind him.

"Oh, man! Whatever's comin', they're not swimmin' like sharks—what's after us *now*?"

Amariel peered into the darkness. Then a smile of relief broke across her face.

"They're not after us," she said. "They're after the men-of-war. Those are leatherbacks!"

"Leatherbacks?" Ven struggled to see better, but all he could make out was enormous shapes streaking toward them.

"Turtles," the merrow exclaimed. "Great armored ones. The men-of-war can't hurt them. In fact, they're the leatherback's favorite food. The leatherbacks see a feast ahead of them—we should get out of the way. Come on, down to the floor, quick!"

Ahead of them, the men-of-war were beginning to tremble, then move. A few of them drew their tentacles in, then opened up like umbrellas, launching out of the group like fireworks going off.

Amariel grabbed Ven's arm, while Coreon took hold of Char, and dove for the ocean floor. It took longer to reach, as the sea had become deeper, and they were swimming into complete darkness, with just the slightest hint of silver shadow from the moon above on the surface to light their way.

"Put your pack over your head," Coreon advised. "Just because this isn't our fight doesn't mean we can't get injured, or worse."

"Watch out for falling tentacles," the merrow agreed.

Ven held his pack over Amariel's head and moved closer to her.

The pressure of the dark sea above them changed again, as it had when Megalodon first passed by, but in patches of heaviness that moved swiftly.

The dark shapes roared in overhead. Ven was shocked to see that some of them were the size of wagons, while others were smaller, about as big as him. They were dark of color, though Ven was not sure exactly what that color was. They had smooth, oblong shells that looked like the armor soldiers wore. Chunky legs with flippers were jutting from that armor, and they bore down on the forest of men-of-war faster than the jellyfish could swim away.

The thrum of excitement and fear filled the sea with vibrations strong enough to stir the drift so that it felt like waves.

Tentacles rained down from above, like strings of beads in the drift. Char and Coreon dodged out of the way of a particularly big tangle of them that floated down fairly quickly.

For much of the night, the feasting and escaping went on, like a lavish ball at a great undersea castle.

*It was strange, crouched on the floor of the sea, watching as the men-of-war tried to escape the leatherback turtles. The colors of jellyfish were beautiful against the moonshine, pink and green and orange and white, like blown glass and ribbon candy. The way they swim is so pretty, like a flower opening and closing, so the giant feast looked like a grand dance of sorts from below.*

*Of course, not from the jellyfishes' point of view, I'm sure.*

*The leatherbacks spun in the sea with tremendous grace for creatures of their size and heft. When I caught a glimpse of one their faces, it looked to me like it was carved from rock, heavy, with a pointed beak that seemed like it could snap a clamshell in half.*

*They reminded me a little of Scarnag the dragon, who literally is made from Living Stone.*

*We remained huddled together until the feasting was over and the remainder of the men-of-war had escaped, billowing their way deeper into the sea.*

*All that was left behind were many glowing strands floating in the drift, filling it with soft colors in the blue sunwater.*

*Which was coming to light with the morning.*

"Wait here."

Amariel pushed the pack Ven was holding over her head aside and began swimming up toward the squadron of sea turtles, who were now circling above them, full and happy.

"Wait! Where are you going?" Ven called nervously.

"Be right back." The merrow approached a large leatherback and hovered in the drift near it for a moment. Then she swam quickly back to the others on the ocean floor.

"We're in luck!" she said, grinning so widely that her porpoise-like teeth showed, something she rarely did. "The leatherbacks are on their way to the Summer Festival. They say it's not too much farther, though it is in its last days. We can follow them if we like. They don't mind the company."

"That would be great," Ven agreed. He turned to see Coreon nodding and Char staring at him as if he were insane.

"Are ya daft?" his best friend asked. "What if they get hungry on the way?"

"Turtles don't eat merrows," Amariel said. "Or humans. Come on. It will be great to have a guide that actually knows where it's going." She looked at Coreon, then smiled. "No offense."

Coreon nodded in agreement. "None taken."

The merrow dove to the bottom and returned a few moments later with some stringy seaweed and a length of algae-encrusted rope. She handed one end of each to Char and Ven.

"Hold tight," she said.

The boys looked at each other. They watched as Amariel swam up to the leatherback squad, which was swimming more seriously now, preparing to depart, and tossed the other ends of the seaweed and rope to two of the giant reptiles. The turtles seized the ends in their beaks.

Then, like a bolt from a crossbow, they shot off toward the west.

Dragging Ven and Char behind them.

Amariel and Coreon swam in their wake.

"Don't let go," the merrow advised. "We'll never catch up with them again."

Ven's stomach had flipped when the turtle on the other end of his seaweed tether launched off, but after a moment it settled back into place and he began to enjoy the ride. He turned his body to the side to see Char was clinging to his slimy green length of rope, his face pale as the leatherback he was attached to swam erratically, dashing up toward the surface, then diving suddenly, then zigzagging.

"You all right, Char?"

"I'm gonna throw up." Char's thrum was as wobbly as his voice would have been. "I think I'm gettin' seasick."

"He's just playing with you, Chum," said Amariel. "Try to be a good sport for once. He'll get tired of it after a while, mostly likely."

Char's reply was lost in a trail of bubbles that swerved through the drift.

Ven closed his eyes. The sickening feeling left his stomach once he could no longer see the ocean floor racing past underneath him. An excitement took its place as he sped along behind the turtle.

The sensation reminded him of standing on the deck of the *Angelia*, the first and only time he went out on an Inspection for his father. The man who would have been the doomed ship's captain had let him hold the wheel, and had laughed at the excitement the speeding ship had brought to him.

*Don't drink too much of the wind, young master Polypheme*, Captain Faeley had said. *It's intoxicating; it will get you drunk more easily than you can imagine. And then you will be lost to it, as we are, and have no choice but to chase it over the sea for all your life.*

The speed of the turtle swimming was a similar sensation—heady, thrilling, making him dizzy. He was enjoying it until he remembered that just after Captain Faeley had warned him not to get carried away, the ship had exploded.

Almost taking his whole life to the bottom of the sea with it.

Ven pushed the thought out of his mind and concentrated on the ride instead.

After what seemed like a very long time to Ven, and even longer to Char, the leatherbacks began to slow down.

Ven opened his eyes.

The surface was now too far above them to see. They were deeper than they had ever been before, the ocean floor at least ten fathoms below them still.

And heading for what looked like a steep drop-off.

The sun was higher in the sky above, he knew, because the bright blue water gleamed around them as they sped along.

"Hold on," the merrow called to them. "We're coming to a rise, and I can't see what's beyond it. It looks to get suddenly deeper."

Ven gripped the seaweed strand a little more tightly, hoping it wouldn't snap.

The leatherbacks swam up the rise, much as if it were a sand dune on the beach, then over it. When they got beyond the ridge of sand, the turtles slowed suddenly, floating in the drift.

"Oh *my*," said the merrow.

The sea basin had deepened to about fifty fathoms. The bottom of the ocean stretched out in glorious blue water and golden light below them, as far as they could see.

And in the middle of it all was an enormous gathering of sea creatures of every kind, with towering plants of many colors waving merrily like flags in the drift. They looked as if they were marking the entrance to a fairgrounds.

In the very center they could see a large shaft of sunshadow. It was so wide and bright that it almost looked as if the ocean was raining light.

"Whoa," Char whispered, pointing. He seemed to have recovered from his seasickness. "Look over there."

Ven followed his finger. In the sunlight below the water were millions of fish, forming a ring around an area of ocean floor wider than the streets of the city of Kingston. They were swimming slowly in wavy lines, as if marking off a circus ground or racing track.

"This is it," Coreon whispered. "The Summer Festival." Ven's eardrums felt the awe in the sea-Lirin boy's thrum. "It's just as my father described it—only, well—"

"Grander," Amariel said. "For me, too."

In the center of the ring stood two enormous chairs on a tall platform of hard coral.

*At first I thought they had been carved with many swirls and details like the finest carvings in King Vandemere's palace of Elysian. Then as I looked more carefully I could see that they were actually made of coral and fine shells, in colors that reminded me of the sky at sea in the morning. The sunshadow seemed brightest there, and so the chairs glowed in hues of soft yellow and pink, pale blue and gold.*

*Sitting in the chairs were two beings that looked at first glance like merrows, a man and a woman. The man was as tall as a human male but with a long, powerful tail. I had always thought that Amariel's tail was amazing, with beautiful colored scales of blue and green and pearl. This man's tail was far more commanding in its appearance, muscular and strong, the fluke almost as big as that of a small whale. It seemed that the scales that covered it were in every color of the rainbow. I knew at once that he could break my back with one slap of it.*

Beside him was a woman with long hair so white that it almost looked clear. Like the man, she wore a crown of mother-of-pearl on her head, but while her body from the arms and shoulders up looked human, her chest was covered with ridges that swirled down into a long, curled tail like that of a hippocampus.

"Crikey!" Char murmured. "What would ya call *her*?"

Amariel rose up a little in the drift for a better look.

"I'd suggest 'Your Majesty' if you get the chance to call her anything."

"No—I mean what kind of creature is she?"

"I think she's an Epona," Amariel said. "They're very rare—and somewhat wild, sometimes even silly. They tell good riddles, or so I hear. They are said to love the human world, and are fascinated with it even more than merrow are—well, silly merrow girls, that is. They live fairly deep in the sea. I'm not surprised she was chosen as queen this storm season."

"And the king?" Ven asked. "Is he a merrow?"

Amariel's brow furrowed. "Obviously. I would think you would be able to recognize one by *now*."

"Well, if I remember correctly, when you first described merrows to me, you told me that while females were beautiful, males tended to be, er, less so." Ven cut off his thrum, remembering the words she had used.

*Now, merrow females are the most beautiful creatures in the world. Everyone knows that. But merrow men, well, that's a different story. It's probably fair to say that, as creatures of the sea go, merrow men are a little bit lazy. All right, a lot lazy. Very, very lazy. They bask for more than just heat collection—they lie around in the sun on rocks whenever they can to get out of helping with the children or the other work that has to be done. As a result, they are fat around the middle—even fatter than you, Ven. And on top of that, they are ugly. Not my dad, of course, but most merrow men. They have noses that are flat and round, with big nostrils that sometimes sprout hair. Their teeth are frequently green, and they tend to burp a lot. Bubbles come out the other end as well, which makes them unpleasant to be around.*

"Well, there are some exceptions, of course," Amariel said. "My dad is not a typical male merrow—obviously the king is not, either."

"He looks like he's part whale," Char whispered.

Just then, an undersea horn blasted. It filled the drift with vibrations that swept over Ven, making his skin tingle wildly.

"Oh no," said Coreon nervously. "Oh no! It's starting!"

# ‑ 26 ‑

# The Wild
# Hippocampus Roundup

W**HAT? WHAT'S STARTING?" CHAR LOOKED DOWN AT THE**
Festival grounds.

"Listen!" Amariel said.

The horn blast had come from the largest conch shell Ven had
ever seen. It was mounted like a giant telescope at the base of the
coral throne platform.

"Does that shell remind you of the Floatin' Island?" Char whispered.

Ven nodded, smiling. He had been thinking the same thing. The
Floating Island was a hollow mountain on a piece of earth born at the
beginning of Time. It sailed the sea like a ship, taken around the world
at the whim of the wind. When he and Char had been inside that
mountain with Captain Snodgrass and the sailors from the *Serelinda*,
they had heard voices from all around the world, messages that had
been spoken, whispered, and shouted into the wind and were caught in
the curls of the shell-shaped mountain. It was a place that sailors and
others who came upon it could send messages home, as well.

Now it made sense to him why the large conch was being used to
send thrum messages to the Festival attendees.

The shell-horn crackled, as if it were being cleared of water. Then
a thrum-voice spoke.

"Your Majesties, distinguished court, honored guests, and general riffraff, may I have your attention, please. The hippocampus reeve has an announcement."

"What's a hippocampus reeve?" Char asked.

Coreon and Amariel shrugged.

"Well, a reeve is someone who's in charge of something, so maybe it's like the master of the sea horses," Ven suggested.

"That seems reasonable," Char said.

Just as he finished speaking, a large male merrow with a dark red-scaled tail swam elegantly to the shell-horn and put the tip against his forehead. His thrum came out in a sophisticated, somewhat high voice.

"Your Majesties, the Grand Derby is almost ready to begin. The Grand Derby is the final event before the closing ceremonies of the Summer Festival. The winning hippocampus rider will be presented with the greatest honor awarded at the Festival, the Grand Trophy."

A smattering of polite applause-thrum rumbled through the depths of the sea.

"We have a very big problem," Coreon said. "If they're running the Derby, then today must be Threshold. We came much later to the Festival than I had hoped. Once the Grand Derby starts, the Sea King will only be in power for a short time longer. I won't get a chance to talk to him and deliver the message the Cormorant sent with me. We'll have come all this way for nothing, and all the people in the Gated City will die."

"We'll just have to find a way to talk to him before his reign ends," said Ven.

The shell-horn crackled again.

"All riders are asked report to the kelp pens to prepare for the race," the hippocampus reeve continued. "At this time, while we are awaiting the running of the Grand Derby, the second-to-last event, the Wild Hippocampus Roundup, will be held. Any prospective rider wishing to take part in the Roundup, kindly come to the center of the racetrack."

Ven felt the merrow tense beside him.

"What's the matter?" he asked. "What does that mean?"

"I'm not sure," said Amariel. "In the Grand Derby, all the racing hippocampi are tamed and all have riders who train them. But the sea is full of wild hippocampi. It would make for a pretty dangerous race, I would think."

"The riders themselves look pretty wild," said Char as a group of male merrows swam into the racing arena from different places in the crowd. They were more like the merrow men that Amariel had described in her stories to Ven, with wild hair, fat stomachs, flat noses and bubbles occasionally trailing behind them. One had an enormous orange mustache that matched the hair on his head, which stood on end like the petals of a sunflower. Another was wearing a large, silly hat and had a nose that looked like a pig's snout.

"All right, gentlemen, begin your calling," said the hippocampus reeve.

Immediately the merrow men put their hands up to their mouths and began making strange, melodic thrum that caused Ven's eyelids to itch.

"Oh, I know what they're doin'!" Char exclaimed. "I once saw somethin' like this in a town when the sailors and I were on shore leave. There was this hog-calling contest, and a whole bunch o' grown men made right fools of themselves, gruntin' an' hollerin' an' squealin' as loud as they could, tryin' to get a pig to pay attention to 'em. It was embarrasing, to tell you the truth."

"Do you think any wild hippocampi will answer?" Coreon asked.

Char shrugged. "Dunno. All the pigs ignored 'em."

Amariel shook her head, then pointed into the drift.

"They must know what they're doing. Look!"

From the shadows beyond the great Festival grounds, large shapes with horses' heads and tails that curled into spirals began appearing. They were swimming quickly toward the racetrack, bucking and rearing as if they were trying to fight the merrows' calls, but were losing the battle. One large dark blue hippocampus with black spots was fighting so hard that he had turned himself upside down, and his curled tail kept unrolling and rolling back up again.

A wide vibration of what Ven recognized as laughter rose from the creatures that surrounded the racetrack.

*Poor sea horses*, he thought. *It's clear that they don't want to be here, but the merrow song is impossible for them to resist.*

"I'm gonna do it," Amariel whispered.

"Do what?"

"I'm going to enter the Roundup."

"What are you talking about?" Char demanded. "I know you want to be a Grand Derby rider, Amariel, but you don't have a hippocampus to ride. An' even if you did, I don't like the way this wild hippocampus roundup is takin' shape. It has *stupid* and *dangerous* written all over it."

"Char's right." Ven was watching a long orange hippocampus with hair as wild as the sunflower-haired merrows drag him around the racetrack by his mustache. Another pair of dappled giant sea horses were wrestling with each other, their long, curved necks clumsily entwined. The laughing thrum of the crowd got louder.

"Yeah, it's humiliating to have lobsters laughing at you," Coreon said.

"And you're sure to get hurt," added Ven. "Those hippocampi must weigh ten times what you do at least."

"Nonsense," retorted Amariel. "By the time they get to the racetrack, they're enchanted."

"Enchanted? Really? Is that what that's called?" Char pointed to a potential rider who was exchanging tail blows with his mount, slapping each other in the face. Another merrow chased down a pink hippocampus and spat in its eye. The giant sea horse spat back.

"I guess I took that spitting too personally," Char murmured. "It looks much more common down here than it is in the upworld."

The merrow pushed past him. "Move out of the way, Chum. I need to get down there before the race starts."

Ven grabbed her arm. "Don't do it, Amariel," he pleaded. "You're going to get hurt, possibly badly."

"Thanks for your confidence in me," Amariel said bitterly. "This is my dream, Ven. I've told you that from the very beginning. I may never have a hippocampus of my own to groom and train. This may be my only chance. So if I call for one, and one comes, who are you to tell me I can't ride it? Let me go, and get out of my way."

She wrenched her arm loose from Ven's grasp and swam quickly toward the center of the racetrack, where the male merrows were thrumming to their mounts. The hippocampi were beginning to settle down, allowing the merrows to put their bridles on.

"Maybe she won't get one," Char suggested to Ven, whose stomach was turning over in worry. "Look at all the would-be riders that didn't get an answer."

A loud roar of thrum laughter from the crowd washed over them. The sea creatures had noticed Amariel, the only female merrow, and the only youngling to come forward, and apparently they found her highly amusing. Even the Epona queen was laughing uproariously. Only the Sea King appeared disturbed by her entrance.

"What are you doing, little one?" he said. His thrum was deep and commanding, and it quieted the vibrations of the laughter into silence.

Amariel bowed awkwardly.

"I'd like to try and call a hippocampus, Your Majesty," she answered.

The Sea King cast a glance at the hippocampus reeve, who shook his head.

"I believe it to be unwise," he said. His eyes took in the sight of Amariel's shoulders sagging in disappointment. Ven was fairly certain he saw them fill with sympathy. "But the rules do not specify an age limit, do they?"

"No, Your Majesty," the hippocampus reeve began, "but—"

"Let her call, then," said the Sea King. "If, like some of these other merrows, she gets no answer, it wasn't meant to be. But if she does, well, then, I will have to assume that it is her destiny to ride in the race."

Ven thought he saw the king's eye wink, even from very far away.

Amariel was quivering with excitement.

"Thank you, Your Majesty."

"Well, get on with it, mer-child," the Sea King said gruffly.

*I wasn't sure what to hope would happen.*

*I know Amariel has wanted this most of her life. To ride a hippocampus in the Grand Derby was a dream she told me about the first time we met, while I was lying on a piece of floating driftwood in the middle of the sea, and she was trying to save me from drowning. She said that most female merrows had a great desire to explore the human world, and were willing to make terrible sacrifices to do so, but she was not. Her dream was of the Grand Trophy.*

*It's one of the things I like best about her.*

*I know this adventure is not at all what she had planned when she asked me to come explore the depths with her. Instead of going where she might want to have gone, we have run afoul of sea Lirin, taken on a mission with Coreon rather than just getting to show me the places she thought were most special about her world.*

*So I hope she gets a chance to ride a hippocampus.*

*But I am also afraid for her.*

Amariel shook her arms to loosen them up.

Another round of laughter-thrum rippled through the crown.

Amariel ignored the laughter and put her hands to her mouth.

At first, no real thrum came out. The chuckling grew louder.

Then, after a moment, it died away, leaving a pure sound, clear and sweet, like the song she had sung to the coral and the elaroses.

Her call echoed throughout the Festival grounds, causing blossoms to erupt on some of the towering plant flags that were floating in the drift. Amariel slowly turned in a circle, sending her call out in every possible direction.

Then, after she had made a full circle, she stopped.

The assembly, including the Sea Queen and King, watched in silence.

Nothing happened.

Amariel looked around intently.

The Sea King and Queen exchanged a glance. Then the king looked to the hippocampus reeve, who shook his head.

"I'm sorry, mer-child," the king said finally. "But you did your best. Perhaps at the next Festival, you can try again."

Amariel look around again, then sighed.

"All right, then, clear the track," the hippocampus reeve said briskly. "Riders, take your mounts to the starting line." He gestured at a row of starfish, which scurried onto the track and formed a colorful marker in the sand.

"Be on your way, mer-child," the king said to Amariel, who was still looking desperately into the drift for a wild hippocampus. Amariel straightened her shoulders and began swimming back toward her friends amid the raucous laughter of the crowd.

The look on her face was the saddest Ven had ever seen in his life.

*What do I say to her?* he thought. *Maybe it's best not to say anything at all.*

The chuckling thrum of the crowd changed suddenly. It sounded like a gasp, followed by even louder laughter. Ven turned and looked in the direction it was coming from.

A hippocampus was making its way slowly toward the track from the north. He was taking his time, sauntering in the drift. The beast was somewhat smaller than the other wild hippocampi that had answered the call, but vastly fatter. He was blue-green in color, puffing as he swam, and heading toward Amariel, who clearly had no idea he was there.

Char pointed over her head as she approached her friends on the sidelines.

"Look behind you."

The merrow's brows drew together. Then she turned around and went stiff in shock.

The crowd laughed again.

Amariel glanced over her shoulder at Ven, who smiled at her. She smiled in return, the toothy grin she usually tried to keep hidden.

Then she straightened her red pearl cap, dashed to the hippocampus, and threw her arms around his neck.

At the throne platform, the Sea Queen was laughing along with the crowd, but the king wore a serious expression. He turned to the hippocampus reeve and gestured. Even across the Festival grounds, Ven knew he was telling the reeve to allow the late entry into the race.

"Better get to the starting line," he advised the merrow, who was happily hugging the hippocampus. "You don't want the race to begin without you."

"Right." Amariel gave the giant sea horse one last pat, then swung herself up onto his back.

The pudgy creature bobbed almost to the seafloor.

The Festival ground exploded with merriment.

Amariel patted the blue-green beast, then turned him gently toward the starting line. The hippocampus curled his spiral tail and chugged off with great effort, like an old, overloaded pony in the upworld.

"Well, at least she probably won't get thrown," said Coreon.

"But she may get trampled," said Char.

"Or she may win. You never know. If she does, that may be our chance to talk to the Sea King." Ven looked anxiously over at the line of wild hippocampi, which, while more calm, were still bucking and biting at each other and their riders. "As my father used to say, let's just keep a good thought, shall we?"

Char and Coreon nodded, then looked at each other doubtfully.

A blast of the shell-horn shattered the thrum of the audience. A clear, commanding voice echoed through the Deep.

"And they're off!"

# - 27 -

# The Second-to-the-Last Race

THE FLOATING FLAGS DROPPED ON BOTH SIDES OF THE THRONE
platform.

The hippocampi reared and bucked, a few of them spinning around
in circles, to the loud amusement of the crowd.

The riders kicked and urged the beasts forward, all except for
Amariel, who patted the fat blue-green hippocampus and gave him
a nudge.

Then, after a moment of chaos, the hippocampi started down the
track.

Immediately a pair of orange and red steeds, including the one
with the sunflower mane, dashed into the lead, creating a huge wake
behind them. The others followed in hot pursuit, dashing down the
track, snapping at each other.

Except for the blue-green one, who puffed slowly behind them.

A yellow and gray sea mare, ridden by the merrow with the pig-
like snout, suddenly veered away from the pack toward the crowd.
She stopped in the middle of the track in an outside lane in front of
a small patch of kelp. She made a quick bob for the seaweed, throwing her rider off. The pig-nosed merrow flipped twice in the drift
and floated down to the ocean floor on his back, while the hippocampus calmly munched away.

The remainder of the hippocampi rounded the first turn, all except Amariel's, who was lagging almost half a length behind them. Ven could see the merrow urging her steed to speed up, but he just kept getting slower and slower until finally he stopped in the middle of the racetrack.

Then relieved himself on the ocean floor.

The crowd roared with laughter.

"Come on, ya fat thing," Char muttered. "You know, Amariel and I don't always get along the best, but she *is* my friend. I hate to hear them laughing at her."

"Amariel doesn't care what the crowd thinks," Ven said, though he wasn't certain he was right. The merrow's face was set in a determined expression. She kept urging the plodding hippocampus along, even though the rest of the pack was halfway around the track ahead of her. "We shouldn't feel sorry for her, or tease her. We'll just cheer for her while she's riding and support her when she's done."

"Right." Char closed his eyes and concentrated on his thrum. "Come on, Amariel! Smoke 'em!"

"Yeah!" Coreon shouted. "Go! Go! Go!"

The boys continued cheering even as the pathetic pack of merrows and sea horses came around the home turn. Amariel still had not made it halfway around the track as the red hippocampus streaked across the finish line, followed by the rest. The winning rider did a flip in the sea, letting loose a stream of bubbles from his backside as he did.

The crowd broke into cheers and hooting laughter.

"Aw, *man*." Char put his hands on his head.

Ven said nothing. He was watching Amariel.

The chubby blue-green horse had bobbed its way to the halfway point of the racetrack in front of the throne stand and was slowing down more at each bob. Finally it plodded to a halt.

The Sea King and Queen stared down at Amariel.

The merrow dismounted clumsily, woozy from her bumpy ride. She bowed deeply.

"Your Majesty," she said to the queen, "may I have the honor of presenting you with a gift—a *human* gift?"

The Epona had been staring at her. Her face lit up and she smiled broadly.

"A human gift?" Her thrum was excited and childlike.

"Yes." The merrow removed the ring the octopus had given her from her hair and looked at it for a moment. "The jewel inside it is very much like your hair, Your Majesty—both white and clear at the same time, depending on the light."

As she spoke, the sunwater around the throne stand dimmed a little. Ven could see the clouds above the surface growing thicker, as if it were getting ready to rain.

"Lemme see! Lemme see!" the queen squealed.

The Sea King coughed. "Some decorum, if you please."

"What does that mean?" the queen asked.

"Calm down, and act a little more regal."

"Oh. All right." The Sea Queen stretched out her palm.

Amariel placed the ring in her hand. The Epona held it up to the dimming sunwater.

"Ooo! Ooo!" she squealed. "It's *pretty!* What is it?"

Amariel shrugged.

"I don't know. But there is a human here who might be able to tell you." She pointed across the Festival grounds to where Ven, Char, and Coreon were standing.

"Ahhh," Ven murmured. "Brilliant. Coreon, I think she may have gotten you your royal audience after all."

"Great," said Char. "Now I get to pretend I know somethin' about jewelry?"

The Sea King gestured from across the Festival grounds. The lines of fish that were swimming in place demarking the racetrack made an opening.

"Let's go," said Ven.

They swam through the break in the fish line while the Festival crowd stared at them in silence, though their thrum was deafening.

When they finally arrived at the foot of the throne where Amariel was floating, the Sea Queen pointed at Char.

"Come up here beside me, *human*," she said sweetly.

"He's close enough," said the king. "What can you tell her about this gift?"

"Er, it's called a ring," said Char, rubbing his neck uncomfortably. "Humans wear them on their fingers to show, uh, that they are important and, well, wealthy."

The Sea King snorted. He held up his hand.

A large ring with a red stone was on the first finger.

"Would you care to tell us something we don't know?" His thrum did not sound amused.

"A ring like that is often given by a human man to a human woman as a promise of marriage," Ven said quickly.

The Epona's eyes opened wide. She turned to the Sea King and smiled a glittering smile.

The Sea King coughed.

"I just think it's pretty," said Amariel.

Ven nudged Coreon.

"Your Majesty, I bring you a message from the Cormorant of the eastern coral reef," Coreon said nervously.

The Sea King looked relieved.

"What is it? Thrum unto me."

Coreon stepped forward, and the king put his enormous hand on Coreon's forehead. They both closed their eyes. After a few moments, the king removed his hand.

"This is disturbing indeed," he said. "Damage to the reef, murder of its residents—and the possibility of war with the humans in the Gated City."

"War with humans?" the queen shrieked. "No!"

"Calm down and stare at your ring." The king exhaled, his gills flapping deeply.

"The Cormorant says he needs your guidance, Your Majesty,"

Coreon continued. "Today is Threshold. He only gave me until today to get your answer. He will attack tomorrow."

"Not if he listens to my direction," said the Sea King. "There is no need to invade the Gated City. I will command him to seal the tunnel in such a way that it would have to be entirely re-dug to be reopened. It is folly for him to attack the Gated City for many reasons. The least of those reasons is that when those who live in the sea, as the Lirin-mer do, fight on land, they are more likely to be slaughtered themselves than to kill those they seek to destroy. But you are right about the life cycles of humans being vastly shorter than our own. Those who came on the *Athenry* are long dead. If even one of their descendants is an innocent captive, then it is worth allowing the city to stand rather than taking that innocent life."

Ven, Char, and the queen all sighed in relief.

"Well, that was a brazen gesture, little one," the Sea Queen said to the merrow.

Amariel beamed. "Thank you, Your Majesty."

"What does your name mean?"

Ven was surprised at the question. It seemed odd, given how many times he had been warned about names in the sea. But the merrow shot him a glance of understanding, and he realized that the Sea Queen had not asked for her name, but for its meaning.

"It means *Star of the Sea*, Your Majesty," Amariel said proudly.

"Ah. Well, then, in return for the ring, I will give you a prophecy. There's an old riddle about a captive like that," the Epona queen said. "It goes like this." Her eyes grew glassy and her face went slack as she spoke the words.

*"Wanderer, out of place in the drift,*
*This riddle is to you a gift.*
*Free the captive who stays by choice*
*Sing a hymn without your voice*
*Find the souls forgotten by Time*

*Believe the view is worth the climb.*
*Follow the path without using your eyes*
*Five gifts the price to spare one who dies*
*Until the stars shine in the depths of the sea*
*Home again you will never be."*

"What does that mean, Your Majesty?" Ven asked eagerly.

The Sea Queen shrugged. "I don't know. I wasn't paying attention during riddle lessons."

"Then you will send your command to the Cormorant?" Coreon asked the king.

The Sea King nodded. "As soon as the Derby is over, and the Grand Trophy presented, I will send a sunshadow message back to him," he said. "But what I want to know is why a human and a—a—"

"Nain," Ven said.

"Ah. Why a human and a Nain are in the sea, traveling in the company of a Lirin-mer and a merrow. It seems rather odd."

"We came to see the Summer Festival," said Ven. "Amariel has been telling me about it since we met. One day she hopes to win the Grand Trophy."

"Not on this hippocampus, of course," said the merrow.

"Good thinking there," said the king.

"And if you will allow me, I should like to tell Vandemere, the king of Serendair—and *only* King Vandemere—about the wisdom and beauty that exists beneath the waves. He has asked me to document the hidden magic of the world—and I think it is important that he know that those who rule in the Deep are as respectful of human life as humans should be of, well—"

"Mer-life?" the king suggested.

"Yes, if that's what it's called."

The Sea King's eyes twinkled darkly in the sunwater that dimmed a little as he smiled.

"You may tell King Vandemere—but only the king—what you have seen here. Since you have just trusted me with his name."

# ~ 28 ~

# A Coming Storm

V EN SMILED, BUT FELT HIS STOMACH DROP AT THE SAME TIME. *When am I going to learn to be more careful with names?* he thought to himself.

The Sea King chuckled.

"Probably never," he said, reading Ven's thrum. "It's not in your culture to guard them, the way it is in the sea. But I suspect it is a lesson that would serve you well on land, also."

"No doubt," Ven agreed. "Might I ask you another question, Your Majesty?"

The king looked out over the racetrack. The hippocampus reeve and his men were rounding up the wild hippocampi and taking them off to the kelp pens in preparation for the running of the Derby. "Thrum quickly, Nain. The race is about to start. And then I must attend to the Cormorant's message."

"I will," Ven said. "Do you know if Frothta, the Tree of Water, is still alive, and if so, where it may be?"

The Sea King shook his head.

"I have always been told that it is a myth," he said. "And if the sea had a real king, instead of just one for the duration of a festival, perhaps he would know the answer. But I do not. I do know, however, where you could find the answer."

"Where?"

The expression on the king's face grew solemn.

"The only beings that know anything about Old Magic, those things that are from the Before-Time, are the ones that were alive during those days, or their descendants," he said. "That means if you want to know what happened to Frothta, you need to find a dragon to ask."

"How did I know you were gonna say that?" Char asked. He looked pleadingly at Ven.

Amariel turned and looked at him also. Ven felt like the water around him was suddenly in danger of freezing.

"Is there no one else who might know, Your Majesty?"

The king shrugged.

"Dragons really are the ones to ask about ancient magic from the Before-Time, because they are the only ones still left from that time. Well, there are others, like the Mythlin, but they are even harder to find."

Ven avoided both Char's and Amariel's threatening glances.

"And—do you know where a dragon might be, Your Majesty?"

The Sea King inhaled, his gills moving stiffly.

"I do. And I suggest you stay far from that place. You would need to leave the Sunlit Realm to find him, anyway, because he lives at the edge of Twilight."

Ven looked at the merrow, whose face was stony.

"What does that mean, sire?"

The Sea King waved his hand in the sunwater. A hazy picture appeared, a map of the ocean, with layers of depth marked on it.

"All natural sea life exists here, at depths that do not go below one hundred fathoms, in the Sunlit Realm," he said. "It is only above one hundred fathoms that the light can naturally reach, where plants can grow. The beast that you seek lives here, in the place known as the Twilight Realm. It is a place of mystery and almost total darkness. The creatures that live there often carry their own lights in order to find their way about in the dark. An evil place, to be certain, but not as evil as that which lies even deeper."

"I'm afraid to ask," Char said. "But I will anyway. What would that be, er, Your Majesty?"

The Sea King smiled, but it wasn't a pleasant expression.

"The vast majority of the sea is beyond the Twilight Realm, in the Realm of Midnight," he said, pointing to the chart. "The weight of the water there is immense and terrible. There are ghosts in that world, lads, and spirits that walk the Deep. You would be well advised to keep far away from those lands. Even deeper lies the Abyss, where the cracks in the world's skin give birth to volcanoes and islands of hot lava, even though the water is all but ice. And deepest still are the Trenches. There is life there, though nothing you would recognize as life. But you would have no way of getting there, no ability to survive there, and no way to see, so there's no point in discussing it further."

"This dragon you mention," said Amariel. "How big is it?"

The Sea King shuddered. "Big as a mountain, it is said. He rules a terrible reef of death and broken dreams in the Realm of Twilight, not very far from this place."

"Are you sure? Because the last sea dragon I met looked like floating vegetables."

"He's very nice," said Coreon defensively. "And a lot smarter than you think."

"This dragon is no joke," said the Sea King. "He could set the sea on fire if he chose to."

"Can you tell us where his lair is?" Ven asked.

"So you can avoid it?"

"Perhaps." Ven didn't want to lie, but he didn't want to argue, either.

The Sea King extended his hands. He put one palm on Coreon's forehead, and the other on Ven's.

Ven closed his eyes.

His whole skull began to vibrate with warmth a moment later. He could feel his brain dancing inside its cave of bone, filling with map pictures so quickly that he could not even make note of what they contained. But when the Sea King removed his hand, he was certain he could follow the maps to where the dragon's lair lay.

"I advise you again, steer clear," the Sea King said. "All are welcome at the Summer Festival, even land-livers—we actually have had a few in storms past. But you are out of place in the sea, boys."

He looked particularly at Ven. "I know your head is on fire with curiosity, lad. I am told in the upworld curiosity is considered a good thing, a gift of a sort. But curiosity has no place in the sea. It is like a sickness to female merrows, as you may well know, something they often cannot overcome. And when a female's desire to explore the human world becomes so great that she can no longer resist it, well, it is the ruin of her life."

"You can say that again," Amariel muttered.

"The greatest secret to surviving and living happily in the sea is to *mind your own business*," the Sea King said. "That, and watch your back. I know you each had your reasons for coming here." He looked at Coreon. "Yours is now successfully completed, Lirin-mer. After the Grand Derby is over, I will see to it that the Cormorant knows my will. The Summer Festival has a no-eating-the-other-guests rule for the duration of the festivities, but once Threshold is over, the law of the sea returns."

"Let me guess," Char said. "'Everythin' in the sea is food to somethin' else.'"

"And the sea is always hungry," Amariel finished.

"Exactly. I can arrange escort for you back to the coral reef, but after that you are on your own. I suggest you go home, remember what you learned here, and forget what you were lucky enough to avoid."

"Thank you, Your Majesty," Ven replied.

Just as the king had finished, one of the hippocampus reeve's men arrived behind Amariel. He slipped a bridle around the head of the blue-green hippocampus.

"Wait!" she protested as he began to lead the beast away. "Where are you taking him?"

"To the kelp pens," the male merrow answered. "Where they all go."

"Why?" Amariel said as she followed him. "Isn't he mine now?"

"No," said the male merrow, swimming away. "He and his like will be assessed by the reeve, and the reeve will decide which to keep for the next Festival. The rest, well, since many of them are barely fit to swim, will be divided up, some of them for work, some for food."

"*Food?* No!" Amariel swam after him.

"Thank you again," Ven said quickly to the king as a group of male merrows appeared, wearing the reeve's uniforms, leading a squad of glossy hippocampi in glorious racing colors to the starting gate. "Enjoy the race, and the rest of your reign. And please don't forget to send that message to the Cormorant."

"I won't," said the king. "Good seas to you."

The boys turned and swam as fast as they could to catch up with Amariel. She was following the reeve's man, nagging him all the way, until he finally stopped in the drift.

"Be on your way," he said sternly. "The Grand Derby is about to start."

He swam away with the blue-green hippocampus.

"Don't worry, Amariel," Ven said comfortingly. "I'm sure he will find a nice owner."

"What do you know, Ven?" The merrow looked like she was ready to cry. "He was pathetic, but he was mine. And if they are judging them by their potential as racing hippocampi, he's sure to end up as seafood."

A blast of the shell-horn vibrated through the drift.

"Attention, all riders to the gate," the thrum-voice announced.

"Come on, Amariel," Coreon said. "Let's get back to the racetrack. You don't want to miss the start of the Grand Derby, especially after all you've been through to get here."

"I couldn't care less about the Grand Derby now," said the merrow sadly. "I don't want to see it."

The boys looked at each other.

"You don't?" Ven asked. "Are you sure?"

"I've never been surer," the merrow said.

"Do ya wanna go back to Kingston, then?" asked Char hopefully.

"Yes. But first I want to go find the kelp pens and say goodbye to my hippocampus. His name is Teel, by the way. He told me while we were in the Roundup race."

"All right, if you want to," said Ven. "I think I saw where the reeve's man went."

They followed the male merrow's trail away from the racetrack to a far part of the Festival grounds where a small kelp forest stood. Inside the waving towers of seaweed, the raggedy losers from the Roundup race were floating, tethered to kelp trees with strong seaweed vines.

The blue-green hippocampus was in a small pen at the end, looking forlorn.

"Poor Teel!" said the merrow, swimming quickly over to him. She threw her arms around his neck. "Look how sad he is."

"He doesn't look like he feels well, Amariel," said Coreon. "Maybe he's sick."

"I'd be sick if I ran the race he did," said Char.

In the distance, the shell-horn blasted, and the thrum-voice started the Derby.

"And they're off!"

A huge roar of thrum rose from the crowd, echoing through the drift.

The sky above seemed to grow a little darker, and Ven could see rain begin to dance on the surface high above.

"Don't worry," said Amariel to the dejected hippocampus. "When the Derby is over, I'll speak to the queen. She likes me—I gave her a human gift. I bet she'll let me have you."

The eyes on each side of the hippocampus's head rolled to look at her, then rolled back again.

The thrum of the massive crowd was so strong now that it shook the ocean floor. Far as they were from the racetrack, Ven could almost tell when the racing hippocampi rounded the first turn, just by the sound of the crowd.

Then it changed.

The thrum grew louder, and flatter, as if the excitement had been stripped from it.

"What's that?" Coreon asked. "What's going on?"

"What?" Char demanded. "I don't hear anythin'."

Ven tried to clear his mind to concentrate on the change in the thrum. At first all he heard was pounding noise.

Then, an instant later, a word became clearer.

*Storm.*

*Storm storm storm storm storm.*

Suddenly, the drift turned gray and dark as the sky above the surface went black.

"What's goin' on?" Char looked around the kelp pens at the hippocampi. The giant sea horses were panicking, bucking and kicking within their tethers, whining in fear.

"I—I don't know," Ven stammered. "I can't believe a thunderstorm is scaring the hippocampi this much. Usually it only makes waves near the surface. Down this far, they should barely feel it."

The thrum from the Festival grounds had also changed. It was higher, louder.

More terrified.

And Ven caught the word it was repeating over and over. It was a word he had only heard once before, in the dark of night, on board the *Serelinda*, when the sailors told tales of storms at sea, and the shipwrecks that followed them. It was a word that was only spoken in a hushed whisper, or in prayer.

Or, below the surface, in a scream.

*Waterspout!*

# - 29 -

# The Waterspout

At first, there was nothing more than rain on the surface of the ocean and black clouds rolling above, something we had seen with each rainstorm since we came into the Deep.

Then, as we watched, a circular, light-colored disk appeared on the surface above us, surrounded by a large dark area that looked like a giant ink stain in the sea. The dark spot seemed to stretch into a pattern of light- and dark-colored spiral bands, a little like a giant pinwheel.

Below the surface, the drift began to churn violently.

A rumble went through the ocean.

B Y THE BLOWHOLE," AMARIEL WHISPERED.

In a twinkling, the entire population of the Summer Festival streamed out of the Festival grounds and vanished into the drift, swimming for their lives. The sleek Grand Derby hippocampi and their riders split apart from the racetrack and streaked off in many different directions, while the sea Lirin and other merfolk dove deeper, speeding away from the spinning circle above them.

Ven and the others watched, stunned, as a dense column of sea spray began to rise from the water, sucking upward into a thin, enormously tall funnel.

"We've got to get out of here!" Coreon shouted. "The winds above are like a tornado—we'll get sucked up into the waterspout if we're anywhere near it."

Amariel grabbed for the blue-green hippocampus as she began being pulled by the churning water up toward the surface.

"We've got to get them loose!" she shouted through her flying hair, which was flapping all around her in the water. "They're tied up—they don't stand a chance!"

Char was already working at the kelp-rope knots.

"No good," he said, his fingers desperately pulling at the tangle. "They don' use regular sailor's knots. I have no idea how to untie this."

Ven patted around in his vest pocket. He could feel the jack-rule of his great-grandfather, Magnus Polypheme, beneath the fabric, and the round bubble of elemental air beside it. *I hope it doesn't slip out in the churning of the water*, he thought as he unbuttoned the pocket. *Well, I guess if it does I can undo that moment with the Time Scissors. That would be a good use of the power.*

He slid the prized tool into his palm and rebuttoned the vest, then opened the knife, remembering the way it had felt the first time his father had put it into his hand.

It was the last time he had seen his father.

*Magnus was the youngest in his family, you know*, Pepin Polypheme had said. *As was my da, as am I. So it's only right that his jack-rule go to you now, Ven. The youngest may be at the end of the line for everything from shoes to supper, but often we are at the head of it for curiosity and common sense. Use it well—it was calibrated precisely to the Great Dial in the Nain kingdom of Castenen, and so it will always measure truer than any other instrument could. It also contains a small knife, a glass that both magnifies and sees afar, and a few other surprises—you will just have to discover those for yourself. Happy birthday, son.*

"Thank you, sir," Ven whispered, just as he had on his birthday.

Quickly he opened the knife.

"Hold the tether taut," he said to Amariel. She pulled the seaweed rope as tight as she could, and Ven began sawing through it with his knife.

The waterspout now towered above them in the center of black storm clouds. Below the surface, the sea was spinning madly. The coral throne stand ripped from its coral bed and hurtled through the drift, narrowly missing the kelp pens. The beautiful thrones tumbled past, breaking into smaller and smaller pieces as they went by.

With a snap, Teel's tether broke free.

"He's loose!" Amariel cried. "Thank you!"

"Let's get the others," Ven said to Coreon and Char. "Amariel, hold on to Teel. Now that he's no longer tied, he may go flying."

"Or *you* may." Char pulled another kelp rope straight. "If you cut this one, Ven, I think it'll turn all the others loose—they're tied together."

A strong underwater wave blasted over them, pulling them up toward the surface. Ven struggled not to drop the jack-rule as he was dragged toward the rising funnel. The wave rolled over completely, returning them to the bottom as it made a full spiral.

"That'll happen again—hurry up!" Coreon was trying to turn the wild hippocampi right side up again as they flailed around, helpless in the boiling foam.

The seat of the Sea King's throne suddenly shot up toward the surface and into the black air above, sucked up into the waterspout. The giant water tornado began moving east, tearing the ocean floor up below it as it went, filling the drift with blinding sand.

Ven felt the seaweed snap beneath his hands as the tether broke free.

"Quick—get on and ride as fast as you can," he thought to the others. "Ride west if you can, away from the funnel." He grabbed Amariel's hand. "Hold on to me. I'm not sure Teel is going to be fast enough."

"We'll just have to help him, then," she thought back at him.

Char pulled himself awkwardly up onto the orange hippocampus with the sunflower mane, while Coreon mounted the blue one with black spots. Ven climbed on the yellow and gray sea horse that had stopped for lunch in the middle of the race.

"Go on," he thought to the other hippocampi. "Save yourselves."

Then he wrapped one arm clumsily around the neck of the yellow hippocampus.

"Get us out of here," he said. The thought burned in his head.

The sea creatures obeyed, dashing off to the west, then veering into several different directions.

Another undersea wave swept past, spinning the mounts around.

Ven lost his grip on the merrow's hand as he and his mount were swung around in a fast circle.

Amariel, on Teel, looked over Ven's shoulder and gasped.

Ven turned.

The waterspout was coming, ripping up the ocean floor as it approached. A swirling wall of black water swept across what was left of the Festival grounds, driving debris in front of it.

Heading straight for them.

"Go!" Ven shouted in his head. "Keep going! *Go!*"

Char's orange hippocampus, along with Coreon's blue sea horse and the yellow one Ven was riding, tore off toward the west, swimming as fast as they could. Only Amariel's mount lagged behind, puffing and panting, struggling to keep up. Ven kept squeezing the yellow sea horse's neck, trying not to get too far ahead of the merrow and her blue-green friend, but it was no use.

Over his shoulder he could see her falling farther and farther behind.

And the waterspout coming closer and closer, the black wall of swirling filth rushing ahead of it.

Then, as he struggled to hold his sea horse's back, the wall caught up with the merrow and Teel.

Ven watched in horror as the blue-green hippocampus and the merrow were swallowed up before his eyes.

He screamed her name, his mouth filling with salt water.

"Ven! Ven! Hurry up! Where are you?" Char's thrum seemed very far away.

A moment later his friend's vibrations were drowned out in the tornado that was splitting the sea.

Despair washed over him only a few seconds before the wave of debris did.

It hit him square across the shoulders, making his head snap back with a sickening *crack*.

*Then everything went black.*

*I think the yellow hippocampus dashed out from beneath me as I lost my grip on her neck, but I can't be sure.*

*I'd like to think she got away, that I was just holding her back, and that she was faster once I was off her.*

*I'll never know.*

When Ven awoke, he was alone on the ocean floor, in the dark.

He thought he might be lying on a piece of broken coral because whatever was poking him in the back was sharp, but there was no way to see for certain. Even the special sight that Nain had in the darkness could not penetrate the complete, overwhelming black of the sea.

*I wonder how long I've been unconscious,* he thought. *It must be night now, by the look of things.* His stomach dropped. *And that means the last day of summer is over. Threshold has come and gone—and the Sea King didn't get a chance to send his message to the Cormorant. Which means the attack will begin when the sun comes up.*

He felt like crying, but no tears came to his eyes, awash as they already were in salt water that was pressing down with great force on him.

He tried to concentrate on the thrum of his friends, but could feel nothing specific in the still-unsettled drift. He closed his eyes again, trying to keep his breathing steady and his heart from pounding too hard. His thrum came out like a call in a wild wind.

*Amariel? Can you hear me?*

Nothing but the slurping and swishing of the drift answered him.

He felt around in his pocket for the air stone. He already knew it was there, because he was breathing, but there was comfort in feeling the bubble beneath his fingers, still with him even after the entire sea had seemingly turned upside down around him.

*If I take it out, I will have light*, he thought. *But if there is no other light, whatever else is around me will see me. That might be worse than being in the dark.*

At that moment, however, it was hard to imagine anything worse.

Far away, he felt a familiar *ping* against his skull. He could almost place the location of the feeling, in his forehead, above his right eye.

*Ven? Ven, is that you?*

Ven's heart pounded harder with excitement.

*Char? Char! I'm over here. Where are you?*

His best friend's answer seemed very far away.

*Here. I'm comin'. Stay where you are and keep thinkin' my name. I'll come to you.*

*Can you see?* Ven thought.

*Not a bit. But I'm human, so I'm prolly more used to it than you are. Hold still.*

Ven exhaled and lay still, trying to keep his thoughts clear.

*Char. Char. Char*, he thought, over and over. *Char.*

The sand beneath him wriggled, and Ven sat up, blind in the dark.

*Ugh! Char!*

"No need to shout." Char's thrum was right next to him.

A blue glow appeared, blinding in the pitch darkness.

Ven shielded his stinging eyes.

Char was hovering in the drift a stone's throw away, his hands cupped around a cold, gleaming pinpoint of light.

"I'm so glad to see you," Ven said, taking his hands down as his eyes adjusted. "Are you all right?"

Char nodded. "Neck's a bit sore, but it's amazin' we both still have our air stones and knapsacks."

"It's amazing we're both alive. I lost my spear." Ven swam up from the ocean floor and over to his friend. His shoulders and back felt bruised, but otherwise his body seemed to be working.

"Any sign of Amariel or Coreon?"

*I'm here*, Coreon's thrum replied from a distance. *Put your light away until I get there. I can see you—and so can a whole bunch of giant squid nearby. They're on their way to find you right now.*

Char quickly slipped his air stone back in his pocket, dousing the light.

The two boys waited in darkness, hanging in the drift, for what seemed like a very long time. Finally they heard Coreon's underwater voice very nearby, its inconsistent tone a little deeper than before.

"You two both in one piece?"

"Yes," Ven replied. "How about you?"

"Fine." Coreon swam nearer. "Any sign of Amariel?"

Ven closed his eyes and tried to find her thrum. After a few moments' concentration, he shook his head sadly.

"Not even a whisper," he said. "I can't hear her at all."

"Me neither," said Char. "What happened to your hippocampi?"

"I don't know," said Ven. "I think mine bucked me off her back, or got swept out from under me. I hope she got away."

"Mine too," said Char.

"Mine as well." Coreon's thrum seemed somewhat more spirited. "Do you hear that?"

Ven concentrated, but felt nothing out of the ordinary.

"No—what are you hearing?"

"There's a strange, sort of sad, helpless thrum not terribly far from here—can you feel it now?"

Ven thought he could, but he didn't recognize it.

"I do, but it doesn't sound like Amariel to me."

"No, it doesn't," Coreon said. "But I think it might be Teel."

Ven quickly unbuttoned his pocket and pulled out his own air stone.

"Where? Can you find a direction?"

Coreon listened again, then nodded. "I think so."

"Then we'll follow you."

The sea-Lirin boy nodded again, then started off into the drift.

With the light out, the black ocean looked ghostly. Both of his friends' faces appeared, disappeared, then reappeared as they passed through the cold shadows cast by the glowing stone. They swam over broken bones of long-buried ships encrusted with claw-like rusticles. Ghost shrimp flitted in and out between the bones, while goliath groupers, enormous pink speckled fish twice as big as each of them, swam slowly past.

It seemed to Ven that he was floating through an entirely different world.

He and Char followed Coreon for a very long time over an ocean floor that was now almost totally absent of plant life. The heavy ceiling of the black water above pressed down on them, making Ven's heart beat hard in his chest.

"It's a good thing Amariel told us Teel's name," Char said as Coreon swam ahead at the edge of the cold blue light. "I'm not sure we'd ever be able to find his thrum in the sea if she hadn't. That thing about names having power in the sea sure seems true."

"Teel trusted her right away," Ven agreed. "She really does have a skill with hippocampi. I bet she wins the Grand Trophy one day, just like she wants to."

"I think I see him," said Coreon.

They quickened their pace.

At the edge of the light Ven could see something vertical in the drift, trembling violently. As they got closer, he recognized the giant sea horse, paler it seemed than he had been before, shaking nervously, his round eyes wide and darting.

"Teel!" he called as they got closer. "Teel! Do you know where Amariel is?"

The hippocampus stared at them.

Then it bobbed forward slightly, as if it were bowing to them.

Ven glanced down at the ocean floor at what looked like a small mound of rags and broken coral, half-buried in sand below the giant sea horse.

He held up the air stone to see it better, then gasped.

"Oh, no," he whispered. "Oh, no. It's Amariel."

# ~ 30 ~

# At the Edge of Twilight

CHAR DOVE DOWN TO THE OCEAN FLOOR, FOLLOWED AN instant later by Coreon.

"Ven, hold the light closer," he said. "Don't drop the stone."

Ven obeyed. His hands had gone numb. He watched as Char turned the motionless merrow over onto her back, clearing the sand away from her neck.

"She's still breathin'," Char said. "But barely. Her gills are barely flutterin'."

"Here, you get out your stone too," Coreon said to Char. "We need more light."

He lifted the merrow off the seafloor while Char fumbled around in his pocket. Char cast a baleful eye at the trembling hippocampus.

"This is *your* fault, ya fat waste o' breath," he said. "If she hadn't insisted on savin' *you*, she'd have—"

"Stop it," Ven interrupted. "We owe Teel thanks—if he hadn't stayed with Amariel, we would never have found her."

"Yeah. Right." Char glared at the trembling beast one last time, then held his light stone aloft in the drift.

The three boys and the frightened hippocampus all winced as the intense blue light brightened the murky black depths.

Now that they could see a little better, Ven was even more

nervous. He could see in the cold light that Amariel had lost a good deal of her coloring. Her skin and scales looked bleached, and her mouth was open, her teeth showing, something she would never had allowed if she were conscious. Coreon lifted her wrist and then dropped it, hoping she would respond, but her arm fell, limp, to her side.

"What do we do now, chief?" Coreon's thrum was even deeper in pitch than before, and more stable.

"I have no idea. Do you have any sense of where we are?"

Coreon shook his head.

"The waterspout tore up a good deal of the seabed," he said. "The ocean floor isn't the same as it was. And if even if it were, there's no way to tell whether it's just a moonless night in the Sunlit Realm, or if we've fallen over the edge into Twilight." He gave the merrow a gentle shake, but she did not respond. "If it's the first possibility, when the morning comes we will know which way to go to get back to the coral reef. I'm assuming you are ready to go home now, and not pursue any more sea dragons or mythical trees, yes?"

"Absolutely," Ven said, struggling to keep the kelp he'd had for lunch down. "Char, you may blame Teel, but this is all *my* fault. You told me from the beginning this was a bad idea, and you were right."

"Hooey," Char said. "If we hadn't o' come with her, she woulda been here anyway. She made it pretty clear that seein' the Festival was somethin' she was gonna do. And it *was* an amazin' sight, before the waterspout, wasn't it?" Ven nodded distantly. "All right. So she got to see somethin' she always dreamed of seein', and we got to explore the Deep. Like you said, one day we'll have a bajillion tales to tell the sailors on board the *Serelinda*, or whatever ship we're on. Things happen sometimes that you can't control. I apologize, Teel."

The hippocampus just stared at him.

"Have you given her up for dead, then?" Coreon asked. "You sound like it."

"Heck no," Char said before Ven could reply. "I just don' want Ven to spend the night beatin' himself up. He does that enough at home. So I guess we wait until mornin', figure out which way is east, then head home, right?"

"Maybe," said Coreon. "That only works if the waterspout didn't throw us too far. I was unconscious during the ride, so I'm not sure how long it carried us. It could have been a few leagues—or for many miles. And if it took us a long way, well, we could have fallen over the edge into Twilight."

"And if we did—"

"Then the sun won't be coming up, or at least when it does, it will only change the water from total darkness to gray total darkness. We could try to find our way back, but we will probably end up wandering, lost, in the sea forever. Or at least until our luck runs out and something eats us."

Char blew out his breath, sending a stream of bubbles into the drift as he did.

Ven bent down beside Amariel and touched her arm. It was hard to tell for certain underwater, but she seemed colder than usual. He fought back the panic that was rising inside him.

"I think we need to find a safe place until morning," he said, looking around at the sea beyond the glow of the air stones. "Do you think there's a shipwreck or something where at least Amariel can be sheltered?"

"You stay with her, an' I'll go look," Char said.

"Don't go far," Coreon advised.

"No worries about that," Char said.

The light around Amariel dimmed as Char swam away, clutching his air stone in front of him. He left a trail behind himself, a little like a tunnel of light, and Ven could see him holding the stone aloft, checking the murky darkness beyond where Amariel was lying. A few moments later he returned, bringing the light with him.

His face was pale in the blue-white glow.

"I don' know *what* this place is, but I'm not sure I want to take shelter in it." His thrum was shaky.

"What's out there?" Ven asked.

"Go look for yourself. It's sort of hard to describe."

"Let's all go," Coreon said. "We have to get Amariel out of the drift. If a predator comes along, or more than one, we won't be able to defend her where we are. Let me carry her so you don't risk dropping your stone."

The hippocampus bobbed its head in the drift. Ven looked over at him.

"Can you carry her, Teel?"

The giant sea horse nodded.

He and the other boys exchanged a glance.

"That's prolly a good idea," Char said. "You lift her, Coreon, an' I'll get her across his back."

Teel shook his head, then curled and uncurled his spiral tail.

"Oh," said Ven. "Well, we can try letting you carry her. But if you think you're going to drop her, tell us quickly."

Together they carried Amariel over to the chubby hippocampus and held her where he could curl his tail around her. The giant sea horse bobbed down to the ocean floor, but then righted himself.

"All right," Ven said. "Let's go see what's beyond the ring of light."

*Walking into the complete darkness is something I'm not sure I could have done alone. Under the sea, the blackness is much heavier than a moonless night in the upworld, especially for me. In the upworld nighttime, even if there is no other light, I can see shapes, and sense what things have weight. It's easy to separate out dark emptiness from solid things that are all around you but not visible.*

*In the sea, there is no weight to feel. Non-living things do not give off thrum, so you can sometimes come right next to something massive that you had no idea was there if there is no light. It would be as if you were walking across a big open meadow in the upworld and suddenly were standing next to a castle you hadn't known was there.*

*Which was a little bit like what happened.*

Ahead of the circle of light, what looked like a giant rock cliff suddenly appeared.

Char held his air stone up to cast the light a little farther.

"What do ya make o' *that?*" he said.

Towering above them was a sunken ship, broken at the keel line down the middle, but almost entirely intact. It lay, partially buried, on the sandy ocean floor, its bones bleached as clean as it might have been in the air of the upworld. Not a barnacle or rusticle or under-sea creature of any sort was visible on its decaying hull. The main-mast was intact, a tattered flag still flapping in the drift off the crow's nest.

"That doesn't look like any other shipwreck we've seen, that's for certain," Ven agreed. "But maybe it's just because the water is deeper here, and it's colder. Maybe it's too cold for the normal ocean life that makes a crust on ship bones to grow here."

Coreon shook his head.

"It's cold, but not that cold here," he said. "I've heard that cold seas can preserve ships, but this one seems too clean to even be possible."

"I've never seen ship bones like that," Ven agreed.

"Well, you would have if you had held your stone a little to the left," Char said.

Ven looked puzzled. He turned with the small bubble of blue light, and almost dropped it in shock.

Beside the enormous galleon was another huge ship, also in al-most perfect condition, with a gaping hole in the hull, but otherwise intact, as clean and free of sea life as the ones outside Ven's family factory in Vaarn.

And, while he could not see very far in the darkness beyond the glowing blue bubble, it appeared that there might be a line of simi-larly broken ships stretching into the gloom, side by side, on a reef of sorts.

A reef that sparkled.

"Criminey!" Char whispered. "Look at all the *gold*, Ven."

Ven didn't need the suggestion. His eyes were already locked on the sight of mountains of coins, of every possible kind, taller than the houses of Vaarn, on which the ghostly ships were seated. Lower down on the reef was a line of ships' wheels, like the ones that steered the *Serelinda*, each carefully mounted in the pile of treasure. There were many more of them, and they were turning slowly in the drift, like windmills on top of a long underwater hill.

But by far the most unsettling sight was what at first had appeared to be a gathering of frozen women, their glassy eyes staring at him in the devouring darkness. Then, as he looked closer, he realized what he was seeing was a collection of figureheads, the wooden sculptures carved into the bows of almost every large sailing ship. His eyes wandered over them, taking in the wide variety of colors of their hair and clothing, their different facial expressions, which ranged from warm and welcoming to stern and forbidding. There was even one that seemed very familiar, as if he had seen it before. He stared at it, trying to make out its details in the pale light of the air stone.

The statue of the woman had its eyes closed, unlike the others he could see in the halo of light. The figurehead had been damaged, as if it had been in a great fire or explosion, but was still intact enough for Ven to tell that it had once been of a dark-haired woman in what had been a flowing blue gown. She was smiling, her arms stretched out behind her, with watery-looking wings dripping from them. The statue looked as if she had once been enjoying the sun and the wind on her face.

Then, in a sickening rush of memory, he recalled where he had seen her before.

It was on the morning of his last birthday, the day of his first Inspection. He had admired her from the pier. He was watching Old Max, his father's master painter, apply the finishing touches to her, just before he painted the name of the ship on the bow above her. The name of a ship was a secret before it was officially launched, but as a special treat, Max had allowed him to look at the oilcloth from which he was copying that name, not knowing what it was himself, because Max couldn't read.

Ven could almost hear his father's voice in his head again, just as he had that morning.

*No one hears a ship's name until she is christened. It's bad luck.*

And now, the figurehead of that ship was here, lying on the ocean floor in the dark Realm of Twilight.

Beautifully maintained.

Carefully collected.

Along with hundreds of others.

In the cold depths of the black water, the enormity of their situation was beginning to dawn on him.

"By the Blowhole," he whispered. He had no idea what the expression meant, but every sailor or merrow he had ever met had used it when they sensed trouble.

And trouble was looming from all around them.

"Char—do you know what this is?"

His best friend was ghostly pale. He could only nod.

Ven replied to his own question.

"We've stumbled into a sea dragon's lair."

All around them, like a great clap of evil thunder, the drift itself seemed to answer them. There was an acid in the thrum that stung the insides of Ven's ears and head.

*Indeed you have. How unfortunate for you.*

Then, like a giant fireball a thousand times brighter and hotter than the explosion that had blown up his father's ship and that of the Fire Pirates attacking it, the sea lit up around them.

Blinding them.

# ~ 31 ~

# *Lancel*

P LEASE," VEN THOUGHT DESPERATELY AT THE DRAGON. "IF you're going to blast me, please spare my friends. The merrow is unconscious, and had no idea we were bringing her here. If she had, she would never have allowed it. Cor—I mean, the sea Lirin and the human were forced to come along. And the hippocampus as well. Please don't flame them."

*Don't be ridiculous,* the hideous thrum-voice answered. It sounded sickly amused. It was so powerful that it shook the drift around them. *The hippocampus, like all of his kind, is a distant cousin of mine, and feeling ill. I would never harm a relative in his condition. The rest of you are another matter, however. You are trespassers, interlopers. Kindly move away from the hippocampus, please.*

Trembling, the three boys started to swim away from the reef of treasure.

Teel's round eyes rolled nervously, and he shook his head. He swam after Ven, dragging Amariel, still curled in the spiral of his tail, with him.

*Teel.* The thrum-voice was disapproving, and it rattled the inside of Ven's skull. *You know better than that. Don't get in the way.*

Ven stopped in the drift. "You know the hippocampus's name?"

*I know your name too, Ven, you fool.* The thrum of the wicked voice felt proud, as if it were bragging. *Each of your names has been spoken in my realm—so I have them all.*

"Wonderful," muttered Coreon.

*That's not a bad thing, Coreon. It's so impersonal to be devoured by a stranger. Now, move aside, Teel.*

"With due respect, we don't know *your* name," said Ven. "That makes you a stranger still."

*Good point.* A massive wave of sand rolled up from the ocean floor, blasting between the ship bones and adding sting to the underwater light that was blinding their eyes.

Behind the wave of sand an enormous head emerged, dwarfing the massive broken ships. It was serpentine in nature, with powerful jaws from which gleaming, sword-like teeth protruded. Its hide was green black, and its eyes burned with a light as intensely blue as the one from the stones of elemental air. Kelp-like structures hung between its teeth and from the pointed horns on its head, and it seemed to slither as it rose from the ocean floor, until it towered in the drift high above them. Its eyes cast a cold blue light over them all.

"I am Lancel," the beast said proudly. "It is a name feared throughout the Deep, which you would discover if you weren't about to be eaten. And I hope you all feel suitably honored. While I have feasted on many humans, merrow, and Lirin-mer in my time, you are the first son of Earth that has had the privilege of being my supper. Congratulations. Now, Teel, drop the merrow and get out of the way."

"That seems a waste," Ven said, thinking as quickly as he could in the heavy pressure of the Deep. His brain was struggling with a memory, and he could feel it rising to the surface, but it was still not within his recollection yet. "I thought dragons were curious to know everything about the world. Do you not want to at least see if there is something I might know that you do not?"

A blast of acid smoke rolled forth from the beast's nostrils. The boys and Teel darted out of the way just as the sand beneath them exploded in fire that burned bright as daylight, even in the depths of the sea.

"Arrogant boy. You have *nothing* that interests me," the beast replied haughtily. "I am the keeper of the secrets of the Deep. In my collection are more than a thousand human ships, each of them full of the stories, songs, dreams, and fears of the men who sailed them—it's a library of the greatest information ever to pass from continent to continent in the upworld. I know the names of each and every one of those ships. What could you possibly know that I do not already know, or have that I do not already own the story of?" The searing blue eyes turned on Char, making him tremble violently. "You do not even know *your own name*, human. What do you think you could possibly tell me that has any value to me?"

I looked at Char.

He was already white in the bright glare that had lit up the sea when the dragon appeared.

But now he was almost colorless.

All the pressure of the salt water had made my brain slow. I had forgotten until that moment what I had known almost as long as I had known Char himself—that he was an orphan, a child with no past, not even the memory of his real name.

Once, within the Gated City, in a place called the Stolen Alleyway, a sweet-voiced woman had offered him the chance to see a memory of his childhood in exchange for a gold coin. Char had not been able to explain to us what exactly he had gotten in return for his money, but it was more important to him than anything. The name Char was a joking one, a reference to his tendency to burn the food he cooked. It had been given to him when he was little more than a baby by sailors who knew him as a fellow member of the crew, a cook's mate, but who had no idea where he had come from. He believed that someone had really named him once, long ago, but he had no idea what that name had been.

*So in mentioning his lack of one now, I knew the dragon was speaking to his deepest and ugliest fear.*

*And I finally understood what it meant to have power over someone by having possession of his name.*

*Because at that moment, if Lancel had told Char's heart to stop beating, it would have.*

---

*Ven.*

A tickle of thrum vibrated on his forehead, almost too weak to have noticed.

But Ven recognized it immediately.

*Amariel?* He turned to the shaking sea horse. Neither of the other boys appeared to have heard it. The merrow remained broken and motionless in the curl of Teel's tail.

*You've—forgotten.* The words formed with painful slowness in his head. *Don't—forget.*

*What?* Ven asked as quietly as he could. *What have I forgotten?*

The thrum seemed to puff against his brain like the tiny seeds of a dandelion caught by the wind, then dissolved in the vastness of the sea.

*Black—Ivory.*

It took a long moment for Ven to catch the words in the drift. Then his head began to burn, not with curiosity, but with memory.

*The scale*, he thought. *The scale!*

The reason he had thought to seek out a sea dragon in the first place.

Lancel was growing impatient with the hippocampus, who was hovering as close as he could to Ven and Char.

"For badness' sake, Teel, *get out of the way*," he demanded. "You are not an actual dragon, you know. Sparing you is my custom and a courtesy, not a requirement. We may be distantly related, but that won't keep even you safe if you continue to defy me. Family connections never win out over supper. Now, last chance. Move, or you'll be the salad course of my meal."

The blue-green hippocampus stopped shaking. He hung in the drift, motionless. A little of his color drained from his hide, but otherwise he did not move.

The great beast sighed. More steam rushed forth out of his nose, making them scurry out of the way again.

"Very well," Lancel said. "Hold still, please. I like it when my food is evenly done. And a nice, crispy skin is a rare delicacy in the Deep."

Ven was fumbling around in his pocket. He ran his finger over the sharp edge of the dragon scale in the Black Ivory sleeve.

"Wait one moment, if you please," he thought desperately. "I believe you will want to see this."

"I doubt it." The sea dragon inhaled, sucking a great deal of the drift in as he did.

Ven struggled to remain upright and to hold on to the Black Ivory sleeve as his feet, like those of Coreon and Char, were pulled forward in the drift.

With shaking hands, he pulled out the scale on which the image and runes of Frothta had been inscribed.

The card from Madame Sharra's deck glowed with an eerie light similar to that of the stone of elemental air.

Only golden.

The sea dragon stopped. He held his breath.

"I've come all this way to return this to you," Ven said.

Lancel turned his head to the side. "Hold it up so I can see it better," he said.

Ven held the scale aloft, his fingers clenched tightly.

The beast's blazing blue eyes narrowed. He stared at the ancient dragon scale while the boys held their breath.

Then he chuckled.

It was an ugly laugh, a laugh that rumbled through the sea, shaking the ships in his collection until the sails and flags on their masts flapped as if in a high wind and causing the ships' wheels to spin violently.

"You think *that* interests me?" he said, a nasty note creeping into his thrum. "A fortune teller's scale? I gave one just like it to your ancestors ages ago. There are five of them in my collection, rescued from the sea into which they had fallen. I have no need of that. It's like, well, like the clipping from one of your toenails, Son of Earth."

Ven could only remain frozen, his hand aloft in the drift, stunned.

"Well, this has all been very amusing, but my stomach is growling," the dragon said. "If it's of any comfort to you, Ven, your race would be glad to know that you ended your days as fuel for the fire gems in my belly. Your life would not have been a total waste, at least in the eyes of the Nain, if they knew what had happened to you. Your friends, on the other hand, will disappear into the ashes, and no one will remember their names—especially *you*, Char. It's ironic that what you were called in life describes your death perfectly. Farewell."

The drift shook as he inhaled again.

Ven's eyes darted about as he tried desperately to pry loose the memory that had been looming near the edge of his consciousness.

Finally, just as the dragon reared back, it was there.

"Wait!" he shouted. "Wait! I do know something *you* don't— something about your collection. And I'm the only person in the whole world who knows it!"

# - 32 -

# A Risky Negotiation

THE SEA DRAGON DREW HIMSELF UP TO AN EVEN GREATER height. His horned head was crowned in the darkness of the Twilight Realm above him.

"That's a lie," he said, but his tone was uncertain, as if he could feel the truth in Ven's thrum. "I know the name of every ship, and have counted every coin, every shiny *pebble* in my hoard. It's my life's work. To suggest you know anything about it that I do not is insulting. I think I will eat you raw instead of roasting you first."

"You know I am telling the truth, because you have my name," Ven said. He was guessing, but something in the dragon's eyes made him believe he was right. "You can feel the truth in my thrum, or you would not have stopped your fiery breath. You know I do not lie, and it worries you. It *should* worry you, because if you kill me, you will never know what I know."

"And what is it you claim to know?"

Ven pointed at the row of figureheads, to the bruised statue of the smiling woman with the dark hair and the flowing blue sleeves.

"I know her name," he said.

The dragon smirked.

"She has no name," he said. "She is like your friend Char in that regard, unnamed. Everything in my hoard speaks to me—and when I asked her name, she did not know it. It was sad."

"That's because her ship was never christened," Ven continued. "It was being inspected when Fire Pirates attacked, and then, well, I did something foolish to drive them away, and blew up their ship, and hers, in the process." He could feel the dragon's eyes upon him, and it made him shiver. "But I know what the ship was to be named—I even carved the name into a piece of driftwood from the wreck before it sank. But she has a name, even if she doesn't know it. And if you kill me, well, I will take the knowledge of that name with me. So you will never completely own your collection, because there will be one small piece that I had, that you never will."

The eyes in the head atop the towering green-black neck gleamed at him for a moment, considering. Then the neck descended, swinging the immense head down until it was directly in front of Ven.

"All right," Lancel said quietly, but with deadly threat. "I'll bite. What is it?"

The smell of acrid smoke filled Ven's lungs, making them burn. Though it took every ounce of his courage, he managed to shake his head.

"With respect. Lancel, I have a friend who is a dragon, and though you may think me a fool, I know at least a little bit of dragons' ways. I need to have your word that you agree to my terms first."

The glowing eyes glared at him, the brightness making his own sting with pain.

"What are your terms?" the dragon asked. Each word had a bite to it.

Ven steadied himself. He looked at the vast hoard of treasure and broken ships rotting quietly on the ocean floor. It seemed to stretch on for miles. *Keep your head about you*, he thought to himself. "Well, first, obviously, you need to agree to grant us safe passage out of your realm."

"That's easy enough," said Lancel. His thrum was smooth and agreeable. "Tell me her name."

Ven shook his head.

"Not yet. I know how dragons can twist words to mean what they want them to mean. So it would have to be more than just a casual agreement, but an ironclad oath to the Earth that you will never do anything to harm me and these friends of mine—including the hippocampus—in any way, *ever*. I need to be sure you are agreeing to let us go and never try to take revenge on us in the future—which to a dragon can mean a heartbeat after you have what you want."

The dragon's eyes narrowed to glowing slits.

"Don't toy with me," the beast said. The threat in the pounding thrum was unmistakable.

"Believe me, I'm not," said Ven. "I just want to make certain we have a clear understanding."

"Hmm. In that case, how's this?"

The drift around them swirled violently as an immense claw, a talon as black as the sea had been, swept out from behind the reef of ship bones and, before any of them could breathe, pinned Char to the sandy bottom of the sea by the throat.

"Let *me* be clear, Ven," said Lancel. "You will tell me the name, or you will watch your unnamed friend be run through with my talon and bleed to death before your next breath. Is that clear enough?"

Ven exhaled, willing himself to be calm.

On board the <u>Serelinda</u>, the sailors are always busy by day. There is a shift that is busy all night as well. But when the wind dies down for a while and there is little to do, they often turn to games of cards.

There is one game in particular that they like to play, a game called by many inappropriate names, but Char and I call it Malarkey, a human word for <u>nonsense</u>. It's a game where the players do not show their cards until the end, but tell the other

*players what they have in their hands—sometimes it's true,
sometimes it's not, but you have to be able to bluff convincingly
when you're not holding many good cards.*

*I'd say at this moment I am only holding one.*

"That's malarkey," Ven said. His thrum was steady. "If I tell you
without your oath, he's dead anyway, as we all are. Do you want to
hear the rest of my terms?"

From beneath the sea dragon's enormous talon, Char shuddered
but said nothing.

The cold eyes stared at him in silence. Then, finally, the beast
spoke again.

"Tell me."

"I want you to answer three questions, truthfully and completely.
They will not compromise your power, or harm you in any way.
Since dragons know things no one else does, I don't want to miss
this chance to satisfy my curiosity."

The sea was filled with a harsh, chuckling thrum.

"You know what they say about curiosity, don't you, Ven?"

"That it killed the cat?"

"I've always heard that it sinks a ship—and since I hoard sunken
ships, that makes me rather fond of the curiosity of humans. And
other land-livers. Well, this has been amusing, but it's growing dull.
If I were to just kill you, then you will no longer know her name,
now, will you?"

"That's right," Ven admitted. "I no longer will. But if you kill me,
you will *never* know it. At least I will have had it for a little while.
Let's trade. I am willing to give you her name and *forget* it, if you
will guarantee our safety and tell me what I want to know."

A gleam of interest made the huge eyes glow even more brightly.

"What is it that you want to know?"

Ven thought hard, trying to see the questions as if they were
moves on a chessboard, as his father had taught him when making a

business deal. He finally decided that he had nothing to lose by asking his most important question first.

"How can I save Amariel?"

The dragon snorted.

"Predictable. Well, I can certainly tell you that—but I suspect it's not the question that is *really* bedeviling you, Son of Earth. If your friend were not injured, what would you have asked me?"

Against his will, Ven's curiosity rose until it tickled the hairs on his head floating in the heavy water of the Twilight Realm. He tried to keep the words in check, but they fought their way out of his mouth in spite of himself.

"How can I find Frothta, the Tree of Water?"

The giant beast threw back his horned head and laughed. The floor of the ocean shook, rattling the mountains of coins and causing the broken ships to pitch about as if on the waves of the surface above. The line of wheels spun crazily and the carefully displayed figureheads trembled as if they were alive.

And terrified.

"We have a bargain, Son of Earth. But you will not like the answer."

## - 33 -

# A Bargain Struck and Fulfilled

WHATEVER THAT ANSWER IS, I WILL ACCEPT IT, AS LONG AS IT is the truth," Ven said.

"Very well," said the sea dragon. "I agree to your terms."

"Not to be offensive, but would you please just say what those terms are, and take the oath?"

The giant sea serpent sighed comically.

"Whoever taught you the art of negotiation must have had some skill at it. All right." Lancel lifted his giant talon from Char's throat, then reached over with it to the figurehead display and wrapped it around the damaged statue of the smiling woman with the closed eyes and the watery sleeves. He set it directly in front of Ven. "In return for the knowledge of the name of this figurehead, which you will forfeit forever, I swear to bring no harm to you, Char, Coreon, Amariel, and Teel, and to answer three of your questions truthfully, to the best of my ability. There. Satisfied? The answer had best be *yes*."

"Yes."

"Very well, then." The sea dragon extended his enormous claw, flexed the talons, then held it directly under Ven's chin. "Give her name to me."

Ven tried not to move. He closed his eyes, remembering the first time he had seen her, the sunlight on her wooden face, the wind shaking the sails above her as if the cloth sheets were itching to weigh anchor and get out to sea. How happy he had been on that day, he thought, when finally he would have the adventure he had been dreaming of.

He could never have imagined it would have led him here, to the blackness of the Twilight Realm, a hundred or more fathoms deep in the sea.

With the sulfur breath of an ancient beast washing over him.

His palm itched. Ven clenched his fist tighter, thinking about the gift of the Time Scissors that the first scale he had drawn had bestowed on him. *If I had it to do all over again, would I have stayed home that day?* he wondered.

Never.

"Her name is *Angelia*," he said.

The water around him swirled as the giant claw swept in front of him as if trying to slash his face. Ven opened his eyes.

The dragon was staring at him, the look of malice gone, replaced by curiosity. He was holding his clenched claw aloft in the drift.

"Wait a moment," Lancel said. Ven could see him shifting his gargantuan body around, searching the vast hoard of treasure behind him with his tail. Finally, when he located what he was looking for, he brought the tail forward over his head, clutching something small and wooden. The dragon laid it in the sand at his feet.

It was a broken piece of the hull of a ship, with a line of rusted rivets down the keel seam. Its edges were singed black, as if by fire that had burned like acid. A single word was carved into it.

*Angelia*, it read.

"Do you recognize this?" the dragon asked. The thrum of his thoughts was soft.

Ven stared at it.

"I think so," he said after a long moment. "I think that may be a piece of a ship my father built that I was inspecting on my birthday."

"Did you carve this word into it?"

Ven's forehead furrowed. "Yes. I believe I did."

"And what does it say?"

He stared at the wooden planks as hard as he could.

*Old Max, the Nain who is the master painter in my father's factory, doesn't know how to read. He used to ask me what various things said, things that I could read from the time I was just a tot of twenty or so years. I could not understand how someone could be that much older than me and yet unable to do so for himself.*

*Looking at the word on the wooden fragment was a little like it must have been for Max. I could see the letters, and individually I knew what they were, but it was as if the word itself was written in another language, or runes, pictures or symbols that meant something to other people who can translate them, but not to me.*

*Even more strangely, I cannot remember them even when I read them in my journals. They scatter across the page in front of my eyes and run from me, refusing to be read.*

*It's like the dragon reached into the recesses of my mind and dragged the word out from within my brain, leaving nothing behind but the hole.*

"I have no idea," he said finally.

The dragon's smile spread slowly across its massive face, its teeth gleaming like swords in the drift.

"Excellent," he said. "Now, what are your other questions?"

Ven continued to stare at the wooden scrap of the ship for a moment longer. Then he shook his head as if shaking off sleep.

"Hmmm? Oh, yes. The ship, the *Athenry*. Is it part of your collection?"

"No," the dragon said. "I have never heard of it."

The boys looked at each other in disappointment.

"Oh, well," Ven said. "I guess that will just have to remain a mystery."

"That happens a lot in life," Lancel said. "Even when one is a dragon and knows the secrets of all the world, there are some things that are just destined to remain in shadow. It makes life interesting, I suppose. I won't count that one—so I'll give you another question out of the, er, goodness of my heart." He chuckled. "What is your last question?"

Ven looked embarrassed.

"Uh—what is the Great Blowhole?" he asked.

The dragon grinned even more broadly.

"I've no idea," he said. "There are many vents in the depths of the ocean Trenches, black smokers where volcanic lava and steam belch forth from the fiery core of the earth beneath the floor of the sea. I was born in such a place—that's where my breath comes from, acidic metals released into the sea in the hot steam of those vents. They could be called 'blowholes,' but bigger ones open all the time, so I don't know that there is one 'great blowhole.' I think it's just an expression, a myth without any truth behind it. Sadly, sometimes that's all there is to the story, Son of Earth."

"And Frothta? Is that just a myth as well?"

The dragon's eyes brightened to an even greater intensity.

"Ahhhh," he said. "No, Son of Earth. The Tree of Water is no myth. It, like all five of the World Trees, was born at the beginning of Time. Those trees grow at the places, the exact spots where each of the five elements—earth, wind, water, fire, and ether, the ancient word for starlight—first appeared in the world. The element of water was the third element to be born, so there are two elements that are older and more powerful than it is—ether and fire—and two that are younger and weaker, air and earth."

"I know of another World Tree, the one known as Sagia," Ven said. "I had a chance to go and see it, but I had to miss it so that I could return Amariel to the sea before she became human forever."

He tried to hold back his thrum, but found that his thoughts were flowing freely to the dragon, almost as if Lancel was summoning the knowledge out of his head.

The dragon chuckled.

"Merrows can be a lot of trouble," he said. "But at least they are tasty."

"Is the Tree of Water still alive?"

The dragon's smile faded, and his expression became thoughtful.

"I cannot say that I know the answer to that for certain," he said. "Frothta grows in a place that it would be almost impossible for me to see her, if I were foolish enough to want to look. But I assume she is still alive, because she is one of the five great sources of magic from the Before-Time in the world. While the modern world either has forgotten that time, or never knew about it in the first place, it is the Old Magic that keeps the fabric of the world intact, Son of Earth. When that fabric is torn, it weakens the world, makes it vulnerable to that which would destroy it. If the Tree of Water had died, the sea itself would know it—and sea dragons especially. Dragons would be the first to know, in fact."

Ven had heard another dragon say almost the same thing.

"Why?" he asked.

"Because, being born of the last element to emerge in the world, the earth, dragons contain a little bit of each of the five elements. Each of the elements has its own magic, but when all five are together, there is greater power, greater magic—some say miracles are possible when it happens. That's why the foolish seek us out—they know we have the answers that no one else knows to questions others have not even thought of. The even more foolish fear our power, and seek to destroy us for the same reason."

"If dragons didn't hate each other, they could rule the world." Char clapped his hand over his forehead as the thought leaked out through his thrum.

The sea dragon laughed nastily.

"Dragons are territorial beings, jealous and even occasionally a bit possessive." Lancel hurriedly returned the figurehead to her place in his collection as he spoke. "But even as violent and destructive as some of us can be—and I must admit, I am among those who like to rip things up a good bit—a dragon would never kill or intentionally harm another dragon, no matter how vehemently it hates its fellow beast."

"Why is that?"

The giant serpent's thrum was as serious as Ven had ever heard.

"Because there are a very limited number of us," Lancel said. "Very few dragon younglings have been born since the Before-Time, and the human spawn have made it a point to try and destroy us. Each dragon is part of the shield that protects the Earth, the element from which we were born, from the evil that lurks within its very heart."

"And what is that evil?"

Smoke began to seep from his nostrils as Lancel's thrum grew angry.

"I will not name it, especially this deep," he said. "But while each of the five elements have the power to both destroy and heal, only one is evil."

"Fire?" Ven guessed.

"Not in its purest form. But there are types of it that are demonic, hungry at all times, not the way the sea is, for sustenance, but for cruelty, for willful and mindless destruction. Those forces are contained, for the most part, deep within the earth. But it is only the shield that the dragons of the world maintain that keep those forces from escaping. One day, when we can no longer maintain the shield—"

The dragon's thrum came to an abrupt end.

"Enough. I have told you more than I should have."

"But where is the Tree of Water?"

"Why do you *care*?" Char demanded. "Aren't we goin' home now?"

"Yes," Ven said quickly. "But I can't waste the chance to find out a piece of lost lore, some magic left over from the Before-Time, from one of the only beings who knows the answer. That's what King Vandemere asked me to do—find and record the magic in the world. Scarnag loaned me a book from his library, with pictures of the dragons of the world in it. For all I know, there is one of you in there, Lancel. I gave that book to King Vandemere for safekeeping before I left on this journey, so I didn't get a chance to study it. There was no text, just pictures. It had a drawing of Sagia, the World Tree that grows in the Enchanted Forest. It may have had one of Frothta as well. Lancel, please tell me—where is the Tree of Water?"

The giant beast eyed him intently.

"Search your memory. What have you been told about it?"

Ven thought back to Madame Sharra's words on the morning when he first pulled the scale from the sleeve of Black Ivory.

*If you are looking for lost magic that was born in the Before-Time, you will need to find a place that no one else could look for it. It might be in a place of extremes—the hottest and coldest part of the sea, the highest and lowest place in the world, the brightest and darkest realms, all at the same time. Or you might have to accept that it no longer exists, as the rest of the world has. And that now Frothta is merely a symbol, just like all the rest of the runes and images on the scales of the Deck.*

*A prediction of your future.*

*What does it mean?* he had asked the Seer about the card in his hand.

*When this card is drawn in a reading it can have many meanings,* Madame Sharra had said. *Sometimes it warns of an impossible task. Sometimes it can mean bringing new power to an old or dead situation, the solving of what had been an unanswerable riddle or a lost cause. It can sometimes warn of something that is too good to be true. Right side up, it can signify breathing underwater, while upside down it can warn of drowning. And sometimes, it just means "the sea."*

Almost all of which seemed to describe the journey that had led him to this moment.

"You're right," he said to the sea dragon. "I'm not going to like the answer to this question."

The dragon smirked.

"And the answer is the same to both of your first two questions," he said. "Because the only way to save your merrow friend from death is to find the Tree of Water. And to find it *very* soon."

## ~ 34 ~

# The Diving Bell

*Maybe it was because he had brazenly told me his name, and so in some small way I had the power to know if he was lying or not.*

*Or maybe it was because I already knew in my heart how badly Amariel was hurt.*

*But Lancel's thrum rang through me like a great ship's bell tolling in the Deep.*

*I knew that what he was saying was the truth.*

*I knew that he was telling me that my friend was dying.*

*And that it would be all but impossible to save her.*

*The dragon was telling me that I had to uncover a miracle, something that even he was not sure still existed.*

*And that a miracle was Amariel's only chance.*

*Not just any miracle. This miracle.*

*It was clear by the sympathy that was below the amusement in his thrum that he did not believe in the possibility of that miracle.*

*I guess we weren't going home now after all.*

Tell me where," ven said. "please help me. i can't find my way in the way in the dark."

The dragon smirked.

"You think this is dark?" he said. "You have not even begun to see dark, Son of Earth. To your night-eyes, this may seem like a dark place, but you are still in the Twilight Realm, where the light from the sun above the surface still penetrates the gloom, at least a little. To find the Tree of Water, you will need to go to the deepest part of the ocean, into the Realm of Midnight, where no light at all is seen. That is the realm of ghosts who wander the deep, lost souls that sought to find magic in the depths—much as you want to do.

"The creatures that live in those all-but-frozen waters of eternal night are the stuff of nightmares themselves: ghostfish and goblin sharks, anglerfish, tripod fish, sea cucumbers and snipe eels, black swallowers and vampire squid, bristlemouths and long-nosed chimaera, light-eating loosejaws and tube-eyes. They haunt the depths, looking for any food they can find, along with the hagfish, the fangtooth, gulper eels and giant tube worms, hatchetfish, six-gilled sharks, lantern fish, and sea vipers. Many of these creatures carry the only light in that realm of endless blackness, so beware of them."

Ven could only nod. He was trembling, and he could feel both Char and Coreon trembling beside him as well, either from cold or fear.

"And going down to the Midnight Realm is only the first step," the dragon continued. His thrum sounded amused again. "You will have to descend even farther than that to find if Frothta still lives. Deeper than the Realm of Midnight is the Abyss, a full three thousand fathoms down into the very cellar of the world. Were it not for the salt in the sea, that water would be ice, it is so cold in the lifeless Abyss. And while that truly is the floor of the ocean, there is a place even deeper."

"The Trenches," Coreon whispered.

"Ah—you've heard of them, then?" the dragon said. "Good— then the sea Lirin remember the tales from the Before-Time, of the cracks in the world five thousand fathoms or more down, where new islands form and the earth splits and spits out lava, even in the freezing black of endless night. It is said that in that empty land of death, Frothta once grew atop a seamount, the highest mountain in the world, in the depths of the deepest trench of the ocean. And if she still lives, that is where she would be found."

Madame Sharra's words rang in Ven's foggy memory.

*It might be in a place of extremes—the hottest and coldest part of the sea, the highest and lowest place in the world, the brightest and darkest realms, all at the same time.*

"That must be it," he said. "If the Tree lives, it's in the Trenches."

"No one would survive to see it, then," Coreon said. "Especially not land-livers. The pressure and the cold of the water would kill any of us long before we even got to the Abyss. We can't even survive in the Midnight Realm. My father warned me never to even go into Twilight—how is it possible to find something that grows in the *Trenches?*"

The dragon shrugged.

"You didn't ask me if it was possible to live through getting to where the Tree grows," he said. "You only asked me where to find it."

"That's true," Ven said. His heart was pounding, and the fear in his thrum was obvious even to him. "But my first question was 'How can I save Amariel?' If you are to keep your word, you can't very well give me an answer that does me no good."

The dragon's eyes narrowed, but his smile grew brighter.

"Actually, I can," he said. "But since I have no stake in whether you live or not, Son of Earth, I will tell you how you can go to the Tree of Water, if you are willing to make the sacrifice."

"I am," Ven said quickly. "Tell me."

The dragon snorted. "You're a fool, Son of Earth," he said. "You should never agree to terms you haven't heard yet. Has our little negotiation taught you *nothing?*" He stared at them for a long moment, then extended his claw over their heads.

In it was a strange sort of metal cage, shaped a little like a woman's skirt, with a chain on the top, a metal lattice bottom, and a smaller cage attached to the slats of the bottom by a hook and

smaller chain. Unlike the other items in the sea dragon's hoard, it was encrusted with barnacles and other grime from the sea, and was large enough to hold several people.

The boys looked at each other.

"With respect, Lancel, what is that?" Ven asked.

The dragon's smile grew even brighter.

"This is a special diving bell," he said. "A diving bell is something humans use to gather treasure and other things they want to salvage from the ocean floor. Of course, that's in the Sunlit Realm, where the floor of the sea is only a few fathoms deep. The shape allows the pressure of the water to trap air inside the chamber. But this diving bell is different, because it's made for just one purpose—to transport the curious to the deeper realms. The sea is full of these, believe it or not."

"How does it work?" Char asked.

The sea dragon laughed. The thrum of it was ugly, and it made the boys shiver.

"You get into the large chamber, and the bell will descend through Twilight to the Midnight Realm all the way to the far edge of the Abyss," he said. He sounded as if he was having great fun. "When it gets to that depth, it will stop in its descent, because the pressure is too great for it to continue. And then you have a decision to make."

"And what is that decision?"

Lancel laughed again.

"Whether or not you are willing to separate your body from your spirit—your soul," he said. "This large metal part is for your body— the smaller cage is a diving bell for the soul. If you are determined to see the deepest part of the sea, you just speak your name, say *going down*, and will yourself to step into the smaller cage. Then turn the key in the lock on the floor, and you will descend into the Abyss—or so I'm told. I've never done this myself, as you may have guessed. Dragons are said not to have souls as other beings do—our souls are part of the Earth. Of course, if you separate your soul from your body, it's only your soul that descends. You leave the mortal part of you behind in the cage, locked, to be safe from the creatures that prowl the Deep, looking for prey in the dark—and if you return, and if the key is still there, you can reunite with your body, say *going up*, ride the diving bell back up through Midnight to the Realm of Twilight, and back you go to the Sunlit waters." He chuckled.

"It sounds like that doesn't happen very often," Ven said.

The dragon shrugged. "Well, as I said, the sea is full of diving-bell cages, and the cages are full of bodies. And the darkness of the Midnight Realm is haunted by souls looking for the cages where they left their bodies, hoping in vain to reunite with them. Sometimes when they actually find their cages, the key is gone. Reunion of body and soul isn't, shall we say, a likelihood. But that doesn't mean it *never* happens."

"Great," Char muttered.

The thrum in the dusky water grew bristly, and Ven knew the dragon was becoming irritated.

"Take my gift, or leave it. My offer only remains open for a moment longer. There is a pathway of pearls in the seafloor past my lair to the place where the Midnight Realm begins. You can follow them in the dark, and when they stop, well, you'll know that you've come to the last place where light touches in the sea. Now, decide, Son of Earth. Do you want the diving bell, or not?"

"We do," Ven said hurriedly before either of the other two could speak. "Thank you, Lancel."

The dragon's eyes narrowed to slits of blue fire again.

"I will give you the gift of one more piece of information, Son of Earth. It is this—you have survived your time in my lair only because you had information that I could not acquire anywhere else in the world, information about something special to me that would not truly have been *mine* if I did not have sole possession of it. You cleverly bargained that information into safe passage for yourself and your friends through my realm, and my promise not to harm you in the future. You also gained answers you wanted to questions you had. But allow me to be clear as the water at the surface of the sea—you and I are not friends, nor will we ever be.

"You claim you have a dragon friend, and your thrum says you believe this to be true. If you do, he is not much of a credit to our race. Real dragons know that friends are a luxury that we cannot afford, and most of us do not want them anyway. Survival in the sea is a constant vigil. One must remain awake and aware almost all the time, and that tends to make those of us who live here suspicious and quick to destroy anything that comes snooping around our lairs. You are *out of place*, Son of Earth, and that is more dangerous than you can even imagine, because you have cheated Death, so you do not know the real consequences of your actions. I advise you not to get used to that, because, sooner or later, Death always wins. Finish your business in the sea and then get out of here while you still can. Our conversation has come to an end. Follow the trail of pearls if you wish, or return to the Realm of Sunlight. But either way, I want you to leave my lair *now*."

The black sea around the circle of Lancel's light rumbled with unspoken threat.

"We'll take the diving bell, with great thanks," Ven said quickly.

The beast opened his claw.

The bell-shaped cage began to sink slowly to the bottom of the sea.

"I suggest you catch hold of it before it becomes stuck in the sand," Lancel cautioned. "It's very heavy."

Char and Coreon exchanged a glance, then swam up to meet the drifting metal cage, taking hold of the chains on top.

"You're not jokin'," Char said. His face turned slightly red with the strain.

"Will you point the way to the pathway of pearls, please?" Ven asked as he swam over to where the hippocampus was hovering in the drift. "I don't want to trespass on your lair any further."

The dragon waved his claw in the drift. Nearby, several of the broken ships in the collection began to rock back and forth, then slid out of the way, opening a tunnel in the lair between them. Coins spun and fell in the undersea waves, then settled back onto the ocean floor again.

"The passageway will close behind you, so make haste," said the dragon. "I do not want any of my ships damaged by falling on you."

Ven put out his arms to the hippocampus.

"Here, Teel, give Amariel to me," he said. "I think you should go back to your home now—I suspect, as she would say, that this is about to get ugly."

The giant sea horse shook its head. Its skin faded to a paler blue than it had been before.

"Hippocampi are faithful creatures," the dragon commented. "Often, when one's mate dies, the other will die of grief. It seems Teel feels strongly about not leaving your merrow friend." He chuckled as Ven pondered what to do. "You may as well take him with you. He's likely to lose her either way shortly."

Ven looked at the sad hippocampus.

"All right, Teel. Come if you wish. But you're not going in the diving bell—you won't fit." He turned back to Lancel. "Since you and I will never be friends, nor are we likely to meet ever again, please allow me to ask one last question, just for the sake of history and curiosity. Your collection seems to contain ships that have gone down all over the world. How did all of these things come to be in your lair?"

"I call to them," the sea dragon boasted. "A ship on the surface will only be mine if I rise out of the Deep and take it down with me, and some of them I have obtained that way. But the broken bones of ships sing their names sadly, over and over again, when they sink to the ocean floor. If I hear them, and I call out to them, they often come to me. They know I will care for them as no other would."

"I see. Thank you," Ven said. "The trail of pearls you mentioned—"

A belch of acidic fire burst forth from Lancel's enormous nostrils.

The boys swam as fast as they could down the open channel in the hoard of treasure. They had gotten past a few ranks of ships when the bright light that had erupted when the beast appeared winked out again, plunging them into total blackness.

Behind them they could feel the drift vibrate as the lines of ships moved back into their places again.

"Keep going!" Ven shouted to the others. "Follow my thrum—at least we'll keep together."

In the distance he thought he heard what sounded like a bell tolling.

"Can you feel that?" he asked the other boys. They both nodded. "I wonder if that is the thrum of a body struggling within a diving bell."

"Don't think about it," Char advised.

"Pearls," Coreon said.

"Where?"

"Down below. Look."

Ven blinked several times. Coreon was right—for the first time since the dragon had sent them back into the Twilight by dousing his light, he thought he could make out something in the gloom all around him.

On the ocean floor tiny spheres were glowing with a blue-white light, neatly positioned in a line that led off into the dark for as far as he could see.

Except for one single pearl floating in the water in front of them.

"That's strange," Char said as they approached the hovering pearl. "It musta been swept up out o' the sand." He put out his hand to catch it.

And could only freeze in shock as a savage mouth with rows of pointed teeth and a jutting jaw roared, open, out of the darkness and snapped shut over his hand.

Filling the sea around him a second later with the thrum of his blood.

# - 35 -

# Descent into Darkness

*For the first few moments I had no idea what was happening.*

*Even when I saw the teeth, and could feel the thrum of Char's blood, the heavy pressure of the water around me was making it hard for my brain to work.*

*Then I felt him gasp.*

*It was the most terrible sound, or feeling, or whatever it is that thrum really is, that I have ever heard, or felt.*

*It made my blood literally run cold.*

*In the sea I thought I had lost my sense of smell. Amariel had told us that the hooded sea slug had a powerful odor, but I couldn't tell. So I thought I was unable to smell anything underwater.*

*Until Char began flailing and shaking his arm beside me.*

*And the blood in the water swept past my face.*

*Then it was all I could smell.*

V EN!" COREON THRUM WAS URGENT. "TAKE OUT YOUR LIGHT!"

Ven fumbled in his pocket and located the air stone and his jack-rule. He pulled out the blue-white bubble, glowing in the same color as the pearls on the ocean floor, but far more intensely.

In the cold light, he could see Char violently waving his hand, trying to shake off a monstrous-looking fish whose jaws had clamped around his wrist. The fish was brownish and round like a ball, and a little shorter than Ven's arm to the elbow, but it had swallowed Char's hand and seemed to be dragging him into its huge mouth, which was opening wider than the rest of its body. Above that massive mouth the glowing ball Char had reached for bobbed on what looked like a small fishing pole attached to the fish's head.

"It's an angler, I bet," Coreon whispered, his thrum high with fear. "The sea Lirin warn about them. We have to pry it off fast, before it swallows his whole arm."

"*Ven!*" Char's thrum was desperate.

"Stop jerking your hand around and hold still," Ven said. He extended the blade in his jack-rule. His hand was shaking so much that he lost his grip on the tool and it almost dropped to the ocean floor. He caught it in the drift, trying to keep his fingers clear of the knife.

Gathering all his strength, he slashed across the top of the fish's head, and struck off the bobbing light.

The fish reared back in shock, its mouth agape.

"Pull it off!" Char moaned. "Get it off me!"

Coreon seized the angler's upper and lower jaws and pried them apart. As he did, Ven grabbed Char's arm and dragged it, bleeding, out of the angler's mouth.

*This is going to get ugly*, he thought as Coreon threw the fish as far away as he could in disgust. *If Megalodon could find me from just three drops of blood, what kind of beacon is* this *going to be, and to what?*

"You all right?" he asked Char.

Char nodded numbly, but his eyes seemed glazed.

Looking through the magnifying glass of the jack-rule, Ven inspected his friend's injured hand. It was gouged and bleeding, but the wounds didn't seem too deep. There was, however, something black at the edge of each tear in the skin, and it seemed to be spreading. "Wrap your shirt around your hand," he said to Char, who was trembling with shock. "We have to get past the Realm of Twilight and into the diving bell as soon as we can, before predators find us."

He looked at the symbol of the Time Scissors in his palm, wondering what moment he would redo if need be.

*This is the closest I've come to needing to use this power,* he thought. It was something he had avoided carefully, uncertain if changing a decision in the past would be better or worse than allowing things to remain as they were.

But somehow, entering a sunless, all-but-frozen part of the sea in a diving bell that separated his body from his soul, with two of his friends gravely injured, seemed to be an action that might need to be reconsidered.

"Can you drag the diving bell yourself if I pull with one arm?" he asked Coreon. The sea-Lirin boy nodded. "All right, then, let's get out of here. Char, hold pressure on the bite with your other hand and I'll pull you along by your good elbow."

"I can swim," Char mumbled.

"No. Your thrum is getting weaker, and we need to douse the light or everything in the Deep will find us."

He held up the tiny glowing sphere one last time.

In the circle of dim light he saw little but the sand of the ocean floor. This realm of endless night, somewhere between Twilight and Midnight in the sea, was a lifeless place, empty and cold, without even dead seaweed on the ocean floor or floating in the motionless drift.

"Teel—how is Amariel?"

The hippocampus shook its head sadly.

Ven inhaled, willing himself to be calm, to be brave. It seemed to work—a moment later he felt as if his brain shut off all ties to his feelings, and was functioning by itself.

"All right," he thought briskly to the other boys and the sea horse. "Let's go."

He put his air stone back in his pocket and buttoned it carefully. The dim light was swallowed immediately, returning them to absolute darkness a moment later. Then he took hold of Char by the elbow with one hand, and the diving bell's chain with other, feeling Coreon's grip on it closer to the end.

He made sure he could feel the thrum of each of his friends. Coreon was nervous, he knew. His gills were opening and closing with more effort than usual. As nervous as the sea-Lirin boy was, Char was fighting full-blown panic, clutching his wounded hand with all his remaining strength. The hippocampus's vibration was mournful and frightened.

He could feel nothing at all from Amariel. He shook that thought from his mind.

Then he made his way back to the water just above the pathway of pearls and started following it.

*Everything Amariel had taught us about riding the drift seemed long ago and far away. There was almost no movement to the water this deep in the sea, just a thick swell here and there, like moving through heavy cream or the air of the upworld in a hard, blinding rain.*

*With the light gone, I began to think of my limited sight as a bit of a blessing. All about me in the heavy drift I caught sight of movement, but little else. Occasionally a glowing light would pass by in the distance, or we could feel the sea above us move as something swam overhead, but considering what Lancel had said about the creatures that lived in the Realm of Midnight, it was probably better that we couldn't see them too well, anyway.*

*Every now and then, I thought I could hear a bell tolling in the depths.*

*The thrum made my teeth sting.*

*Usually I have a terrible time controlling my curiosity. But for once the vibration of those distant bells did not catch my interest even a little bit.*

"What do ya suppose *that* is?" Char's thrum was sounding even weaker.

Ven looked in the direction where his friend was staring above them. A blue-green blob of light, large from what he could see, was pooling higher up in the drift. It seemed to be spreading widely through the water not too far away.

"Squid," Coreon said. "They usually float on the surface, but sometimes they come down looking for food. I didn't know they could dive this deep. Keep away from the mouths—and the tentacles. If just one catches you, you're squid food."

"The only squid I've ever seen are kind of pale and pasty-looking," Ven said, watching the beautiful blue-green flow. "But I've seen patches of that color on the sea in the dark from time to time—I never realized it was squid having a party."

"When that color shows up in the air or around the mast, sailors call it Saint Elmo's fire," mumbled Char. "They think everything weird they see is a sign of somethin' haunted."

"If only they knew," Ven said.

As if to prove him right, ahead of them something clear and filmy appeared in the drift. At first it looked like a jellyfish, a man-of-war without the tentacles. But as they stopped and looked harder, they could see it had a human form, a billowing shape wandering in the drift ahead of them, its human-like hand shading its eyes, searching the blackness. It was wearing what looked like translucent human clothes, tattered and torn the way a ship's sails sometimes were in a terrible wind.

"Oh man," Char whispered.

"Just hold still," Ven whispered back. "Let him pass."

"Do you think we're gonna end up like that?"

Ven watched as the translucent figure floated away on the black drift. He couldn't bring himself to answer honestly.

"Come on," he said. "Keep your wits about you and your eyes on the pearls."

They waited until they could no longer see the wandering

spirit, then began following the tiny markers in the glowing path again.

After a while, they lost track of time. The kelp packets the Cormorant had given them were almost gone. There was no plant life left in the sea, and no fish that they would have considered eating, even if there was a way to catch them. Fortunately, their hunger had vanished along with the light, and now they made their way in the dark, focused on the pathway, with all other thoughts of a world beyond the endless black drift gone from their minds.

It was a little like sleepwalking, Ven thought.

He had no idea how long they traveled, whether it was days, or weeks, or months, or even years. The seasons of the upworld could have changed, for all he knew, because it was bone-chillingly cold all the time. Char was so weak that Ven could barely feel his thrum. He knew the hippocampus was still with them, but he got no vibration at all from the merrow it was carrying.

Every now and then, the blackness would brighten with thousands of tiny lights, or snap with red sparks, or a glowing flash would swim by, reminding him that even though he saw nothing in the deep blackness, it was still full of a haunted kind of life.

"How long do you think we have been following the pearls?" he asked Coreon.

"A long time," the Lirin-mer said. "Several hours at least."

"Several *hours*? Seriously?"

"It may seem like we've been traveling a long way," Coreon replied. "But we're not traveling far out to sea anymore—we're going *down*. If you were to stop swimming, take a deep breath, and let go of your air stone, you'd start rising to the surface again. Eventually you'd float up out of the Midnight Realm, through the Twilight and finally find yourself in the Sunlit Realm once more. Far out to sea, of course."

"That sounds great," Char mumbled weakly. "Why aren't we doin' that?"

"Because you could never hold your breath that long," said Coreon.

"You need to go back to the surface slowly, or you get the bends. And that can kill you pretty quick."

"We couldn't do that—but *you* could," Ven said. "You have gills, Coreon. You've finished your mission. There's no reason you can't go home now."

"Sure," said Coreon bitterly. "I can go back to find the mess the Cormorant has undoubtedly made of the attack on the Gated City. A whole bunch of people are probably dead, maybe even my dad. I'm not in a hurry to return to the reef. Actually, I'm trying not to think about it."

"Sorry," Ven said. He sank back into the silence of the Deep, where thrum was heavy.

They went on, swimming in impenetrable darkness, for what seemed like forever.

And then, suddenly, there were no more pearls.

The pathway came to an abrupt halt in the darkness.

Ven exhaled.

"Well, I guess we've gone as far as we can without the diving bell," he said. "I'm going to take out the air stone—close your eyes."

He waited for a moment to make sure the others wouldn't be blinded by the blue-white light, then carefully fished the stone out of his buttoned pocket and held it in his clenched fist. Even with his eyes closed, the light that leaked out between his fingers made his eyes sting.

He opened them slowly.

They were standing at the edge of a sandy cliff, like a giant dune under the sea. The dropoff to the bottom was steep and long, with not a shell or a broken piece of a ship in sight.

*True nothingness*, Ven thought.

"Midnight—and the Abyssal Plain," Coreon said in return.

With great effort, Char lifted his head.

"Criminey," he whispered.

Ven looked up.

Above them, the drift was swollen with eyes.

Schools of lantern fish, the tiny, minnow-like flashes that brightened the drift every now and then, hung, as if stunned, all around them, like great reflective curtains. A smaller group of fangtooth ogrefish were similarly shocked, their mouths agape, with oversized teeth gleaming in the reflection of the air stone's light. Gulper eels, creatures with whip-like tails and massive mouths lined with rows of teeth, were slithering on the sand dune below them, their black skin flashing red. And above, six-gilled sharks were circling, long, gray beasts that looked like great whites but without the dorsal fins on their backs.

They were completely surrounded by monsters.

Beside them, Teel began to shudder violently. His tail spasmed, uncurling suddenly, as all the color drained from his blue-green body.

Dropping the broken body of the merrow into the dark drift.

# ~ 36 ~

# The Abyss

"Teel!" ven shouted in his mind. "What are you *doing?*"

The trembling hippocampus just looked at him, glassy-eyed. His skin got even paler.

"Coreon—get her!"

The sea-Lirin boy stared at the sinking merrow, then at the diving-bell chain in his hand. A split second later he dropped the chain, kicked down toward the ocean floor, and caught Amariel.

Ven was locked in a staring contest of his own with the creatures of the Deep.

The six-gilled sharks circled a little closer.

"Close your eyes," he thought to his friends. He gave them a moment to comply, then shut his own and opened his hand, letting the full brightness of the air stone penetrate the gloom of the Deep.

"*Get away from us!*" he screamed in the harshest thrum he could summon.

Stunned, the curtain of lantern fish swelled and disappeared rapidly into the dark, as did the fangtooth ogrefish.

The six-gilleds veered off in their paths and swam away.

The gulpers shut their gigantic mouths and skittered from the light as well.

As the monstrous creatures vanished into the darkness of their realm, one thought of common thrum was left behind, hanging in the thick drift.

*Out of place!*

"Do you have her?" Ven asked Coreon. The sea-Lirin boy's thrum replied that he did.

"Teel? Are you all right?"

As if in response, the front part of the giant sea horse's stomach looked like it was splitting open.

Ven watched in horror, then amazement, as a cloud of tiny creatures spewed forth from a pouch of a sort on the beast's belly and filled the area of light surrounding them. As he looked closer, he could see that they were dozens of tiny hippocampi, each a perfect replica of its father, down to its tiny spiral tail.

"What the *heck*?" Char's thrum sounded a little stronger.

"Oh—of course!" Coreon said. "Now it all makes sense! He's not sick, or even fat. He's been pregnant all this time!"

"He's—been *what*?"

"Waiting to give birth. With hippocampi, it's the fathers that carry the eggs around until the babies are born."

"I wanna go home *now*," Char muttered.

"Are you all right, Teel?" Ven repeated. The hippocampus did not answer, but hung motionless in the drift, his grape-like gills flapping heavily. His hide had lost all its color, his shell-like scales pasty and white in the light of the air stone.

"I bet that hurt," said Char.

"More than you realize," said Coreon. "This is really bad. When male hippocampi are getting ready to hatch eggs, they normally don't move very much. The mothers do all the hunting for food, swimming for a long ways to find it and bring it back for them. Hippocampi like to dance with their mates, and they do it every day. They usually only ever have one mate, and, like Lancel said, they can die of loneliness if they lose their partner. He must be feeling pretty awful right now, for a whole bunch of reasons."

"And we've dragged him halfway across the sea," said Ven. "Poor guy. I'm sorry, Teel."

"Well, we sure can't take him into the Abyss," said Coreon. "You should go home now, Teel."

The pale sea horse looked at them sadly.

"I wonder why the enchantment of her song didn't break when she lost consciousness," Char said. "That seems strange."

"Maybe he didn't stay with her because he was enchanted," Coreon noted.

"Don't worry about Amariel," Ven said comfortingly to the giant sea horse. "I know you're fond of her, but we are, too. We'll do everything we can to save her. I promise."

The hippocampus watched them a moment longer. Then he gave his head a shake and let out a thrum that made Ven's eyelids hurt.

The dozens of tiny baby sea horses stopped floating and playing in the drift and hurried to their father. They crept back into his pouch.

"Good luck, buddy," Char said.

"Yes, and congratulations," said Ven.

"I hope you make it back safely," said Coreon. There was an uncertainty to his thrum.

Teel nodded. Ven could almost hear words in his thrum, though it was more like an understanding than a statement.

*You too.*

The hippocampus sounded less sure than they did.

He turned and swam off into the darkness, a little faster than before.

"Now what?" Char asked. His thrum was growing dim.

"Well, we're at the edge of the Abyss. The only way to find Frothta and see if doing so saves Amariel is to push on," Ven said. He looked at the diving bell, which had fallen into the sand on the ocean's floor. "I guess we're headed for the Trenches now."

He glanced at Coreon, who was silently staring above them.

At the light's edge he could see a number of cages floating in the drift, much like the ones attached to the bottom of the diving bell.

"And I guess this is where we do it," he said.

"I'll get the bell," the Lirin-mer boy said. "We should hurry, before the light attracts even bigger guests." Carefully he handed Amariel over to Ven.

"You going to be all right on your own for a minute?" Ven said as he released Char's elbow to take the merrow.

"O' course." Char's thrum was cross.

"Just checking. We have to stick together."

"No kidding," Char said. "At least ya finally got that straight."

"You might want to stay here, Coreon," Ven said as the sea-Lirin boy swam down to the seafloor and grabbed hold of the chain on the diving bell. "We got ourselves, and you, into this mess, but there's no point in you taking a ridiculous risk."

"Sure there is," Coreon said. "If we find the Tree of Water, I'll have seen something no one in my whole nation has ever seen. It will erase my disgrace and let me return home. And if not, well, as I said earlier, I have no reason to go back now, anyway."

Madame Sharra's voice rang in Ven's memory.

*One does not always know the reason at the beginning of a journey. Sometimes you find the reason in the course of it. What matters is that at the end, you know why you undertook the journey in the first place.*

When he had begun this journey, finding the Tree of Water had been one of the main reasons he had thought to go. That reason dimmed as other things happened, other missions, other problems, became the focus. Now it had become the only goal, because without it, he would surely lose one of the most important people in his life.

"All right then," he said. "Let's go."

Coreon was struggling with the heavy diving bell.

"I don't think I can get this back high enough up in the drift to swim under," he said. "The dragon was right—it's miserably heavy."

Ven peered over the edge of the dune into the depths of the Midnight Realm.

"Can you shove it off the edge?" he asked. "We can swim under it as it descends and get up inside it."

"I think so."

"Good. Char—can you take out your air stone without dropping it? We don't want to risk that again, and you look sort of woozy."

"I'm all right," Char insisted. "If I can't hold on to a bloody *air bubble*, I'm not gonna survive the Abyss anyway." He fished around in his pocket. "Got it."

"Let's trade," Ven said. "On the count of three, you take yours out and I'll put mine away." He waited until Char nodded that he was ready, then switched the air stone back into his pocket and buttoned it with one hand.

Just as he did, he took a last look at Amariel's face.

*I didn't think she was still alive.*

*I remembered how bright she looked, smiling broadly, her teeth showing, her skin gleaming in the light of the moon on Skellig Elarose, laughing smugly at her victory over the sea lion. I thought about her singing to the coral and the creatures of the reef, when real elaroses grew just to hear the sound of her voice.*

*And I remembered how frightened her face had been at the thought of meeting a sea dragon. It's a good thing she was unconscious for the meeting with Lancel, because I'm not sure she would have made it through.*

*I recalled, in the haze of my own woozy memory, her singing to me while I floated on the piece of my father's broken ship, songs of the sea, telling me tales of the Deep and the glories I would find there, if I stayed alive long enough to see them.*

*As the light from my air stone went away, it seemed to me like I was looking at the shipwreck of Amariel's body. Lancel said that the bones of ships sang sad songs as they were sinking into the depths of the sea. I realized that Amariel's thrum, whether in the sea or the upworld, was a music of a sort, a song that rang from her with every breath she took.*

*A brazen song.*

*There was no music coming from her now.*

*It's almost as if her soul had already descended into the Abyss.*

*Then I remembered what else the dragon said about the sinking ships.*

*If I hear them, and I call out to them, they often come to me. They know I will care for them as no other would.*

*I wondered if she might hear a call like that. A call from her mother—or perhaps her father, who I know she loved very much. She told me he had swum across a good deal of the sea with her once to take her to a place he wanted her to never go, just to show her why she should never go there. He didn't want her curiosity to win out and her to go alone.*

*Then I knew what I had to do.*

*I had no idea if it would help or not. But I still had to do it.*

Ven put his head down next to the merrow's.

"Amariel," he whispered. "Amariel, stay with me, please. Wherever you are in there, stay with me." The voice in his head caught in his throat. He cleared his thoughts, then tried to imagine himself singing to her, the way she had sung to him on the wreckage of his father's ship, the name of which he could no longer remember.

He sang her name in his mind, over and over, as Char's stone began to glow in his hand. He kept singing as Coreon shoved the diving bell, with great effort, off the side of the underwater cliff, and swam up inside it. The diving bell began sinking slowly into the black drift.

"You comin'?"

Ven nodded to Char. "Go ahead," he said. "I'll follow your light."

His best friend nodded, then dove as quickly as he could.

Ven pulled Amariel up against his shoulder and followed him.

The diving bell was sinking slowly, but it weighed a good deal more than he did, so he had to kick hard to catch up with it. He could see the light of Char's air stone as his friend crawled up inside the large bell. Now the smaller cage that was attached to the bottom of the door in the diving bell cast shadows into the deep, slashes of foggy darkness against the foggy light.

"Hurry up, Ven! I can't see you!"

"I'm coming. I'm almost there."

With a few more kicks he was just below the edge of the sinking bell. He tucked Amariel up inside the rim and released her into the hazy light, knowing she would float up as the bell sank. Then he grasped the rim and pulled himself up inside it.

Char and Coreon were seated on a small ledge that ran all the way around the inside of the bell, belted in with a length of chain across their laps. Char had caught the merrow and was holding her steady in front of him. He passed her back to Ven as he took a seat beside Coreon and strapped himself in.

"Going down," he said.

Char snorted. "I think it's already got the idea, mate. How long ya think this is gonna take?"

Ven shrugged. "I don't know—but if you can keep the light out I bet it will seem like it's not as long as it will if we have to descend in the dark."

"Good point," said Char. "An' even if I let it go if I fall asleep for a minute, it should just float up inside the top of the bell."

"Let's not take a chance with that," Ven said, brushing Amariel's hair away from her colorless face. "We'll take shifts. Let me know when you get tired."

"That would be now," said Char. "I can barely keep my eyes open."

"Why don't you both sleep?" said Coreon. "I'm not tired—Lirinmer only sleep at the turning of storm. And I don't mind the dark, so put your air stone away, Char. I'll wake you both if anything changes, and that way we don't risk losing either of your air stones."

"Thank you," said Ven gratefully. "I could use the sleep, too. Even though I'm sorry about the circumstances, I'm glad you came with us, Coreon. We'd be dead without you."

"Well, you still may be, even with me," said the sea-Lirin boy. "Get some sleep."

"What's that for, do ya think?" Char asked, pointing to a hole in the top of the diving bell with a sealed cover.

"I think it's for the air hoses," Ven said. "On some of the ships my father builds there are diving bells, though I've never really looked at them carefully before. I think they work a lot like the airwheel in the Drowning Cave. The pressure of the water outside keeps the air inside."

"Good to know," Char muttered, trying to get comfortable beside the merrow. "Just in case we find air down here in the dark."

"*Go to sleep*," Coreon repeated. "You may not get the chance again."

Ven stared down below the slatted metal door of the diving bell at the black Deep into which they were slowly sinking. A moment later, when Char's air stone was back in his pocket, that blackness swallowed the inside of the diving bell.

He was now more aware of the descent, like a slow falling to the bottom of the world. His mind did not want to think about it, so he let sleep take him.

His dreams were filled with eyes that watched him from the dark, glassy eyes belonging to creatures with terrifyingly large teeth that carried their own light as a lure to unsuspecting victims longing for a little bit of the sun. Every now and then the diving bell would shudder, and in his sleep he knew that a deep-sea shark was ramming its body against it, trying to jostle them free from the protective cage.

His nightmares were all the more frightening because they were reality.

How long he slept, he could not tell. He awoke to the sound of Coreon's voice. It was cracking both high and low.

"Uh, guys—I think you better take a look at this."

## - 37 -

# All the Way Down

*I opened my eyes, then closed them quickly.*

*A strange hazy light was filling the inside of the diving bell, not as piercing as it normally was when one of us took out our air stones, but stinging nonetheless.*

*From Char's reaction, I could see he was surprised as well.*

*I wondered why Coreon would risk taking out one of our air stones while we were asleep.*

*Then I realized he hadn't.*

*The light was coming from below us.*

*Where it looked like part of the sea was boiling.*

BELOW THE SLATTED FLOOR OF THE CAGE, IT SEEMED AS IF A river of light was flowing into the black depths, along with clouds of billowing smoke.

"What the heck is *that*?" Char asked.

As if in answer, the diving bell suddenly stopped in its descent.

"Oh boy," said Coreon. "I think we're here."

"Where? Where is 'here'?" Ven asked.

"We've descended all the way through the Midnight Realm, and the Abyss as well, I guess," said the sea-Lirin boy. "You've both been asleep for a very long time. Lancel said the diving bell would take us to the far edge of the Abyss, so we must be at the Ocean Basin, a full three thousand fathoms down. The basin is the ground floor of the sea. The only place in the whole world deeper than this is the Trenches." He shuddered visibly.

"Sort of like the creepy dark root cellar in the basement of the Crossroads Inn," Char suggested.

Coreon shrugged. "I don't know what that means. I only know that if we're at the bottom of the Abyss, we should be being squashed by the weight of the water. The only thing that is saving us from the pressure is the diving bell."

"Why is there light in the Trenches, when most of the rest of the ocean is so dark?"

"The skin of the earth is thin at the bottom of the world, they say," said Coreon. "The fire at the Earth's heart melts the earth into lava. Sometimes it leaks out—that must be what we're seeing."

Char's thrum was tight and nervous. "Like Lancel said—black smokers, whatever *that* means, rivers of lava—"

"Wonderful. Well, I guess here is where we have to make that choice the dragon told us about," Ven said. "Our bodies will never survive outside the bell—the only things that can go on from here are our spirits."

"Yeah, like the poor chap we saw floatin' in the Midnight Realm." Char shuddered as well. "I hope we don' end up wanderin' the black sea like that forever."

"It's a pretty big risk," Ven admitted. "I don't feel my curiosity itching at the moment, just my stomach flipping over and over. If there was any other way to save Amariel—and get home—I would say we should head back up for the surface now."

"She really hasn't been breathing much this whole time," said Coreon. "I've seen her gills open every now and then, but that may just be from the water passing over them. I think you're already too late."

Ven looked down at the merrow beside him.

Coreon was right. Her gills were barely moving, and her body was cold.

"I wish I'd never come here," he said, his thrum choking as his throat tightened. "I should have known better. I'm out of place in this world, even more than you are, Char. Everything we've met in the sea so far has said so—the marble ray, the Sea King, the dragon. I've probably killed her."

The boys fell silent in the dim light inside the diving bell. Then Char spoke.

"Remember that prophecy the Epona gave her? The one about the wanderer out o' place in the sea?"

Ven nodded. He squeezed Amariel's limp hand. Her webbed fingers were cold and bony.

"Do you think that might have been about you?"

Ven looked up in surprise.

"I—I don't think so," he said. "The queen said it was an old riddle, something she had studied during her lessons a long time ago. And if it was long ago to her, I can't even imagine how long it would have been in our years."

"You said Madame Sharra told you that the card you drew could represent an unsolvable riddle, right?"

"Yes."

"What was it again? The one the Epona told to Amariel?"

Ven thought back. "Wanderer, out of place in the drift," he repeated slowly,

*"This riddle is to you a gift.*
*Free the captive who stays by choice*
*Sing a hymn without your voice*
*Find the souls forgotten by Time*
*Believe the view is worth the climb.*
*Follow the path without using your eyes*
*Five gifts are the price to spare one who dies*

*Until the stars shine in the depths of the sea*
*Home again you will never be."*

"Well, I hope it's not about you," said Coreon. "Because there is no way for the stars to shine in the depths of the sea, as you can tell. This place is miles below the surface, and even the light of the sun can't penetrate the darkness, let alone starlight. And this isn't even the deepest part of the sea."

"Maybe it's just a fancy way of sayin' you'll never see home again," Char said gloomily.

"You really are a cheerful fellow, aren't you?" said Coreon. "It must be such fun being you."

"I haven't thought about it at all since she gave the prophecy to Amariel," Ven said. "The waterspout came along right after she finished the prophecy, and we've been just trying to survive ever since."

"Well, you may want to take a moment and think about it before we go any farther," said Coreon.

"Especially if you were thinkin' of usin' another weird gift that a strange person gave you," Char added. He tapped Ven's palm where the image of the Time Scissors was. "If it's still there, that is. I never have been able to see it."

Ven examined his palm. In the dim light he could see the hour-glass and scissors, and even the thread, very clearly, almost as if they were glowing with a light of their own.

"It's still here," he said.

"Well, maybe you should undo us comin' here in the first place. We would never have met Coreon, and he would still be in good graces with the Cormorant. Amariel would still be alive—"

"But I don't have any idea which single moment of Time I would like to redo," Ven interrupted. "Messing with Time is something you should only do when there's no other choice—and you know what you're doing. If we were to redo a single moment, do we keep the knowledge of why we did? Who knows—if I pick the moment just before we entered the sea, but don't remember why, we'd probably just go again in the next moment anyway."

"What's a hymn?" Coreon asked.

"A song that's also a prayer," Char replied. "Sailors sing 'em all the time. An' that part about the stars shinin' in the sea—maybe that's the Sleepin' Child! Remember that place we sailed past on our way here, in the northern islands? The grave of the Sleepin' Child. It was a legend about a star that fell from the sky into the sea, and we could see the steam, remember?"

"We'll drive ourselves crazy if we try to figure out the prophecy, especially since it probably doesn't have anything to do with us," Ven said impatiently. "Lancel also said that there are some things that are just supposed to remain mysteries. Sometimes I think they are there just to distract you, to keep you from doing what you know you're supposed to do."

"So what do you want to do now?" Coreon asked.

Suddenly a face and a pair of ragged hands appeared at the grate below them. The skin was pale and filmy, but the eyes were black as the depths of the sea. It let loose a howling thrum that sent shivers through all three boys and caused them to draw their legs up quickly beneath them.

"Ven—Ven!" Char whispered, his thrum shaking. "What *is* that?"

"I'm guessing it's a lost soul, looking for wherever it left its body," Ven answered quietly. "Hold still. It should figure out that its body is not here in a minute and move along."

The filmy hands reached through the grate, grasping at their legs.

"Ven?" Char began again, but Ven waved him into silence.

"Keep your thrum calm—think of things that make you happy," he said. "If we learned anything from the great whites it's that nervousness just attracts bad attention."

He closed his eyes and thought about the forest outside of Vaarn, where colorful kites danced on the warm spring wind above green, fresh-smelling branches.

When he opened his eyes a few moments later, the face and hands were gone.

"We had best be on our way, if we're going to do this," said Coreon. "Nothing natural lives in the Abyss—it's too dark and cold for ordinary sea life, as the dragon said. But there are legends about the things that do—and obviously the stories about ghosts walking the Deep are true. So let's go on—or let's go back."

"Agreed," said Ven. "I'll go first. And if anyone wants to stay behind, it's probably safer."

"What about Amariel?"

Ven looked down at the merrow.

"She's coming with me. We're here to find a miracle for her. I can't very well leave her behind."

"How do ya propose to make that happen?" Char demanded. "She has to be able to say her name in order to get into the smaller divin' bell, doesn't she?"

Ven exhaled. "Right." He leaned over the merrow. "Come on, Amariel," he thought to her as he did before. "Come with me." In his head he chanted her name, over and over again, then picked her up in his arms. "All right Char," he said. "Unlock the grate."

"Careful, mate," Char cautioned as he turned the key in the lock.

"Good luck," added Coreon.

*Amariel, Amariel, Amariel,* Ven thought as he lowered himself through the opening into the smaller diving bell. *Amariel.* Then he spoke his own name. After all the times he had been told to keep it to himself in the depths of the sea, it seemed particularly odd to be pronouncing it now. As he did, the diving bell rang with it and echoed the name over and over until the sound disappeared.

"Charles Magnus Ven Polypheme."

He felt a slipping, as if he were coming down a slide. With ease he passed out of the metal diving bell and down the tether into the smaller basket below.

When he looked down, he saw his arms were empty.

The merrow's body had remained behind.

But in his hand was her red pearl cap, her most prized possession. It was the object that merrows entrusted to a human man in order to grow legs and walk on the land of the upworld—as she had done with him not long ago.

Ven looked up through the gate.

And saw himself sitting on the seat beside Amariel, fast asleep. Char and Coreon were staring back at him.

He felt the same as he had a moment before, though a little lighter. Seeing his body in the metal diving bell should have been unnerving, but he felt calm and confident.

"Whoever else is coming, be quick about it," he said. "We have to get that grate locked."

Coreon said something that Ven did not hear, then sat back on the inner ledge of the diving bell and seemed to fall asleep. A clear shadow of the Lirin-mer boy stepped away from his body, much as Ven's must have, and swam through the grate into the smaller cage, followed a moment later by Char.

The body his best friend had left behind was sleeping fitfully, as if it were partly awake, Ven noticed. In addition, the spirit form was much fainter than his or Coreon's, leading Ven to believe the strength of their names may have determined how strong those forms could be. Char's could only be faint because he knew so little of his own identity.

A tiny blue-white light glowed in Char's pocket.

He looked down at the red pearl cap in his hand. Inside his buttoned vest pocket he could feel something with weight, but otherwise he was as light as air in the drift. He closed the top of the smaller diving bell.

"All right," he said to the other boys. "Into the Trenches. *Going down.*"

# - 38 -

# At the Bottom of the World

It was really hard to leave the second diving bell.

The first one, the dark metal cage, was one of the most unpleasant rooms I've been inside in my life, a little like the dungeons and prison cells I've spent time in, only smaller.

And miles deep in the sea.

You would think that it would be a relief to get out of such a place.

But I had a very hard time taking my eyes off of Amariel, broken and quiet, leaning up against my own body. It was strange enough seeing myself from the outside.

It was even harder seeing it for what might have been the last time.

It is one thing to face your own death. Char and I had done that many times before. But facing the future as wandering spirits, separated from our bodies, haunting the sunless sea forever, was more than my mind could handle.

It was time to go.

I took a last good look at myself, just in case.

Then I turned the key in the lock, opened the grate, and dropped out of the diving bell and into the dark drift.

Char and Coreon followed a moment later. Char was almost

*impossible to see. The glow in his pants pocket where he kept his air stone weighted down with pebbles was far brighter than the light of his spirit.*

*I waited until they were free of the diving bell, then pushed the grate shut.*

*Then I turned the key in the lock. The thud of its thrum was a sickening sound.*

*A little like the tolling of a bell.*

*The second diving bell, the little cage below, was even smaller, as well as flimsier.*

*What Lancel had called the diving bell of the soul.*

*It was lucky that we were nothing more than spirits, because it was too fragile to hold anything else.*

---

THEY DESCENDED FOR A LONG TIME INTO THE DEEP TRENCHES.

Far below, a split in the ocean floor crawled with lava, like a glowing thread of light. Clouds of smoke rolled upward in the drift, then were devoured by the dark.

Above them they could feel vibrations, slow and lonely.

"More diving bells?" Char guessed.

"Let's go see," Ven suggested. "We're not mortal at the moment. We may as well take a look."

"Leave the cage?"

"Why not? We can bring it with us—but it's not going to keep anything with teeth from eating us anyway. It will be good to be out in the drift, I think."

"After you, mate," said Char.

Ven grinned, then swam out of the bell, followed a moment later by the other boys.

They floated along in the misty light from the Trenches below them. Above them, hanging in the black drift, were rusted bells and cages, many of them empty, but most with their grate floors closed, the keys missing.

Wandering below the old diving bells were what at first looked liked patches of light, but as they watched, their shapes became clearer. Like the few they had seen before, these spirits had faces and hands, though it was hard to tell if some of them had legs, because their clothes were tattered and raggy as they hung in the blackness above the world's root cellar.

Every now and then one of the spirits would float up toward one of the diving bells and bang piteously in the grate, or shake a small cage of rope like the one hanging at the bottom of the bell Lancel had given them. Sometimes it howled with rage or sobbed in grief, but eventually it would turn and glide away, seeking other bells in the dark water.

Char's filmy form was shaking beside Ven.

"Do ya think we'll end up like them?" he asked. His thrum was weak and wavery.

"No," Ven said, trying to sound confident, but he had been thinking the same thing. "I wish we could help them—this is so sad. I think that one over there was a sailor."

Char nodded in agreement as the hovering spirit with what looked like a peg leg and an eye patch drifted past them as if it did not see them. "Maybe a little light might help—maybe they just can't see inside the diving bells."

Ven patted his buttoned pocket. The weight was still there, even as it had left the rest of his body.

"I'm not sure it's a good idea to take out the air stone," he said. "What if it falls through my hand?"

"Are you sure it's even still in there?" Coreon asked. "It may have stayed behind on your body—otherwise, wouldn't you have drowned already?"

"Good point," Ven said. "I'm not sure what is still with me and what isn't." He unbuttoned the pocket of his vest and felt around inside.

He knew at once that the jack-rule had not come with him. His heart sank. The tool had been his prized possession, something he had wanted most of his life even before his father had given it to him. *I hope I can get it back*, he thought as he felt around the corners of his pocket.

The sleeve of Black Ivory was still there. Ven sighed in relief. The dead stone was working its magic on him even in the depths of the sea. If he was not touching it, most of the time he forgot it was even there.

The gleam of light from the corner of Char's pocket was matched by his own. His air stone was still there.

And still in the pocket was the long thin tool with the skull on the top. Ven pulled it from his pocket and rebuttoned it.

"Hmmm," he said. "I had forgotten all about this. What did it say on it, do you remember?"

"Somethin' about freein' the only innocent prisoners she ever held," said Char.

"Well, this may not work, because if any of these spirits have something to do with the *Athenry* it's purely a coincidence," said Ven. "But if you were right, and it's a skeleton key, or a lock pick, it might open the locks on the grates where the keys are missing. And then if there are souls that have found their way back to their original cages, only to be unable to reach their bodies, well, maybe they'll be reunited."

"I suppose these could be the souls forgotten by Time that the Epona's prophecy mentioned," said Coreon. "If that is about you after all."

"Nothing ventured, nothing gained, as my father used to say," Ven said. He swam to the first of the diving bells and peered insider, then jumped away.

Parked on the rim much like the one in Lancel's diving bell was a skeletal being, its bony hands grasping a wooden sea chest. The chest was open, and empty. The creature's eyes were open and hollow, its face drawn into a skull-like mask, and its lips skinned back in a ghoulish expression. A metal hose swung lazily around in the drift. No air bubbles came out of the loose end.

"I'm—I'm not sure what to do," Ven whispered. "I think he's dead."

"Whether he is or not, he's a prisoner," said Char. "Ya may as well set 'im free. It's not like he can do us any harm.

"I hope you're right." Ven inserted the long thin wire of the tool with the skull on the top into the lock in the grate below the shrunken man.

A loud, scratchy *plink* vibrated through the drift.

The grate opened slightly.

"I guess this is a skeleton key after all," Ven thought to the others. "Probably from a pirate ship, or—"

"Uh, Ven—move out of the way—quickly," Char murmured.

Ven turned to see the floating spirit that had looked like a sailor to them streaking through the darkness at him. He hurried back to his friends in the drift below the diving bell, just in time to be out of the way when the lost soul reached the metal cage.

From inside the bell they saw a glow brighten intensely, then fade again.

Then the bell began to toll joyously.

From the bottom a spirit appeared. It was shining brightly and looking whole, not ragged and pale as before. It shot out of the bell and rocketed toward the surface, its thrum merry and light.

As it did, something that looked like falling ash quietly floated down into the dark sea below the diving bell, then spread out in the drift and disappeared.

The bell fell silent.

"What the—what just happened?" Char whispered.

"I'm not sure. But I think it was a good thing."

"Me too," said Coreon. "There's something not right about bodies trapped in all those bells. I think it makes this part of the sea sick and haunted. Do you want to open more of them?"

Ven considered. "If we find them as we go," he said finally. "If

that prophecy was indeed about us, we may have to fulfill the different parts of it to save Amariel. And if that's the case, I'm willing to
do whatever we have to do. But Lancel said we would need a miracle
to save her, and that finding the Tree of Water was the only way that
would happen. So I think we need to keep going down into the
Trenches and keep searching until we do."

"Why do ya suppose her cap came along with us?" Char asked.
"That seems odd, doesn't it?"

"Not really. I think a lot of a merrow's spirit is tied to her red
pearl cap. That must be why when they give the cap to a human
man it lets them grow legs and leave the ocean. They also lose a lot
of their, well, *brazen* spirit and become very quiet, like Amariel did
before we got her back to the sea. So I think her spirit is with us—at
least most of it."

"I feel another bell thrumming in the distance," said Coreon.
"Deeper, I think."

"Down we go," said Ven.

Without the crushing weight of the water against their mortal
bodies, the boys passed almost effortlessly through the drift. Coreon
dragged the small diving bell behind him by the tether, because
when Char tried to grasp it, his filmy hand passed right through the
chain.

They swam slowly to the bottom of the world, stopping wherever
they saw diving bells hanging in the drift. Sometimes the spirit was
just outside the door, but mostly there was nothing there. After a
few times, they gave up looking inside the bells, because what they
saw was always terrifying. But every so often, as they were moving
deeper into the Trenches, closer to the river of lava, they heard the
thrum of a bell ringing happily above them.

As they descended, they discovered that going down was easy,
but swimming higher in the drift was almost impossible. While the
lack of a body meant they could float downward with almost no re-
sistance, the absence of their muscles and bones made them weak.
Coreon almost lost the diving cage several times.

"Don't let go if you can help it," Ven said the third time the tether slipped through the Lirin-mer's hands. "It's going to be too hard soon to get back on our own to the diving bell."

"I hope we live long enough to have that problem," Coreon muttered.

Finally there were no more bells. The pressure around them was so great that Ven could feel it in his eyes, even without his body.

The floor of the trench into which they were descending was coming closer all the time. Unlike the bare sandy floor of the Sea Desert, the bottom of the sea in the deepest of its depths was alive.

And terrifying.

As freezing as the black water was, there was heat rising from the ocean floor. The ground was bursting with smoke that was belching forth from what looked like chimney vents, rolling in great black waves toward the surface. Some of the vents were taller than buildings Ven had seen back in Vaarn.

Waving from the knobby floor were fields of long thin noodles that Ven realized after a moment were tube worms, giant creatures that resembled the coral of the reefs, but many times larger. Spidery crabs with ten legs walked among the worms, fishing out shellfish and snapping them into their mouths with claws attached to their front legs.

He felt Char gasp beside him as his best friend realized that those giant spider crabs trolling the floor near the vents, feeding on blind shrimp and starfish, had legs that were longer than the two of them would have been together standing on top of one another. Clams of immense size were filtering water near the white smokers, vents belching lighter smoke than their counterparts, snapping their giant shells shut from time to time and spraying forth water into the darkness.

"When are we gonna wake up from this nightmare?" he whispered to Ven.

"Not until we have Amariel back, safe." Ven dodged as another vent erupted like an undersea volcano, spewing harsh ash into the drift, ash that smelled like the sea dragon's acidic fire.

"Look." Coreon pointed into the distance.

Rising up from the seabed was a mountain. It was visible in the light of the glowing lava that ran down its sides, streaking its black surface with veins of bright orange. The mountain reached up into the black drift farther than they could see.

And filled the ocean floor from side to side.

As did the thousands of others in the mountain range it was part of.

"Which one do ya think is the tallest?" Char asked.

"No idea."

"Well, you had best figure it out—since Frothta supposedly grows on top of the tallest mountain in the sea. And from where we stand, all I can see is mountains. More than we could climb in a lifetime if we all were Lirin-mer."

## - 39 -

# Letting Go of the Last Lifeline

I try not to whine. I really do.

My mother has no tolerance for whiners. I have learned, as the youngest in the family, that you risk having your ears pinched until they bleed if you whine in her presence.

My brother Jaymes wears a small gold ring in the top part of his left ear to fill in the hole she left there after one particularly bad temper tantrum on his part.

But after traveling far out to sea, then down into its depths, after dodging giant sharks and leaving our bodies behind in a giant bell-shaped tin can and everything else we've gone through, a range of enormous mountains suddenly appeared before us.

And all I wanted to do was throw myself on the ocean floor amid the giant tube worms and the eyeless shrimp and have a tantrum that would put Jaymes's to shame.

Of course I didn't.

But I thought about it seriously.

COREON BROKE THE SILENCE FIRST.

"Now what?"

Ven sighed, a deep, painful sigh that came from the bottom of his spirit.

"How are we supposed to find a tree on top of a mountain in a range of mountains we can't even see the tops of?"

He looked down at the red pearl cap in his hands. It was beginning to fade, to curl slightly at the edges. If, as he believed, it was a sign of Amariel's spirit traveling with them, it made him fear for her.

Her voice rang in his memory.

*The bigger something is, the louder the thrum it makes.*

Ven took a breath.

Lancel's voice replaced Amariel's.

*If the Tree of Water had died, the sea itself would know it.*

He closed his eyes and concentrated.

At first he could feel nothing but the ferocious pressure of the sea. The weight of the water was heavy even on his spirit, and seemed to block out the thrum from almost everything else around them. The vibrations of the hydrothermal vents, the giant tube worms waving in the drift, the enormous clams filtering water on the seafloor, the thousands of starfish clinging to the mineral chimneys of the black smokers, were all very slight compared to the heaviness that surrounded everything.

But then, high above it, he heard, or more likely felt, a sound.

The thrum was bell-like and clear, with a sweet, deep tone. It did not ring desperately like the harsh clanging of the diving bells, but rather rolled through the drift, like tides of breath. It seemed like it was coming from very far away, and yet it hung in the water around him at the same time.

If he hadn't been specifically listening for it, he never would have heard it.

Now that he *could* hear it, the sound reached down into the depths of his soul. He felt lighter just knowing it was there, and a moment later it was as if he had breathed in sweet air, or sunshine, something that banished the darkness from inside him, even though it was still all around him.

"I think I hear her," he said.

Char's eyebrows drew together.

"Who?"

"Frothta."

"Really?" His best friend listened carefully. "Sorry, mate, but I don't hear anything except the thuddin' o' the sea."

Coreon, who had been listening as well, nodded in agreement.

"I could be wrong, but I can't imagine what else would make a thrum like I'm hearing," Ven said. "I guess we should just follow it, at least as long as we can. Unless someone else has a better idea."

"No better idea—but you have to lead," said Char. "Where are we headin'?"

Ven pointed to the towering mountain range. "Over there. Then up."

"I don't think I can carry this diving bell any longer," said Coreon. "I can barely drag it along here at the bottom. If you think we need to climb, I don't think it's coming with us unless we're inside it."

"I guess we're going to have to decide if we believe we're going to find a miracle, then," said Ven. "Because you can get back in that diving bell, say *going up*, and it should take you back to your body. It may be the last chance either of you have for making it out of the Abyss. I don't blame you if that's what you want to do."

"You're sayin' *you*—not *we*," said Char. "I guess this means you've already decided you're not goin' back in the divin' bell?"

"Yes," said Ven. "I'm going to the mountains—and I'm going to find the Tree of Water, or die trying."

Char sighed. "Well, then, ya know what I'm gonna say."

"Me too," added Coreon. "There's no point turning back now."

Ven smiled in relief. "Good. We'll just start climbing the first mountain we come to, and keep going as long as we can."

Coreon let go of the chain tether. The small cage floated away from them and into the black water outside their sight.

"Goodbye!" Char called after it. "Well, there goes our last life-line."

"We'll have to make our own way out, then," said Ven. "Let's get to it."

The black drift was heavy, and it took all their strength and concentration to move upward in it. Every now and then a crack in the floor of the sea would spew forth acidic spray. They dodged out of the way, forgetting for a moment that they had no bodies to be harmed by it.

They soon lost all track of time. The mountains they had seen in the light of the river of lava were much farther away than they had seemed, and after a while it felt like they were traveling in vain, not getting any closer.

"You know, I really hope that stupid hippocampus made it back," Char muttered. "I hope he's home, tendin' to his babies."

"With his mate," Coreon added.

"I hope so too," said Ven. "He really was a trooper."

"Are you still tryin' not to think about the Cormorant?" Char asked Coreon.

"Trying, but not succeeding," the sea-Lirin boy said. "My dad is the division leader of the eastern part of the coral reef. He would have been one of the first ones in."

"Sorry to have brought it up," Char said.

"Focus on hearing the song of the Tree," Ven advised. "Once you do, you'll feel better, I bet."

Coreon nodded. "I think I do hear it," he said. "It has a hopeful ring to it, doesn't it?"

"Yes."

Finally the mountains were within plain sight. They reached up into the black drift, lighted by the blazing lava oozing from the cracks in the skin of the world. The haze and smoke from the mineral chimneys on the seafloor made them look like a nightmare fairyland.

*This is a little bit like what the Nain kingdom of Castenen, where my ancestors come from, might have looked like if it were in the upworld,* Ven thought as he stared up from the base of the towering mountains.

*Strange that Nain fear the water so much, and in fact in the deepest depths of the sea the world looks almost the same.*

He tried to remember what it felt like to ride the drift, the way Amariel had shown him and Char at the beginning of this long, terrifying, amazing journey. None of the lift the ocean had provided then, back in the Sunlit Realm, was in the heavy salted water at the bottom of the world. He pushed his arms through the drift, and his spirit form rose slightly, with great effort. He took another stroke. He rose a little farther up, feeling tired.

The other boys joined him. Char took twice as long as he and Coreon, his dim spirit form all but disappearing several times. Ven set a slow and steady pace, swimming until he was finally within reach of the side of a mountain of towering rock formations.

All over the surface, millions of tiny starfish clung to the mountainside with several of their arms while they waved others in the drift, catching the occasional eyeless shrimp for food. Light from deeper within the mountain chain glowed, making the drift almost as bright as moonlight when it shone on the surface.

"This is so weird," Char said as they struggled past the cliff faces swarming with starfish. "It looks like the reverse of the sky in the upworld, like all the stars fell right into the sea."

"Are any of them shining?" Ven asked. "Because until they do, we won't be seeing home again, according to the Epona's riddle."

"Well, they kinda glow every now and then when a burst of lava shoots out. I don't think any o' them are shinin'. " Char's spirit form dimmed again.

"Try not to thrum too much," Ven advised. "We have an enormously long climb ahead of us. I can't even see the peak of this mountain, and I know there are more than we can count on either side of it and beyond. It may take us the rest of our lives to find Frothta."

"I stopped thinkin' a long time ago," Char answered. He paused for a moment. "Can you imagine what Amariel would have said in response to that if she was with us?"

"She *is* with us," Ven said. "I have to believe that, or there's no point in going on."

"How is the pearl cap?" Coreon asked.

Ven looked down at Amariel's most prized possession. It had shrunk considerably, and was now fraying at the edges.

"Let's just keep going," he said. He was finding it hard to get his thoughts out of his head in the heavy water.

They climbed the drift, swimming up along the mountain face, stopping to rest every so often, until it felt almost as if that was all they had ever done in all their lives. The starfish-covered mountain seemed endless in height, and Ven was beginning to despair of ever reaching its summit, when something shot off above them like a firework in the depths of the sea.

It seemed to come from beyond the mountain.

"We're almost at the top," Ven said excitedly. "Keep going if you can. We're almost there."

"You go on ahead," Char said. "I have to stop."

Ven saw his best friend's spirit all but disappear into the drift.

"No, we'll wait until you're ready," he said. "No point in getting separated now. You all right, Coreon?"

"Right here beside you," the Lirin-mer boy said.

"Good." He tried to force back the excitement he was feeling as they neared the summit of the mountain. His curiosity was pulsing through him like a strong heartbeat. But he kept his thoughts to himself and struggled to be patient until Char became more clearly visible again.

Then he waited until the deep thrum song he had heard filled his ears again, and followed it once more.

Once they started climbing again, they kept going until they could see the summit. Beyond it, the tips of many more mountains rose, even taller above the distant floor of the sea below them.

"Don't look down," Ven advised Char, whose pale spirit had dimmed even more when he cast a glance at the seafloor. "We can't fall—our bodies aren't really here."

"It still feels like they are," Char said. "Now I finally get what Amariel meant when she said everythin' in the sea was bigger or taller than everythin' on land. I don' think I've ever seen a mountain this big. And they seem to never end."

Ven turned around as they reached the summit and looked at the seafloor below. The tube worms, giant clams, and starfish were much too far away to be seen now. Rolling clouds of gas from the vents in the ocean floor bubbled up occasionally, and the rivers of bright orange lava now looked like tiny threads so far below.

"I guess that riddle can't really be about us," he joked as he watched the lava wind its way thought the undersea canyons in the dark. "I don't really think the view from up here was worth the climb."

"That's because you aren't looking in the right direction," said Coreon. "I think you might feel differently if you turned around."

# - 40 -

# The Real Queen
# of the Sea

VEN TURNED SLOWLY.

As he did, an enormous display of what looked like undersea fireworks exploded above him. Red and gold sparks sped through the drift, leaving glowing trails hanging in the water before they began sinking slowly to the floor of the sea.

Beyond the summit of the mountain they had just climbed were more mountains filling the Trenches for as far as they could see. Unlike the view from the bottom of the world, however, these mountains were lit by a ring of glowing red vents that exploded molten fire into the drift around them like a giant cauldron of bubbling lava. It reminded Ven a little of the huge pumpkin shell full of boiling squash soup in the Gated City that he and his friends had sampled on Market Day when they had visited there.

Great molten lava bubbles three feet or more across floated past, then burst into the freezing cold seawater all around them. Farther off in the range of endless mountains, volcanos erupted, filling the drift with rolling smoke. Hazily Ven was aware that they would never have been able to stand so close to such things in the upworld if they were still in their bodies, and it was only the intense pressure of the water that had suppressed the violence and heat of the undersea volcanoes.

Madame Sharra's voice echoed in his memory.

*If you are looking for lost magic that was born in the Before-Time, you will need to find a place that no one else could look for it. It might be in a place of extremes—the hottest and coldest part of the sea, the highest and lowest place in the world, the brightest and darkest realms, all at the same time.*

"Criminey," Char whispered.

Ven looked up even higher, following his gaze.

Rising into the drift beyond the summits of the mountains was another peak, larger and taller by far than all the others. It stretched up like a wide flagpole in the middle of the mountain range.

High atop it was a giant tree, a tree bigger than anything Ven had ever seen before.

At first he did not know what it was.

The enormous trunk and arms, branches, twigs and leaves all seemed to be made of water, water that pulsed clear in the hazy black drift, running like a stream flowing upward, gleaming with a light of its own and rippling with power. Ven was not certain that there was anything solid to it, as if it were made of the same kind of elemental magic as his air stone. Its thrum rang all around him, shouting joyously over the mountaintops and echoing through the drift until it filled his spirit with the same vibration. He could see that Char and Coreon were feeling the same thing.

The song they had all been following.

The tree's gigantic supple arms reached far out over the mountain range, swirling and dancing in the moving drift and the flickering light from the flowing lava of the sea volcanoes. Its lacy leaves cast shadow patterns all over the mountainsides, making the depths of the seabed flicker and swirl with light. The leaves resembled those of an upworld oak tree, but the body of the tree was more like an undersea kelp plant, fluid and flexible, unlike the solid bark of oaks that lived on the land.

*What is an oak tree doing at the bottom of the sea?* Ven wondered, amazed.

Even more amazing, however, were the creatures that had taken shelter within its boughs. Bright fish in every color of the rainbow, and some colors Ven had not seen in the upworld, hovered amid its branches, decorating them with their hues. Dolphins with a metallic shine to their skin chased each other playfully through the giant tree's boughs, and shimmering silver whales circled the upper limbs, singing in high, sweet tones.

*I wasn't sure if the sea creatures were spirits, like Coreon, Char, and me, because they seemed almost clear at times. I was certain there was something special about them, because a normal whale, fish, or dolphin could not have survived the pressure and the temperature of this place.*

*Any more than we could.*

A word formed in Ven's head. He was not certain if the thought was his own, or if the great tree had put it there with its pounding thrum. Either way, he wanted to give voice to it in his brain.

"Frothta," he whispered.

The song he had been hearing for so long echoed in agreement, ringing through his spirit.

"We've found her," he said to the others.

"We sure have," said Char in awe.

Coreon said nothing. He just stared above him, then pointed at the base of the tree.

*Then suddenly, like a rock falling out of the sky and smacking my head, I remembered something.*

*The drawing I had seen of Sagia, the oldest of the World Trees, was in a book of pictures that all had one thing in common.*

Coiled around the giant trunk, almost invisible against the gleaming bark, was a dragon. Just as Lancel had seemed enormous after the tiny Spicegar, this beast was many times the size of Lancel, who by comparison would have seemed like floating weeds. Ven knew immediately that the creature was female. Her scales were all shades and hues of blue and green, like the colors that were seen in the water of the sea, with frosty white tips that looked like sea foam. Her body was filmy, almost clear, like their spirit forms, but her eyes glowed intensely with a clear, almost unnatural light as intense as that of the air stones, only vastly brighter. The shape of her body was fluid, and her enormous head was crowned with ridges where horns might have been, scalloped like the waves of the sea.

The giant beast rose up and looked over the edge of the mountain at the three boys below. As she did, she resembled a great wave rising to a crest before it crashed to shore.

"Welcome," she said. Her voice vibrated in their heads, ringing with a deep and beautiful music that had a comfortable, reassuring sound, a little like the patter of steady rain on a roof in the night. "I imagine it feels like it has taken you a long time to get here."

Ven and the other boys could only nod in response.

"My name is Dyancynos," said the beast. "I bid you welcome, Char and Coreon. It has been a very long time, even by my measure, since anyone of your kinds have ridden a diving bell to the bottom of the sea." Her vast head swiveled, and she looked directly at Ven.

"As for you, Ven Polypheme, a special welcome is due. You are the first son of Earth ever to come into the Deep—and certainly the only one to live. A few of your race have fallen from ships or met their ends in the Sunlit Realm, but none have ever ventured past where the light ends—especially on purpose."

"You know—how we came here?" Ven asked.

The massive beast's eyes blinked, and her jawline seemed to expanded into a large smile.

"Anything the sea touches is known to me, Ven Polypheme. I heard your name in the Sunlit Realm when you first thrummed it.

I had hoped you would survive until I could come to know more about you. We are distantly related, after all."

Ven almost swallowed his tongue. "We *are*?"

The beast chuckled, a merry sound that thrummed through the moving water at the base of the Tree.

"Dragons and Nain are both children of the Earth," she said.

"Oh."

"And your coming was foretold long ago."

"It was?"

"Of course, we didn't know what your name would be, or anything about you. But the prophecy said that one day a son of Earth would come to the depths, as impossible a task as that seemed."

Ven's head was ringing. "An impossible task? Foretold?"

A huge spray of bubbles rolled out of the great beast's nostrils. Ven was fairly certain that she was chuckling.

"Not all of Time runs forward, Ven Polypheme. There are some that see it in reverse—that have lived in the Future and are growing younger as the rest of the world ages. Those that have been to the Future often speak of it in riddles, because their way of seeing the world is topsy-turvy to us. So your coming here must have been a very important event, because the sages of the Future spoke of it."

"Why—why would there be a riddle about my coming here?"

The dragon's face lost its wide smile, and grew solemn.

"To give us hope," she said.

"How—what do I have to do with that?"

The dragon's massive eyes narrowed. The light from them hit Ven like a shining beacon, making him squint from the brightness.

"Why do *you* think you came here—to the depths of the sea?"

Ven swallowed hard. "I don't know," he said finally. "I've been trying to learn the answer to that from the beginning of my journey. Why—why was it foretold that a Nain would come here?"

Dyancynos watched him for a long moment. When she finally spoke, her voice was low and serious.

"The sea needs a miracle—and the only way for it to happen was to have a Child of Earth come to the depths, where all five elements, all of the Five Gifts of the Creator, could be present at the same time."

Ven's head was throbbing so hard he could barely form thoughts to thrum in response.

"The *sea* needs a miracle? How can that be?" He shook his head, trying to clear it, but the vibrations of the tree, and the dragon, the molten bubbles of lava, the explosions of fireworks, and the pressure of the sea all pressed against his spirit form so hard that he felt it might explode and vanish. "That's why I came here, to the Trenches. But I was looking for my own miracle. I am trying to save the life of my friend."

"I can understand that," Dyancynos said. "I, too, am trying to save the life of my friend."

"Who is your friend?"

The dragon exhaled a great stream of bubbles.

"Frothta. The Tree of Water is dying, Ven. And when she dies— all the magic of the sea will die with her."

# ‐ 41 ‐

# The Fulfillment of Most of Two Prophecies

At the moment the dragon's words sounded in my head, I had the distinct feeling that my brain was drowning.

My thoughts had been overwhelmed ever since I came into the sea, but those words of thrum were like a great tidal wave blasting through what little awareness I had left. I could only blink and stare at the towering tree above me, humming and alive with rings of swimming fish, dolphins, and whales, its arms dancing in the heavy drift at the bottom of the world.

Dying.

Only two thoughts were able to form.

The first was the unsuccessful attempt to imagine what Frothta would have looked like in health, if she was this magnificent in dying.

The second, and far more terrifying, one was the idea that I could do anything about it.

Because in the deepest part of my heart, I had no clue about how to help save her.

"WHAT—WHAT DO I HAVE TO DO?" VEN'S THRUM STAMMERED. His thoughts echoed extremely slowly, between the pressure and his fear. "I don't know how to heal the Tree of Water. I can't even imagine how to try."

The dragon's gigantic body stretched and uncoiled a little, sending gusts of sand and starfish swirling upward. "You've already done it—you came."

"That's—that's it? That's all I had to do?"

A throaty laugh vibrated through the depths.

"That's all? Look what it has cost you to come here, Ven Polypheme. You have come close to meeting Death many times on your journey. And, worse, you have had to watch your friends do so— death of their bodies *and* of their souls." Her thrum grew solemn. "Even now, you still are facing that." She nodded, and Ven felt a gentle tap of pressure on his hand.

He opened his hand and looked at Amariel's red cap of woven pearls.

It had shrunk to nothing more than ashes. A gust in the heavy drift lifted them, and before he could catch them, carried them away among the floating lava bubbles. He was able to seize just one small pearl as the rest of the cap disintegrated.

Ven gasped. His mouth opened, and the bitter water of the Deep started to swell in.

The dragon's eyes gleamed a little brighter. The water in his mouth vanished, and his teeth banged shut.

"Can—can you fix it?" he thought desperately to Dyancynos. "Can you—make it whole again? Get the pieces back?"

The dragon shook her massive head solemnly, or at least to Ven it seemed she did.

"The merrow's cap is gone, Ven Polypheme," she said. "Gone, and not able to be replaced."

Ven felt his throat start to close. He turned to Char, who looked back at him. The sadness in his best friend's eyes was visible, even in the dark water.

He glanced over at Coreon, but the Lirin-mer boy was still staring at the revolving rings of fish and sea creatures swimming through the arms of the Tree of Water.

"So—she is dead?" Ven asked. "Amariel is—*dead*?" His thrum choked on the word.

The dragon's thrum grew even more solemn.

"She may be—it is *very* likely. But I cannot tell for certain, because it seems you left her within the diving bell—so at the moment, the sea is not touching her. I can only see what the sea touches."

"What do I have to do?" Ven asked desperately. "What do I have to do to make your miracle, and mine, happen?"

"Well, the prophecy given to me by the sages of the Future has been fulfilled—a son of Earth has come in the time of Frothta's dying. But I do not think it will matter, unless you are able to fulfill the destiny that was spelled out for you. What was the prophecy you were given, Son of Earth?"

He thought back to the last time he had seen the light of the sun below the surface of the ocean, to the magically colorful Summer Festival. Until he had seen the glowing lava of the seafloor, the fireworks, and Frothta herself, he had thought the Festival grounds to be the most amazing thing he had seen beneath the waves. He remembered the Epona's words, even as she had spoken them in her flighty, singsong voice. He closed his eyes and thought them to Dyancynos.

*"Wanderer, out of place in the drift,*
*This riddle is to you a gift.*
*Free the captive who stays by choice*
*Sing a hymn without your voice*
*Find the souls forgotten by Time*
*Believe the view is worth the climb.*
*Follow the path without using your eyes*

*Five gifts the price to spare one who dies*
*Until the stars shine in the depths of the sea*
*Home again you will never be."*

The dragon looked thoughtful.

"I'm not certain that prophecy applies to either of our needed miracles, Son of Earth," she said sadly. "It really only tells you what you need to do to return home."

Ven shook his head against the pressure of the heavy drift.

"I'm not going home," he said softly.

Both Char and Coreon turned to him in shock. The same word thrummed forth from them both.

*"What?"*

"I mean it," Ven said. "I am not leaving. If Amariel is dead, if the Tree of Water is dying, and I cannot save either one of them, I have no need of going back."

"Why?" Char's thrum demanded. It was not angry, just weak and resigned.

"Because nothing I do makes any difference," Ven said. "What's the point in returning to the Crossroads Inn—to let the Thief Queen find me? I've—we've—come all this way, through all these trials, and it was all for nothing." He pointed to the ancient tree towering above him. "Is she any better, Dyancynos? Has she stopped dying, just because I am here?"

The dragon exhaled, a long, slow stream of fizzy bubbles that took on the color of glowing lava.

"No," she said.

"See?" Ven's thoughts were growing so heavy that he could barely thrum. "I am done," he said to Char and Coreon. "You two, go back now, while you can. Find the diving bell, get your bodies back, and go home—"

"Stop it, Ven," Char said. "You know better than that by now. If you're really stayin', then I'm stayin', too."

"Let's look at the prophecy again," said Coreon. "It seems to me we've accomplished most of the things on your list. I'm not sure about the captive who stays by choice—"

"Maybe it was one o' those ghost spirity things in the diving bells," Char suggested. "They chose to come down in those cages into the Deep."

"Perhaps," said Coreon. "But it seems to me the one you're really missing is that 'Five gifts the price to spare one who dies' part. I know you have at least two of the Five Gifts of the Creator that Lancel told us about, Water, *obviously*, and Earth, meaning you. But what about the other three?"

"Well, there's Fire all around us," Char said. He pointed to the rivers of lava flowing brightly over the seafloor and the bubbles floating above their heads.

"What about Air?" Coreon asked.

Char's brow furrowed. "Goodness knows there's none o' that down here." A moment later his eyes stretched wide in wonder. "Wait—o' course there is!" He put his hand into his filmy pocket and drew out the air stone, the only solid thing on his spirit form. It gleamed in the darkness, forming a circle of blue light around them all.

The greens of Coreon's eyes glowed brightly.

"That's it—that's it! Now all we need is starlight—Ether—the first of the Five Gifts."

Char released the bubble of elemental air, keeping his hand above it. It floated upward, glowing brightly, and hung without moving in the thick water.

"That's gonna be a bit harder," he said reluctantly.

"No, it's not," Ven said. His thrum seemed to be speaking only to himself. "No—it's been here all the time."

"Whaddaya mean?" Char demanded.

Ven held up his hand, just as Char had done the moment before.

In his palm was the last tiny pearl from Amariel's red cap.

## – 42 –

# Another Riddle Answered

*I wasn't sure if I was awake any longer, though it didn't really seem that I was dreaming, either.*

*I thought about how her eyes lit up when she talked about the Deep, how excited she had been for me to see it with her.*

*And now I was here, at the bottom of deepest trench of the ocean, at the foot of the most powerful ancient magic of her world.*

*Without her.*

AMARIEL," VEN SAID. HIS THRUM VOICE WAS HEAVY. "HER name means *Star of the Sea*. She was angry with me whenever I would forget and thrum it in the drift, but really, it's pretty much all that's left of her now." His spirit-eyes began to sting with salt that did not come from the seawater. "I wish she was here—that she is still alive up there, miles above us, in the diving bell. Amariel, look—here's a wonder you deserved to see, and probably never will. Thank you for bringing me here, for letting me see this amazing, watery world of yours, which I never would have seen without you."

Below him, the ground began to glow, it seemed.

The three boys looked down at their feet.

The millions of starfish that covered the seamount on which Frothta stood were growing brighter each second, as if they were the heavenly objects for which they were named. The glow grew more intense, until the dark water of the drift at the bottom of the sea was alight, shining like a bright day in the upworld.

And as they shone, the starfish began to rise in the drift, turning slowly, almost as if they were leaves dancing in the wind. Stars falling upward.

Spreading their new light to every dark corner of the sea.

Beneath their feet, the boys could feel a rumble, a thrum that was louder and stronger than that of Megalodon, of the waterspout, or any other massive thing that they had met up until that point in their travels.

Frothta was soaring upward, revived and growing with the speed of a traveling waterspout, reaching its ropy branches out across the undersea mountain range, lighting the peaks with a golden power. Its voice, beautiful as it had been in dying, was ringing through the Deep, causing the lava to erupt in laughter and the black smokers to split in two.

From everywhere, it seemed, fish and sea creatures appeared, joining in the eternal dance that had been within the Tree of Water's arms from the beginning, expanding it as far as Ven could see.

Out of the corner of his eyes he could see his two friends, their faces slack with wonder, frozen in the light that was washing over them all. Higher above, he could see the head of the dragon Dyancynos, glowing as the Tree was glowing, watching him.

"What's happening?" he asked her silently, his thrum lighter than it had been in the Sunlit Realm. "Has the Tree of Water stopped dying?"

"So it seems," the dragon replied. "This great being, one of the five World Trees, has been healed, reborn, because the five elements that were present at the moment of her birth have come together once again, because of you, Ven. And you saw it. And now you know that she is not a myth, that she lives—and you can tell those who have forgotten her story what you've seen." She looked directly into his eyes, and Ven knew by the feel of her thrum that she was smiling. "That alone has helped to revive her. When all but a few beings in the world have forgotten your name, your story, it's a little like dying."

Ven thought of his family back in the seaside town of Vaarn, half a world away. He remembered how he had felt their sadness when they believed him dead after the Fire Pirate attack, and how much it had meant to him when the albatross that had helped to rescue him returned with a letter from his father, celebrating the news that he had been found alive.

"I think I know what you mean," he said.

The dragon smiled.

"I had a chance once to meet the sister of Frothta, the World Tree known as Sagia, in the forest of the Lirin back in Serendair," Ven continued. "My curiosity was boiling when I got the invitation, but I had to pass it up, to get Amariel back to the sea."

"I suspect you will have that chance again one day," said the dragon.

"I'm not sure I want to go back to the upworld, where that tree lives," Ven admitted. "It was a long and painful journey to get here. Going back may be even more painful—I've heard tales of sailors dying from the bends, and it's a fairly horrible way to go. Couldn't we just stay here now, Dyancynos? I can't imagine returning to the Sunlit Realm without Amariel."

The great beast eyed him with sympathy, but shook her head.

"As important as it is that you came here, Ven, you are out of place. We can sometimes observe each other's worlds, but that does not mean we can live in them. Think of Coreon's people, who gave up the air to live within the sea—and they can never go back. It's time for you to return to the place where the Creator put you, where you are meant to be."

"I'm not sure where that is," Ven said. "The Nain, my people, mostly live within the depths of the Earth. My family chose long ago to live in the upworld, by the edge of the sea, building ships to carry people across that sea, though none of them would ever have dreamed to go themselves. I live in a place far away from my family—I don't really know what is meant by 'home' anymore."

"You are young," said Dyancynos. "You have a lifetime to discover where 'home' will be. Know this, Ven Polypheme—you are always welcome in this place, if ever you are in need."

"Thank you," said Ven gratefully.

"And do not spend too much time wondering why your arrival was foretold," the dragon continued. "You were not chosen to come to the bottom of the sea—*you* chose to do so. You curse your own curiosity, but you have something else that makes you special—courage. And a kind, loyal heart. You seek the magic in the world, but there is much of it in you—not in the way there is in Frothta, or me, but in the simple willingness to see a journey through to the end, taking care of the companions you have brought with you. That is sometimes the greatest magic of all, Ven Polypheme."

"Magic," Ven murmured. His head was still spinning from the power that was surging all around him. "Wait—wait! I almost forgot—what started me off on this quest in the first place, besides Amariel's desire for me to explore the Deep with her." He fumbled around in the buttoned pocket of the filmy vest that was part of his spirit form, then pulled out the sleeve of Black Ivory.

"I have something that belongs to you," he said.

Then he drew the dragon scale from its sheath.

The dragon's eyes widened in surprise.

Then filled a moment later with a shine that looked like tears.

"Oh, my," Dyancynos murmured. Her thrum was soft with wonder. "My scale. You have brought me back my scale."

"Yes," said Ven. It was the only word he could form.

*The ancient dragon was silent for what seemed like forever. But finally she nodded at me, and the scale rose from my hands, as if the drift itself had plucked it from them. It floated up until it came to a stop, hanging in the now-bright water of the depths, in front of her gleaming eyes. The dragon stared at it for even longer than she had been silent.*

*And then she told me the story of how it had come to be separated from her.*

*Her thrum was as clear and clean as the whistle that starts the work shifts each day at my father's factory. It's a silver sound that can be heard all over the harbor when it blasts each morning, impossible to miss. And as she told me the tale, I took note, because I knew I was hearing a special story, lore that had never reached the ears of my kind before. No Nain had ever heard the story, nor any other land-liver.*

*She was trusting me with it. And even before she was done, I knew that I had to go back, back to the upworld, back to the king, and tell him this story.*

*Because it was my job to do so.*

*Because it was my honor to do so.*

How long he stood there after the dragon was finished with her tale, Ven was unsure. He did not know if Coreon and Char were hearing the same story. The boys were still staring at the great convention of sea life that was joining the dance through the arms of the Tree of Water.

Finally, when the great beast had completed her story, she nodded to the boys. Her thrum changed.

"Thank you for all you have done, Char, Coreon, and Ven Polypheme," she said. "Frothta thanks you, as do I. But now it is time for you to return to your own world. I will see to it that you will do so in safety, protected from anything that would harm you in our realm. Hold tight to what you brought with you—your return journey will be swifter than the one that brought you here." She waited while Ven tucked the sleeve of Black Ivory back in his spirit-pocket, and Char hastily took his air stone from the drift and returned it to his own.

"Take these," she continued as five of the smallest glowing stars spun slowly toward them in the drift. "One for each of you, one for your merrow friend, if she lives still, and one for the king of the land-livers, so that future generations will know just enough about Frothta to keep her safe—and no more."

"I understand," Ven said as he plucked three of the stars from the drift and added them to his pocket.

"In the upworld, they will be out of place, you know," said Dyancynos, smiling.

"I know."

"And one more thing before you ascend—Frothta has a gift for you as well."

Ven looked up. As he did, he saw a single leaf, like that of an oak tree in the upworld, falling gently down in the drift. He caught it carefully and turned it over. Its veins were green as the kelp in the forests through which they had traveled.

"Thank you," he said.

The dragon nodded.

Then she sang a single note, pure and sweet, that echoed through the Deep.

The boys looked up.

Like bolts of lightning, breaking through the darkness of the depths, three enormous whales appeared, clear and silver, from the branches of Frothta. They swooped down elegantly, like giant birds of the sea, to where the boys stood, and, before they knew what to do, the three of them were riding on the backs of the great beasts, or, in Char's case, on the tip of its nose.

*They sped us through the darkness of the depths and up toward where the sea began to lighten, at least a little. They followed our thrum, and we followed that of the tolling bell in which we had left Amariel's shrunken body, as well as our own. It did not seem to take long to find ourselves at the bottom of the diving cage, and the whales waited patiently while I fumbled with the skeleton key, almost dropping it several times from my filmy hands.*

*It was pretty strange to look up through the grate in the bottom of the bell to see our earthly bodies, asleep, on the small ledge. We looked pretty much as we had left ourselves, but Amariel, to our dismay, had shriveled to little more than scales and dry skin.*

*I watched as Char and Coreon both swam over to themselves and slipped inside their bodies. They began to yawn and stretch, and once I was sure they were safe, I did the same myself. It felt for a few seconds like I was caught in a giant whirlpool, sucking me down in a spinning riptide, but a moment later I felt solid again.*

*Real, as Char put it.*

"Now whadda we do?" Char asked as Ven began to dig around in his pocket. "I hate to say it, Ven, but it looks like we're too late."

Ven didn't answer. He took one of the tiny gleaming sea stars out and laid it carefully on what he thought had at one time been the merrow's heart.

The three boys watched in amazement as Amariel's body began to swell in the light of the sea star. It filled in, almost like a flower that had been dried too long in the sun of a rainless summer, until the merrow was whole again, curled up asleep on the tiny shelf of the diving bell.

"Don't wake her," Coreon advised as Ven started to gently shake Amariel by the shoulder. "She's been through a lot more than we have—and when she finds her cap is gone, it may take a while for her to get over it. Merrows believe their red pearl caps are part of their spirit, their soul."

"But they can live without them, right?" Char said worriedly.

Coreon nodded. "She doesn't need it to live."

"But it's part of her soul," Char insisted. "Will she be herself without it?"

"Perhaps," the Lirin-mer boy said. "Who knows? But I'm guessing all it means is that she will never walk on the land again—and that's not necessarily a bad thing. She said she didn't want to be like the stupid merrow women who give their caps to human men—she's done that already once with you, right?"

Ven nodded sheepishly.

"So maybe her soul will always be here in the sea. That's probably for the best."

Ven was about to respond, but just as he was forming his reply, the whales nudged their metal room with their giant heads, eager to get going. He lifted the still-sleeping merrow up and followed the other two boys out of the diving bell and into the sea again.

Below them, the black water seemed lighter, still glowing from the celebration miles below. Ven thought he could hear the thrum of the singing from the swirling rings of fish, but decided a moment later that it was all in his memory.

*Goodbye, Dyancynos,* he thought. *Goodbye, Frothta. And thank you.*

At the base of his brain, he felt a gentle thrum, or at least thought he did.

Replaced a moment later by the echoing, vast emptiness of the ocean.

Ven looked into the great face of the giant whale hovering below the diving bell, waiting impatiently for him.

"Sorry," he thrummed at the annoyed creature. "We're ready to go now."

He struggled to hold tight to Amariel, gripping the whale's dorsal fin with one hand and the merrow with the other, as they streaked through the ever-warming water, which was growing lighter all the time. Amariel grew more and more restless and awake the longer they traveled, and just as they were approaching Coreon's reef, she finally opened her eyes and stared wildly into Ven's.

"What—where?—"

"Shhhhh," Ven thrummed in return. "You're safe—and we're on our way back to the Lirin-mer settlement."

The merrow shuddered. "I thought you just said we were safe," she said.

"Coreon's with us," Ven said. "And he's grown up a heck of a lot since we left. I think we will be fine."

*And I was right.*

*Coreon's father was waiting anxiously at the edge of the reef when we arrived. He was floating above the colorful coral, which was waving its tiny arms in welcome. The Cormorant watched as the whales offloaded us and said farewell in the high, squeaking thrum in which they sang as we had been traveling. We thanked them as best we knew how and watched them swim away, back to the depths, back to the world we could never have imagined if we hadn't seen it for ourselves.*

*Coreon's father swept Coreon into his arms as soon as he was close enough, then turned him loose and pulled back to look at him. Whatever they thrummed to each other stayed between them, but it was clear by the way that the Lirin-mer man looked at his son that he had found a new respect for him. I was glad— I have a father a lot like that, someone whose respect I was always trying to earn, who seemed to think of me as a baby, but I have since come to know loves me and misses me when I am away.*

*I am glad for Coreon. He deserves it.*

*Char and I got to speak to the Cormorant for a few moments before he, Coreon's father, and Coreon went back to the reef. The Cormorant told us that he had indeed received the Sea King's message, and had stayed the attack on the Gated City as a result. They had instead undertaken just to seal the underwater tunnel, and had set off an explosion so enormous that they could see the walls of the city shake with dust from outside the harbor. He said the tunnel had collapsed completely, and in the half-turn of the moon since the explosion, there had been no sign of anyone from within the Gated City leaving or harming the reef.*

*He told us something interesting about the tree stump we had seen in Spicegar's kelp forest—that it was definitely not the remains of the Tree of Water, but rather a massive oak tree that had once grown on the border of the Lirin-mer lands before they had gone into the sea.*

*And had been cut down to make the airwheel.*

*Coreon, Char, and I just looked at each other and smiled.*

*The Cormorant gave us each another flask of fresh water, and another packet of kelp.*

*And that was it. No goodbye, no lingering, no other comments.*

*But as they were swimming away, I saw Coreon stop and turn back to us one last time. He held up his hand, and smiled slightly. I found myself matching his gestures in return.*

*And somehow I know, deep in my guts, that the world of the Lirin-mer and that of the land-livers has become closer, more peaceful, even if he, Char, and I never meet again.*

The closer to the surface they got, the brighter the water and Amariel's mood grew. They were swimming on their own, now that the silvery whales had returned to the depths, and she seemed to get stronger as they passed the skelligs and approached Kingston Harbor. The boys took turns thrumming to her, filling her in on what had happened since the waterspout and the diving bell. Amariel shuddered, but she seemed happy enough to have escaped with her life.

She did not mention the loss of her red pearl cap. But she did put the glowing sea star at her throat, like a necklace, and caressed it every so often.

"I can see her," she finally whispered to Ven as they approached the seawalls that marked the underwater opening to Kingston Harbor.

"See what?" Ven asked.

"You know," Amariel said. "The tree, and her guardian."

"Really?"

"Really. And everything around them. It's like—it's like part of me is down there with them."

Ven smiled in relief. *That's because it is*, he thought. The merrow nodded, and Ven remembered his thrum still could be heard, even as close as they were to home.

Their excitement grew as they approached the surface. Amariel was the first to break out of the waves, and she waved excitedly to the boys as she did.

Char and Ven surfaced at almost the same time a moment later, laughing.

"Ven!" Char shouted.

"What?" Ven shouted back.

"I have no idea what you're thinkin'!"

"What a relief," Ven chuckled, trying to breathe lightly and adjust to the thinner air of the upworld. "I don't have any idea what you are thinking either, Char."

"*I'm* thinking you both are bonkers," Amariel said cheerfully. "Only humans—er, land-livers—would prefer to be ignorant. Oh well."

Her words were interrupted by a harsh scream.

# ~ 43 ~

# A Familiar Friend

A GIANT WHITE BIRD WITH GRAY-TIPPED FEATHERS WAS CIR-cling overhead.

"The albatross!" Ven cried. "Look! It's the albatross!"

"That's just what she looked like on the day I first found you in the sea," Amariel said, grinning widely. "She was flying in great circles around where you had fallen from that exploding ship—what was it called?"

Ven thought, then shook his head.

"I don't remember," he said. "But it hardly matters now." He waved as much as he could from the water, trying to keep from sinking. "She's always been a great friend—and Madame Sharra told me that she was the eyes of someone else who was watching out for me."

The great bird banked on the wind, then began slowly flying east.

"Do you think she's leading us to shore?" Char asked, struggling to keep above the waves.

"I hope so," Ven answered. "Wherever she's leading, I think we should follow."

"I can see the shoreline from here," said Amariel. "We're not too far from the northern end of Kingston, up past the Gated City. The skelligs aren't too far from here either, just outside the harbor, farther north."

The boys squinted as they looked east.

"You have great eyes, ya know that?" said Char. "All I see is waves forever."

"Well, trust me, we're not that far away. You probably would be best off to float on your backs, so you don't have to keep catching your breath. I'll let you know when to stop swimming."

"Good idea," Ven agreed. "That way I can watch the albatross as well. I'm so glad to see her."

"Is it just me, or is the wind a lot colder than it was when we started?" Char asked.

"It's autumn now," Ven said. "Summer's gone." He felt a bit of sadness creep through him at the thought, but pushed it away and concentrated on the sky above them, clear and blue with traces of fragile white clouds spun like cotton candy through it.

The swim was longer than he had imagined, and by the time the merrow told them they were nearing the shore, the clouds had thickened and the sky above the albatross had grown darker and gray. The sun still hung in the sky, well above the horizon, but had turned a bloody shade of orange.

"What are we gonna do when we get to land?" Char asked, staring nervously above him. "If we're north o' the Gated City, the Thief Queen may be nearby."

"Not if the Cormorant was right," Ven said. He closed his eyes for a moment as a stray wave slapped over them. The tide was getting stronger, and the waves were beginning to crest with white foam, pulling them toward shore.

"You should probably turn around and look now," said the merrow. "It's getting pretty shallow here. I can't go too much farther without scraping my tail on the bottom—and I *hate* that."

Ven rolled over and floated upright, treading water. The coming of night had turned the waves dark blue, and the shoreline ahead was rocky and gray. He could see the northern end of the Gated City off to the south, but it was still too far away to see any people on its walls.

"Are you going back to your school now?" he asked anxiously.

Amariel shrugged.

"I don't know," she said. "I think I'll stay around and follow you both down the coast until you get home—especially if the albatross leaves once you get to land. Then, when I'm sure you're safe, I may go out of the harbor, call for my school, and see if they're near enough to catch up with. Winter is coming—it will be time for them to head home soon."

"I'm going to miss you so much," Ven said. "I just got you back."

"I'll miss you too. But I miss my family as well. I've been following you around the sea for the whole summer. I need to go home."

"Fair enough. Make sure you say goodbye before you leave, if you can. We'll meet you at the old abandoned dock north of town."

The merrow nodded. "Good luck. Come back to the sea if you get into trouble."

"We will," said Char. "Thanks."

The albatross banked to the south. Ven watched as she sailed over the rocky beach, then began flying in circles around a pile of rocks at the water's edge.

"What do you suppose she's up to now?" Char demanded. He spat out the seawater of a wave that had caught him in the mouth.

"I don't know. Let's go see. You want to come along, Amariel?"

The merrow sighed. "I guess so. But I can't get too close. I've lost enough scales off my fluke already."

They swam south until they were within better sight of the rocky outcropping. By now many boulders and large rocks dotted the water's edge, and they had to swim carefully around them to avoid being grazed by them. The albatross seemed to be circling one particularly large rock ledge, half in, half out of the water, most of it buried in sand.

As they got closer, Char stopped suddenly, treading water.

"Ven," he whispered. "Do you see something odd about that huge rock?"

Ven stared as best as he could in the dim light of dusk, but his eyes were stinging from the combination of salt water and fresh air. The sun was beginning to set, and the sky was taking on colors of pink and orange and a deep, forbidding purple.

"It does seem odd," he agreed. "But I'm not sure why."

"Well, do you see that half-round indent on this side?" Char asked.

"Yes."

"It looks like a porthole."

"A porthole? Like a window in a—"

"Criminey!" Char exclaimed. "That's no rocky ledge. That thing's an old, dead ship!"

"Or what's left of one," Ven said. "I'd say it's less than half a ship."

"So what do ya suppose has the albatross so interested?" Char asked. "There are dozens of broken ships along the water's edge in Kingston."

"I don't know. That one looks pretty old."

The ruined vessel appeared to be wedged largely in the sand at the water's edge, so that waves swelled around it, splashing it with white foam. There was something about the sight of it that burned Ven's already stinging eyes.

*It was a little like the feeling of thrum, though that was something I had usually felt in my skin or my ears. I wondered if in fact the wreck was calling out to me, its vibration catching me in the eyes. Amariel had said that things in the upworld had thrum like the beings and places and storms of the sea, but that their vibrations got lost in the wind.*

*Then I saw the name, all but gone, carved long ago and once painted in thick black paint that had all but worn off completely over time and in the surf.*

**Athenry**, it said.

"Do you see that?!" Ven shouted.

Char was already swimming straight for the shipwreck. Ven followed him, slowing down only to avoid the coastal rocks and small jellyfish that were floating along the water's edge.

"No—wonder Dyancynos—couldn't—feel—it," he said in between waves. "She said there were places of water that didn't count as the sea. Technically, I guess this is the harbor."

Char had gotten as far as the porthole. He peered inside.

"What's in there?" Ven called.

His best friend lifted himself up even closer and leaned forward through the opening. The portal was barred like a window in a prison cell, but the bars were rusty and cracked with time.

"I don' see anything," he called.

Ven looked out to sea, where Amariel was floating, far enough away from shore to be out of the rolling tide. The merrow shrugged. He turned back toward the shore, and as he did, a shiver went up his spine, as if someone was watching him. He looked around, but saw no one nearby. The Gated City was still too far away to see any details, and was slowly being swallowed by darkness. He shook his head, and the feeling went away.

"Do you think it's safe to explore?" he called to Char.

His best friend replied by crawling through the porthole and disappearing into the shattered ship.

Ven hurried to catch up. The opening that Char had slid through was a little small for him, so he crawled through as carefully as he could. He found himself in the old ship's hold, the rotten wood floor wet from the water that had splashed through the porthole, but otherwise dry.

The hold was empty, except for a few pieces of rusty hardware, hinges and metal plates bolted into the ship's interior walls. A few links of what had once been chains were attached to the plates.

"This musta been a horrible ride," Char mumbled. "It's easy enough to get seasick when you're free to move around. But being chained day after day to the wall of a prison ship? Gives me the willies just bein' in here, all these centuries later."

"I don't see anything of interest," Ven said as he walked carefully around the hold. "I'm not surprised it's so solid. My father has built a few prison ships, and they are as sturdy as ships come. They can't sail very fast because they're so heavy, and they put extra strong wood and iron in them to make sure none of the prisoners escape."

"What did that key you found tell you to do in here?" Char asked. "Because I want to get out of here right now. I'm startin' to get gooseflesh."

Ven fished the skeleton key out of his pocket and held it up to the porthole to catch the last of the day's light.

*"Free the only innocent prisoners she ever held,"* he read.

"Well, we're clearly too late for that," said Char. "Anybody who was imprisoned in here, innocent or not, is long gone."

"So it seems," Ven agreed. "We should search the place carefully anyway."

"What's to search?" Char asked crossly. "This is just the hold, the very bottom o' the ship. All o' the cabins and cells and decks are long gone as well. It's just a big, empty, broken wooden box now. Which is good, because even as dead and shattered as it is, I can still feel the sadness, and the evil that it was built to contain. It's makin' me shake. C'mon—let's get outta here."

Ven was pacing back and forth across the length of the rotten deck.

"We're missing something," he said.

Char sighed. "We sure are. We're missin' *supper*. And the hearth and the fire and the kitchen o' the Crossroads Inn. And Mrs. Snodgrass. And our friends. And Felitza. C'mon, Ven—let's go."

Ven shook his head. He turned and walked back to the front of the shipwreck.

"I know we're missing something," he repeated.

Char threw up his hands in disgust. "What? *What* are we missin'?"

Ven shook his head, trying to clear it of salt water and confusion. There was something nagging at the back of his mind, but he couldn't force it to come forth. He decided to try not to concentrate too hard.

As he did, a picture came into his mind. It was the image of a fish, one of the many odd creatures they had met on the coral reef before venturing into the Deep. There was something particularly odd about it, ugly and spotted, with yellow fins. He thought back to where he had seen it, then realized that it had inflated into a ball almost as soon as they came upon it.

Then, suddenly, he understood.

"Remember that poisonous puffer fish from the reef?" he asked. "The one that swelled up out of nowhere?"

Char nodded.

"I think Amariel said he had a stretchable stomach that could fill with water or air to keep him upright, didn't she?"

"Yes—so what?"

"Well, a lot of ships have something like that, too." Ven knelt down and tapped on the rotten floorboards.

"A stretchable stomach?"

"No—but something that fills with water or air to keep it upright. It's called a ballast tank. My father put them in almost every ship he made—the big ones, at least."

"I've been on plenty o' ships in my life, an' I never saw nothin' like that," Char said suspiciously.

"Unless you see the ship out of the water, you never would," said Ven as he continued to tap on the floor. "The ballast tank is at the very bottom of the hull. It's either sealed to keep air in, or there are tiny slits that keep it filled with water." He stopped when he heard a hollow sound beneath the floorboards. "I think I found it."

"Criminey." Char crouched down on the floor and joined in the search. Within a few moments they discovered a long regular crack in the floorboards that appeared to be the seam of a hatch or doorway.

Ven took out his jack-rule. He extended the magnifying glass and found the lines of a door. He folded the glass back in and pulled out the knife blade, then cleared away a lot of the gunk from the seam. He tucked the tool back in his pocket when he was done.

"Watch your fingers," Ven advised as they tried to pry the hatch in the floor up. "The wood of the door is almost as thick as your arm—it has to be in this part of the hull."

They struggled, lifted, and pulled until finally the hatch gave way. It swung up, revealing a small ladder with three rungs, one of them broken.

And darkness.

"Whaddaya know," Char whispered.

His question was answered by a deep, threatening growl that made the hair on both of their necks stand on end.

And two yellow eyes, glowing at them in the darkness.

A hair's breadth away from them.

Then, before they could breathe, the beast leapt from the darkness and lunged at Char's throat.

Knocking him to the ground.

## — 44 —

# A Mysterious Reunion

Ven's hand went immediately to his jack-rule. He pulled the tool from his pocket again and quickly extended the knife. His hands were shaking.

Then he looked down in surprise.

Char was lying on his back. Standing on top of him, looking confused, was a slender dog the color of butter and cream, with long ears the color of toasted marshmallows. He was staring down at Char as if he knew him.

Ven realized a moment later that he did.

"Finlay!" he exclaimed. "What are you doing here?"

Char's eyes were closed tight. He opened them slowly.

"Is—isn't this Mr. Coates's dog?" he asked. "From the weapons shop?"

"One of them," Ven said. "Hey, boy! What are you doing here? How did you get out of the Gated City?" He crouched down and held out his hands to the yellow dog.

Finlay leapt off Char's stomach and trotted over. He licked Ven's hands while Ven scratched his ears.

"I assume you're not expectin' him to actually answer you," Char said, slowly standing up. "The only talkin' animal in the upworld I know is Murphy the cat—at least if I'm rememberin' correctly. My brain is boiled since we've been in the sea."

"What could he be doing here—in the wreck of the *Athenry?*"

"Dunno," said Char. "Could he be one o' the only innocent prisoners she ever held?"

As if in response, the dog ran over to the dark hold opening and began to bark.

Ven followed him. He peered through the opening.

Cowering in the back of the ballast tank at the bottom of the ship were two human children, a boy and a girl. Ven guessed them to be about Char's age. They were ragged and thin, and their eyes were wide and hollow in their faces, which Ven could barely see in the slashes of light that came in from a pair of small slats on each side of the ballast tank, too narrow for a person to fit through.

But just wide enough for a skinny dog.

They looked scared to death.

Ven's heart leapt into his throat.

They looked more afraid than I had ever seen anyone look in my life.

Their raggy clothes were ill-fitting, as if the children had shrunk since putting them on. After a moment I realized it was because the clothes were made to fit human adults, and were just too big.

Both of them were chained to the wall with leg irons that were probably left over from the <u>Athenry</u>'s days transporting criminals to their prison-colony home. There were two small cots with thin blankets behind them, with chamber pots underneath. An empty flask and a few scraps of bread lay on the floor near them.

Otherwise the ballast tank was empty.

And as my heart sank all the way from my throat to my stomach, I realized we must have found the only innocent prisoners the <u>Athenry</u> had ever held.

"Water—please," the little girl whispered.

Ven and Char looked at each other. Then they dug furiously into their packs and pulled out the half-full flasks of fresh water the Cormorant had given them. Ven pulled out the cork from his, hurried to the girl, and held the flask to her lips. She drank greedily as Char let the boy drink the rest of the contents of his flask.

"Don't be afraid," Ven said to the boy, who was shaking so hard that the water was spilling over his face. "We'll help you. Who are you?"

The little girl leaned forward. Just as she did, the last light of the day splashed through the slats in the tank. In that dim light Ven could see that she had dark eyes with dark circles beneath them and similarly dark hair. The boy, on the other hand, had hair that was almost colorless and eyes the color of the sky.

The girl said nothing.

"Ahem. Maybe they'd be less afraid if they weren't *chained to a wall*," Char said pointedly.

"Oh! Yes. Sorry. My brain is still addled from the salt water." Ven took the skeleton key out of his pocket. He read the inscription again.

"All right," he said. "Here goes."

He reached for the leg iron that was clasped around the little girl's leg. The girl shrank back, trying to scramble away. Ven put his hands up.

"Whoa. Don't worry," said Char. "He's just tryin' to help. If ya hold still, he might be able to set you free. Hold still a minute."

The children looked at each other. When they did, Ven noticed that in spite of having totally different coloring, they both had the same long thin nose that hooked slightly at the bottom.

Ven held up the skeleton key,

"May I?" he asked. He tried to keep his voice as gentle as he could. Finlay came over to him and sniffed at the long thin tool, then walked away, seemingly satisfied.

The children exchanged another glance. Then the girl nodded.

Ven took hold of the padlock on the girl's ankle. He winced at how bony and bruised that ankle was. Then he slid the skeleton key inside the hole in the padlock and jiggled it around.

A solid *thunk* echoed through the ballast tank.

The children's faces lit up. The little girl pulled the shackle off her foot and tossed it across the ballast tank and into a wall. Then she grabbed the shackle around the boy's ankle and held it still for Ven. He quickly freed the boy from his chains. The key almost fell out of his hands as the girl threw her arms around his neck and hugged him.

"Thank you," she said. Her voice was stronger than the first time he had heard it.

"Will you please tell us who you are?" Ven asked. "We've been looking for you for a very long time."

"How can that be, if you doesn't know who we is?" the girl said.

Ven and Char exhaled at the same time. Then Ven held the key up where she could see it.

"I found this in a glass bottle floating in the sea on one of the skelligs outside the harbor to the north," he said. "There was a scrap of oilcloth wrapped around it with just one word—*Athenry*."

"What does that mean?"

Ven blinked. "Well, it's—this place, where we are. The prison ship, the *Athenry*." The children just stared at him. "This was once a small part of a gigantic ship that brought prisoners from far away to the Gated City, to live in it as kind of penal colony."

"I didn't know that," said the girl. "I don't know what those words mean. None of them ever told us anything about where we is."

"Them?"

The girl hesitated. "The guards," she said finally.

"Guards? There have been people holding you captive here?"

She nodded. "They brought us food and water every few days—until about ten days ago. That night, there was a big *boom*. We could feel it, even in here. The tide was high, because the water was coming in." She pointed to wet spots on the floor. "And it will be coming in again soon. But after that night, no one comed. We runned out of water two days ago."

"That must have been the attack on the Gated City," Ven said to Char. "The Cormorant said the tunnel was sealed half a turn of the moon ago—that means about two weeks. They must have been held captive by the thieves from inside the city—probably Felonia's thugs from the Raven's Guild. Once the tunnel was sealed, the guards couldn't get out to bring them supplies." He turned back to the girl. "You've been without food and water for ten days?"

The girl shrugged. "Only water. The animal has bringed us food. He comed not long after the boom. He bringed us some bread. He goes out every night and comes back with something to eat. But I don't think he can carry water."

"He must have escaped during the attack," Ven said to Char. "The sea Lirin wouldn't have paid any attention to a dog fleeing the tunnel."

"How long have you been here?" Char asked.

The children stared at them.

"We don't remember ever not being here," the little girl said.

"You're kiddin'."

"You've lived here all your lives?" Ven asked in disbelief. "Have they ever let you out?"

"Never," said the little girl. "At least not when we're awake. Every now and then they gives one of us a drink that makes us fall asleep. Then they comes in and takes that one out in a blanket. When they comes back, we're still asleep. But they never takes both of us at the same time. Just one. I heared the guards talking once, and they said they were taking us to him, but we never get to see him, because we is asleep. But he comed to see *us* once, I remember. We both was awake. That was a good day."

"He? Who? The dog?"

The children exchanged a glance. Then the girl spoke again.

"Our father. The guards bringed him one night when the moon was full, a long, long time ago. We was very little then. He wasn't allowed to stay very long, just long enough to hug us and tell us our names and not to be afraid, that he would find a way to get us out one day. But he never did. He never comed back. I don't think he ever will. It's been a very long time."

Ven scratched his head. His curiosity was blazing like wildfire, making his scalp and skin itch. "You're brother and sister?" The children nodded. "Twins?" They looked at him oddly, and he realized if they didn't know the word for *dog*, they probably didn't know what he meant. He thought about every warning he had been given in the sea about telling names, and then threw caution to the winds. "I'm Ven—and this is Char. Can you tell me your names?"

"I'm Hannah," the girl said after a moment. "And my brother is Sam. He doesn't talk much, so I do it for him."

"Who teaches you things?" Ven asked. "How did you learn to talk?"

Hannah shrugged. "I listen to the guards when they don't know it."

"We need to get them outta here," Char said. "The tide's comin' in, and soon it will be Total Dark. They probably can't swim."

"You're right," said Ven. "This dog is Finlay, by the way—he belongs to a friend of ours inside the Gated City. I'm glad he has taken care of you." He helped Hannah to stand, while Char helped Sam, then signaled to Finlay, and slowly helped them out of the ballast tank and into the dark core of the prison ship.

"It's prolly a good thing it's dark," Char said as he pulled Sam's arm up over his own shoulder to steady him and help him walk. "After spendin' their whole lives in darkness, the sun's gonna burn their eyes at first."

"Very true," said Ven as he helped Hannah out of the shipwreck and onto the rocky sand of the windswept beach. "Plus it should help hide us until we get back to the Crossroads Inn. We're going to have to walk right past the Gated City—and even if the thieves aren't able to get out right now, they still always have guards on the walls and people on the Skywalk. I think we should try very hard not to be seen. I want Felonia to think I'm long gone."

"Yeah, and we don' wanna tip her off that these two are free," Char said. "I don' know why they were so important to the Thief Queen, or whoever was keepin' them prisoner, but there's sure to be some fallout when they find out they're missin'."

"If they ever do," Ven said. He looked back at the broken piece of the *Athenry*. It looked like nothing more than a large black rock formation in the dark. "No wonder no one knew what had become of it. It must have run aground in the harbor just outside the Gated City, probably in a storm. All these years it's been here, the last dozen or so serving as a prison for these guys. I wonder what's so special about them."

Char looked back at the Gated City in the distance. The torches had been lit all along its high walls, filling the darkness with thin wisps of smoke rising ominously into the air.

"We prolly will never know," he said. "At least *I* won't. I'm never goin' back in there again—and that's prolly the only place to find out."

Ven came to the edge of the beach where the dry, rocky dunes met the wet sand. He squinted in the darkness, but could see nothing but the rolling waves.

"Amariel? Are you there?"

"Yes." Her voice floated over the wind and the crashing of the waves. "Can't you see me? I can see you clear as day."

"Not a bit," Ven admitted. "Can you follow us down the coast back to central Kingston?"

"Certainly," shouted the merrow over the noise of the ocean. "Who do you have there?"

"The innocent prisoners."

"Ah! So that's the *Athenry*," Amariel said. "I guess that makes sense. By the way, there's someone watching you from the wall of the Gated City."

Panic coursed through Ven, quenching his curiosity and leaving him weak.

"Where?"

"About midway down the wall, towards the Outer Market. On the good side of the tunnel. Near the torch that keeps flickering."

"Hannah, do you think you can stand without help for a minute?" The girl nodded. Ven dug into his vest pocket and pulled out the jack-rule. He extended the glass that magnified things from far away, thankful that he had not dropped the tool in the sea the many times he had come close to doing so.

He held up the jack-rule's glass to his eye.

And gasped.

# ~ 45 ~

# A Rescue, Long Time in Coming

**W**HAT LOOKED LIKE A GIANT WATERY EYE, BLACK AS THE COM-ing night, was staring back at him from within a dark, floating ring.

Ven almost dropped the jack-rule.

He blinked quickly, then held the glass up to his eye again.

The floating eye was gone.

In its place he saw a man in a long, dark cloak and hood. He was standing near one of the large streetlamp torches, half turned away, putting a spyglass of his own into the folds of his cloak. Then he turned back to Ven.

As if he could see him.

*I must have been looking straight into the lens of his spyglass,* Ven thought.

The man stood motionless for a moment. Then he grabbed his hood and pulled it down.

Ven gasped again. Even in the almost-complete dark he recognized him.

"It's Mr. Coates!" he shouted. "Char, it's Mr. Coates!"

"Seriously?" Char's voice rang with excitement. "Oh, I'm so glad he's alive. Last time we were in his shop, I wasn't sure he had made it out, blood on the floor an' all."

Ven turned the tiny ring on the edge of his telescoping tool to try and focus better. Mr. Coates's dark eyes above dark circles and beneath dark hair came into view. That hair seemed a little grayer than the last time Ven had seen it a few months before, but perhaps he was imagining it.

He stepped back a little farther, and saw through the glass that at the man's side was an enormous dog, muscular and shaggy, standing atop the Skyway with the weapons maker. The giant beast shook, and tufts of hair exploded into the air around him and were carried off a moment later by a gust of wind into the dark. Ven broke into a wide grin.

"It's Munx!" he called to Char. "Munx is on the Skyway with him!"

Char exhaled happily. "Good. Good—he's all right too, then. I love that dog."

Mr. Coates held out both his hands in front of him, palms down. Then he put one hand flat on his chest, near his heart.

"He's trying to tell me something," Ven said as the weapons maker repeated the gesture. "But I can't tell what it is." He held the small telescope out for Char to look through. Char did, then shrugged.

Ven peered through the glass again. Mr. Coates was patting his chest harder now, insistently.

"It looks like he's trying to say that something belongs to him," Ven said. Through the glass he could see Mr. Coates look over his shoulder anxiously. The man reached back into the folds of his garment and took out his spyglass again. He extended it toward them, looked through it, then began sweeping his left arm violently, as if to hurry them away toward the north.

"He wants us to get out of here, that seems clear," said Ven. "We had better do as he says." He heard a bark, and turned around to where the two young former captives stood, fighting to remain upright in the sea wind.

Finlay, Mr. Coates's other dog, was running in circles around Sam and Hannah, chasing the foaming waves away from the children as they skittered back into the sea. Char chuckled, but Ven felt the backs of his eyes burn with sudden curiosity.

And realization.

"They're—they're *his*," he said slowly. "That's what he's telling us, Char—Sam and Hannah are *his kids*!"

"Criminey," Char whispered. "Are—are you sayin' he's the one that put the skeleton key in that bottle?"

"Makes sense, doesn't it?" Ven said as he hurried toward the little girl. "When you saw the skeleton key, you remembered you had seen one like it in his shop. And he told us that while he knew about the tunnel out of the market, he couldn't leave, didn't he? *There are many layers in a prison—it all depends on who's doing the watching*, that's what he said, remember?" He stopped in front of the young girl. "Hannah—can you look through this, please? Up on the wall."

The girl stared at him, then reluctantly put her eye to the glass.

She stood still for a moment, then began to shake with excitement.

"That's him! That's our father!"

"Oh, man, we gotta get them outta here," Char said. "If he's on the north wall of the Gated City, he's real far away from his shop in the Outer Market. In fact, he's a deep as you can get in the Inner Ring—right in the middle of the Raven's Guild territory. He's prolly watchin' to make sure we get the kids outta the *Athenry* and to safety."

"Let's do that, then," Ven agreed. He took hold of Hannah's arm. "Come on—let's get out of here."

"I want to see him! I want to see my father!" the young girl squealed, twisting away.

"Come with us—please come with us," Ven begged, pulling her as gently as he could. The sand was slippery, and he was having trouble standing upright after all the time in the sea. His lungs and skin were still waterlogged, and even the weak girl was more than he could hold on to.

Hannah twisted free and stumbled toward the city in the distance. She had only gotten a few paces before Char tackled her, pulling her down with him in a heap on the sand. "It's all right," he said, grabbing her arms as she scratched at him. "I know—I really do—but we can't go there right now. We have to get you and Sam to safety before we do anythin' else—your dad wants it that way, too. Come on. Please. Just come on."

Weeping, the girl pulled away and tried to drag herself toward the city.

Night had fallen completely, and the moon had not yet risen. All around them was dark wind and crashing sea, and the flickering lamplight in the distance. Over the sound of the waves, Ven suddenly heard a voice floating on the wind. It was sweet and warm, a wordless tune he thought he knew, and he smiled.

The children stopped. Hannah ceased her struggle, and Sam froze where he stood. They turned toward the south, following the sound.

Ven sighed in relief. The merrow's song had not only enchanted the frantic children, but made the buzzing in his ears from the salt water and the ache in his head disappear.

*Thank you, Amariel,* he thought. *You are always there when I need your help.*

Maybe it was just his imagination, but he thought that the song grew a little louder, a little more amused in reply. The merrow had said that thrum in the upworld got lost in the wind, but now that they had been to the edge of life and death together, maybe their messages would still be able to find each other.

Ven took hold of Hannah's limp wrist, while Char put his arm around Sam's small shoulders. Together they helped the frail children along the beach, long into the night, as the moon rose and set again, over the pebbles and broken shells, around the fragments of lobster traps and scraps of rope wedged in the sand, away from the walls of the Gated City, all the way south until the lights of Kingston finally came into view as the sky was growing paler with the coming of Forelight.

At the edge of an old abandoned dock.

Just as the merrow's song ended.

The twins collapsed, exhausted, onto the sand. Char bent down beside them, puffing as well.

"I thought movin' through the water was harder than the air," he said between breaths. "But now I miss how much the sea carried me."

"Rest for a minute," Ven said. "I'll be right back."

He trotted to the dock and out to the end of it, taking care to avoid the rotted planks. His face, dry and sore from salt, broke into an enormous smile.

Floating in the water, where she had been so many times before, was a girl with green eyes and long, wet hair, beautiful multicolored scales peeking out of the water below her armpits.

She was grinning broadly in return, unbothered by the fact that her porpoise teeth were showing.

"Thank you so much," he said earnestly. "It's amazing how a merrow song can calm down even the most panicking land-liver."

Amariel shrugged. "I've gotten used to having to do that, ever since I rescued you. It is, however, getting a little old."

Ven thought back to his birthday, to the thrill of the Inspection voyage, the terror of the Fire Pirate attack, the explosion of the ship whose name he could no longer remember, and the beauty of the songs that greeted him as he lay on the piece of floating wreckage.

"Well, we did it," he said. "We finally did it! You've shown me the Deep—"

"Keep your voice down," the merrow interrupted. "As you know by now, that's hardly something for me to brag about."

Ven laughed. "I don't know about that. You brought the first son of Earth to the bottom of the world, fulfilled a couple of prophecies, saved the Tree of Water, helped return the dragon scale to Dyancynos, and lived to tell about it. I think that may make you more famous one day than—what's her name? The merrow from your school that the skellig is named after?"

"Lilyana," said Amariel, smiling more slightly. "And you did a lot of that while I was sleeping."

"It doesn't matter. It was always your idea."

The dragon's words returned to his mind.

*We can sometimes observe each other's worlds, but that does not mean we can live in them. Think of Coreon's people, who gave up the air to live within the sea—and they can never go back.*

"I'm so grateful for the chance to have seen your world, Amariel," he said. "And I appreciate that you came to visit mine as well."

"Well, now that's done, I guess it's time to say goodbye for real this time," the merrow said. "It's time for me to go home. Winter is coming, and I want to be with my family for the swim to the Warm Waters."

"What are the Warm Waters?" Ven asked, his curiosity flooding over him and erasing the sadness that had begun to take hold.

Amariel sighed.

"I'll tell you what," she said. "You get those younglings to some sort of safe harbor, and get some sleep. I'll wait until tomorrow morning to say goodbye. And maybe I'll tell you one last tale—the story of the Warm Waters—before I go. One last story to remember me by. But only maybe—we shall have to see what comes with the new day. I may be tired, or feeling grumpy, and if I am, you will have to wait for the tale."

"All right," said Ven. "That makes sense. Besides, I think you should stay at least one more day anyway. Don't you want to find out what the king's surprise is?"

"Surprise?"

"Yes, every time I come home from an adventure, I tell the king a story. The last time I saw him he said he had a surprise for me when I got back. Don't you want to know what it is?"

The merrow considered for a moment.

"Yes, I suppose I do," she said. Her face got brighter, and Ven laughed, knowing that she was the one person in the world he knew that was as much a slave to curiosity as he was. "All right. I'll see you here tomorrow."

## – 46 –

# The Return

*While the thought of sleeping in my own bed at the Crossroads Inn, and seeing all my friends again, and hugging Mrs. Snodgrass, the innkeeper's wife, and happily stuffing Felitza's griddle cakes into my mouth made me so happy that my nose itched, I decided it was better to pay my debts first.*

*So, difficult as it was, just before dawn I put Char, Sam, and Hannah in a delivery cart full of late-season squash that was headed for the inn and went back to the fishing village, down to the docks where we had met Asa.*

*I had, after all, promised him the tale.*

T HE SUN WAS JUST BEGINNING TO LIGHT THE EDGES OF THE eastern sky toward the inn when Ven came to the dock where had seen the fisherman.

And Madame Sharra.

He looked toward the Gated City, hoping for and dreading the sight of a rainbow flash, but saw nothing but the gray haze of the morning. He shielded his eyes and watched, hoping to see Mr.

Coates again, but the walls of the city were silent, with not even a scout visible on the Skyway in the distance.

He sighed, then turned west toward the sea and made his way down the pier to the place where the red-bottomed boat was moored.

He nodded politely to the fishermen who passed him on the dock, who nodded politely in return, but didn't seem to really notice him. Asa's boat was halfway down on the right, and he could see the kind man's shadow growing longer in the rising sun as he sat on a barrel, stripping a length of rope.

"Good morning," Ven said. "I've come to tell you your tale."

"Excellent," the man replied. He put down his rope, then turned and raised the brim of his cap.

Ven gasped out loud.

"Your Majesty?"

From beneath his soiled fishing cap, the king smiled.

"What—what are you doing here?"

"I'm here for my story, of course," King Vandemere said merrily.

"How—how—?"

"Shhh," the king said. "Your friend, the albatross, has been flying around my castle battlements each morning for the last few days. She makes one full circle around the tower where I have my tea in the morning, then flies straight out to the fishing village. I decided to come and see what was going on—I suspected it had something to do with you. And I see I am correct. Where have you been? Pull up a barrel before you begin."

*The tale that Dyancynos had told me was still ringing in my ears—either that or the salt water was still swashing around in there. So I sat down beside the king on a salt-crusted barrel and told him the story I had heard in the darkest and brightest parts of the sea, at the highest and lowest point in the world, in the coldest and warmest realms in which I had ever been.*

*I tried as hard as I could to duplicate the dragon's thrum.*

My efforts fell short, but I forgave myself. Because even if we are both Children of the Earth, as Dyancynos had said, there is no comparison between the words of a Nain and the thrum of a dragon. Fortunately it was a pretty short tale, so I think I got it all.

## The Gift of Scales

Deep within the Earth lies an evil that cannot be named, especially by dragons, for reasons that cannot be spoken. It has been there since the early days of the world, and it grows in the cold and dark, silent place beyond the fire at the Earth's core. In this cold darkness, it sleeps.

And it must ever do so.

Because, on that day when it wakes, it will consume the Earth.

May that day never come.

At the Earth's fiery heart, in the core, dwell beings, demons that seek to see the beast awaken. They are set on one thing, and only one thing delights them—destruction. It is the energy off which they feed, and they care nothing for the consequences. Even if their own destruction would result from their deeds, they care not, for destruction, any destruction, is the one thing they seek.

Long ago, in the Before-Time, when a great battle raged between the Firstborn races of the world, the dragons made a monumental sacrifice to ensure the safety of the Earth. That sacrifice helped build an enormous Vault, a prison of impenetrable walls that held fast the demons who sought to destroy the Earth. For a great, long time, the demons were contained, and the Earth was allowed to grow and bloom in all its realms—the plains, the mountains, the seas, and the downworld, where your ancestors, Ven Polypheme, lived and prospered, completely unaware of what dwelt deeper within.

And then, one day, the Vault was cracked.

Those who stood guard at the Vault fought bravely to keep the demons within it, but those demons were too strong, and many of them escaped. The dragons, who, like the Vault itself, were made of elemental earth, known as Living Stone, each made a sacrifice to seal the Vault again.

That sacrifice was the gift of a scale, one from each dragon living in the world at the time.

You tried in vain to offer the scale you were carrying to Lancel, Ven Polypheme. While that was a noble effort, he scoffed at you because he is a young dragon, only a few thousand years old. He does not know much about the Gift, because if he did, he would have offered you his entire hoard in exchange for what you were carrying.

The scales were not easy to give, because, unlike snakes or other animals you may think are similar to dragons, we do not shed our scales. They are alive, just as our eyes, our hearts, our flesh is alive, and to give one up in sacrifice was a painful, difficult undertaking. Be that as it may, each dragon alive on the earth, and there were many more then than are even remembered now, made the sacrifice. We tore them from ourselves and used them to seal the Vault, so that the remaining demons could not escape. Added to a small number of even older, more powerful scales, from a being I cannot speak of, they formed a patch of Living Stone that sealed the Vault and kept the demons, who had been driven back inside, prisoners once again.

And there they have remained, screaming in the darkness, waiting, and trying, to break free once again.

Over time, as the Living Stone of the Vault has healed itself, the scales fell off, one by one, when they were no longer needed as a patch. Eventually they were found by a wanderer, out of place in the depths of the Earth, and brought upworld. Because there were traces of magic in them, coming as they did from the hides of dragons, they fell into the hands of a tribe of Seers, who, like the woman Sharra you thrummed of, were tall and golden-skinned with eyes of the same color, and able to use the scales to predict the future, or read the past, or in some other way utilize their magic.

This should never have been done, Son of Earth. Those were sacred gifts, given willingly and at great sacrifice, to protect the world. They were not toys for the vain or those seeking fortune, as they became in the hands of the Seven Seers like the one who gave this to you. It was a terrible insult, at the best. The fact that this Seer seems to understand this, and now seeks to return them to their rightful owners, is a hopeful sign for the world.

For in the days since the last battle, the thousands of years that have passed since the Vault was repaired, many of the dragons who gave of their bodies and souls to keep the world safe have passed into the next world. There are very few of us left, hunted as we are by men who do not understand what they are doing when they kill one of us. If they knew what lies within the world we guard, and that each dragon's death leaves a hole in the shield that protects the Earth from within, they would never seek to harm any one of my kind.

But the return of this scale is a hopeful sign, Son of Earth. It may mean that man is beginning to understand how important it is to protect those who protect this land—or at least not try to destroy us for sport or vanity.

And your return of this scale to me will help ensure that the floor of the ocean, the very bottom of the world, which you can see burns and erupts with volcanic fire, will stay as strong as it is possible to remain.

And that the Tree of Water will grow and bloom again.

## - 47 -

# The Surprise

THE KING WAS SILENT FOR A LONG TIME.

Finally, as the sun was beginning to turn the sea blue from the gray-green of Foredawn, he spoke.

"I see that I made a wise decision to hire you as the Royal Reporter, Ven," he said, staring out at the sea. "There is so much I did not have a chance to learn when I was about your age, wandering the world, learning its ways, before my father's death put me on the throne. You are a much better person to be traveling the world, being my eyes, seeing these things for yourself. Thank you for doing it—I know it is not easy."

"No need to thank me, Your Majesty," Ven said hurriedly. "Even when it's frightening, it's lots of fun."

"So you did not mind this last journey? Even with all you might have lost?"

Ven thought hard. "No, sire. In the end, I think a lot of good was accomplished, in spite of the hardship. So I'm satisfied—that is, if you are."

"Did you have any idea what you would be doing when you agreed to go into the sea?"

"No—but I think that's not a bad thing. Madame Sharra said that it wasn't always necessary to know the reason for your journey when you begin it, as long as you discover why you undertook it when it is over."

"And did you discover the reason? What was it?"

Ven pondered for a moment. The chilly air of autumn was heavy with salt and the rain of morning.

"I guess it depends on who you ask," he said finally. "Amariel thought the reason was for me to finally make good on my promise to come and see where she lives, to explore the Deep with her, as I had agreed to do when we first met. Coreon had a mission assigned to him by the Cormorant—and the Cormorant thought our reason was to find out what he needed to know about his plans to attack the Gated City. Madame Sharra herself might have thought that the real reason for my going into the sea was to return the scale to Dyancynos. The dragon thought my purpose was to fulfill an old prophecy and bring about the miracle that we all needed. I'm sure Mr. Coates would say the reason was to rescue Sam and Hannah. Char's reason was simple—if I was going, he was going too. Captain Snodgrass's orders."

The king nodded. "All of those seem like good reasons," he said. "But what do *you* think the reason was?"

Ven exhaled. The air he had inhaled a moment before was heavy. Now his lungs felt lighter, as if the wind he was breathing was drying them out.

"I think each of those reasons was in some ways my reason as well," he said finally. "I began the journey thinking I was hiding from the Thief Queen, something I may have to do for a very long time—though with the tunnel closed, I may be safe for a while. But in the end, I believe that I was doing what you asked of me—looking for the magic hiding in plain sight, and recording it, so that one day you might have a book of all human knowledge, and of all the world's magic. I guess I was just doing my job. And to a Nain, there is nothing more important than that. So I think that's my reason."

The king's blue eyes crinkled as he smiled widely.

"That seems like a very good reason, then," he said. "And if that is going to be your main reason for all your adventures, I have something for you that I think might help you."

Ven's ears perked up.

"Is it the surprise you told me about before I went into the sea?"

The king laughed.

"It is indeed. Come, and I'll show you. Tell me more of your story on the way."

We tied up the boat, left the dock, and headed south to where the royal boathouse stood, even farther down the coast than the fishing village. It was a towering building with bright flags flying, far more grand than my father's warehouse in Vaarn. It had the smell of fresh wood and varnish to it, so even from a few streets away it made me feel homesick.

The king had taken off his fishing hat and coat, so by the time we reached the doors the guards recognized him, and quickly obeyed his order to stand away. He held the door open for me, then followed me inside.

In the dim light I could see the outline of several ships, all of them moored in the shallows of the southern coast. King Vandemere led me up to a long dry dock and invited me to follow him down it.

Alongside it stood the most beautiful ship I have ever seen in my life. I felt suddenly guilty, disloyal to my family's business, because this vessel was as magnificent a sailing ship as I had ever seen, even more splendid than any ship my father had ever manufactured. Then, a moment later, I noticed some scrollwork on the hull and some cables that looked very familiar.

My father's hallmarks.

"You—you bought a ship from my father?" Ven stammered, delight giving way to confusion.

"Actually, I have bought many ships from Pepin Polypheme," the king said, chuckling at the look on Ven's face. "But this is one I have commissioned specially—just for you."

"For *me*?"

The king's laughter grew louder.

"Good heavens, Ven, you're turning white! Yes, for you." King Vandemere grew more serious. "It's clear to me that you should go exploring for a while—get off the Island of Serendair and go out into the wide world. The tunnel from the Gated City into the harbor has recently been destroyed, but one should never underestimate the power and determination of Felonia, the Thief Queen. It's best if you are not around for a while. And besides, this way you can travel *on* the water, and go to many marvelous places, maybe even home for a visit. Then come back and tell me what magic you have seen in places beyond my realm."

Ven was speechless. He could feel his ears burning, and his curiosity was blazing like the fires in the depths of the sea.

"Thank you, sire," he said finally when his voice returned.

The king patted the hull of the beautiful ship. "You're welcome. Do you like her? Don't be polite—she's your ship, and you need to be happy with her."

Ven hurried down the dock, taking a good look at the new vessel.

"Well, I'll have to conduct an Inspection," he said. "But, given my history, I'd like to do it here in the boathouse, rather than on the open sea, if possible."

"Whatever you think is best."

Ven stopped at the prow and stared up at the figurehead.

It was the likeness of a beautiful girl, with glorious-colored scales beneath her armpits that continued on down into a magnificent tail inlaid with mother-of-pearl. The scales of the tail gleamed even in the dim light.

The statue's emerald-green eyes were open wide, as if they were taking in the world with excitement. Her rose-petal mouth bore a wide, happy smile, *brazen*, Ven thought in delight. And on her head, a red cap embroidered in pearls was carved into the wood of her hair.

"Oh, my" was all he could bring himself to say.

"I've spoken to Oliver Snodgrass, who's come home while you were away. He said he would be willing to captain her for you, at least for your maiden voyage, if you want him to—"

"*Want him to?* Are you kidding, Your Majesty? *Want him to?!*"

The king smiled broadly. "He's been putting a crew together— should be ready by tomorrow morning, I would guess. He's at the Crossroads Inn, signing up a bunch of new sailors—"

"My—my friends? They can come?"

"Of course they can come—it's *your* ship." The king laughed out loud at Ven's now-red face. "So what are you going to name her?"

Ven took a breath. Then another. Then finally, after three more, he could speak.

"I have the perfect name for her," he said. "But it's bad luck to tell it before the ship is christened—believe me, I know. Is there any way we can get a bottle of rum down here tomorrow, sire? We can name her right before we launch on the morning's tide."

"As you wish." The king patted his shoulder. "Now, we'd best be off to the Crossroads Inn and get you set up with Captain Snodgrass. I'm sure you two have a million things to discuss before you set sail."

"Thank you, Your Majesty!" Ven shouted. "Thank you so much— but, er, I have one more thing I have to do before we head home. I'll be right back."

The king nodded, and Ven bolted out of the boathouse. He ran down the dock outside it as fast as he could to the water's edge, put his hand to his brow, and scanned the water, which was just beginning to turn gold in the light of the morning sun that had finally broken through the clouds.

"Amariel!" he called softly, hoping not to draw the notice of the local sailors and any fishermen heading north to the pier. "Amariel!"

A moment later a beautiful multicolored tail broke the surface, waving.

"Amariel!" Ven called again. "You have to meet me here tomorrow morning, at Firstlight."

Amariel's head popped out of the waves.

"Why?"

Ven grinned broadly.

"It's a surprise," he said. "But you won't have to wait very long to see it—because it's named after you."

# Acknowledgments

After such a long stretch between the discovery of Ven's first three journals, a number of my colleagues deserve recognition and thanks for sticking with the project:

Eloise Breadwater, my fellow documentarian and research archanologist, for her patient assistance piecing the fragments of Ven's journal together with wax,

Professor Lee Butterscotch Kalin, for his sweetness and good humor in last-minute reviews,

Zovenistra Deswatch, oceanographic researcher, for the loan of her human-to-whale/whale-to-human dictionary,

Dr. Susan Persimmon Chang, for once again fighting off brigands on the Ivory Coast who were either trying to steal the chest with Ven's water-soaked journals or the expedition's precious supply of chunky peanut butter (it's not exactly clear which),

The Royal Undersea Institute of Arcane Creatures in London for its kind help in identifying some truly revolting sea animals from Ven's time,

And Miss Zoe Goodtowne, record keeper.

All of your help is greatly appreciated.

Read on for an excerpt from Ven's first adventure, The Floating Island.

– 1 –

# The Albatross

The morning of my fiftieth birthday found me, as the last twenty had, sneakily examining my chin in the looking glass, searching for a sign, any small sign, of a whisker.

And, once again, as on the previous twenty birthdays, I found nothing.

Absolutely nothing.

It may seem strange to you that I was able to reach the age of fifty years and still have my face remain as smooth and hairless as a green melon, and you would be right. Many lads of my race begin sprouting their beards by the tender age of thirty, and nearly all of them have a full layer of short growth, known as their Bramble, by forty-five. It is all but unheard of among the Nain for a boy to reach his fiftieth year without at least some sign that his beard is beginning to grow in.

But then, this is certainly not the first thing about me that the rest of the Nain in the city of Vaarn think of as odd.

If I were a human, by the age of fifty I would be entering the later years of my life, and my hairless chin would be of no consequence. In fact, it might even be seen as an advantage, since human men have the rather astonishing habit of removing their beards with a sharp knife known as a razor each morning, a practice that horrifies the Nain. This intentional sliding of knife over throat also permanently cements the distrust they feel for the race of humans. A man's beard is the story of his life to the Nain.

And on that morning it didn't seem as if I would ever have one—a beard, a life, or a story worth telling of it.

How quickly Fate turns things around.

Being fifty years old as a Nain is the same as being about twelve or thirteen in human years. We live about four times longer than humans, and grow more slowly. You might think that living four times as long as humans we would have special wisdom upon reaching those teenage years that humans do not have. I certainly thought so. On the night before my forty-second birthday I floated this theory past my mother, who looked at me doubtfully.

"Neh," she said, scorn in her voice. "It merely means you have four times as many years being pigheaded and stupid."

She had a point.

But while Nain can be somewhat pigheaded, I know they are not stupid. They are just uncomfortable in the air of the upworld, with the wind blowing and the bright sky and the commotion of those taller people walking about.

Nain much prefer the dark tunnels of the earth, the warm, solid feel of mountain rising around them, the clanging of anvils and the noise of digging that their deep world absorbs. Being out of the earth for any length of time bothers them. It makes them feel as if things are, well, <u>loose.</u>

So when my great-grandfather, Magnus Polypheme, chose to leave Castenen, the underground kingdom of the Nain, and make his way in the world of human men, it was considered more than strange.

It was a scandal.

Magnus the Mad, as he was known, was by no means the first Nain to leave Castenen. Nor was he the first Nain to choose to live among the humans that were the largest part of the population of the Great Overward, where I was born. Nain, in fact, lived in cities all over the vast continent. Oftentimes they were the merchants who sold the wares that were produced within the mountain kingdom of Castenen to humans in their towns and villages.

But not my great-grandfather. He chose instead to move to the city of Vaarn.

By the sea.

To work on building ships.

Even the upworld Nain couldn't figure that one out.

On the morning of his fiftieth birthday, as Ven Polypheme hurried excitedly to the docks, the light of the sun disappeared for a moment, as if it had been suddenly blotted out.

Ven shielded his eyes and looked up into the dark sky just in time to catch sight of the largest feather he had ever seen, wafting down toward him on the hot wind.

Momentarily blind as the sun returned, he reached out and caught it, an oily white feather tipped with blue-green markings.

It was as long as his forearm.

He had no time to wonder where it had come from. His father's voice filled his ears.

"Ven! *Ven!* Did you see it?"

Ven looked down the long wharf. Pepin Polypheme, a rather portly Nain of close to two hundred and fifty years, was hurrying toward him, puffing and wiping the sweat from his forehead with his pocket handkerchief.

"Did you see it, lad?" his father asked again.

Ven held up the feather.

"Not the feather, the bird!" Pepin gasped as he came to a halt beside his son. "The albatross—did you see it?"

Ven shook his head. "I saw its shadow as it passed overhead, but I was too busy trying to catch the feather to see the bird."

The older Polypheme shook his head as well, spattering drops of sweat into the hot air, and sighed.

"I fear that may turn out to be the story of your life, my boy," he said regretfully. "Catching the useless feather, missing the giant, rare, *lucky* bird. Ah, well. Come along."

Ven sighed as well, wondering if he would ever be able to do anything but disappoint his father. He slid the feather into the band of his cap and followed Pepin along the planks to the pier where the ship his family was outfitting was moored. Like all Nain he was stocky, but he was tall for his age, so he kept up easily with the old man.

"Have they decided what to name her yet?" he asked Pepin, who was waving to the head shipwright.

His father scowled at him. "You should know better than that. No one hears a ship's name until she is christened. It's bad luck."

"But someone must know what she is to be called," Ven said, mostly to himself, as his father was now talking to the shipwright. "Someone will have to paint the name on her prow before the christening ceremony."

"That won't be you."

Ven jumped at the sound of his second-oldest brother's voice behind him.

"Morning, Nigel."

"Morning, and many happy returns of the day, Ven. I'd say 'bless your beard,' but of course you don't have one yet. Now get your oversized fanny to the end of the causeway where the others are waiting. We're drawing straws to see who has to do the Inspection. Now that you're of age, you have to throw your lot in with the rest of us. No more free ride for you, little brother. Even if it is your birthday."

Ven nodded excitedly. He had long been aware of the need for the final check of the ship's fittings that was made on the open sea outside the harbor just before its christening. It was the last chance the ship's builders had to make certain the vessel was seaworthy before turning it over to the new owner.

His brothers dreaded Inspections. They feared the water and could not swim, so the eight-hour voyage on seas that were often rough was torture for them. Whenever it needed to be done, they had drawn hay straws, making the loser in the game undertake the Inspection.

Unlike his brothers, however, Ven could swim, and he loved to sail. His heart was always dreaming of adventure beyond Vaarn, the bustling seaside city in which he lived. So the opportunity to do an Inspection—taking a ship with a small crew out of the harbor and into open sea—made his skin prickle with excitement. *I hope I get the straw!* he thought, but he said nothing, following Nigel over to meet with three of his other brothers.

He could see them from quite a distance; his siblings, like Ven himself, had hair the color of ocean sand, and their heads stood out in the sea of darker-haired people milling about the docks, despite their being shorter than everyone else. Besides, most folks knew to give the Polypheme boys plenty of room in case one of their frequent scuffles broke out. Their good-natured horseplay had bumped more than one innocent bystander into the water.

Vernon, Osgood, and Jasper didn't appear especially happy to see him. They glanced up from the model of the ship's hull they were examining, then went back to arguing among themselves. Arguing was how the Polypheme family communicated.

Ven watched nervously as Jasper squatted down and pointed to a line of miniature lead rivets that fastened a small board to the keel of the ship's model. He grew even more anxious as his brother spat on the pier and continued to point at the model's hull. Ven had worked on that part of the model, and had forged many of the actual iron rivets for the ship himself.

Scale models of the ships they built were the Polypheme family's stock-in-trade. They fashioned whatever vessel they were crafting in perfect miniature detail, from stem to stern, in all its fittings, down to the last rivet and dead-eye, at one-tenth the size it would be when the ship itself was finished. In this way the Polyphemes could be certain the design was sound, and catch any problems before the vessel sailed into the harbor for Inspection.

At least that was the hope. It didn't always turn out that way.

On Osgood's first Inspection, a design flaw with the bilge pump caused the ship to start taking on water at alarming speed. By the time the leaky sloop returned to the pier, it was riding very low in the water, and Osgood was gibbering like a panicked monkey.

But for the most part, these models served to prevent problems in the enormous projects of building sailing vessels. Whether it was a frigate, a sloop, a galleon, or a fishing boat, before the first iron rivet or steel nail was forged to fasten it together, the Polyphemes had already built a smaller version of it. The model for this one was lying in great sections on the planks of the dock in front of their family factory.

Jasper pointed a stubby finger at Ven, then indicated the bottom of the model again.

"There's twice as many fastenings here as there needs to be," he said, scowling. "Ya think we're made of gold or something, Ven? Do you have any idea of the *cost* of this?" Jasper was in charge of the factory's finances.

"I know that the ship stands twice as good a chance of holding together if it hits a reef because of them, Jasper," Ven replied. "Since that might save the entire cargo and crew, by my reckoning it's cheap. Just looking after the family's reputation." It was his birthday, so he decided to risk a playful poke at his brother's stinginess. "Wouldn't want skimping on rivets to cause the loss of the ship and the business at the same time."

Jasper's face turned an unhealthy shade of purple. Even though he was half a head shorter than his youngest brother, he strode over to him angrily and bounced his belly off of Ven's.

Ven knew the belly blow was coming and braced himself. So when it came, Ven didn't move an inch, but it sent Jasper sprawling backwards, landing on his backside with a resounding thump.

"Stow your bickering," ordered Nigel, holding out a curled fist from which five straws popped. "Time to draw. Short straw inspects. Since it's your birthday, Ven, you can draw first."

Swallowing his excitement, Ven stepped forward to get a better look at the ends of the straws, trying to determine which of them was the shortest. He inhaled the salty air, hoping it would bring him luck. Then he took hold of one end, closed his eyes, and plucked the straw from Nigel's hand.

At first he thought he must have dropped the straw because of his eyes being closed. Ven opened them quickly, feeling nothing in his hand, then looked.

The straw between his thumb and forefinger was not even the length from his fingertip to the first knuckle.

Nigel opened his palm. Every other straw was at least the length of his hand.

"Tsk, tsk; hard luck, bucko," said Osgood in obvious relief, wiping the nervous sweat from his forehead with the back of his hand. "Your first draw, and your first short straw. Too bad."

Ven nodded but said nothing, knowing that any word out of his mouth would betray his jubilation. He turned away from his brothers and walked slowly down to the end of the pier, where the all-but-finished ship was moored, still waiting for its sails to be brought aboard.

As Ven moved beyond earshot, Vernon turned in disgust to Osgood.

"You sniveling baby," he said contemptuously. "Why are you sweating like a prisoner about to be keel-hauled? You knew all along the draw was rigged."

Ven was too far away to hear when Osgood tackled Vernon, too caught up in excitement to notice his brothers rolling around on the docks, pounding each other's heads into the planks. The sight was a common one anyway.

Instead, he was listening to the call of the sea wind, to the scream of the gulls, to the glad song his heart was singing of adventure beyond the harbor of Vaarn, where he had spent his entire life.

It was an excitement none of his family could possibly understand.

In the distance he could make out a tiny moving shadow against the sun, flying in great circles on the warm updrafts.

The albatross.

Ven touched the long feather in his cap.

"Thank you," he whispered into the wind. "Seeing you seems to have brought me luck this day after all."

He had no idea how much—or how bad.

# READERS' GUIDE

## About This Guide

The questions and activities that follow are intended to enhance your reading of *The Tree of Water*. Please feel free to adapt this content to suit the needs and interests of your students or reading group participants.

## Before Reading the Book: Writing and Discussion Activities

The pre-reading activities below correlate to the following Common Core State Standards: (W.4-9.3) (SL.4-9.1, 3)

- Ask students about a time they might have had to keep a difficult promise. Why was it hard? What are the choices they have to make—to stay true to the promise versus disappointing or making someone they care about angry? Would it be difficult to keep a promise that they were afraid of or that required them to give something up? Which choice did or would they make?

- Invite students to discuss times when they may have thought they understood what someone else wanted, only to find out that the person wanted something entirely different. Have they ever described something they wanted to another person only to get something very different? Discuss.

- Discuss times when tasks required of students were or are more challenging than they expected. Did they feel they could accomplish those tasks or did it make them nervous? What are some ways to get past those worries?

- Pose these questions to students for a general discussion: Have you ever taken a long journey that did not turn out exactly as planned? What was supposed to happen that didn't? What happened instead?

## Discussion Questions

The discussion questions below correlate to the following Common Core State Standards: (SL.4-9.1, 2, 3, 4) (RL.4-9.1, 2, 3) (RH.4-8.6)

- Different people want Ven to do different things for them. Amariel expects Ven to come explore the sea with her. Char wants Ven to refuse Amariel's demand and stay on land. The Cormorant wants Ven to go to the Summer Festival and get some guidance about the attack on the Gated City from the Sea King. Why does Ven decide to do or not do what each of these people expect of him?

- The Lost Journals of Ven Polypheme series is what the publisher refers to as "faux nonfiction." This means that while Ven is called the author of the journals, the actual author is pretending that Ven existed in the real world. Why would a writer put part of the story, the "journal" pages, in Ven's voice? How is Ven's voice different from the third-person narrator's voice?

• Merrows, Sea-Lirin, the Epona, and the Vila are all human-like creatures of the sea. How are they alike and how are they different?

• Ven gets redirected several times in the course of the book. Do you think that each time someone changes his original plan, it confuses and frustrates him, or do you think it leads him in better directions in finding out the purpose of his journey by the end, as Madame Sharra tells him must happen?

• In Chapter 18, the worst fight to ever happen between Ven and Char takes place. What do you think would have happened if the Vila had not attacked Char at that moment?

• At various parts of the story, different characters have to apologize in some way for another character's presence or behavior. List some examples. List some apologies that work and some that do not.

• When Coreon introduces Spicegar to his new friends, each of their expectations about this sea dragon turn out to be wrong. How does each person handle being incorrect? How does his or her opinion of Spicegar change? In your opinion, what does Spicegar think of each of the children?

• Make a list of all the mistakes Ven and Char make in the sea. Then make a list of all the positive outcomes that came of them.

• Do you think Ven is responsible for the death of the herring in the herring ball? Or do you agree with Amariel that what he called "terrible," most people would call "lunch"?

• Do you think the Cormorant is a good or bad person? Why? When he sends the children on their mission to the Summer

Festival, how does Coreon decide that the Cormorant will not be guided by the Sea King's answer? Is he right?

- From the very beginning, Ven has had the power to undo any moment of time that he wanted if he thought things had gone too far. Should he have? Which moments? Have you ever wished you had that power, and if you did, when would you have used it?

- The book introduces the concept of thrum, talking underwater by way of thoughts. How does thrum make the action of the book easier? If there was no thrum, how do you think communication would have happened?

- In *The Tree of Water*, we see words that mean one thing to one person and something different to another. Ven explains that he has heard both his mother and Amariel use the word "brazen." To his mother, the word is negative, meaning something inappropriate or pushy. To Amariel, it is a positive word, meaning brave and proud. Do you know of any words that mean different things to different people?

- The friends learn things in each of the different realms they travel through. What does the setting of each place they go to— the kelp forest, the Lirin-mer Drowning Cave, the skelligs, the Sea Desert, the Festival grounds, Lancel's lair of lost ships, the Abyss with the soul cages, the Trenches—have to do with what they learn there? How does each place limit or encourage what they can do?

- What does Teel the hippocampus have in common with Ven? List physical characteristics, how they treat the people they care about, and their reasons for being with Amariel.

- How much of Ven's journey would you have been willing to undertake? At what point would you have stopped, or would you have finished the journey as he and Char did? Why?

- How does the author make you like Amariel even though she is obnoxious? The Sea King does not particularly like the Sea Queen—why? How is humor used in this scene?

## Writing and Research Activities

The writing and research activities below correlate to the following Common Core State Standards: (L.4-8.4) (RL.5-6.5) (RL.4-9.6) (RL.4-9.7) (W.4-9.2, 7)

- In the kelp forest where the children meet Spicegar the sea dragon, they come upon the stump of a giant oak tree, a kind of tree that grows on land, not under the water like kelp. Because Spicegar is annoyed, Ven and his friends are asked to leave, and they do not get a chance for him to tell them the story of that tree. Pretend that you are Spicegar, and are not as offended as he was. Write a tale telling the story of the giant oak tree. Why it is under the water, and what happened to it? Illustrate your story.

- The major places to which Ven and his friends travel in *The Tree of Water* are mostly known as realms, and they correspond to the actual zones of the sea. Look up the zones of the sea (Sunlit, Twilight, Midnight, etc) and make a chart of them. Write words or draw pictures of some of the plants and creatures that can be found in those zones.

- Create a PowerPoint or other multimedia presentation showing the actual creatures, plants, and formations in the sea that you found most interesting in *The Tree of Water*. Share that presentation as a report on magic hiding in plain sight to your class, explaining what you think is most magical or interesting about them.

- If you could be any one of the people or any type of creature in *The Tree of Water*, who or what would you be? Write a one-page account telling the story of your birthday as that person or creature, and what you did to celebrate it.

- Not all of Ven's diary entries survived. Find a place in the book where there is narration about something that happened, and write Ven's account of it, complete with illustrations. Notice that each of Ven's illustrations in the book are signed, and remember to do that on your illustrations as well.

- Skelligs are actual geological formations off the coast of Ireland. Research the skelligs, and then build your own skellig out of modeling clay or papier-mâché. Make birds, animals, and structures (like the beehive huts on Skellig Michael in Ireland) that you want on your own skellig. Write a poem about your own mountain island.

- Imagine Ven is a travel agent, writing about the places he has been for other people who want to explore them. Make an itinerary (look this up if you don't know the word) in list form with comments about the places he went, in order (reference the book). Have him use a five-star rating system (1 being awful, 5 being wonderful) to rate each of these places. Write the comments as if you are Ven.

- Fantasy as a genre is supposed to make you use your imagination to envision places that do not exist. Of all the places or creatures in *The Tree of Water*, which place, creature, or thing was, in your opinion, the most beautiful? The most interesting? The scariest? Draw three pictures depicting each of those places, creatures or things.

- Many times Ven and his friends are reminded that "everything in the sea is food for something else, and the sea is always hungry." Look up what a food chain is, and make one, using the creatures and plants from Ven's world.

- In Ven's world, there are five elements—earth, air, fire, water, and ether—that are the basis of all life and all magic, that need to be brought together to make a miracle. Research the origin of these five elements in ancient Greece. If you were forming a world of your own, what would your elements be? Make a poster illustrating the ones from Ven's world and contrast them with the ones from you own world. Which would be the same?

• Much of the "magic hiding in plain sight" in the sea is real. Many of the sea creatures, such as the sea dragon, the sunflower starfish, and the green sea slug all exist in our world. How does the author blend actual scientific information about existing creatures with those that are made up? Which beings and animals do you think really exist or once existed, and which do you think are imaginary? Make a list of creatures or parts of the sea you think might be real, and look them up online to see if you are right.

• Turn one of the scenes in *The Tree of Water* into a play. Get some friends who have also read it to act out the parts with you. Present the play to your class.

# CHARLES MAGNUS VEN POLYPHEME
## —known as Ven—
### is setting sail on the journey of a lifetime....

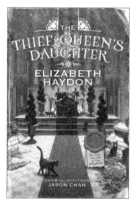

Starscape TPB and eBook

Visit us online at venpolypheme.com to download a
**free, Common Core compatible curriculum based**
on The Lost Journals of Ven Polypheme.

tor-forge.com/starscape